IGNITED

A reverse harem bully romance

STEFFANIE HOLMES

JOIN THE NEWSLETTER FOR UPDATES

Get bonus scenes and additional material in *Cabinet of Curiosities*, a Stephanie Holmes compendium of short stories and bonus scenes. To get this collection, all you need to do is sign up for updates with the Steffanie Holmes newsletter.

www.steffanieholmes.com/newsletter

Every week in my newsletter I talk about the true-life hauntings, strange happenings, crumbling ruins, and creepy facts that inspire my stories. You'll also get newsletter-exclusive bonus scenes and updates. I love to talk to my readers, so come join me for some spooky fun :)

A NOTE ON DARK CONTENT

This series goes to some dark places.

I'm writing this note because I want you a heads up about some of the content in this book. Reading should be fun, so I want to make sure you don't get any nasty surprises. If you're cool with anything and you don't want spoilers, then skip this note and dive in.

Keep reading if you like a bit of warning about what to expect in a dark series.

- There is some intense bullying in the first couple of books, but our heroine holds her own. Our heroes have been born into cruelty and they'll need to redeem themselves.

- This series deals with themes of inequality and cycles of violence – there may be times where this is tough to read, especially if it hits too close to your lived reality.

- This is a reverse harem series, which means that in the end our heroine, Hazel, will have at least three heroes. She does not have to choose between them, and sometimes her heroes like to share. Although this book is set in high school, I'd call it R18 for sexual content.

- Subsequent books contain violence, threat of sexual violence (that doesn't succeed), and cruel and capricious cosmic deities.

Hazel and her friends are deep in a cruel, bloodthirsty world. It's not pretty, but I promise there will be suspense, hot sex, occult mysteries, and beautiful retribution. If that's not your jam, that's totally cool. I suggest you pick up my Nevermore Bookshop Mysteries series – all of the mystery without the gore and trauma and violence.

Enjoy, you beautiful depraved human, you :) Steff

To James,
Who didn't just stand up for me,
but taught me how to stand up for myself

"Who knows the end? What has risen may sink, and what has sunk may rise. Loathsomeness waits and dreams in the deep, and decay spreads over the tottering cities of men."
    – HP Lovecraft, *The Call of Cthulhu*

"He stepped down, trying not to look long at her, as if she were the sun, yet he saw her, like the sun, even without looking."
    – Leo Tolstoy, *Anna Karenina*

CHAPTER ONE

Let them burn. Let them all burn.

Ayaz jerked me back as flames poured from my fingers, dragging the fragments of my soul along with them. I clenched my teeth as heat burst from my body – a broken hydrant that couldn't be turned off.

The fire aimed at the Deadmistress went wide, but the other hit Vincent Bloomberg square in the chest. He staggered across the stage as flames enveloped his torso. His scream was like poetry, like music – high and ravenous and beautiful. I reveled in the joy of his song.

Let him sing a whole fucking aria of pain.

"Vincent!" Damon Delacorte vaulted over the last row of chairs and launched himself at the stage. As Damon reached out to his friend, the flames tore along his arm, ripping through the expensive fabric of his suit and sending him reeling, howling, bawling – another voice in the choir of horror I now conducted.

"What have you done?" Ayaz tried to wrestle my arms behind my back, but I slammed my elbows down, breaking his grip. A little trick Dante taught me before I roasted him.

I planted both palms on Ayaz's chest and shoved, spinning

away from him as he floundered on the edge. Through the haze of my fury, I knew that I didn't want him anywhere near me, that just to touch me might kill him.

"You're only hurting those you care about, Hazel. Perhaps that is your destiny." Ms. West stalked toward me. I whirled around and aimed both palms at her. From the well of hate inside me I drew up all the evil things she'd done, all the lives she destroyed in service to her god. I took the hate and twisted it until it burned molten hot, until it boiled in my veins and melted away my skin until it burst through my palms and flew straight at her.

She slammed her body to the ground, flattening herself against the stage. The fire sailed past her and hit Ayaz's legs.

Fuck.

No.

The world stopped.

Someone screamed. The god screamed too. Pain rippled through his consciousness – a pain that bubbled up from within, that attacked the parts of him that weren't used to feeling. But the other scream drowned him out, the scream of a soul being torn from its mate.

It took me a moment to realize the one screaming was me.

Ayaz's face twisted in surprise and agony as the flames circled his legs, devouring his clothing, stripping him bare to gorge themselves on his skin. I stared, hopeless and helpless, at what my rage had created – fingers of fire consuming my love.

Why did this fire feel so different? I'd already burned two people I loved, and I'd gone numb to save myself from the pain – this time, I felt *too much*. Ayaz's pain seared me as though it was my own.

He crumpled to the stage, his mouth open in a wordless cry.

His silence chilled the fire inside me more than any scream. A spasm shook my body, dredging up the last flickers of heat. Flames spewed from my fingers and rolled across the stage. My body pushed them out in a final splutter before the urge to maim, to kill, to destroy left me completely.

I was nothing.

I do not know, the god cried – a choir of merciless horror. *He burns and I burn.*

"Ayaz." Trey leaped across the stage, diving and ducking between the flames. He grabbed one of the heavy velvet curtains that made up the wings and tore it from its rail. Trey flung the curtain over Ayaz's legs and rolled him inside it. Back and forth, back and forth, smothering the flames while Ayaz's silence tore through me.

I hurt him. I thought at the same time the god thought, because our minds were one.

I can't hurt him I love him I can't lose another that I love I can't I can't...

The god's pain pushed me out of my own mind. My body pitched forward, the stage rushing up to meet me. I hit the ground hard, my fingers clawing at the wood. "Ayaz, Ayaz..." I cried.

The stage buckled. The whole room trembled. I thought it was just my body crumbling under the strain of the god's possession, under the guilt for the hurt I'd done to Ayaz, to Dante, to my own mother. But then Quinn slid across the stage in front of me, his arms wheeling in the air as he fought for balance.

All around me, kids and adults dropped like flies, fragile against this new onslaught. *What's happening? Why is the room shaking? Is it an earthquake—*

Cracks opened in the walls. The wooden planks of the stage bent and buckled, nails pinging from their places and flying about the room. Quinn dragged himself forward on his elbows and reached out to me. As his fingers brushed mine, his face twisted with indecision, as if he couldn't decide whether to embrace me or fling me away.

From between the boards of the stage, a black tendril shot

out, wrapping around my wrist. Its touch was pure ice – so cold it burned my skin. Quinn cried out and jerked his hand back, rolling away as another inky tendril reached for him.

My servants are yours to command, the god roared in my head. Of course, I'd forgotten that he gave me his shadows. It appeared they'd come to my aid.

More tendrils shot through the stage, wrapping around limbs and trapping students and parents in place. Dark creatures pulled themselves from the cracks in the walls and stalked over the seats, their growls as deep and dark as fear itself, the kind of sound that made your teeth sting and your knees buckle in terror.

The shadows stalked and circled, snarling and snapping jaws of midnight, driving the students back toward the center of the room. I scanned frightened faces until I saw Andre and Loretta huddled together, hemmed in on all sides by other students. I had no way to get to them.

Pull out Andre and Loretta. I gave the thought as a command. *They don't belong here.*

Two of the shadow creatures leaped into the crowd, their teeth closing around Andre's leg and Loretta's arm. Students dived out of the way as the shadows dragged my friends to the exit and dropped them over the threshold. Andre bundled Loretta away, and the creatures sat down, guarding against anyone else who tried to escape. Behind me, I sensed shadows moving to block the stage door – as if the wall of fire wasn't deterrent enough.

Quinn's wide eyes bore into mine. His fingers froze in midair. He knew without knowing that I was in control here. "Hazel, what are you doing?"

I opened my mouth to tell him to run, to take Ayaz and Trey and get out. But I was distracted by what was going on in the auditorium.

Are the seats... warping?

I assumed my ruined mind was playing tricks on me. But no...

the seats sloped inward, disappearing into the floor, where a cold wind blew from someplace far below. Dust and debris rained from the ceiling, and the cracks widened. The earth rolled and rumbled. My nails clawed for purchase on the pitching stage.

Inside my head, the god cried. *Together, we crack open the ebony gates of oblivion.*

Something shot from the center of the room, spewing mangled chairs and stone and plaster in all directions. Tremors coursed through my body, shaking me with such force and ferocity I couldn't breathe, couldn't think. My eyes glued shut. Whatever was coming for us from below, I couldn't face it. I didn't have the strength.

Quinn flattened his body over mine as debris rained down on us. I felt rather than heard him yell as the stage cracked and jerked, sending us sliding. We slammed into another body. The world spun out of control.

The god screamed in triumph.

The tremors stopped.

Silence reigned.

White, hollow, deathly silence – even the god didn't trouble my mind. He had gone somewhere. He had no more need of his conduit.

I opened my eyes.

What.

The.

Actual.

Fuck?

CHAPTER TWO

In the center of the room stood a square pillar with four sides, its pointed tip nearly touching the collapsing auditorium roof. It reminded me of the obelisks of Ancient Egypt, only the geometry didn't seem correct. If I stared at a single point for too long, the angles appeared to recede into and overlap each other, revealing layers beneath that my human eyes could not fathom.

The smooth sides caught the light of the intact chandelier and the scattered fires, illuminating pulsing veins against its sleek black surface. About halfway up one side, I noticed a sigil ringed in fire. A coldness not unlike the chill of the god's void emanated from the stone.

What fresh horror is this?

I staggered to my feet. Quinn clung to my arm, but I shoved him off. I stepped over a squirming Vincent Bloomberg, still pinned down by the shadows and by the pain of his wounds. He hissed at me, the sound of air rushing from a tire. I opened my mouth to speak, but I didn't remember how.

I kicked Vincent in the head. It felt good.

Around the room, others lifted their heads and noticed the

pillar. Some wept, others cried or whimpered or screamed. I could no longer distinguish student from parent or faculty. My ears buzzed, and the rising noise around me receded into the background. I transcended the pain in my body until it became a siren call, urging me forward. The pillar called me, begged me to come closer.

"Hazel, what are you doing?" Trey cried.

I jumped off the stage, crashing my way through the smoldering orchestra pit. Smoke and shadow curled around me as I vaulted the broken chairs, kicking Damon Delacorte's hand from around my ankle.

The pillar towered over me, ice and malevolence rolling off it in waves that shook my bones. I pressed my palms against the stone. A hum that was more than sound pulsed through my fingers – the heartbeat of the universe coursing through the monument.

Come home.

Come home, a voice that was not a voice called to me, in a language that wasn't words.

The ice collided with the flame inside me, dragging up all the rage I thought had been spent. All that horror and pain and fury soared through my veins... it had to go somewhere. It had to be unleashed.

I am the conduit.

Above my head, the sigil glowed with a blue flame. And although I had no idea what any of this meant, I understood what I had to do. I curled my fingers against the stone, letting the hum pulse through me. I piled up everything inside me – my regrets, my righteous anger, my hopelessness, my love – into kindling. A scream escaped my throat as I ignited that fuel. As the fire roared through me, soaking my veins in crippling emotion, I *pushed* with my mind.

My power, my fire, my essence, flowed into the pillar.

My fingers shuddered as the fire raced along my arms and

poured through my fingers, like magma bubbling from an active volcano. That was what I felt like – a mountain that had suddenly been blown apart.

My entire body convulsed with light and pain and desire, all of it pouring into the stone.

CHAPTER THREE

Fire crackled along the stone, latticing in all directions – forks of lightning earthing themselves to whatever was in reach. Chairs crashed against the walls, and the room trembled from a violent quake. People might've been screaming, but I couldn't hear them. The hum shook me inside and out until I didn't know myself anymore.

Beneath me, the obelisk rumbled to life once more. The stone rose higher, cracking the floor beneath it. The tip punched through the roof, sending a fresh avalanche of plaster down on the room.

Behold, for I have waited and dreamed in the deep, that what has sunk may rise again, the god screamed in my ears.

My bones cracked. My veins boiled. I longed to release myself from the hell that captured me, but my fingers remained glued to that stone. I felt my own mind slipping away, my organs turning to rocks, my body becoming one with the god.

"Hazy!"

A voice broke through the hum.

Three faces flashed in my mind – three broken Kings who needed me.

Trey. Quinn. Ayaz.

I drew up every last ounce of self I had left, every semblance of human emotion, every memory of safety and kindness and love.

I yanked my hands from the pillar.

The shaking stopped.

The shadows retreated.

Silence fell on the room, punctuated only by the steady crackle of fires not yet contained and the subtle sob of a student. Smoke and plaster dust clung so thick I could barely see a foot in front of me.

"Hazy?" From the smoke emerged figures, hands outstretched toward me. One had a body flung over its shoulder.

My Kings.

Quinn stopped just short of touching me. Tension crackled between us, rutting deep lines across his handsome face. "Hazy, you... you tried to *burn* them."

I had no response to that.

"And where did the pillar come from? What possessed you to touch that thing?"

That, either.

"What the fuck is it?" Trey glared up at the pillar. Ayaz's head flopped against his bicep, dropping my heart to my knees. *Is Ayaz okay? He's not dead. He can't be dead.*

Trey's words broke the spell that held the room entranced. As the shadows retreated, parents and teachers and students leaped to their feet and fled to the exits, crawling over themselves in a mad frenzy to escape the alien monstrosity. I watched them through the haze with an odd detachment. I knew I didn't want them to leave, but I couldn't remember why.

"Trey, don't you dare leave with that girl." From the stage, Vincent's glacier eyes met mine. He staggered to his feet, his hands clenched in fists at his sides as he fought against the horrific pain that must've been attacking his body right now. His smartly-tailored suit was now a mess of charred fabric and ruined skin. He roared as he shuffled forward, every step a fresh agony.

That's right. Vincent is here. That's why they can't leave.

"What are you going to do, Vinnie boy?" I yelled back, stepping close to the pillar. My fingers itched to touch it again, to pull from it enough power to raise the shadows and send them to torment him. "It looks like the god isn't under your thrall any longer."

Hands shoved me toward the exit. "Don't worry about him now. We've got to get out of here."

Trey and Quinn closed in behind me, blocking me from returning to the pillar. I reached out, but Quinn knocked my arm away. He shoved me toward the exit.

"No, I need it." I wrestled against Quinn, kicking at his shins, clawing over his shoulders. But he held fast. With every step away from the stone, it released more of its hold on my mind. By the time we reached the bottleneck at the auditorium doors, I'd regained my faculties completely. Vincent's gaze still burned into my back, but he was right at the rear of the stage, penned in by frightened parents and the raging fire that now tore through backstage. He'd never move fast enough with his injuries to catch up to us.

We had no time to digest what had just happened. Not with Vincent Bloomberg ready to gut me. Not with students stampeding toward the atrium, desperate to escape the building, to put some distance between themselves and that freakish pillar and the flames. They'd already died in a fire once before – no one should have to live through that hell *twice*.

Students and parents shoved past us as Trey struggled with Ayaz's dead weight. My Turk's head flopped back, his eyes glazed over. His legs were no longer on fire, but a glance at the charred curtain wrapped around him told me he was in bad shape. Even an Edimmu who couldn't die would pass out from the pain. A smell like roasting meat rose from his velvet-clad body, turning my stomach.

"We've got to get Ayaz to the infirmary."

"Don't you think I know that?" Trey's eyes burned as he shifted Ayaz's weight to his other arm. "But that'd be an easy way for Dad to corner us. That's why you need to run – he can't do anything to me or Ayaz, but you're mortal."

As if underlying his point, a loud noise punctured the air.

BANG.

Fresh screams rose from the student body as a bullet left a smoking hole in the plaster above my head. *Someone shot at me.* I burst out laughing.

BANG BANG.

Trey shoved my head down as more shots rang out. Whoever it was had terrible aim. A gilded painting depicting one of the past headmasters fell off the wall and smashed on the marble.

Loretta and Andre pulled up beside us. "We'll take him," Loretta said as Andre grabbed for Ayaz's shoulder. "You guys protect Hazel."

"Fine." Trey dumped Ayaz into Loretta's arms. She sagged under his weight. Andre threw Ayaz over his shoulder, and the two of them half-carried, half-dragged Ayaz away. Trey yanked my arm in the opposite direction just as another shot rang out.

The three of us elbowed our way through the crowd to reach the front doors. We shoved them open, allowing the crowd to spill out into the moonlight. The kids took off into the forest while parents leaped into their cars. Vehicles tore down the drive, kicking up clouds of dust and fumes as they fled the horror of their own making.

Vincent reached the top of the steps and surged after me, screaming as he came. He must've been in tremendous pain, but his rage kept him coming. My base instincts took over – I spent most of my life hiding from bad guys. I grabbed Quinn's arm to yank him behind a flower bed. He jerked his arm away, but slid down behind the low wall. Trey dived over the low stone wall and pressed up against me.

"Your dad is crazy." Quinn poked his head up above the garden to see what Vincent was doing. "He's going to shoot one of the parents if he's not careful."

"Or someone else," I snapped, trying to shove his head down while at the same time get a view myself. Vincent hobbled through the panicked crowd as fast as his old legs and ruined body would carry him, arms raised, his lip curling back in triumph as he lifted a trembling arm and pointed the gun right at my face.

Beside me, Quinn froze. The poor dear had never had stared down a barrel before. Back in Philly, I called that Tuesday.

I yanked Quinn's neck and flattened myself against the stone just as Vincent fired. The edges of the bed chipped away, sending flakes of stone flying in all directions. Better the precious school flower beds than my brains.

Adrenaline surged through me, and faint embers of my flame sparked to life once more. Not enough to hurt Vincent, but perhaps enough to call for help.

Hey, Great Old God. I need those shadows now like I've never needed anything in my life.

Beside me, Quinn whimpered. I braced myself for another barrage of bullets, but none came. Instead, fresh screams choked the night. I dared a look around the corner. Shadows spilled from between the window panes, creeping and curling across the parking lot toward Vincent. He caught their approach out of the corner of his eye and dropped the gun. He turned and tried to run, but his burned body declared no more and he toppled into a screaming, writhing heap.

Senator Hyde-Jones drove past in a Lamborghini and slammed on the brakes. In the backseat, Damon Delacorte shoved the door open. "Get in!"

Vincent twitched on the ground. "Get the AR-15 from my

Porsche. I've also got enough fuel to burn the entire state. She won't get away with this. I won't let her take—"

"Don't." Damon reached out with his remaining good hand and grabbed Vincent's wrist. Vincent howled as Damon dragged him up. I couldn't even imagine the pain of running and falling and being dragged after you'd been that badly burned, but the sound of Vincent's scream was pure sweetness. "You think fucking bullets are going to stop that thing? The whore's right – we don't have control over the god anymore. Which means we *can't be here.*"

Vincent yelled and fought for freedom, but both of them were too old and weak and burned that their fight looked pathetic. Somehow Damon dragged him inside and slammed the door. The car tore off down the drive.

"They're getting away," I growled, leaping up.

"Let them." Quinn shrunk away from me. "After today, no student is going to doubt how they came to be here. We won this battle, Hazy. We showed them the truth."

The fire inside me burned bright and hot as I watched the taillights recede into the trees. *That's right, you cowards. Run away. Leave us trapped here with that... pillar thing.*

Whatever it was.

Right now, it wasn't the most important thing. The parents were gone. They wouldn't try anything else tonight. The pillar was... doing whatever it was doing. The god rumbled within his cage, content with the chaos we had wrought together. But there was a boy with dark eyes and burnt flesh, and he needed me.

"We have to get to Ayaz." I stood up. "Even for an Edimmu, wounds like that... I have to know that he's okay—"

Trey gripped my shoulder, dragging me backward. I flailed for Quinn, but as he reached for me, he froze in place. He didn't want to touch me.

I didn't blame him, not after what I'd done to Ayaz. But it hurt.

It *fucking* hurt. Much more than my arm being twisted out of its socket – and that wasn't exactly comfortable.

"Let go of me," I yelled. "I have to see Ayaz."

"Hell no. Andre and Loretta will look after him. You have bigger things to worry about." Trey let go of my arm and wrapped his across my chest, holding me in place against him. With his free hand, he pointed toward the front steps.

"But Ayaz—"

"Hazy, *look*." Quinn's eyes followed where Trey was looking, and a fresh shudder of fear tore through his body.

I squinted into the shadows that hung over the school, like a curtain falling on the final act. Ms. West stood between the stone pillars, her arms folded across her chest and a look of complete triumph arresting her solemn face. Behind her, Dr. Atwood, Dr. Halsey, and Mr. Dexter formed a triangle, their robes fluttering in the breeze as they watched the last car tear around the bend in the drive.

Silence descended – an eerie stillness punctuated only by the roar of the ocean beyond the trees and the sound of the god hissing in my ear.

"I know you're out there, Hazel Waite," the Deadmistress called into the trees, where the students cowered. "You and I have unfinished business."

CHAPTER FOUR

Trey, Quinn and I spent the night in the mouth of the cave where they'd first hidden me from Ms. West at the end of first quarter. We leaned against cold stone, just far enough back to be hidden from view, but with a clear line of sight, and huddled together for warmth. Quinn still refused to touch me, so Trey had to act as the middle of our sandwich, smothering my body in his as much as possible.

All around us in the woods, students whispered and shuffled and sobbed, moving in their hiding places to huddle in small groups. In the bitter-cold night, the truths I'd laid down in the auditorium burrowed into their psyche and took root. Spending the night cold and uncomfortable in the woods did more to alter their minds than I could have ever achieved on my own.

Sleep eluded me. I reached out with my mind, trying to touch the god, but he'd gone quiet, as if joining with me and raising that pillar had sent him into a slumber of his own. That was annoying. I had so many questions – I desperately needed his confusing non-answers. I tried to summon the shadows to look in on Ayaz, but since they were part of the god they too were silent.

When the first light of morning crept through the trees, I

shook Trey awake. "Get up. I want to be back at school before the teachers start—"

He shook his head. "You should be in Mexico by now, not here where both West and my father have seen you. I'll walk you down to Arkham. Deborah can take you to an airport and—"

"Not happening. I'm not leaving Ayaz, and I'm also not going to ditch you with that weird pillar thing." I brushed cave mud off my clothes, trying to ignore the cold that seeped into my bones. I desperately needed sleep and warmth and a safe place to think, but I'd be o-for-3 where I was going. "C'mon, we don't want to miss breakfast."

"Quinn." Trey poked him in the side. "Wake up and help me talk some sense into our girl."

"Noooo..." Quinn mumbled in his sleep, gripping Trey's sleeve like it was his lifeline. "Please, don't burn Ayaz... he's my friend... and I don't have friends..."

His words sent a jolt of cold through my already freezing body. *He's talking to me. He's begging me for his friend's life.*

I'm a monster.

"Quinn." Trey landed a kick in his side. Quinn bolted upright, his eyes darting around, searching for something familiar. When he saw me, he slunk away, although he tried to hide it with a half-assed stretch.

"I was having a nightmare." He ran his hand through his sandy hair, averting his eyes to the cave wall. With grey light dripping through the entrance, I could just make out the edges of the cave-in that Ms. West had used to trap Zehra.

"It's not over yet." Trey hauled him to his feet. "Hazel wants to go back to school."

"Huh?" Quinn rubbed his eyes. "That's one of her most insane suggestions. And she's set a high bar."

"We *have* to." I rubbed my arms. I was still wearing the dress from last night, although now it was torn and dirty and bloody and the hem had been singed. Trey had loaned me his jacket, but it did little to hold off the chill now I didn't have his body heat. "Ayaz is there, and Greg and Zehra. And let's not forget the black phallus that so rudely interrupted our little performance."

Quinn shuddered, whether from my presence or the memory of the pillar I couldn't tell, and I didn't want to ask for fear of the answer. "Why did you raise that thing? Everyone was already terrified. They'll be too scared to go back to school."

I snorted. "Don't make the mistake of imprinting your fear onto them. One night sleeping rough under the stars and the Miskatonic students will be gagging to return to their espresso machines and 400-count Egyptian sheets and solid gold vibrators. They don't know Trey's secret about moving the boundary sigils, so they don't have any other choice *but* to go back. As for the pillar, I have no idea what it is or how I made it rise. But the god said he'd help us, and I have to believe it might be his contribution. It's worth investigating." I narrowed my eyes at Quinn. "If you don't want to come with me, that's fine. Courtney's here in the woods, and I'm sure she'll need comfort."

"I'm coming with you." Quinn's voice was dark.

"Really? Because I need people who will have my back, and right now you're afraid to touch me."

And I don't blame you.

Quinn whipped his head around. His eyes fixed on mine, and my breath caught in my throat. To see the broken edges of him, the battle he waged inside himself between the person he believed I was and the evil he'd seen me do, tore me apart as it was tearing him. "I'm with you, Hazy."

"Okay then." I sucked in air through my teeth. Quinn needed time and space, and I could offer neither. It occurred to me that it was easier this way, that if Quinn was afraid of me, he would not mourn me when I become the god's companion. I made a deal with the god, and with myself. *Free the Kings of Miskatonic Prep at whatever cost.* In order to free them, I had to let them go, and that would be much easier if they didn't cling to false hopes about what we could have together. My crimes gave me the perfect reason to pull away from all the Kings, to let them take their freedom, even if broke me utterly.

No one mourns a murderer.

Trey stepped between Quinn and I, breaking the spell that kept me suspended on the edge of pushing him away. He pressed his chest against mine. "If we're gonna go, we should go now, before the sun is too high. We should make sure it's safe for everyone to return."

There Trey went again, thinking like a leader, making sure he was the first one to storm the castle gates.

As we picked our way down to the pleasure garden, I felt the prickle of eyes on me. Students in the trees and sleeping under bushes. When we descended the steps, a shadowy figure darted from beneath the rotunda to hide behind the grotto.

I crouched low and shuffled along our secret tunnel, one hand in front of me, guiding the fire that would light our way. Quinn hung way back, and even Trey drew ragged breaths, as though being in the confined space with the flame made him anxious. Because of course it would. No matter how much Trey said he didn't care what I'd done, he couldn't quash the fear that had rooted itself in his bones to see me wielding my fire, to know I'd used that fire to take life.

But they followed my light despite their fear, and that meant everything to me.

I stepped out of the tunnel into the storage room, listening hard. The school was silent. A faint *scritch-scritch-scritch* circled overhead. My rats, welcoming me home.

I swung my flame toward the door. The light caught a message scrawled across the wall.

AYAZ IS SAFE. IN INFIRMARY.
– LORETTA

I knew we should move cautiously, that the teachers were still here, lying in wait for me, that we should check every room methodically. But one thought ran through my head, over and over, driving out all rational sense.

Ayaz.

My feet moved of their own accord, dragging me up the stairs, across the dorms, over the skybridge into the classroom wing. I knew exactly where I was going – some invisible force pulled me to him like a magnet. Like a moth to a flame.

The boys followed me, and the rats scritch-scritch-scritched overhead, no longer confining themselves to the lower floors. Our footsteps echoed along empty corridors that bore the scars from the production – torn costumes strewn across the floor, blood smeared along the lockers from where students had been injured trying to get away from the pillar. A ring of soot from the fire burned through the wall. I suppressed a shudder as I noticed the bullet holes in the plaster. From somewhere in the building, I caught the faintest sound of voices. A conversation? No. It was too regular, too rhythmic.

Chanting.

"Where are the teachers?" Quinn scanned the empty halls, his eyes widening as he took in the blood.

I stopped at the top of the staircase leading down to the gym. It was obvious where they were. Murmured voices rose from below, chanting in their strange tongue. One piercing wail soared over all of them.

"Oh, Great Old God, who came to our young world from the sky on a trail of devoured stars," Ms. West's voice floated up the stairs. "We have seen your beautiful pillar, and we humbly inquire as to what you wish for us to do next. We know you must be hungry, for you have not consumed for some time. We come bearing this gift."

"Shit." Trey started down the stairs. "She's going to sacrifice someone."

"Wait." I threw my hand out in front of him. "Listen."

"What if it's Andre or Greg or—"

"I know." I gritted my teeth. "But barging in there isn't going to save their life. Just *listen*. I got this."

The chanting rose, and a woman's scream pierced the air. It sounded like Zehra. My stomach plunged. *Please, please let the god stay true to his word.*

The scream faded into a yell of triumph and some commotion. Lots of voices shouting. Over it all, the god's voice rushed my ears. *I am a truth-teller. I will not consume until your friends are free.*

"Does she not please you?" Ms. West's voice wobbled. "Why do you refuse our gift? Please, star-devourer, please tell us how we can appease you—"

Quinn looked at me, the horror and surprise evident on his face. Trey's look was more searching, suspicious. "Hazy, what did you do?" he demanded.

A slow smile slid across my face. The god was obeying our agreement. He wasn't taking sacrifices. He refused to give Ms. West a thing – not his power, not even answers to her questions.

And although I was desperate to see Ayaz, I recalled Loretta's scrawled message. He was being cared for. If I could bring him *answers* about the pillar, about how I could help him get his real life back, then maybe I could... I could...

Maybe I could make him remember me.

Maybe I shouldn't want him to remember.

I balled my hands into fists and turned away before Quinn's eyes made me break things. "We need to see that pillar."

"What do you suppose it is?" Trey circled the pillar, his eyes widening as he took in the sigil. I knew he couldn't see the flames tearing along the lines, but even without them, the obelisk was impressive. It dominated the ruined auditorium, its strange hum vibrating in my bones.

Around us, the auditorium bore the scars of my rage. My fire had blown massive holes in the wood of the stage. The curtains no longer existed, save for thin ribbons of torn fabric dangling from the rings. The orchestra pit was just a gaping hole exposing bare rock beneath. There didn't seem to be a single seat in the audience that wasn't mangled or broken or torn from its brackets.

"That's why we need Ataturk. He knows all about ancient wossits. He'd figure this out." Quinn pulled a bag of weed from his pocket and proceeded to roll a joint. I glared at him.

"What?" Quinn looked down at his joint. "No one's gonna notice. This whole place reeks of smoke."

He wasn't wrong. The scent of fire scratched the back of my throat. Hot air clung to my skin as if somewhere in the room, the flames still burned. Unlike the fire that gutted my old apartment building, there was no damp furniture or buckled floors from the water sprayed in by firefighters. No firefighters had been called. The fire had burned itself out... somehow.

Stop calling it the fire as if it is somehow an accident. It wasn't the fire. It's my fire.

And it didn't burn out. I poured it into that pillar. I sucked the flames and the heat from the room and gave it to that strange obelisk. And I've got no fucking idea why.

I picked my way across the ruined stage, staring up at the pillar. *Is it my imagination, or has it grown since we fled the auditorium?* Fresh cracks latticed themselves across the ceiling, and the top of the sigil had disappeared into the roof above.

I jumped down from the stage, picking my way around mangled chairs and singed carpet. The pillar called to me, drawing me into its dark depths. The rest of the room receded as I leaned close, studying the polished surface of the stone.

Quinn called out to me, but I ignored him. I pressed my fingers to the stone.

Something inside *pressed back*.

The god tugged inside my head, his cry without form or meaning. For the first time since I'd stared into the void, I had a sense of him as he was, *right now* – not as he liked to show me in his visions. He slumbered in his prison, teetering on the brink of death, but could a god made of the stars even die? He'd collapsed in upon himself in his prison – a black hole of cruel energy growing denser and more dangerous as he faded. In his dreams, he called to me, the same way I called to him...

A thread of darkness poured through the pillar, coiling around my fingers. It stretched down, down, down, to the slumbering god at the other end. The pillar connected us somehow, but I didn't understand. Weren't we already connected by our dreams?

Scritch-scritch. Scritch-scritch.

That wasn't the god speaking. I tore my eyes from the depths of the stone to glance over my shoulder. The familiar scrabbling of tiny rodent feet called me back from the hum. Trey and Quinn dived for cover as rats leaped over the chairs, tumbling down the aisle and catapulting from the stage. They circled the pillar, their noses turned toward me – twitching, expectant.

Scritch-scritch-scritch-scritch-scritttttttttch.

I hadn't seen them since the day we found Greg and Zehra, when they led me to my friends and showed me the names they'd scrawled in the wall. But they followed us across the school to the auditorium, and there had to be a reason for that. The rats always looked after me. They urged me forward when I was on the right track, and forced me back when I was about to do something stupid. *Why are they here? What do they know about the pillar?*

They circled the pillar, spinning in alternate circles before breaking in half. They formed up two jagged lines, rearing up on their hind paws before running and crashing into each other, forming a mass of indistinguishable bodies. They separated along the same jagged line, creating a gap down the middle like a lightning strike. As I watched in amazement, they ran at each other again and again, their bodies fitting together into one big mass before separating once more.

What are they showing me? It's like a zipper being pulled or... or...

Hands wrapped around my waist, tearing me away. My fingers scraped at the pillar, desperate to retain my tether to the god. But they grabbed only air. I yelled as the darkness tore from my mind, flaring pain across my temples.

"You shouldn't touch that thing," Trey whispered. "You don't know what it does."

"Actually, I think I do." I grinned down at the rats, who had stopped their strange dance and stared up at me expectantly. *You guys always have the answers, if only I'd listen.* "It's a lock. And I'm the key."

CHAPTER FIVE

"A key to what?" Trey asked as we slipped out of the auditorium.

I shrugged. "I could start guessing. The destruction of all humankind. A treasure chest of unimaginable riches. An entire mansion filled with gummy bears."

"What are the chances it's the latter?" Quinn had his eyebrow raised in his cheeky way, but there was no smile in his voice. He looked completely rattled.

We rounded the corner, our voices echoing in the vast atrium as we took the marble stairs down to the ground floor. "You're right about one thing, Quinn." My gaze flicked over to the blinking screens that hung over the staircase, flashing the class lists with their scores. Ayaz's name was at the top of the list, with Tillie Fairchild underneath him. I could have beaten them both, if this was a normal school and points weren't awarded just for being rich, and Trey would've wiped the floor with Ayaz if he hadn't given me half his points to save me. "If anyone can figure out what this pillar is about, it's Ayaz. We need him. We need—"

A dark shadow stepped in front of me, blocking our path. Not one of the god's shadows – this one was pure flesh and blood and human evil.

Pale hands reached up to flick back a black hood, revealing the cruel, hard face of the Deadmistress.

I spun around, but more robed figures teamed up the stairs, black robes flapping as they moved to surround us, blocking our exits.

I turned back to the first shadow. Ms. West flashed me her cold smile. Her talons tightened around my shoulder. "Well, well, well. Hazel Waite returns."

CHAPTER SIX

The Deadmistress folded her arms and studied me with those piercing eyes of hers. "That was quite a stunt you pulled, Ms. Waite. I don't believe the senior Eldritch Club will set foot in this school ever again."

"Good." I folded my own arms, hoping they'd disguise my heart thundering inside my chest. "If you're trying to make me feel guilty, you've failed."

I'm already drowning in guilt for much worse crimes, for the things I've done while my fire burned bright that haunt me once the flames died down. This doesn't even register.

"Oh, no." A smile played across her lips. "I'm pleased to see you. Your little performance has worked nicely into my own plans. I think you and I might be able to help each other, Miss Murderess."

Is she serious? Help her with what? I remembered the faculty arranging to kidnap Courtney's mother. I assumed my 'little performance' would stop their ridiculous plan, but maybe it hadn't? I hadn't seen Gloria since the fire started. I don't remember seeing her in any of the cars, but in the chaos of the pillar and my fire I might not have noticed. I probably created the perfect opportunity for the teachers to grab her. The smile playing on Ms. West's face certainly suggested so.

I might've played right into her plans.

So what? I don't care.

We'd achieved what we intended – for better or worse, the students of Miskatonic Prep knew the truth about their parents, and I'd had my revenge by bringing down a reign of terror on those who'd tried to terrify me. "Oh yeah? Seeming as you're the one who sent me away to Dunwich and tried to make me believe I was insane, how do you figure that?"

She waved a dismissive hand. "That was Vincent's grand scheme to neutralize your influence on his sons and the god. I told him it was too risky, that you would be better kept here for close study, but he underestimated you. Men like him often do when confronted by clever women like us."

I narrowed my eyes. "Don't pretend we're rah-rah feminism buddies. Not after the things you've done."

It shouldn't have been possible, but her eyebrow arched even higher. That thing was like the *Arc de Triomphe*. "The things I've done? That's high praise from a girl who burned her mother and best friend alive, who just tried to raze a room filled with her classmates because she couldn't control her anger." Ms. West took a deep bow. "Hazel Waite, I am not worthy."

"I know about Arkham General Hospital. I know that you were forced to resign because you experimented on bodies in the morgue. I know Vincent and the hospital board let you off and brought you here even though you're not a qualified teacher. And I know that it was your experiments and not the god that are responsible for the hell each of these students now endures."

"Hell? I gave them a great gift." Something flashed in her eyes. Part anger, part admiration. "I see we both hold each other's secrets, Ms. Waite. Very well, if you come to my office, I will give you a full account of what your little stunt may have unleashed. Mr. Bloomberg and Mr. Delacorte may join you."

"Not before we see Ayaz."

"Your friends have barricaded him inside the infirmary. With wounds like that, he's unlikely to be responsive for hours or days yet. Come if you want your answers. Stay if you want to be torn to pieces when the students return inside. No one rewards a revealer of ugly truths, Ms. Waite."

Ms. West turned on her heel and flounced into the shadows. Even though I hated myself for it, I scrambled after her, registering Trey and Quinn falling into quick steps behind me.

"Hazy, wait up!" Quinn's boots beat a fast rhythm on the marble as we turned into the faculty wing.

I exchanged a glance with Trey and Quinn. "One of you should find Loretta and Andre, see if Ayaz is all right."

"We're not leaving your side." Quinn huffed as he came up alongside me. I noticed that he still didn't touch me, unlike Trey, who slipped his fingers through mine and squeezed. "You're fast when you're after a maniacal Dr. Frankenstein."

"Quinnanigans has a point. Why are we following her?" Trey growled. "*She* should be running with the Eldritch Club."

"She's got nowhere to run," I said. "She's just as trapped as the rest of us. And we're following her because she has Greg and Zehra. And because she's done something to Ayaz's memories. Also, there's a huge-ass obelisk in the auditorium and we need answers."

We ducked into the darkened corridor, our feet sinking into lush red carpet as we kept our distance from Ms. West. Her swirling black skirts flicked around a corner, past locked offices and pigeonholes for internal mail, past a dusty suit of armor and her secretary's desk to the twin wooden doors of her office. She shoved them open and beckoned us inside.

The guys flanked me as I stood in front of her desk. Ms. West shut and bolted the door. Tension plucked the air taut. I didn't want to be here – I longed to lay eyes on Ayaz, to make sure he was okay. The guilt of what I'd done to him gnawed at my gut.

Ms. West crossed to a wooden cart and lifted a crystal decanter filled with brown liquid. "Drink?"

"I'm not touching anything poured from your hand to my lips," I spat.

"Funny. You never have a problem with the dining hall food I supply." Ms. West licked her lips as she sipped her drink. "Perhaps I should simply cut off the food and see how you and your friends fare."

I snapped my mouth shut. Even now, she still had some power over us. Trey and Quinn and the Miskatonic Prep students didn't need food, but Loretta and Greg and Andre and I still did.

"I'll take a drink," Quinn quipped. I glared at him. He shrugged. "What? That's a fine Scotch, and poison can't hurt me. Besides, I don't want to be cut off from the bacon. It still smells amazing."

When she handed Quinn his glass, he went to stand beside her bookshelf, where unbeknownst to her the oak paneling could slide away to reveal a secret passage. Quinn and I used it in the second quarter to sneak into her office to copy the key to her laboratory. Why did he stand there now? He wasn't looking at me. I didn't want to see in his eyes the reason he was avoiding touching me or standing near me.

That he was afraid of me.

I couldn't blame him. Not after what he'd seen me do, after what he'd heard last night. Quinn *died* in a fire. They all did. He'd always been jumpy around my powers, and now he knew the secret I'd tried to keep shut away – that I'd ignited the fire that killed the two people I loved most.

Fuck.

Why are you even here? I glared at the side of his head. *You should be running away from me as fast as you can. I'm no good for you,*

Quinn Delacorte. I'm all burned up, inside and out. I don't want to pull you into the inferno.

"Why are we here?" Trey demanded, mirroring my own thoughts as he stepped closer to me. "Did you know anything about the pillar?"

"The obelisk is a mystery to me, as it appears to be to you. But I believe the god will reveal his purpose in time." She said nothing about his silence to her, which was more revealing to me than her total honesty. She was growing desperate, grasping at straws to try to understand why the star-devourer she'd served was suddenly changing. "As to your first question – you're here because we can help each other."

"What makes you think we would ever help you?" Trey said. "You did *this* to us."

He gestured to his body, to his frozen state of perpetual youth.

"I gave you the greatest gift that could ever be bestowed upon a human. And now I am just as much a prisoner as you are," she shot back. "But I don't expect that to convince you. We'll help each other because I can give you what you desire."

"And what would that be?" Quinn asked as he moved back to the cart to pour another drink. He still wasn't looking at me.

"Your freedom, of course. The chance to step outside the school gates. A second chance at life."

Trey's face froze. Quinn sloshed whisky over his shoes. The thing they'd wished for twenty years, a thing they'd convinced themselves had to be impossible, and here she was dangling it in front of them like candy.

What the fuck?

"I *knew* you had a way to reverse what you did. But you're not offering this to all the students." I folded my arms. "Only Trey and Quinn?"

You, Hazel Waite, don't need my help. You can walk out of the gates at any time. In fact, I expected you to be in Buenos Aires or New Zealand by now. As for the other students of Miskatonic

Prep, if my plan goes as intended, they will *all* have the freedom to walk unhindered out of the school grounds for the first time in twenty years. That's what you want, isn't it?"

Ms. West leaned back in her chair, crossing her long legs. I was reminded of the day I saw Ayaz fucking her, his nails digging into the curve of her ass as he bent her over an old desk. The way her neck bent back when he pulled her hair, exposing a long, pulsing vein...

Bile rose in my throat.

Unstoppable, my mind filled with another image of Ayaz – his eyes wide and his pain-soaked silence as flames engulfed his body.

Please be okay.

"We'd be fully human again?" Quinn asked in an awed voice. "We'd be able to age?"

She shook her head. "There is no reversing the gift, but what I can offer is even better. You would be immortal and free. You would never age, nor could you be killed by any conventional means. You would not get sick. You would not even need to eat to survive. At least, not conventional food. All would be the same as it is now, except that you could roam the earth, untethered to this school. Not only would you be free, but you would have the means to enjoy that freedom to its fullest extent."

This is pointless. She's not reversing what she's done, only enabling them to walk outside the grounds, which we already know we can do by carrying around the sigils. But she doesn't know that.

One glance at Trey's face and a new fury burned inside me. She offered them nothing they didn't already have for themselves and acted as if it was some great boon. Trey's hands curled into fists. "We don't want to be immortal. We want normal lives."

"Why be normal when you are extraordinary?" She licked her lips. "You can sup of the riches and wonders of life at your own pace, over and over again until the sun swallows this feeble planet. What you see as a curse is truly a *gift* – the greatest gift the god has given us."

"You're immortal, too," Trey blurted out.

"Not exactly. Your parents' power and the longevity granted me is nothing on what you are capable of. The god extended my life – and the lives of the faculty – but we cannot heal ourselves, nor do we possess the powers you haven't even touched yet... such as the ability to walk in dreams."

Hmmmm. I thought of Trey speaking to me through my dream when I was trapped in Dunwich. *Little does she know...*

"That's not true." Quinn's eyes darted to me briefly before flicking away. "Even if the god isn't giving them power anymore, they've been drinking his Kool-Aid for a long time. The god is where the real power comes from, and to him we're nothing but a tasty snack."

That mirthless smile spread across Ms. West's lips. "No, no. You are so much *more* than that. How much do you know about the human soul?"

I narrowed my eyes. "I thought you were a scientist."

"I *am* a scientist – one with an academic interest in souls as a body of energy." Her eyes swiveled to the ceiling, a smug smile playing across her lips. "The concept of a soul is unique in that it is present across practically all earth religions and cultures. On some innate level, we all *know* that while our human body can die, our consciousness – what makes us who we are – lives on as a separate entity. Souls are key to our belief in a future after death. Without the soul, the world can only possibly exist in the moment. The soul gives us subjectivity. While we believe that the world has an objective truth, when observed through the lens of our own experiences and biology the world will present a *subjective* truth, unique to each person. Subatomic experiments bear out this fact. The universal rules we've bound ourselves to – rules of space and time and gravity and relativity – are tools we've designed to hold the subjective together. Some members of the scientific community, myself included, believe this is because the soul itself is made of a kind of energy not found elsewhere in our universe – energy that arrived on earth from somewhere or some-when else entirely."

"Like the god?" Quinn asked. Ms. West nodded.

"We know the god came here from a far corner of the known universe, perhaps even from outside our universe. We know he requires souls to survive, but perhaps it was he who brought the soul here in the first place. For he was present on earth long before Thomas Parris, before the human race was birthed, perhaps even before the first spark of life ignited. Perhaps he *was* the spark. He has been lying in wait, dead but dreaming, ever since. We do not know why he came, but he has revealed his intention – to colonize our galaxy and to build on earth a factory of souls to fuel his expanding race."

"He's never said that to me," I said.

"You do not ask the right questions. He revealed this to Vincent Bloomberg during their first meeting, when Vincent took over the role of President of the Eldritch Club from his father."

Trey snorted. "Trust my father to see a malevolent cosmic deity as a kindred spirit."

"Vincent is nothing if not brilliant." Ms. West's voice took on this wistful tone I'd never heard before. She turned to me, but her eyes were far away. "You may not know, but your boyfriend's father is the director of one of the biggest aerospace technology companies in the world. The combination of his astrophysics background and his judicious imagination meant he was the first member of the Eldritch Club to discern the god's true purpose. That's why Vincent contracted me to study the god. He knew I was uniquely suited to help both the god and him achieve their aims."

"What aims were those?" Trey demanded.

Ms. West waved her hand. She was clearly going to tell this story in her own time. "Before I knew your father or had contact with the god, my early experiments looked at how to separate the soul from the body – the subjective from the objective. I figured out that trauma severs the soul/body connection. And, of course, the greatest trauma a human can endure is their own death. The soul as energy is then reabsorbed and reused as part of the world, in a similar way that all life on earth is made from the dust of stars. What this reabsorption involves is unclear – are souls reincarnated, or does that energy become something else? These are the questions I wanted to answer but have not yet fathomed. What I *do* know is that the most traumatic deaths can damage a soul so it cannot be absorbed, giving us ghosts and spirits who linger on our plane."

Easy pickings for a god who devours souls – like the ghosts of the witches that haunted Parris. I shuddered at the memory of the names scratched on the walls of the weight room. I still didn't know how they tied into all this, or why the rats scratched them for us to read. And I didn't want to ask Ms. West. I had a feeling she hadn't noticed the scratches, and I didn't want to give away the rats' secret.

"After many months of unsuccessful attempts, I was able to intercept the soul on the very point of transition," Ms. West explained. "The soul is just energy, and any standard conductor of energy can then be used to direct that soul wherever I wish."

"You did experiments on cadavers at Arkham General," I said.

"Of course. To test my theory, I needed subjects on the brink of death. I needed to be able to capture the soul at the very point of its observable transition. And it proved successful – I was able to isolate and trap the human soul within an occult sigil."

I wondered about the sigils I found on the Miskatonic Prep graves. Had the sigils somehow trapped their souls? But there wasn't time to consider it – I had to focus on Ms. West's words, for each sounded more insane than the last.

She continued. "Now that I had captured a human soul, what could I do with it? I wanted to know what happened if I placed the soul in another body. What if I could move a dying soul into a new body and therefore eliminate death entirely?

"But before I could explore further, the hospital discovered my experiments. There was an inquiry. I explained the importance of my work, but they could not see beyond the potential litigation into the wider benefits for humanity. Luckily, Vincent sat on the hospital board and immediately recognized my brilliance. He stepped in at the last minute with an offer I couldn't refuse.

"He introduced me to the god. When he opened those trapdoors, what rushed at me was the sensation of a soul leaving, only amplified a hundredfold. I knew then that Vincent was right in his theory – what for centuries has been called a god or a demon is really an alien entity that required no food to exist, but a kind of living energy that originated from its home across the stars. It had been starving for millennia, for it was trapped beneath the earth, starved of souls, the very thing which I could supply.

"Vincent explained that he could kill a person and throw their corpse into the prison, and the entity – the god, if you prefer – would give off a small burst of power that Vincent could use. He wanted a way to make that power grow and last. I knew immediately what was happening – in the same way we eat food to give our bodies energy, the god devoured the soul and took the nutrients of life itself to give off an energy that has never before been discovered in our world. And that energy was absorbed by Vincent and other members of the Eldritch Club – all descendants of powerful witches and occult leaders. The answer to Vincent's question was therefore simple – if he wants a great release of this energy, his god requires a great feast of souls."

I sucked in a breath, willing down the heat that flared in my palms. Beside me, Trey gripped the edge of his chair so hard his knuckles glowed white.

"I also knew that if I told him this, Vincent would cast me aside. I'd lose access to the god forever. I was the only scientist to make these breakthroughs in the study of souls, and the only one who would have access to this new energy. I alone had the opportunity to reveal the deepest hidden secrets of the universe. I couldn't allow the Eldritch Club to close off my access to the god. This discovery was bigger than them and their petty squabbles for dominance.

"And so, I did what no one else had done since they discovered the god – I asked him what *he* wanted. The answer was also obvious, although not to Vincent Bloomberg. If the god had come to colonize our universe, he must have had a mate with him. But his mate died on the journey. The god was unable to complete his mission, so he slumbered beneath the earth until he was awoken by Parris. More than anything else, our god wished for progeny to carry on his dynasty of star-eaters."

"What does that even mean?" Trey demanded.

"It means, boy, that I saved your pointless lives *and* gave the god what he wanted. Instead of killing you like Vincent would have demanded, I blessed you with the god's gifts. You were to be his firstborn – the first generation in an evolutionary chain that would lead eventually to a race of new star gods. Your teachers volunteered to leave their lives and accept immortality – without the associated gifts of his energy – to act as your nursemaids and tutors, to ensure you continue the god's race to the next generation, and the next. Your father – your *new* father – is patient. He can afford to wait a millennium or two for the last of your frail human genes to be flushed from the system."

Trey stalked across the room, his eyes ablaze. He grabbed her shoulders, yanking her forward on her toes until her face was an inch from his. "Stop trying to make poetry from your butchering. What have you done to us?"

Cold realization sliced through my chest as Ms. West's words clicked into place.

I knew. I understood.

The Edimmu. The undying. Human, but not human. All my questions about how the Kings were dead and yet they breathed and hurt and acted as living people. About how they saw cruelty as the answer to all their problems.

They weren't dead at all.

They were *changed*.

This is madness.

"You're not dead," I whispered. "You were never dead. This school... it's a nursery. You're the god's children."

CHAPTER SEVEN

Ms. West nodded. "I knew you would understand, Ms. Waite."

Trey's eyes blazed. "That's absurd. How could my mother have slept with a creature made of shadow and malevolence? *I am Vincent Bloomberg's son.* It's *his* cruelty that runs in my veins."

Ms. West laughed, the sound like shattering glass. "Cosmic gods do not rut in the dirt like humans. His reproductive process involves an exchange of energy. Some of yours for some of his. You were born of your parents as a boring human and then we created you anew, the god and I, from his recipe and my skills. In some ways, you might say I am your real mother."

Trey's face betrayed his horror and disgust. The Deadmistress tossed back her head and laughed – an unhinged, maniacal sound.

"Trapped in this school, at the mercy of your teenage hormones, you were supposed to breed like rabbits, and your children would have been less human than you, and on it would go until the god's race reigned over our universe. But of course, we didn't know how human physiology would react to the god's energy – it appears the ritual has made you all sterile."

"You're sick." Trey grabbed her shoulders and shook. This only made her laugh harder. Quinn finished his drink and poured another. He still wouldn't look at me.

My mind swam with thoughts and memories, putting together everything she said against what we already knew. "Only the teachers knew about this... this *breeding*."

"The Eldritch Club wanted the god's power for themselves, not to create a race that would one day rise up to surpass them. They could never know the truth. And so, I told the stories I had to tell to make myself indispensable to them. I told Vincent what he needed to hear – that I could obtain this power for him, but it would come at a price. For the first three years, I conducted preliminary experiments on lower life-forms – rodents, dogs, sheep, the vagrants Vincent found to act as caretakers at the school. I moved souls around between bodies, carving them into pieces, mingling them with the god's energy to see how they reacted. Then I experimented on the ghosts and ghouls that haunt this house. These old stones contain a lot of restless spirits – the perfect vehicles for further experiments. I achieved exceptional results, but none that pleased the god as his first progeny. Interestingly enough, it was the family history of an old work colleague that gave me the final answer."

Deborah? I leaned forward. "Let me guess – something to do with Parris and his final ritual."

"Indeed. Parris had figured out some aspects of the god's being. Back in his day, science and the occult were intrinsically linked – both concerned with knowing the secrets of the natural world, and with controlling it. Parris also conducted experiments, sacrificing many members of his coven in his quest to uncover the god's secrets. Finally, he thought he had the answer – he'd designed a ritual that was a crude version of the one we used on you boys, only he thought it would bind the god's power to himself so he could control it. One of his foolish acolytes, a Rebecca Nurse – from whom my colleague was descended – decided to stop him. From across the country, her ritual blocked

Parris' at the exact moment a mob from the town set fire to this place. Parris was thrown into the ocean by the mod, where he drowned. The fire tore apart his home, but it also raged *through* the connection between the two rituals, burning Rebecca and her coven to a crisp. And so, my idea was born."

"The fire," Trey said bluntly. A shudder ran through Quinn's body.

"Indeed. Fire is raw, pure energy. It also acts as a conduit that can carry different types of energy – that's why it's used so often in ritual magic. I wondered, what if I repeated that ritual, but instead I used the fire to bring the god's energy into the bodies he had chosen?" Ms. West beamed. "I know. It's genius, and somewhat above your comprehension. Allow me to attempt to explain. As you writhed in the flames, the trauma made your souls pliable. I pulled out pieces of your soul and gave to you a piece of the god in return, then I bound you together and placed you in the ground while the binding took hold. When you rose from your grave like a butterfly emerging from its chrysalis, you were born anew."

The sigils carved into their tombs were the binding. I remembered how Ayaz explained that sigils could be used to control a demon or spirit or to bind them to a place. *I knew the sigils had to be important.* My legs wobbled from the horror of it. I slumped into the chair and sat on my hands, hiding the curls of smoke that rose from my palms as my anger bubbled inside me.

Across the room, Quinn squirmed. He grabbed the Scotch from Ms. West's desk and took a glug straight from the bottle.

Trey's fingers dug into Ms. West's shoulders so hard he tore the fabric. "You're saying that... that you chopped off *a piece of my fucking soul* and replaced it with a piece of the god?"

"You should be proud to be chosen by him! I told Vincent that every Eldritch Club member who wanted power from the god would have to offer up one of their own children for sacrifice. I knew that the child they each chose would be a product of their own cruelty and avarice – the perfect receptacle for the god's first offspring. Everything you have been tasked to do from that moment on has been designed by me to mold you in the god's image."

"Everything you told us and made us do – hurting the scholarship students so they would make fitting sacrifices... it was a lie." Trey's hand slid away from her throat. He stepped back, anger rolling off him.

"Oh, please. You stepped so easily into your role of chief torturer that if I'd told you the truth, it wouldn't have made a difference. You're cut from the same cloth as your father – he thought I was his loyal servant, but I've manipulated him this whole time. It was so easy – you were all too consumed by lust for power and control that you could not see my deception. The whole trick was too easy. I told the Eldritch Club that any member who wished to partake of the ritual should invite their sacrifice to the dance, and that they must be prepared to bury their corpse. I thought we'd have only a handful of willing parties, but in the end, the temptation proved too great for any of them to resist.

"245 students with souls to be sacrificed. 42 faculty members who volunteered to run the school and nurse the god's children in exchange for immortality. And a freshly dug graveyard, ready for a second birth. We organized the dance, invited the chosen students, and made sure the doors were locked. We stoked the flames and lay down beside you, knowing the fire would bring us greater rewards on the other side. While the god's servants gave us his immortal touch, the Eldritch Club did the rest – carrying the corpses down to the graveyard and burying the bodies in their designated places so the severed souls would find their way back to the right vessels.

"Then the god took over. For three days he roared and screamed, gorging himself on the most innocent and delicious parts of your souls. The earth shook with such violent earthquakes the fire investigators could not get their vehicles up the peninsula to study the fire. When he was finished, the god gave of himself, reducing himself to a fraction of his own power, carving his own essence into 245 pieces and placing one inside each of you. You became his – no longer innocent, no longer entirely human. Then, he returned to his slumber.

"The god spared the faculty from the flames so we could watch over your graves. For three long days we stood vigil, long after your parents grew bored with their tears and returned to their lives. We helped the first of you to claw your way to the surface, and then left you to free the others.

"Every year since, the god has demanded four sacrifices – just enough energy for him to provide the boost of power the Eldritch Club needs to keep them in the dark about what's really going on. Meanwhile, you fulfill your true purpose. You feed the fire of the god inside you with your cruelty and vice. Each day you become more like him, and your children – once we figure out how to make you viable – will be even closer to his image. Now, we don't even have to guide you – you torture the students for your own amusement. I kept detailed records observing your behavior." Ms. West's gaze fell on me. "I must say, you two boys have made a fascinating study."

"We're... we're lab rats?" Trey growled. I was amazed he was able to cling to a single element of the litany of horrors she'd just outlined.

"Inaccurate. My experiments have shown rats do not possess the brutality to be the chosen children of the god—"

SMASH.

Quinn tossed the bottle across the room. It hit a portrait above Ms. West's fireplace. Glass exploded everywhere. The gilded frame fell to the floor, bent out of shape. Slivers of glass glittered on the rug – beautiful in their capacity for cruelty, like my Kings.

Shattered glass for a shattered soul.

I expected Quinn to yell, but instead, he stood frozen. His eyes focused on something behind Ms. West's head none of us could see. I longed to embrace him, but the rage rolling off his body called to me, begging for permission to be unleashed – for a spark to set him off. If we touched now, the explosion of emotion might burn this place down.

Ms. West continued talking as if all these rending souls and immortal children were completely normal.

"As I said, I've never before acted as midwife for the birth of a new race, and as such, we've had some hiccups; namely, the fact you haven't yet bred. I've tried everything, including using my own body as a vessel, but it appears what makes us immortal also makes us unable to bear children."

"Ayaz." Bile rose in my throat as I realized why she had pursued him, why she was prepared to use her position of power to sleep with him. She was trying to have his child.

It's sick. She's sick. And mad. In this whole fucking wackadoodle school, she's the craziest of them all.

"Mr. Demir did his duty with enthusiasm." She laughed again, and the sound turned my stomach. "Alas, it was in vain. And then, Hazel Waite appeared and affected our god, and I started to wonder if perhaps the god sensed something in her that would be perfect. And once again, you boys did your duty without prompting from me. All three of you! The god inside you must be attracted to her cruelty."

No.

My heart plunged to my toes.

That can't be true. Everything I feel for the Kings – it means something. It can't simply boil down to me being a vessel for a fucking god-baby.

It can't it can't it can't.

Trey looked ready to explode. "You can't force us to *breed*."

"I don't have to. All these years you've carried off our plan perfectly without my prompting, excited to do your parents' bidding and torture the sacrifices in a state fit to be fed to the god and fuck like rabbits as the teenage hormones continued to rush through your veins. Don't act as though you're a victim here, Trey. You've had free will to resist at any time. But the god is inside you. He is part of you and you of him. You *wanted* to hurt and torture and bully, just as you now want Hazel. At least with her, you get to have your fun at the same time."

"Only because we were lied to!" Trey cried. "If we knew the truth, we never—"

"You never would have tortured those who had less than you to raise your status? You never would have lashed out because you were afraid of something different? You never would have done his bidding if you knew your father's empire was built on the god's brutality?" Ms. West silenced Trey with her penetrating stare. "Is that true? I think Hazel would tell a different story."

I bit back my answer. I didn't want to admit it in front of the guys, but Ms. West was right. The Kings of Miskatonic Prep didn't need their parents' encouragement or the knowledge of the god to bully the scholarship students. They'd been raised to believe that was their right. The choices they made belonged to them.

Just as my choices – my *terrible* choices – belonged to me.

Ms. West steepled her fingers together, studying me with that hard, cold face. "The god very much wants you, Ms. Waite, but not as fuel. He reads your crime on your soul as easily as you might read words on a page. Long before I figured out what you and Ms. Putnam were hiding, the god had set his sights on you as his consort."

"Yeah, well, he can keep on dreaming. He's so not my type." I wanted to steer her away from that line of thought, in case the guys started to suspect the relationship I had with the god. "If the god has his children, why raise the pillar?"

The Deadmistress' mouth tugged up at a corner. "As I said, the pillar is a mystery. Perhaps it is part of a fertility rite from the god's own culture, meant to inflame the loins. Tell me, Trey, does staring into its blackened depths bring the stirrings of lust?"

"You're *sick*," Trey spat. "Why are you telling us this now, when you've gone to such great lengths to hide the truth?"

"If we are to work together, I demand complete transparency. That is the only way our efforts will be a success. It is why I have told you everything."

Complete transparency? Was she serious? After everything she'd done, how could she expect us to trust her? And yet, our best chance at surviving this was to make her believe it. She gave us her secrets, and we owed her something in return.

"If you want transparency, you should probably know we over-heard Vincent and the others talking before the performance," I said.

Ms. West raised a perfectly manicured eyebrow. "How did you manage that?"

"There's a secret passage Quinn knew about – it leads from the forest cabins into the faculty wing. We hid inside during their meeting."

"You are resourceful. What did they talk about? No doubt they're all *deeply concerned* about their imminent aging." She let out a dry laugh, touching her alabaster cheek. "The god is now too weak to give them the power that keeps them young. You have injured many of them with your fire. They will need to lick their wounds for a while. Perhaps some of them will even die. But they will want to regain control."

I nodded. "They do want to regain control. They're planning to release the Great Old God from his cage."

"A bold plan, if a foolish one." Ms. West's lips pursed. "Such arrogance to assume the god cares for their petty power squab-bles. Our god cannot be controlled – even from within his cage he exerts his own will and works his schemes. We saw this with the presence of his pillar. If he is free, he will not waste a moment helping the Eldritch Club. He will be with his children, teaching them the wonders of the universe. He will destroy the human race to make the planet ready for his children."

"Yeah, that's not good."

"Agreed." She waggled a finger. "No destroying the human race until we've perfected breeding. We need at least ten generations of evolution before we can be certain of the viability of the god's progeny. But if he is freed, I cannot promise he won't be overcome by the deliciousness of our feeble race. But not to worry, the Eldritch Club won't attempt anything so stupid after that fire. Especially not when they see what we have."

She drew a mobile phone from the folds in her coat, tapped her fingers on the screen, then passed the phone across the table. I picked it up and hit play on a queued video.

Gloria Haynes was tied to a chair, her mouth gagged, her eyes wide with fear as robed figures flocked around her, leering over her with menace on their minds. She cried incomprehensible words, her voice muffled by the gag and the large room.

I recognize it. She's in the weight room. But are Greg and Zebra still there with her?

Ms. West hasn't said anything about the god's silence, or about his refusal to devour Zebra. She wants me to believe she's still in control.

Ms. West replaced the phone in her robe. "I'll be sending that to Vincent within the hour along with our demands. We cannot allow them to free the god."

"How do you... I mean, *we* plan to stop them?"

"First, Hazel will return as a student."

I snorted. "Even with the other problems he's dealing with, Vincent Bloomberg will have something to say about that."

She smiled. "Thanks to you, after tonight the Eldritch Club will no longer exert any power over what happens at this school. Think about your future, Hazel. If you return as a student, you can graduate with a diploma. When this is all over, you will be able to leave and continue your life elsewhere, with all the clout a

Derleth education could offer. And perhaps, a celestial baby in your belly."

I snorted with laughter, thinking of the absurdity of what she just said. *Never have I been so fucking grateful to my mother for the bad example she set. Thanks, Mom, for making me gun-shy. All those times with the guys and we used condoms even when we didn't have to...* "What clout? There have literally been no graduates of Derleth Academy. *Ever.* I'd be the first. But fine, I'd get a diploma. You try to use my uterus for your own ends. Good luck with that, but whatever. Say I agree to come back. What's after that?"

"We need you and your boyfriends—" she let the word dangle on her tongue like a bungee jumper "—to take back the school. You must regain control. We will host a formal dance on the anniversary of the first ritual. It's the only time the sigils can be broken. The Eldritch Club will return for that if I have Gloria, and I will make them break the sigils that bind us to this school. I need every student to attend and to fight with the faculty if the club tries any tricks, which they no doubt will. We may be immortal, but they are the descendants of great witches and occultists. Vincent will throw his full weight at us, and I need every student on our side. If we are triumphant, every Miskatonic Prep student will be free. Immortal and free."

I glanced between Trey and Quinn. Neither of them moved a muscle, nor gave any indication of what they were thinking. They didn't have to – I knew their hearts well enough by now to know what they thought of Ms. West's offer. But it was important to keep her on our side... for now. "And you'll return Greg and Zehra?"

"They are safe. You do not need them, but I do." Her smile chilled my bones.

"I don't care. We want them back. After tonight, you don't need to pretend that Greg went to the god. Release Greg and Zehra. Otherwise, there's no deal."

"Very well. If you get me what I want, I will return them to you. Show me you can be trusted, Hazel Waite." Ms. West stood, towering over me in that sweeping black dress. A hand with nails like talons crept toward me.

I shook on it, sealing my new deal with the Deadmistress.

A deal written in blood and lies.

A deal that gave me a ticket back into the school, and the chance to study the pillar and the god, to find the solution that would restore the lives of all the students.

What Ms. West didn't know was that while her cold fingers gripped mine, I'd already made a deal of my own – that I would end her reign of terror, and the god would help me do it.

CHAPTER EIGHT

Our business concluded, we rose. My legs shook, but I held out my hands to steady the guys. Trey leaned against me, his features pale and drawn. Quinn shrunk away, not wanting to be touched.

As soon as the Deadmistress' door slammed behind us, Trey sank to his knees, burying his face in his hands. I stopped in my tracks, frozen by his pain.

This was Trey Bloomberg, undisputed King of the Kings of Miskatonic Prep. This was a guy who'd known cruelty his entire life, who'd taken those lessons he'd learned from his father and internalized them until he became the very person he hated and feared.

Yet he'd still clung to one sliver of hope – that deep inside, he was someone different than his father. That his dreams and his soul were his own to command. And Ms. West had just shattered that hope.

Trey's shoulders rocked, and my chest ripped open as I felt his heart shatter like it was my own. I staggered toward Quinn, desperate to hold him. But Quinn flinched away.

He wouldn't break like Trey. No, Quinn had been broken long

ago. His father had beaten the soul out of him and then I'd gone
and set his world on fire. Now, Quinn looked over at me with
cold, calculating eyes.

"You should run," Quinn whispered. "Take Greg and Andre,
take Zehra. Run as far as you can, as fast as you can away from
this hellhole."

"You know I'm not doing that," I said. "We're going to fix
this."

"Don't you understand? There is no fixing this. Our souls have
been *severed*. They can't be put back together again. I'm not
Quinn Delacorte any more. I'm a demon spawn, a fucking
monster."

"So what? We're all monsters. But you're right about one
thing," I whispered, my nails digging into the burn on my wrist.
"You can't go back. But after twenty fucking years, you get to
move forward."

"What she's offering isn't a life." Quinn turned his head away.
"I couldn't walk out with my head held high, not with a piece of
that... that *thing* rattling around inside me."

"I agree, but it is a start. It's the chance to stand outside the
grounds of Miskatonic Prep without carrying a giant-ass stone
around your neck. It's being able to have ice cream with Trey and
me, pat some dogs, drive a motorcycle really fast. It's the ability to
experience new things, new people, new ideas. Don't you deserve
that?"

Quinn didn't reply.

"You're right about another thing, too. You're no longer
Quinn Delacorte. The Quinn I met when I first arrived at
Derleth believed the world owed him a good time just because he
existed. That was the Quinn who gave in to his base urges, who
took pleasure in torturing new students because it made him feel
good about his own life. But the guy I fell in love with..." I choked
back a sob. "He's brave and loyal and he makes me laugh and he
can't stand injustice. So don't you—"

"You'd know a lot about base urges," Quinn's face twisted into an ugly scowl.

I tried to fight down the pain that threatened to overwhelm me. *Right now, I'm the physical embodiment of Quinn's greatest fear. Cut him some slack.* "You know what? Yeah, I fucking do. Because I've spent my entire life trying to hide who I am, and maybe if I'd embraced the fire instead, I might've been able to control it and I never would have hurt the people I loved most. I know I scare you right now, and that's okay. Being scared at Miskatonic Prep is so mundane, it's ridiculous. But don't let that fear make you forget who you are. Besides, if you think we're going to blindly do whatever Ms. West wants, then you don't know me as well as you think. I want her to believe we're on her side – that buys us time to find a real solution. And there *is* a real solution, I know there is. There's a fucking giant-ass obelisk in the middle of the auditorium – so we know there's more going on here. But being able to leave Miskatonic Prep without having to sneak around would help a lot. Deborah could do more tests and—"

"No." Quinn's voice was pure ice. "No, no, and no."

"It's not for us to decide," Trey whispered, his chin rocking against his chest.

"You don't know," Quinn snapped.

Trey jerked his head up. His eyes swam with a pain so intense I staggered back in shock. Yet when he spoke, his voice carried a calm authority. "Exactly. I *don't* know. We can't make this decision for everyone. This isn't about us anymore, Quinn. It's about every Miskatonic student."

There he was – Trey Bloomberg, class president, future world leader, squaring his shoulders and stepping into his *true* power. My chest swelled with pride for how he was able to pull himself through this haze of pain. Dicksome rich boys could be an asset, after all.

Quinn gaped at him. "What's your fucking game, mate?"

"This isn't a game," Trey growled. "Ms. West wants to make an army out of the students. Fine. We'll show her an army. It's time we take back this fucking school."

CHAPTER NINE

Trey's jaw had set into that hard line, his eyes glaciers – immovable, remote. He'd shut away the parts of him that felt the sting of Ms. West's revelations. His focus became his armor. He knew he needed nerves of steel for what would come next.

I knew that look all too well, for it was what I did – I shoved all the feelings down deep so they wouldn't cripple me under the weight of my guilt. We had shit to do – a student body to win over, a creepy pillar to decode, and only the final quarter of the school year to make it happen. Trey took Quinn's arms and dragged him into the atrium. I followed, my eyes locked with Trey's. Wordlessly, we formed a plan.

First, Ayaz. Then, sleep. Then, taking back the school.

As we approached the infirmary, Quinn clawed his way out of his stupor and was able to walk under his own weight. As we rounded the corner a cry echoed down the hall, so filled with pain it rent my heart.

"Ayaz!" I broke into a run. Trey grabbed my arm and yanked me back.

"Don't go in there guns blazing or you might... start blazing," he hissed. "At least he's conscious."

I nodded. Trey was right. I needed to be calm, or the guilt and the pain would make me boil over. I hated that Ayaz was hurt because of my fire.

He's a child of the god. His wounds will heal.

Courtney appeared at the door, her skin pale, her usually-perfect hair matted and dull. Her eyes narrowed as they landed on me.

"Get out." She backed up and slammed the door.

Quinn shoved his foot into the door, catching it just in time. His nose hovered inches from hers. "We're seeing him, Courts."

"*She's* not coming in here. She burned him." Courtney slammed the door against Quinn's boot. "Get. Your. Foot. Out."

Trey added his foot to Quinn's, using his shoulder to muscle the door open wider. "I get that you're scared, but Hazel isn't the enemy here. We've got bigger problems than her fire. Like that creepy pillar in the auditorium and the fact our parents are going to try to finish the job they started twenty years ago."

And discovering we're the children of the god, I finished for him inside my head. I guessed now wasn't the time to spring that one on Courtney.

"I don't care! Ayaz is my boyfriend and *she's not coming in.*"

"Forget about Hazel for a moment. Look at me, Courts." While Trey maneuvered the door open with his shoulders, Quinn slipped behind him and reached for Courtney, his fingers trailing under her chin. "It's really important that we see Ayaz. You know I'm not one to exaggerate and be overdramatic, but our very future could depend on it. Do you think I'm lying?"

After a moment staring at his serious, freaked-out eyes, she shook her head.

"Okay then. Let us in."

"Not her." Courtney spat. "She burned him. No way is she going to finish the job."

I'm done with this.

"Get the fuck away from *my* boyfriend," I snarled, slamming my body into the door and thrusting my palm into her face. I wasn't going to burn her, but she didn't know that. Courtney screamed and dropped her grip on the door. Trey shoved. *CRACK*. The door slammed against the wall.

"He's not your boyfriend. *He hates you.*" Courtney careened across the room, toppling over the back of Ayaz's bed and landing in a heap on the floor. I stepped over her and plonked down in the chair beside the bed. Behind me, I was dimly aware of Courtney shrieking while Trey hauled her away. I heard her yell in anguish. I didn't care. The world narrowed into a dark tunnel – at the end of which was Ayaz, broken and burned and maimed beyond belief.

Because of *me*.

I refused to see my mother and Dante's bodies after the fire. I needed that last image of my mother's halo of flames to be the one burned into my memory, to be the flag of my guilt and anger. Anything more and I'd have come apart completely. And so I was unprepared for the trauma of Ayaz's injuries.

He lay on the infirmary bed, naked apart from some areas of his leg where his jeans had fused to his skin, the fabric garishly bright against blackened chunks of flesh. His legs didn't look like legs anymore, and around his torso, his beautiful tattoos had been reduced to weeping blisters. Someone – Courtney, I guessed, since Old Waldron was with the teachers – had started to dress the wounds, but the job looked insurmountable. There was just so much damage.

Ayaz breathed through a mask, his body shuddering with each gasp. I thought he was unconscious, but then his dark eyes swiveled toward me.

His whole body jerked with shock, which caused him to let out a pain-soaked scream.

A tear fought its way out of the corner of my eye and rolled down my cheek. I'd never wanted this to happen. He was never supposed to get hurt. *Never.*

Fire burns. But that's what happens when you unleash your monstrosity on the world. People you love get hurt.

"Fuck, Ayaz." My hand hovered over him, my fingers itching to touch him, to feel the softness of his skin against mine. But touching him would only bring us both more pain. *How will his body ever heal from this?*

How will he ever forgive me? How could I ask him to? He's lost to me now.

I turned away, disgusted with myself. I shouldn't be in the room with him. Courtney was right – he shouldn't have to look at the face of the one who did this to him.

"Wait," he croaked out, his voice muffled by the mask.

The word tugged at me. *Don't turn around. Don't give him a chance to—*

I turned around. Of course I did. I would do anything that boy asked of me.

Ayaz leaned back on his pillows and raised his arm, his breath ragged as the pain of it tugged at his ruined muscles. I was too shocked, too frozen to force him to stay still. I watched, mesmerized, as he reached toward my face, his rage twisting his features into an ugly mask. A well of emotions flooded up inside me. All I wanted was for him to wrap those strong arms around me and pull me into a hug. All I wanted was his lips on mine, his fingers tangled in my hair, his heat enveloping me.

All he wanted to do was kill me. And I didn't blame him.

At the last moment, Ayaz snapped his fingers back, his mouth twisting – not in rage this time, but confusion.

He reached up to his own face and tugged off the mask. "Who are you?" he demanded.

My whole body trembled. "You know who I am."

"I don't! They told me that you were a dangerous bully who had to be stopped, that you were trying to destroy this school. That you were something evil and wrong and... and last night I saw it with my own eyes. But I get this *feeling* when I'm around you—" he scrunched up his face and jerked his head like he was trying to shake me off. The movement made him cry out in pain. "I'm going fucking *nuts.*"

Seeing him suffering like that, not trusting his own mind while he fought against the injuries I inflicted, made me long to pull him against me. I stepped toward him, but he glared at me with those dark, untrusting eyes.

Ms. West did something to him. I know it.

"They lied to you – about me, about us, about Zehra, about everything. I don't know why you believe them over your own best friends." I nodded to Trey and Quinn in the corner of the room. "Maybe if I stayed away from you in the first place, none of this would've happened. But it's okay. I have to believe it's okay that you forgot me, forgot everything. You don't even remember that night in my room."

The stumped look on his face revealed the truth. Rage bubbled up inside me. *They've already taken everything from Ayaz. How dare they take that, too?*

Heat rocketed down my arms. *How dare they rip away the tiny shreds of happiness we eke out of this hellhole?*

"It's probably a blessing that you don't. It might be keeping you alive. You think Ms. West gives you the truth, but she's the biggest liar of them all. You think Vincent Bloomberg is like a father to you, but you're wrong," I spat, fighting to control the fire beating against my palms. The fire had already burned too much already. "Everything you heard last night is true – Vincent is the architect of Derleth. He chose to sacrifice you all. Do you know what he's doing with all that info you gave him about the god's prison? He and the Eldritch Club were planning to kill you all so they can free the god."

"How do you know about that?" Ayaz demanded, his shoulders tensing as he struggled against his internal demons. "How can you—"

Ayaz tried to roll toward me. He winced as he put weight on his arm, his body convulsing with pain.

"Don't move." The fight fled me at the sight of his pain. I placed my hand on his chest, shoving him back down. Where our skin connected, a wave of heat sailed along my veins, touching every part of me with sizzling warmth. It took everything I had not to wrap my arms around Ayaz and press myself against him.

I closed my eyes, tried to draw my hand away. Warm fingers clamped around it, holding it in place. My eyes flew open.

Ayaz. My beautiful dark King. My artist with the brilliant mind trapped in a world where his talents held no value. My man of myth from across the sea. In the corners of his eyes, the faintest flicker of his former self danced.

"That was a hell of a fireworks display you put on last night," he said. "When I first came to America, Trey took me to a Fourth of July display in New York City. We sat on a million-dollar yacht and watched the sky burn. You made that look like kiddie shit."

"It had to be done." I tried to make myself sound confident – more confident than I felt. Ayaz must have been able to see my heart pounding against my chest, my whole body poised. After he let me walk away with Parris' book I thought there was a chance he might remember me. But just yesterday he handed the Eldritch Club everything they needed to fuck over the world, so now I couldn't be sure. "You all had to know the truth."

"You used Tillie's own sister against her." His words dripped with hate. I had a feeling he wasn't talking about Bianca, but about Zehra.

Zehra, who's still locked in the gym, with only Greg and an army of rats for company.

It was on the tip of my tongue to blurt out where she was, but Ayaz probably knew. After all, I was pretty sure he betrayed me to save her. I couldn't hate him for it – just the opposite. I missed him more than ever.

"I didn't want to, but it was the only way. It's more important for me to show you the truth than for you to... to remember me."

"You've explained to me, at least twice, what I am to you," he said, his voice hoarse.

"Don't speak." I shook my head. "Not if it hurts. Focus on getting better. You *will* get better."

"My body will heal from this, as it has from all wounds. My heart, on the other hand... what I'm trying to say is that I still don't remember you. All the evidence I've seen is that you're here to destroy us. You broke into my room. You burned me. You know things about my sister that you're not telling me. You have the students enraged and the teachers afraid and you're bitter enemies with the man who's treated me as his own son."

I dared a smile. "You're not allowed to write my obituary."

"Ever since the day I saw you, I've been drawn to you. It's like..." he looked puzzled for a moment. "My body remembers you, even though my mind draws a blank. You're imprinted up here." He tapped the side of his head, then winced. Apparently, he'd momentarily forgotten he'd been burned over most of his body. Lifting his arm over his head was a no-no.

My mind cast back to the first time Ayaz and I spoke after he'd forgotten me. I snuck into his room to steal Parris' skin book and discovered Ayaz's sketchbooks filled with drawings of me.

He must've been thinking of them, too. "Last time I came to in the infirmary, near the end of second quarter, Ms. West handed me a fresh sketchbook. She said that I'd been horsing around with Trey and Quinn and had a bump on the head, that my memories may feel fuzzy and disjointed, but drawing was something I loved and it may help me to transcend my confusion."

He's talking about the scuffle in Trey's room, where Ms. West and Vincent dragged the Kings away as I escaped out the window. But Ayaz wasn't there, so the only reason he'd have to be in the infirmary is if Ms. West did something to him. If she's moving souls around to different bodies, it wouldn't be a big deal for her to alter Ayaz's memories. She told me she could do that.

"After I got back to my room, I opened the sketchbook and started to draw. It was a compulsion – my hand moved on its own. I had no control. When I had finished, you stared back at me from the page, defiant, radiant, mesmerizing.

"Every time I sat down to draw something, the lines turned into you. I told myself, 'I'm going to sketch a kitten,' and I'd imagine all the planes and curves of the creature in my mind and then I'd look down at the paper and you'd stare back at me. I couldn't understand it – they told me you were dangerous. Obsessive. A liar. A bully. And yet, some part of me saw you differently."

"Is that why you trusted me that first time, with the book?" I asked. "You could have given us up to Courtney and taken the book back, but you didn't."

He nodded. "I wanted to see what you'd do. I wanted to see if I *could* trust you."

My Ayaz. I couldn't even imagine what it felt like to grasp at a memory but have it constantly slip away, to feel as though your mind and body were at war. *There must be something that could help him remember. Or, if not remember, then reimagine.*

Flames licked at my heart, urging me to act. Never one for impulse control, I slid from the chair and stood over his bed, leaning down so my face was an inch from his. This close I could see a nerve in his temple jumping. He swallowed hard after every breath, as though willing the air to stay in his lungs. He was in greater pain than he was letting on.

Perhaps I could take a piece of that pain away.

I leaned in closer. His breath touched mine. Behind the sickly smell of the creams slathered on his wounds, the metallic tang of blood, and the unmistakable charred meat scent of burnt flesh, I caught a whiff of honey and sweet blushing roses. My beautiful Turk.

You remember. I know you remember! The words screamed inside my head, but instead of yelling them, I brushed my lips to his – so gently, so softly that I could pretend I'd never kissed him at all.

But that touch was enough to send fire racing through my limbs, to grab my heart and shake it like a fucking earthquake, to leave me breathless, gasping, desperate for him.

Ayaz's eyes widened. In those dark pools, I caught a flicker of the wounded boy who'd come into my room in the second quarter, who'd shared a piece of his shattered soul with me, who'd let me leave my monster at the door and just be Hazel in his arms.

Please remember. Please...

Every stolen moment, every wish I'd had for a future with him, every emotion I'd stamped down and refused to acknowledge, I poured into that kiss. *Please remember. Please remember.*

Fire coursed through my body – a line of flame connecting my lips to my heart to the throbbing heat between my legs. Tendrils of flame broke through my skin, reaching for him, not to burn him again but to bring him back to me.

It took everything in me to tear my lips away. I dared a smile. "Did that bring anything back?"

"Just that I've been fucking stupid wasting the last quarter with Courtney." Ayaz grinned. His hand reached up, and even though he winced, he gripped my neck with surprising strength, pulling me against him for another scorching kiss. "Where have you been all my life?"

I sat back, the taste of him sizzling against my lips. "You remember me now?"

Ayaz's eyes swept across my face again.

"No. But I remember... that I know you," he whispered.

"In the biblical sense," Quinn piped up helpfully.

"You do know me," I whispered. "Everything I've told you is the truth."

"I don't know how, but I know... I will never forget you. I remember that you're more important to me than myself. And that's enough for now."

My heart soared. I touched my hand to his, stroking his fingers. It felt so good to touch him. "I have so much to tell you. I don't want to melt your brain while you're still trying to recover."

"I can handle it." He nodded at his legs. "This is going to take a bit of time to heal. You might as well fill me in."

I glanced over my shoulder, checking the room was empty. Old Waldron wasn't hovering as she normally did. Of course, she'd be with the other teachers, going over their plan. Trey and Quinn slid out the door, but I knew they'd be right outside, keeping guard. I took a deep breath.

Between more tender kisses that melted like chocolate, I told him everything that had happened since he'd betrayed me in Ms. West's office until last night, when he'd walked into that Eldritch Club meeting and then appeared on stage with Ms. West.

"Shit." His face wrinkled in pain. "I told Vincent what I discovered in Parris' book. I gave him a recipe to destroy us."

"Yup. You fucked things up for us a bit there. But the teachers have Courtney's mother, which means it's a stalemate between the adults, for now. This next bit is the rough bit. Are you sure you want all the gory details?"

"I can handle it." He gritted his teeth, his body stiffening as another spasm of pain rocketed through him. I bent down to kiss him again, wishing I could sweep up his pain into myself. The good news was that when I gathered my strength to look at his legs again, a few of the blisters seemed to have gone down. He was healing... slowly.

As best as I could, I told him everything I remembered from West's insane tale of souls and progeny. Ayaz shuddered again, but whether from the pain or the news that he'd been intended as a child of the god, I couldn't tell. When I finished, he didn't say anything for a while, just kept gasping his shaky breath.

I hit Ayaz with the last piece of the puzzle, praying that I'd read him right and he really was back on our side. If he betrayed us to the Deadmistress, it would be all over. "Ms. West wants us to be her pawns so she can force the Eldritch Club to break the sigils that trap you in the school. She doesn't know that we can already get past them."

"You can?"

"Yup. But I want her to keep believing we need her as much as she needs us. We can't do anything without control of the school. For that, we need you."

Ayaz laughed bitterly. "After you burned the auditorium, didn't you summon that crazy pillar thing? Courts told me about it. I'd say you've got control."

I shook my head. "People are afraid of me. I like it, actually, but I know from the Bloombergs that having followers who fear you isn't the same as people who adore you. I'll deal with the god and his weird pillar and his soul-eating ways, but I need you to convince the others to listen to me. You're loved at this school, Ayaz. The other students look up to you. I think it's no accident that Ms. West targeted you with her... charms, and that you had your memories of me wiped. Of all the Kings, you're the most dangerous, because people actually trust you. And now you're the only King left."

Ayaz's eyes swam with pain and confusion. "Is it really all true... Ms. West swapped part of my soul with the god?"

"I swear it on a mountain of bacon."

The corners of my Turk's mouth twisted up into one of those rare, dazzling smiles. "Then whatever your plan is, count me the fuck in."

CHAPTER TEN

No way was I leaving Ayaz alone. Quinn and Trey stayed in the hall, keeping watch, listening for the return of the students. I searched the infirmary cupboards and found a couple of scratchy wool blankets and a supply of Scotch hidden in Old Waldron's desk drawer. I crawled up on the bed beside Ayaz and slipped under his arm, placing the blanket over my knees and being careful not to touch him anywhere below the waist.

"You'll heal, right?" It was hard to tell if his burns had actually improved or if the horror of looking at them had simply faded a little.

Ayaz shrugged, then winced. "I fucking hope so. In twenty years I've never been this badly injured. I can feel things happening down there, but I'm too afraid to look."

"He'll heal fine." Quinn strode into the room and tossed me my mobile. "Once Trey cut my arm off just to see what would happen. It took a week but it came back. Hurt like you wouldn't believe."

"I bet. What's this for?" I stared down at the phone, not understanding why Quinn had brought it. Outside the walls of the school, I had nothing and no one. Deborah... maybe? But who was she apart from a stranger who got caught up in something she didn't understand. I didn't know how much we could trust her. Judging by the way Quinn immediately slid into the corner of the room – as far from me as he could get – I wasn't sure I still had all my Kings.

If the students are all as afraid of fire and that creepy pillar as Quinn is, I'm going to have a hell of a time getting them to trust me.

Which was super annoying, because I wasn't used to needing others and I didn't know the first thing about inspiring trust. At my old school, I didn't give a fuck about the other kids. I was perfectly happy flying under their radar, especially since half of them were in gangs or worse. But if I was going to pull this off, if I was going to find out why I was the key and what the pillar unlocked, I needed the Miskatonic Prep students on my side.

All of them.

Even though it would be easier in the end, I couldn't do that if Quinn was afraid of me. I searched his face for some clue as to how he was feeling, but apart from the distance between us, he appeared his normal, happy-go-lucky self. No trace of the ice king from earlier.

"I went back to the dorm to see what was going down. While I was there, I went to our rooms for supplies," Quinn's familiar grin churned me up inside as he emptied his pockets, revealing my knife, several smushed Twinkies, and a box of condoms. "The phone was beeping."

"How are the other students?" I asked. "Have they come back yet?"

"They're starting to trickle in. Everyone looks horrible – like they've been living feral for months. Court's is holding court, of course." He tried to smile at the feeble joke, but it didn't reach his eyes.

"They haven't hurt Loretta or Andre?"

"Nope. They're mostly standing around in a daze. The girls are gathered in Courtney's room, whispering and crying and holding each other. I thought maybe Ataturk would like to go back with me in case it devolves into a pillow fight?" A hopeful eyebrow shot up as Quinn locked eyes with Ayaz.

Ayaz's chest heaved as another spasm of pain shot through him. "Perhaps another time."

"You two should go back to the dorms," I said. "Your presence could do a lot of good. I don't want them to think you abandoned them after our performance, lest they get any wild ideas about my loyalties."

Trey plonked down in the wooden chair I'd left. "I'm staying right here."

"Ditto." Quinn pulled open the infirmary door. "I mean, I'm going to be outside, keeping watch in case anyone wants words with Hazy. But that's basically here."

Ayaz managed a shaky half-smile. "Thanks, guys. I probably would have missed you if I didn't believe you'd been brainwashed by a witch named Hazel."

The door closed behind Quinn. The audible click of the bolt sent a shiver down my spine, as if it foretold a void between us. I hoped Quinn knew he could find his way back to me, as soon as he was ready to step through the door and face what that meant.

Desperate for a distraction, I unlocked my phone. The screen flashed with messages from Deborah.

"How's the production going?" she asked. "I haven't heard anything. I hope that means things went without a hitch."

A half-hour later. "Hazel, are you okay?"

"Hazel, please answer."

"A ton of cars just sped down the peninsula and careened through town. A bunch of them pulled up at my hotel. Doors slamming. People yelling. A few are being carried on makeshift stretchers. They sound freaked out. WHAT HAPPENED?"

"What happened?" I texted back. "Oh, nothing. Just your typical night at Miskatonic Prep. The god showed up at our little production and gave a performance of his own. Now there's a weird stone obelisk in the middle of the auditorium. Oh, and I got overwhelmed and burned some shit, but we knew that might happen. We're all fine. Ayaz is burned, but he's slowly recovering."

Ayaz leaned over my shoulder. "How do you have a phone? And who's that?"

"I have a phone because I'm not technically a student anymore, so I snuck a new one in. And I'm talking to Deborah. She's a descendant of Rebecca Nurse and she used to work with Ms. West at Arkham General Hospital. It's a long story. I'll fill you in when you have brain cells to spare to process it."

A moment later, Deborah replied. "Phew. I'm so glad you're okay. Don't go dark like that again! Vincent Bloomberg arrived a while ago. Four men were carrying him because he's all burned up, but he's yelling at the other parents to join him in the woods. Do you want me to follow them?"

Fuck no. Don't be an idiot, Deborah. I jabbed the screen so hard I worried I'd break it. "NO. Stay where you are. Lock your door. Don't let them see you. If they recognize you, they'll figure out we're working together."

My stomach tied in knots waiting for Deborah to reply. When it finally came through, it made me smile. "Okay, no amateur heroics. The dogs and I are going to lay low. If possible, can we meet tomorrow? I think you really need to see what I have to show you."

I glanced at Trey. "Do you think you'd be up to lugging that sigil into Arkham? Deborah wants to meet. She's still on about this important thing she needs to tell us."

Trey leaned forward. "Does she have the dogs with her?"

He kept his voice nonchalant, but I noticed the glimmer of hope in his eyes. "Yes, they're here, too. A bunch of the parents are staying in the Arkham Grand as well, so we'd have to wait until they leave and things have calmed down here. She doesn't want to tell us over the phone."

Trey nodded once, desperately trying not to betray his enthusiasm in front of me or Ayaz. Even in front of his friends, he still struggled with that need for control. If anything could break him of that habit, it would be Roger, Leopold, and Loeb – Deborah's delightful dogs.

I typed out a response to Deborah, telling her to let us know when the coast was clear. I settled back into the pillow, placing my arm around Ayaz's shoulders and staring down at him. Was it my imagination, or had the burns on his lower torso diminished a bit? I hoped so... a body that fine and a heart that broken didn't deserve this cruelty.

Ayaz blinked. His dark eyes clouded with pain as another shudder rocketed through him. "I think... I should rest..."

"If you're trying to kick us out, you can forget it."

"Trust me, she'll crowd you out of that bed, so you'll need us on call to wrestle her back to her rightful place. Quinn and I are taking turns outside. Hazy, you need sleep. I know you didn't get any last night, and there's nothing you can do for the students right now."

"We'll make sure no one comes in," added Quinn, poking his head in the door. "So close those eyes and dream of bathing naked with lots of sweaty guys in your harem."

"A Turkish bath is called a *Hammam,* not a harem, and it is sacred. Don't disrespect my culture..." Ayaz murmured, but he dozed off before he finished the thought.

"Yeah, Quinn. Get it right." Trey squeezed my shoulder. "Hazel's the one who has the harem."

I snuggled in against Ayaz's shoulder, pressing my lips to my forehead as he let out a tiny, adorable snore. Trey's eyes bore into the back of my head, his gaze hot enough to make me melt. That was exactly what he was hoping to do – melt away the layers that protected me and expose the truth.

No one could lay me bare quite like Trey Bloomberg – my mirror. In his cruel smile, I saw the worst of myself, and also the best. As soon as Ayaz slipped into sleep, Trey's eyes had me in his grip, and he wouldn't let go until he had stripped me back to nothing.

"Hazel." Trey's voice was firm. "You have to talk about it."

"About what?" I feigned innocence.

"About what Ms. West said on stage. About your mother and your friend and the..." even Trey struggled for words. "The fire that killed them."

"What's there to talk about? I ignited that fire. I killed them. I'm a murderer."

I met Trey's eyes with the fury of my own. I poured every last ounce of rage I could muster into that stare, willing him to see what I needed him to see.

I *wanted* Trey to squirm in his seat. I wanted him to back away from me in horror. I wanted him to accuse me of being a monster, to tell me what my heart already knew – that I was no good. That I was evil.

Because that was what I believed.

Instead, he shook his head, his throat making a sound that might've been a laugh. "You couldn't control your powers. That's not murder, Hazel. That's a tragic accident."

"Nope. That's you trying to get me to escape responsibility, something you Kings are particularly skilled at. I can't let myself off that easy." *Shit.* My words wavered. I stared at my hands so I wouldn't have to keep Trey's eye contact. "You want to know the truth? In the moment, I *wanted* them to die."

"So what?"

"That's *sick*. That's murder. I'm a murderer. Talking circles around it won't make it any less true."

"You're determined to take the blame for that night, for all of it?" Trey's voice took on a dangerous edge. "Even for what they did to you."

"I'm not 'determined' to do anything, except to get your ass out of this hellhole they dare call a school. Let's talk about that instead, because as far as I'm concerned the topic of the fire is well and truly burned out."

I didn't even apologize for the terrible pun.

"Fine." But Trey didn't talk. He stared at the wall, his face frozen in deep thought. Above my head, a clock ticked away the seconds. *Tick-tock. Tick-tock.*

Tick-tock. Tick-tock.

Scritch-scritch-scritch.

Tick-tock-tick.

From inside the walls, the faint scratch of rats feet against wood and stone. I hadn't heard them all night and now here they were, reassuring me that I'd done the right thing. *Don't let Trey get too close to you. Don't let any of the Kings get close. Now that you know what's happened, you can get them out of here, but to do that will mean you lose them forever. You might as well practice saying goodbye now—*

"It's not fair."

Trey's words thudded inside my head, each one stinging like a punch from one of my mother's dead-end boyfriends.

"What's not fair?"

"I finally have something in my life that's good. I met this amazing girl. She doesn't stand on fucking pretenses. Hell, half the time I'm convinced she was sent from the god himself to torture me. She constantly surprises me, but the good kind of surprises – the kind I'm not used to. I keep thinking that eventually she'll wake up to the piece-of-shit I really am and kick me to the curb. But for some reason, she stays, and she looks at me in this way that makes me feel as if I must've done something right. This girl is the brightest spark in all my darkness, but she's stuck in the past. She forgives everyone else for their shitty decisions and half-cocked impulses. She forgives her bullies for all the horrible shit they did to her, but she won't forgive herself. She doesn't believe she deserves forgiveness. But that's not true. It can't be true. If she can't forgive herself, then how the hell is there any hope for me?" Trey's icicle eyes stabbed me, twisting deep into my skin. "We're exactly the same, Hazy. You believe I'm worth saving. I believe you're worth saving. And one way or another, I'm going to make you see it for yourself."

Before I could throw something at his sentimental ass, Trey Bloomberg rose from his seat, stalked to the door, flung it open and stalked out. It slammed behind him, the *CRACK* of wood splintering imperceptible over the fracturing of my wounded heart.

CHAPTER ELEVEN

Sleep must've found me in Ayaz's arms. One moment, I was curled up beside him, carefully avoiding touching his healing flesh as I watched his chest rise and fall, the next I lay on a cold stone floor. A familiar, unearthly pulse tingled the ends of my fingers where they touched the stone.

As I sat up, a wave of hatred rolled over me, crawling over my skin and standing every hair on end.

The god is in the house.

By way of greeting, he offered up a cacophony of screams that echoed between my ears. Torches flared to life along the walls. As my eyes adjusted to the burst of light, I saw the platform in front of me, the chains hanging loose and the doors flung open. The god remained inside, but his presence seemed... closer. Lighter. Almost... jovial.

I have not feasted for many days. It has been difficult, for I have been offered delicious fruits of your race. My grip on the waking world grows weaker. But I made you a promise, and I am a truth-teller.

He means Greg and Zehra. They're still safe, no thanks to Ms. West. I folded my arms across my chest in the hopes I could hide the pounding of my heart. "Good. Thank you for keeping your end of our bargain. I am working on keeping mine. I gotta ask, though. What's the deal with the ugly-ass obelisk? If you're so weak, how could you make that giant thing rise up?"

It spoke little of my self-preservation skills that I'd just called the god's architectural statement 'ugly-ass.' The god turned in his prison, sending a fresh wave of nausea-inducing horror from the open trapdoor. A sound like blood bubbling from a wound reached my ears – *is that... laughter?*

Did the god find this *amusing?*

"What?" I demanded. "Tell me."

It is a figment from a time long past, that had almost been forgotten even by me. It was hidden, but your power revealed it.

I sighed. *I guess we're having another incomprehensible conversation.* "Fine, so it's my fault, as usual. What is the pillar?"

It is a piece.

"A piece of what?"

A piece of the star-journey. There are other pieces, also hidden. You will reveal them in time, as we grow closer.

An involuntary shudder pulsed through my skin. I knew what I'd promised the god – that he would set the students free as long as I joined him as his consort – and I would promise it a thousand times over if it meant saving my Kings, but the thought of being closer to it... I swallowed hard against the bile fighting its way from my stomach. "You say you are a truth-teller, but you weren't being truthful to me before. You didn't tell me you were trying to make children."

I did not make a lie. I said their souls were given to me, and they didn't know pain as you do. I did this only to protect my nest. It does not matter now that my race will continue.

"That's not fair. They didn't ask to be your children. You took their lives without permission."

What child asks to be born? Their own parents pushed them away. I took what was unwanted and I gave them gifts greater than they could ever wish for. I protect them and send my servants to guard them. Their descendants will rule over this galaxy from their castles made of stars. It is an honor to be chosen.

He had a point – from where he sat, what he offered the Miskatonic Prep students *did* seem better than what they had.

"You won't give them up," I said, understanding dawning. "When the time comes, you won't give me what we agreed. You love them."

I do not understand. They are my children. Their souls have given me these... feelingsss. I could not leave them even if it were possible to return to the stars, or if it were possible to bring back the one who is my twin.

The one who was his twin – for a moment I thought he meant me, but then I remembered what Ms. West had said. The god came to our galaxy with a mate, but she died on the journey. "You mean your soulmate? When you came to our galaxy, you weren't alone. You had another like you." *Like Noah's Ark... all the cosmic gods, two by two.*

The god's pain welled inside me as a deep and fathomless hole. I teetered on the edge of his loss, flailing my arms to keep from falling in, to becoming lost in his misery. *We danced among the stars, and their brightness lit the cosmos – a lantern to guide our way. But your universe was so far, and I had no brightness of my own. My twin burned and burned until their light faded, but I wanted so badly to reach the shores of our new home. I wanted to be first among us. I drove us onward, until their brightness was swallowed up in the cold depths of nothing. Their light went out. It was just me.*

I clutched my heart as his anguish cut through me. My mother's face flickered across my eyes – her hair ringed in orange fire. It was my mother, and yet it was not her. Her face wasn't quite right. There was another image beneath her – I could only see the edges of it, only enough to know it wasn't something that could be seen with human eyes. But it was the same. Because the god and I were the same. We'd both lost the people we love.

Because we are the murderers.

This was why he craved me and not Loretta. Because Loretta had no love for the man she killed. Because the god could not understand her emotions, but he knew mine all too well.

I sucked in a breath. My mother's angelic face continued to stare at me, her eyes haunted, edged with the god's inky darkness – the memory of his own crime had fused with mine, becoming one singular horror. "What you're describing is love – or as close an approximation as your race can get. You loved your soul twin, and you love your children. You want to hold them close, to protect them, to watch them grow up, to make sure their light never goes out. But your children are my friends, and I love them, and you promised you would free them if I found a way."

I promised. I am a truth-sayer. I love them and I will lose them, because I promised you. You must keep your promise. You must stay with me and be my new soul-twin.

"I haven't forgotten." Another shiver rocked my body. I hugged my arms around myself, trying to shut out the wave of jubilant despair the god threw my way. "I know you used the fire to give part of yourself to your children, and you took a piece of them in return. If I made you another fire, could you just swap the pieces back again?"

If I were to take back the spirit pieces, I would be tainted by their... feelingsss. I would not be able to make more children. We would be lonely together, you and I, without children.

I thought I understood. The pieces *could* be switched, but then the god would be so broken that he could not continue his race. And that was his whole reason for coming to our planet in the first place. He was supposed to colonize our universe.

I tapped my chin. "What if I found you some other vessels to be your children? What if they were *better?*"

Yesss. The god's voices crackled between my ears, the sound like an ice shelf breaking into the sea. *I could take my gifts from my children and give them to others, as long as they were worthy.*

A slow grin spread across my face. "I have the perfect candidates in mind. You tell me what you need, and I will make it happen. Mr. God, I think you and I finally have a plan."

CHAPTER TWELVE

I woke to shooting pain down one side of my neck from sleeping curled around Ayaz's body. Quinn slouched in the chair, his chin against his chest and an ugly sword he probably stole from that suit of armor in the faculty wing resting across his lap. He must have traded places with Trey during my slumber.

I reached across and poked him in the arm. Quinn snorted and leaped to his feet, crushing his back against the wall as he surveyed me with wild eyes. The sword clattered uselessly to the floor.

When he realized I hadn't set him on fire, his shoulders sagged with relief. Angry tears welled in my eyes, but I forced them back. *It's better this way. If he is afraid of me, he'll be relieved when I leave him to join the god. This way, I won't hurt him.*

"Morning, Hazy." Quinn turned on that megawatt smile of his, the one that melted all the hard things inside me. He ran a hand through his surfer hair. For an instant, the tension between us shifted from wariness to attraction. *Quinn still cares. He's afraid, but he's trying to fight it.* "I swear I wasn't sleeping on the job. I just closed my eyes for a moment—"

"It's fine. We're all tired." An awkward silence stretched

between us. Beside me, Ayaz still slept, his chest rising and falling in a steady rhythm. His head had bent toward me in the night. As I slid my legs out from under the blanket, his stubble tickled my leg, sending a delicious flare of heat right to my core.

Mmmmm. I'd missed Ayaz – so much it was a physical ache that dragged in my limbs. I'd missed his lips on mine, the way he stared at me so intently, unraveling my secrets with his eyes. I missed his scent on my clothes and the warmth of his fingers tracing my jaw – the artist becoming one with his muse.

Don't think about it. Don't think about things that can't be and feelings that won't last. Focus on your task – freeing the Kings of Miskatonic Prep.

I tore my eyes from Ayaz's sleeping figure, whirling around so I wouldn't be confronted with more painful memories of what we had and could never be. Only instead, my eyes met Quinn's again – amber orbs swimming with fear and confusion, torn between the desire to run and the desire to hold me close.

Another memory flashed in my mind. My back against a stone column in the garden, Quinn's mouth pressed against mine while his cock slammed into me—

I turned my head to the wall so I didn't have to confront his fear. "You don't have to be in the same room as me if it freaks you out. You can leave. I've got Trey and Ayaz – I don't need you if you're not—"

"I want to be here." Quinn's voice sounded hard, determined.

I snorted. "No, you don't. You're afraid of me, even more so now you know I'm the key to whatever the fuck that pillar is. You think I'm gonna burn this place down at any moment."

"Okay, yeah." Quinn's voice wavered. It took every ounce of self-control not to turn back to him and wrap him in my arms. I longed to kiss away his fears, but I couldn't do that when *I* was the one who frightened him. "I am afraid. Not of you, Hazy. But of the fire. I just... I can't go through that again. And I tell myself that you'd never hurt me, that you have control, that you love me.

But I used to tell myself the same things about my father, and... and Ayaz is all burned up and the god stuck a giant black phallus in the middle of the school and I just *don't fucking know what's real anymore*. You don't know how much I want to—"

His voice cracked. *Oh, fuck.* My resolve slipped. Heat sliced down my arms. I drummed my fingers against my arm so I didn't reach for Quinn.

"Shut up." I needed a distraction, something that would make me stop thinking about how much I needed the Kings, and how much I hated myself and this power that I never asked for and didn't want. Responding to my ire, the fire flared within me – reminding me that Quinn would get his revenge on his father soon enough. But what would he do to me?

I swung myself down from the bed and padded around to the end, flipping back the covers. I gasped as I saw Ayaz's legs.

He hadn't completely healed, but they were better than last night. Fresh skin peeked out from patches of charred and blistered skin. The burns were still horrific, but they no longer looked as fatal.

This is incredible. The god truly has given them a gift.

I'd never witnessed the healing powers of the god's spirit in person before. Quinn's eyes had healed quickly after Trey threw the itching powder in them, but I hadn't been close enough to Quinn back then to notice the change. I touched one of the patches of new skin, astounded at the speed to which Ayaz's body repaired itself.

Ayaz jumped, curling the blankets to his chin. "It's still tender," he muttered.

"Tender like your bruised ego, from getting beat up by a girl," Quinn said behind me. His words lacked their usual jovial tone, and the joke sailed over Ayaz's head unacknowledged.

"I'm glad you're awake. I had a little meeting with the god, and I have the best news." I threw the infirmary door open, expecting to see Trey standing in the hall. He wasn't there. I glanced both ways – nothing.

"Where's Trey?" Quinn shrugged. A noise hit my ears – a commotion. Voices shouting from somewhere in the school. *What the fuck is going on now?*

"Wait here," I ordered Quinn, and took off at a run. The noise echoed down the empty corridors. It was coming from the dormitory wing. I crossed the sky bridge, shoved open the doors, and strode into the wide hallway. Students gasped as they saw me, flattening their bodies against the walls to escape my touch. Their fear gave me a clear view of what transpired at the foot of the grand staircase.

Trey stood at the foot of the stairs, holding a pile of his folded clothes in his arms. He faced off against Courtney, Amber, John, Derek, and a couple of others, who'd linked arms human-chain style to block the staircase that led to the second floor.

"You can't come up here. That's not your room anymore," Courtney flipped her hair over her shoulder. "You think just because your little girlfriend summoned fire and a chunk of stone you get your old room back?"

"I don't think that. I know it." Trey's ice-blue eyes sized her up, finding her wanting.

I strode down the hall, inserting myself between Trey and Courtney. "There a problem here?" I cocked an eyebrow.

"Your toy-boy seems to believe he's entitled to his old room." Courtney's voice dripped with saccharine sweetness.

"That's because he is." I waved my hand. "Scoot aside. You're blocking the stairs. That's a fire risk."

At the word *fire*, an audible gasp rippled through the students. Courtney couldn't win this game because there was one person they feared more than her now – me.

I gazed down the hall, meeting the eyes of those gathered, taking stock of the terror that lurked there. Yup, they were all afraid. Which felt good but could backfire on my ass in a big way if I wasn't careful. As much as I wanted to push the Kings away now, before I got even more attached to them and our goodbye was too painful to articulate, I needed them.

I slid closer to Courtney. She blinked but didn't move. Beside her, Amber and John broke the chain and scooted away. It was just me and her, nose to nose.

"You don't have power here any longer." I held up my palm, pointing it to her chest.

A muscle in Courtney's eye twitched. "You wouldn't dare, gutter whore."

"Wouldn't I?" I grinned, although the smile probably looked more like a wolf baring its teeth. "If I were to burn you to ashes right now, would anyone try to stop me? Would your death matter to anyone?"

Courtney glared at me, but she darted out of my path. She knew she'd given us more than just a staircase. Trey smiled. "Thank you kindly."

He marched up the stairs and flung open the door to his old room. He must've taken the keys from Ayaz. He dropped his clothes onto a chair and went to open a window.

"It smells like a Turkish bathhouse in here."

I thought it smelled amazing. Touches of Ayaz were everywhere – the stack of art and architecture books piled up beside the TV, the boxes of weird spices and strong coffee scent in the kitchen, the heavy metal playlist flicking across the sound system. I picked up a black hoodie draped over the back of a chair and pulled it over my shoulders, breathing in Ayaz's rich honey and rose scent.

He's back. My heart did a little dance. *He might not remember everything that happened between us, but he remembers how I made him feel.*

That's enough. That will always be enough.

Trey sank down into his expensive sofa and pulled Parris' skin book across the table toward him. Already, his mind worked over the next phase of our plan. I knew him well enough to see that the showdown with Courtney in the hallway was for the benefit of the whole school. Trey had already started to take back control.

My King. My mirror.

I shoved my hands into my pockets. My eye sockets ached with tiredness, but I needed to get this out. "The god spoke to me while I was asleep."

BANG. The book slammed on Trey's knees. He whipped his head around, fixing me with that ice stare. "What's he got to say for himself?"

"The usual nonsensical gibberish. I asked him what the pillar was and he said, 'it is a piece.' A piece of what? He wouldn't elaborate. He didn't explain how I was the key or what it unlocked. But he did give me some good news about you guys." I relayed what the god had told me about taking away his gifts to give to a new brood of children, leaving out the bargain I had struck. If Trey knew what I was planning, he'd try to stop me, and that wasn't happening.

I'd already agreed – the price of my Kings' freedom was my own servitude.

It was a price I'd happily pay a hundred times over to give the Kings a second chance at life. What did my life matter? I wasn't giving up much of value – as soon as the police caught up with me, I'd be going to jail anyway.

I just wish...

Trey's face remained as impassive as stone. "All this time, the god had a solution, and he was willing to help. I guess no one ever thought to ask him."

"I don't think he's as evil as everyone makes him out to be." I shuddered as I heard the faintest shadow of the god's voice screaming between my ears. "I'm mean, he *is*, but only because his rules of right and wrong are completely different than ours. I guess it's kind of rude to hold him to our ideals. But at the heart of it, there's something universal that connects us – otherwise, the god wouldn't be drawn to me. He's lonely and he feels guilty about the death of the cosmic deity he loved. And maybe he couldn't articulate that until the Eldritch Club stuffed him full of human souls, but that doesn't change the fact he *feels*."

"Mmmm." Trey patted the cushion next to him. "Sit with me."

The command in his voice stoked the fire inside me. No one else but Trey could order me around and make me love it so much, make my body bend toward him and my core throb for more.

I plopped down on the couch next to him. Trey wrapped his arms around me. I sank against him, breathing in his scent, so different from Ayaz's, so utterly not what I'd expect. It always made me smile that a guy who was supposed to a King of the undead smelled of all things fresh and living – of spring herbs and wild-blossoms and cypress wood coated with dew.

"You're something else, you know that?" Trey murmured against my throat, his lips grazing my skin. "Only you could find something *relatable* about that ball of malevolent shadow. But that's why you're the first person who I ever truly believed could lift this curse. You're one-of-a-kind, out-of-this-world..."

A moan escaped me as Trey used his lips on mine to continue his thoughts. My exhaustion fell away under his touch. I tangled my hands in his hair, bringing his cruel lips to mine. Trey pulled me against him. His hard body pressed against mine, all our angles and corners fitting together, smoothing out and softening. I arched toward him, desperate to claim more of him.

"Shouldn't we..." I nudged the skin book with my foot.

"Not now." Trey shoved Parris' book off the couch and pulled me onto his lap. I straddled him, grinding my hips against his hardness as I plunged my tongue inside his mouth, claiming my first taste of him in far, far too long. Trey brushed his hand over my thigh and shuddered with want. "Right now I need you."

This is a bad idea.

Being close to Trey was like falling over a waterfall – once you jumped, you'd committed yourself to drowning. Sure, the fall was exhilarating, but under the water lurked all the things that would wreck your life forever.

To him, I was the same – a current dragging him under, knocking his carefully-curated world off-balance. But as much as we knew the pain we could cause to each other, we couldn't help ourselves. The thrill of the fall and the lure of those dark, unexplored waters was too strong.

I pulled back, struggling to catch my breath, to give myself a moment. Trey thought I was changing positions, so he scooped me in his arms, lifting me off the couch and heading for his room.

"Trey... mmmm..." His mouth crushed mine, driving away my protests. My body succumbed to his. I wrapped my legs around his back, grinding myself harder against him, feeling the rush of heat as his hard cock brushed my clit.

Trey threw me down on the bed and climbed up next to me, his hands skimming my body, stoking my nerve endings to life. Fire tore through me – flames to turn the waterfall to steam, to burn away my doubts. I succumbed to it, letting the heat soak me, igniting my body into a torch that burned bright beneath Trey's fiery kiss.

He tore at my clothes, shedding his own as though they were poison to him. Hot skin met skin, stoking the fire inside me into a raging inferno. Trey cupped a breast, roughly tonguing my nipple until I gasped. My nails raked down his back hard enough to draw blood.

I still wore the tattered dress from last night's performance. He pushed up the hem and dived between my legs, his tongue flicking over me with relentless speed. I bent my hips toward him, needing, wanting, hoping. A flame darted from my palm to lick the pillow, and I snuffed it out before Trey noticed.

He lifted my hips, bringing me closer to him. His eyes flicked up, meeting mine, arresting me there. Fire and ice locked together – each needing the other to survive.

A hard lump formed in my throat. In all the times we'd slept together, it had never felt like this before. It felt... like having the god inside my head during my dreams – invasive and raw and too, too real.

He'd become the air I breathed.

I can't do this. I can't let him go.

I opened my mouth to tell Trey to stop, but the words wouldn't come. There was no word for what I was feeling, because I desperately didn't want him to stop. The orgasm built inside me as the heat thrashed against my palms, desperate to escape. I needed him, like water or sunlight, but my need could risk everything we'd fought for.

I need to be strong.

My hand flopped over the edge of the bed, searching for something to break the moment.

As Trey's tongue beat a furious path across my clit, my fingers closed around the spine of a thin volume. I gripped it and swung. The flimsy pages fanned across Trey's face.

"What the fuck—"

The book flopped onto my stomach. Trey tore himself from me, his hands slack at his sides. I'd hoped to surprise him, but the look of horror on his face told me I'd done worse than that.

I glanced down at the book I'd flung at him. It wasn't a book really, more of a pamphlet, and it had fallen open on a familiar scene. Bright faces stared out from computer labs and walked amongst leafy grounds. Scrawled across the page – the pen pressed so hard it broke through the page – were the words:

NO FUTURE. NO HOPE. NO TOMORROW.

The college prospectus. The one Trey defaced because he was the smartest guy at Miskatonic Prep and he would never be able to go to college.

Mood officially killed.

Trey's mouth froze in a hard line as he stared down at the page. I caught the slightest tremble in his shoulders – the only sign that he'd been affected by it at all. But I was his mirror and I knew what would hurt him, and this sliced him open and tore out his heart.

I slammed the prospectus shut and tossed it into the corner of the room. It hit the shelf, knocking over Ayaz's paint bottles.

I'm sorry, the words danced on the tip of my tongue. But I wouldn't apologize. I needed to keep him distant, for both our sakes. He'd understand one day.

Trey shook his head. "Why did you do that?"

"I needed you to stop."

"You could have said that." Cruelty edged into Trey's voice – my old bully putting his defenses up. How I wanted to take it back, but I wouldn't. It brought me the distance I needed. "You didn't need to hit me over the head with my own shattered dreams."

"Don't be like that. You *are* going to college." I grabbed his shoulder and shook him. His head rocked, his eyes staring dead ahead but not focused on me. Trey had gone somewhere inside his head, somewhere I couldn't follow. "And you're going to be an engineer and work in renewable energy and fuck your father and his evil plans. Not just you, but *every student* is getting out of this hell."

"No, we're not."

"You're not afraid, are you? The god says—"

Trey's eyes flicked to the discarded prospectus. He shook his head. "We can't, Hazel. Seeing that page confirms it. I've spent my whole life inflicting misery on others because I thought that was what I had to do. Because I didn't know there was another way to be. Now I know. I *want* to be different. I can't doom another person to this fate. If I save the students of Miskatonic Prep, then other innocent people will become the god's children.

They'll be tainted by his power. They'll do more evil things. We can't do it."

I smiled. "What if those children were locked away where they couldn't do harm? What if those children were your parents?"

Trey reeled, touching his hand to his cheek as if I'd slapped him. He froze, his eyes glazing over, going deeper into that place inside himself where he kept all the evil things his father did to him. His legacy of blood and violence and greed – the legacy he was strong enough to overcome, even if that meant a little more blood had to be spilled.

Two orbs of pure ice searched my face, different in color to mine but shining with the same defiance. Trey lowered his hand, placing his fingers over mine. Fire sizzled beneath my skin.

When Trey spoke again, his voice was made of flint. "If my father is so desperate to obtain the god's power, then this is merely granting his wish. Yes... you're right. As long as there's a way to stop them using their powers in the world, our parents are the perfect choice for the god's children."

CHAPTER THIRTEEN

"Yoooooo-hooooooo, are you in here?"

My eyelids tangled together as I struggled to open my eyes. White walls greeted me. Sunlight from an open window reflected off rows of trophies, splashing colorful prisms across the walls. Warm flesh pressed against mine. For a moment I didn't remember where I was, and then it all came back to me in a rush – the performance, the pillar, Trey's dad shooting at me even though I'd burned him good, sleeping in the cave, Ms. West's confession, Ayaz in the infirmary, the god's dream, falling into bed with Trey...

The last thing I remembered was talking about offering the god Trey's parents as his children, and then I rested my head on his chest and we must've both fallen asleep. Between everything that happened in the auditorium, the cold cave, Ayaz's uncomfortable hospital bed and the god invading my dreams, I couldn't have slept much before. No wonder I'd crashed. But now...

"Wakey, wakey." Quinn's voice called from the living room.

"Mmmmph." Trey threw his arm across my chest, pinning me to the bed. "If we ignore him, he'll go away."

"Have you *met* Quinn?" I slid out from under Trey's arm and threw off the covers. "If we ignore him, he'll get five times more annoying—"

As if on cue, Quinn kicked open the bedroom door. He brandished a large frying pan and a metal spatula, which he clanged together. "Rise and shine!"

CLANG CLANG CLANG.

Trey tossed a pillow at him. "Get the fuck out."

"Not until you get up. We don't want to be late for class."

I rubbed my eyes. *Fuck, why was that sun so bright?* "I hate you, but you're right. Whatever goes down in school today, we need to be there. How's Ayaz?"

"Still crispy. Loretta is watching him while I get my groove on." Quinn gave an exaggerated twirl. "Do I look like a King again, Hazy?"

For the first time since he walked in, I noticed Quinn had changed into a uniform, but it wasn't that of Derleth Academy. The Miskatonic Prep crest with its five-pointed star stood in sharp relief over his breast.

Instead of the red and black of Derleth, the Miskatonic colors were a soft blush pink and a strange green that seemed to be many different shades at once. It reminded me of the glowing veins in the stone of the obelisk – of all the reasons I never wanted to step into a uniform again.

And yet, on Quinn, it made me ache with desire. It might've had to do with the way his shoulders filled out the blazer, or how the lapels and low double-breast accentuated his narrow waist, or how he'd taped together my gold tiara from the performance and wore that lopsided on his head, or how for the first time in too long his smile reached all the way to his eyes.

Quinn danced away from me, and I knew it was because he didn't want to touch me. But he was here, he was *trying*. And I wished like hell I didn't have to prove him right.

I was going to hurt him, only not with my fire.

"You don't need a crown to be a King." Trey went to his own

closet and emerged a few moments later in his own Miskatonic Prep uniform. My breath caught in my throat at the sight of the two of them together. Trey was broader in the shoulders than Quinn, and when he stood with his legs slightly apart in his slacks – creased to a knife-edge, of course – and his wing-tips all shined up, he could melt panties at fifty paces. Trey smoothed the cuffs of his blazer, his eyes searing over my body.

That boy was King.

And he fucking *knew* it.

All he had to do was go out there and claim his crown. And damn if I didn't want to—

Keep it in your pants, Hazel. You can't be weak. You can't let what just happened with Trey happen again, or you won't be able to leave them. It's better this way.

Quinn had brought my Derleth uniform from downstairs. I tugged that on in the bathroom and stuffed my textbooks into my satchel. I linked my arm through Trey's and held my other out to Quinn. He hesitated, driving the breath from my lungs.

"Quinn, stop being a loser and take the damn woman's hand so we can do this," Trey barked.

Quinn's arm slipped through mine, raising the hairs on my skin. His eyes met mine, and in those amber orbs was a pleading innocence. And I realized that for all Quinn had done and seen and experienced, for all he'd reveled in every wanton fantasy he could imagine, he'd closed himself off from this particular intimacy – from placing his life in someone else's hands.

He used humor to keep people at arm's length because he didn't *trust*. He couldn't. Not when his father – the very person who should protect him and love him and nurture him – raised his fists and broke his spirit. Not when his own mother let it happen, let the blows rain down on her son so she would be spared.

I gave Quinn's arm a little squeeze. "Wait until you hear my news, straight from the mouth of the god."

"You haven't told him yet?" Trey looked surprised.

"Tell me what?"

"I was going to," I said quickly. "But then we—"

Quinn waved a hand dramatically, as if it was no big deal. He didn't want Trey to know he'd told me he was afraid of me. "Tell me now."

"When I drifted off in Ayaz's bed, the god drew me into a dream. He told me that the pillar is so old he doesn't know what it is anymore. But the important thing is that he'll take away the gifts his spirit gives you – the immortality, the fast healing, all the stuff that makes you not human – but only if you can find other children for him to bestow those gifts and continue his race."

"Our lovely girlfriend thinks our parents would make the perfect candidates," Trey added.

Quinn's mouth froze in a hard line. "Give our parents immortality?"

"They've worked so hard. I think they deserve this. Don't you?" I explained my plan to him as we checked ourselves one last time in Trey's mirror. Quinn's crown slid down over his eye, and I reached up to adjust it. He didn't flinch when my fingers brushed his face.

Yes," he whispered. "Yes, I think they will get exactly what they deserve."

CHAPTER FOURTEEN

"This feels like the worst idea ever." I smoothed down the front of my Derleth uniform. The red-trim on the blazer swam in my vision, the same red as blood.

On either side of me, Trey and Quinn looked resplendent. The pink of the tie brought warmth to Trey's icicle eyes, while the green blazer and crest gave Quinn's savage expression an other-worldly glow.

Behind them, Andre and Loretta wore their Derleth uniforms. Sadie wore Loretta's spare uniform – they were about the same size. Andre had insisted she be part of whatever happened today, and I agreed. This was as much her decision and her battle as anyone else. For the first time since I'd met silent, angry Sadie, I could picture her as a student here. Young and fierce and naive and innocent – until Derleth Academy had taken everything from her.

Edimmu. Scholarship students. Maintenance staff. All the people who'd been wronged by the Eldritch Club and faculty.

A united front.

A recruitment drive for the damned.

I squared my shoulders. "Let's do this."

We'd deliberately ignored the first bell in order to make an entrance. Homeroom was in session, so the dormitory was empty of students as we headed toward the main classroom wing. The place looked like a tornado had blown through. Doors hung open, and rubbish had been flung all over. My shoes scuffed papers littering the hall.

Every noticeboard stood empty — strips of paper hung from bent thumbtacks. Every last student photograph and memento had been torn down and trampled underfoot. Memories too painful to bear after I'd shown them the truth.

We shoved our way through the double doors and across the sky bridge into the classroom wing. The bell sounded. Students poured into the hall, their conversations rising through the high rafters and bouncing off the rows of lockers.

They saw us. They stopped dead, freezing like statues. Conversations cut off like someone had hit a mute button. Even though some of them had already seen me in the dorm earlier, I still inspired enough fear to render them silent.

I folded my arms, moving my head to meet each and every single pair of eyes. Many of them looked away. At the front of the crowd, Courtney fixed me with her panther-stare, but she didn't intimidate me anymore.

The last person I locked eyes with was Ayaz, who shuffled out of Dexter's classroom on crutches. The sight of him shuddered through my body like an earthquake. His eyes swept across my Derleth uniform, and I felt like I was wearing nothing at all.

You're mine again, Ayaz Demir. At least, for now.

I stepped back and nodded once. "Glad to see you've all missed me."

"How are you back, gutter whore?" Amber demanded. "You died in the Dunwich fire."

I breezed past her without answering the question. They were smart enough to figure out that fire wasn't my enemy.

Trey and Quinn edged forward, escorting me toward my

locker. Students parted for us to pass — like I was a plague victim they were afraid to touch. I slammed my locker open and grabbed a stack of textbooks at random, hugging them to my chest as I grinned at Courtney. "It turns out I'm only slightly dead. Like you."

Courtney's eyes blazed, but there was no real fury there. We faced off across the corridor. Tillie stood behind her, flicking her gaze from me, back to Trey and Quinn and the others, then back to me again. She looked like she didn't know where she wanted to stand. Behind them, Ayaz looked on with intense interest. Everyone wanted to know how this was going to go down.

"It *was* you on stage," Tillie said in a small voice. "I thought maybe it was just a trick."

I nodded. "I was really me, alive and with my soul intact. And apart from a few projector tricks, the rest of it was real, too. The fire. The pillar. The truth about what your parents did."

Tillie flashed me a tentative smile — a smile as a peace offering, as an olive branch. She'd been the first one to start to believe me during the performance. She and Trey had suspected the parents for years. Not only did she believe me, she wanted to be a part of putting it right. I wasn't ready to trust her, but I was ready to make an attempt to try.

It took every effort to return her smile. I didn't make a habit out of smiling at my ex-bullies, but I needed as many people on my side as I could get.

Silence again. Courtney cleared her throat. "My parents had told me the fire had been a horrible accident. They really agreed to this... mass sacrifice?"

"Yes. Everyone's parents did. I have a list they made at a club meeting where they each volunteered a child, and I've heard it confirmed from Ms. West *and* from the god himself. I think your mother agreeing was a condition of her joining the Eldritch Club."

Courtney stood back, her face pale. "I hate you for ruining

everything," she whispered, but her words had no venom. We both knew she wasn't talking to me.

"You're a cold-hearted bitch, Courtney Haynes. But you don't deserve this. None of you do."

Around the room, students nodded. They may have tormented me, hated me even, but they believed me. Right now, that was all that mattered.

"You've all been complicit in this plot your parents cooked up," I said. "You tortured scholarship students because you enjoyed it. You knew what would happen to them at the end of each quarter, and yet you let it continue. You'll have to do your own penance for your part in those crimes, but right now you're also victims. You've been trapped here for too long and deprived of a piece of yourselves – a piece that might have urged you to act more humanely. It's time for the lies to stop and the truth to set you free."

That old feline fury flickered in Courtney's eyes. Only this time, it wasn't for me. "I don't know what you're planning for them, Hazel Waite, but you can count me in."

My grin widened. I held out my hand. Courtney stared at it for a moment, like she thought it might burst into flame at any moment. *Which I guess is true.* Then she reached out and gave it a firm shake.

"I can't believe it. I'm gone, like, five minutes and you're making friends with the Queen Bee."

My heart soared at the sound of that familiar voice. *I must be imagining it. I can't...*

I turned my head, slowly, because I still wasn't at a point where I wanted to take my eyes off Courtney, to see a hand running through sandy blond hair.

Greg grinned up at me like a cat who'd just caught one of those catnip mice and never intended to let it go.

"Greg?" I threw my arms around him. "It's really you."

He nodded, then winced as if the very act of moving his neck gave him pain. "She let me out," he whispered. "A good-faith gesture to make sure you guys held up your part of the plan."

"What about Zehra?"

Greg shook his head. He tucked something into the pocket of my blazer. "She gave me this. She said you'd know what to do with it."

I didn't dare open my pocket in the hallway, fearing what Zehra might have given me. Instead, I hugged Greg harder. He felt so good, so alive.

"What's going on?" Amber asked. "Wasn't that queer guy sacrificed?"

"'That Queer Guy' has a name." Greg extended a hand to her. "Hi, I'm Greg."

She looked confused for a moment, then reached out to shake. Greg grabbed her arm and folded her into a hug. Students laughed – not cruelly, just releasing tension. Amber's face burned red with shock and embarrassment before she succumbed to the charm that was Greg and crumpled into his arms.

Trust Greg to slay them with his charms.

"I was never sacrificed." Greg ran a hand through his hair. "But I've been locked in a room beside the gym, inhaling that foul rotting meat smell all day and night while our headmistress took vials of my blood for her experiments."

"I thought you were into meat," Derek jeered, grabbing his crotch. For the first time, no one laughed. He stared at his friends before quickly dropping his hands.

"This shit stops now." I raised a hand, palm out in an obvious threat.

Silence fell.

Quinn stepped away from me, his eyes wide. "Hazy, you shouldn't..."

"No, I *should*. These bastards have done so much worse. If I burned them all now, they'd heal overnight, like Ayaz. But the scars from what you've all done to the scholarship students over twenty years – those will never go away."

I looked to Sadie for confirmation. She nodded fiercely.

"But I won't." I lowered my arm. Derek let out a sigh of relief. "I won't, because we've got a bigger goal in mind that requires us all to work together. You're welcome to stick with your beliefs about certain people being beneath you, but that's your loss. You can stay here and rot, because we're the ones with the plan to get your lives back."

"What?"

I gestured to my friends standing around me. "You've been trapped here for twenty years, and you've done *what* exactly to save yourselves? You've been so distracted with petty vendettas and bullying people you consider less than yourselves that you haven't considered how you came to be here or how you might get your lives back. Well, those very people you tormented are standing here before you with the beginning of an answer. We could have run away and left you to your fate, and I'll admit, it's fucking tempting. But I don't believe in running, so here we are with a plan, if you want to hear it."

I didn't really have a plan, yet. But that little fact was on a need-to-know basis.

Students exchanged glances. Amber's eyebrows lifted so high they practically crawled off her face. They *wanted* to believe me, but I wasn't going to give them the option until they asked nicely.

"Cut the dramatics, Waite." Courtney flipped her hair over her shoulder. "We want to hear your plan."

Well, as nicely as a monarch was capable of. She didn't call me 'gutter whore,' I guess?

I smiled. "Good. The first thing you need to know is that whatever the faculty want you to believe, Ms. West has her own agenda. On the surface, we're playing along, but we're not their pawns. We're hosting a party in true Miskatonic Prep fashion on Friday night, down at the pleasure garden, no teachers allowed.

I'll reveal the details then. Bring the last of your drugs and your booze and be prepared to burn your inhibitions, because this is your farewell party. At the end of this quarter, you'll be saying goodbye to this hellhole forever."

A cheer rose up from the students – the sound resonating through the vaulted corridor, bouncing off the marble floor and the shiny lockers to feed back into itself, growing in power and intensity until it became a bugle calling us to war.

A black cloud swirled through the crowd, knocking aside students. My heart plummeted, thinking it was the shadows. But it couldn't be – I controlled the god's shadows now.

Ms. West stormed through the students, her black gown flapping around her and her eyes narrowed to slits. Teachers in their black academic gowns tore after her, struggling to keep up with her determined step. Of course, we all turned tail to follow them.

Voices bounced off the walls as students poured into the atrium, crowding the staircases and blocking the exits in flagrant disregard for fire safety protocol. Ms. West strode through the assembled students, flanked by Dr. Atwood and Dr. Halsey. They reached the Derleth Academy crest hanging above the stairs. Ms. West snapped her fingers.

Dr. Atwood and Dr. Halsey lifted the wooden crest from the wall, revealing another underneath. A crest familiar to me now, even though I'd never worn the uniform.

Miskatonic Prep.

CRASH.

They tossed the Derleth crest over the balustrade. It flipped once before smashing into the marble. Students leaped out of the way as splinters flew in all directions.

"We're done pretending," Ms. West roared at the cowering students. I could practically see smoke coming out her ears. "You have learned the truth about your enrollment here. You were chosen because your parents deem you expendable. But there is one here who truly loves you, who wants the best for you. Your god."

A ripple of disbelief echoed through the crowd. Trey glanced at me, silently asking what we should do. I shrugged. We had to let her talk, or it looked as it the top of her head would explode.

"He has cared for you all these years as if you were his children." I bit my tongue not to yell the truth, but it wasn't time for that yet. "Each of you carries him inside you. Over the years I have tried to mold you into something that pleases him, but again and again, you have failed us both. Your god has given you a great gift – immortal blood and endless good health, and powers you haven't begun to explore, but you feel it is worthless while you are trapped inside these walls. But the god did not trap you here – your parents did. And by your god's grace, we shall all be free again."

Another cheer rose from the students, more subdued, unsure. Eyes turned to us, looking for direction. In the front, the Kings and I cheered loudest of all. My eyes met Ms. West, and I tried to convey through the curl of my lip and the tightness of my fist that I had the students in her thrall.

"We will be hosting a graduation ball at the end of the quarter, on the anniversary of your imprisonment here. If you wish for your freedom, you will show up at this ball in your finest clothes. You will do your school proud. If you stand with the faculty against your parents, you will walk out of this school as free spirits, with the god's gifts still intact."

Only a smattering of applause greeted her words, and not even Trey's enthusiastic shout could bring them around. Ms. West stared down at us as though she expected flowers to be thrown at her feet. Instead, all we had were the rotting tomatoes she deserved.

I stepped forward, my voice ringing clear. "We'll do what you ask, but the students want something in return, a show of good faith. If we're all to graduate this year with real diplomas, we want the points table set back to 0. For *everyone*. It's about time we *all* knew what it's like to start life without advantages. We're going to be even, and at the end of term, the valedictorian will be chosen based on merit alone."

Trey stared at me gape-mouthed, like I'd suddenly sprouted a second head. But I knew what I was doing... I thought so, at least. I needed the students to see me command Ms. West and have her obey. They needed to see who was in control here.

"Great idea," Tillie called from the back of the room. Courtney shot her a dirty look, but a number of other students echoed her agreement.

"You ungrateful brats," Ms. West hissed, wrapping her shawl around her shoulders like a vampire making a dramatic exit. Above her head, the merit points boards flickered once, then every single total was reset to 0. "This isn't a holiday. Get to class."

CHAPTER FIFTEEN

"A key?" Greg squinted at me like he was seeing me for the first time.

We'd gathered our crew – Greg, Andre, Loretta, Sadie, and Trey and Quinn – in Trey's room to report on how the first day had gone. Quinn tried to find Ayaz to join us, but he wasn't in his room or the art studio – I wondered if seeing how afraid everyone was had made him rethink the things he'd said in the infirmary. My stomach twisted up in knots about it, but I tried to ignore it and focus on Greg.

"I don't get it either, and we're not supposed to be talking about it now. We're supposed to be figuring out how to sneak out to see Deborah, Mr. 20 merit points." Greg already jumped ahead on the points table for answering a difficult question in physics.

"Yeah, brainiac." Quinn thumped Greg on the back. "I need you to tutor me."

"I don't think tutoring is going to help you," Greg grinned. "Mostly you just need to shut your face." Quinn was at -13 for talking back to Dr. Atwood.

Quinn clutched his chest. "I'm wounded. I shall never recover from this slight—"

Trey rolled his eyes at me. "Maybe we could get back on topic. Hazel, you might as well tell Greg about your key theory, since we can't focus on anything else."

I shrugged. "I don't know how to explain it, but when I was touching the pillar, it's like I could see right through to the god as he is. The god is sort of... asleep but dreaming. It's through his dreams that he talks to me and shows me things, and I think that's how he talks to Ms. West, too. But I saw him as he truly was – like peering through a keyhole."

"That's what the rats were trying to show – a key and a lock fitting together," Trey said. "I'm guessing the pillar unlocks—"

"The god's prison," I finished. "I think so, too. Which means this information *cannot leave this room*. If any of the senior Eldritch Club find out about this, they're going to make it their mission to force me to open the lock. I don't know how to do that yet, but I bet Vincent has delightful ways of finding out."

"I'm not likely to tell," Quinn made a zipping motion. "Greg has taught me the value of shutting my face."

Trey snorted. "You have a mouth the size of the Grand Canyon. You're a security risk."

Quinn pouted. "Hazy has no problem with the size of my mouth, or what I do with it—"

I punched him in the shoulder, hard enough to make him wince. Greg and Andre laughed.

"Can we get through *one conversation* without Quinn being gross?" I touched my fingers to the scar on my wrist. *I wish Ayaz was here.* "I'm serious – this key idea is just a theory, but it can't get out. I'm not even telling Deborah when we see her tonight—"

"Who's Deborah?"

I whirled around at the familiar voice, deep and exotic.

"Hey," Ayaz hovered in the doorway. Apart from the single crutch he leaned on, his body showed no signs of the literal hell I'd put him through. He held up a set of keys, indicating he'd unlocked the door since it had previously been his room.

"Hey," I choked out. My throat had dried up. I couldn't believe he was standing there. It hadn't been lies. He hadn't changed his mind. *He's here.*

"Glad to have you back, Ataturk." Quinn slapped him on the back. Ayaz winced as the force jostled his body. Quinn's eyes glinted with mischief. "We're off to do something reckless and dangerous. Want to come?"

"That depends. I just need to talk to Hazel first."

Trey and Quinn exchanged glances. The two of them grabbed the others and backed out of the room, leaving me alone with Ayaz.

Traitors.

Ayaz's dark eyes regarded me, his expression unreadable. Ayaz always held his emotions close, never giving too much away. "I am sorry I missed you after class. Courtney cornered me and asked me to be her date for the graduation dance."

A wave of jealousy shot through me. Even now, after everything that happened and our supposed truce, Courtney was still determined to stir shit between us. I guess you couldn't expect a panther to put away her claws.

It's a good thing. Ayaz should go with Courtney. She obviously really likes him, and it's not like I'll be able to have him after graduation.

I couldn't help the tightness in my voice when I asked, "What did you say?"

"I said that I didn't know anything about a dance, or why we'd be having one in the middle of the chaos. I wanted to hear from you first. What's going on?"

"What's going on is a Mexican stand-off between the faculty and the Eldritch Club, with us in the middle," I said. "And that's exactly what I need them to continue to believe. The teachers and the parents underestimate the students. They believe you're beholden to the base instincts of the god's spirit, that you all want to be immortal and powerful and filled with the god's wrath. But I've mostly figured out a way to reverse what was done to you. All the students and teachers would be free. *Truly free.*"

Ayaz's eyes fluttered closed. Dark lashes tangled together, and I held my breath. "In your scenario, would we be the age we are now, or will we be the age we *should* be? I don't want to suddenly be in my forties with a bald spot and wrinkles, complaining about my knees all the time."

"Honestly? I don't know. I don't think even the god knows. You're refusing his gifts, which apparently has never happened before. I think it's most likely your physical body will remain the same, but I'm not the expert."

"I'll take the chance." Ayaz swung the crutch as he hobbled across the room. He half-sat, half-fell into the sofa. I'd never seen him so awkward before, and judging by the scowl on his face, he didn't like it.

"So you're in? You trust me? But you haven't even asked what the god wants in return."

"I don't care. I'll help any way I can." Pain-filled eyes stared up at me, begging me for something I couldn't give. Ayaz's brow creased in concentration as he bent his will toward trying to place me inside the gaping hole in his memory.

"You might not thank me when you find out what we have to do. The god needs to give his gifts to others to make more children. That means others will have to become his children in your place. The only people Trey and Quinn are willing to sacrifice are the Eldritch Club."

Ayaz pursed his lips. "Vincent has been good to me."

"He used you – you told me that yourself. You're a political pawn, a way for him to show his buddies that he has powerful connections all over the world. Just because he was kinder to you than to Trey doesn't change that fact, or any of the things he's done since. Do you believe he's responsible for sacrificing the entire class so he could gain power?"

The forehead crease appeared again as Ayaz considered this. Finally, he nodded.

"And knowing what the god's gifts mean, are you willing to give them to Vincent? After all, power is what he craves – it's not cruel to give someone what they want."

"But once he has this power, we can't stop him using it against vulnerable people. We've seen what he's capable of when he controls this school. What if he controlled the world?"

"That's the major snag." I shuddered. "The others are all for this justice by revenge – the punishment fits the crime. They don't want to ruin the lives of more innocents, but I think that will happen anyway if the Eldritch Club become children of the god. I was wondering if you could help? You know more about this occult stuff than anyone else. I've heard you talk before about binding spells. Can you find something that will enable us to bind the power of the Eldritch Club so they can't destroy the world?"

"I can try." Ayaz leaned over, wincing as the movement tugged at his new skin. As he grabbed the corner of Parris' skin book, his arm brushed mine.

Sitting this close to him and breathing in his scent made all the memories rise to the surface. His kiss last night burned on my lips. I couldn't kiss him again. I couldn't risk it. *I need a distraction...*

"I have something for you," I whispered.

As I reached across the table, my finger brushed his hand once more. A flare of heat jumped from my skin to his. Ayaz jerked away, but a moment later his hand returned.

He's still afraid of me. I squeezed my eyes shut. *I can't blame him.*

I pulled the tiny box across the table. Ayaz sucked in a breath as he recognized it. It was the lockbox the Kings used to keep things in the cave that they didn't want the teachers or parents to discover. The last thing I'd hidden in it was the imprints of the keys for Ms. West's laboratory, but we didn't need them now. Now the box held something more precious.

"I was hoping to find a chance to give this to you all day." I lifted the lid and slid the box in front of him. "She gave this to me, but I think it's really meant for you."

Inside was a small pendant on a leather thong – a glass bead with concentric circles of dark blue, white, and light blue with a black dot in the center. It looked a little like an eye. Ayaz touched the object, the look on his face rapturous.

"Zehra," he whispered.

"What is it?"

"It's a *nazar* – an amulet worn to ward off the evil eye." Ayaz rolled up the corner of his shirt to show me a tattoo of the same design under his ribcage. "Zehra made one for each of us when she was eight. She mailed mine to me so I'd always have something to remember her. I wore mine every day until my first year at Miskatonic Prep. The others bullied me about it so much that I threw it into the ocean. I regretted it ever since – that is why I have it tattooed. She must have seen I wasn't wearing it..." A shudder racked his body. "That's Zehra; even though she's the one in danger, she's still thinking about me. We have to help her."

"I'm trying. Ms. West still has her locked up." I curled my fingers around the *nazar*. "This is my promise to you that I will get her back. Ms. West is supposed to return her as part of our deal, but I was a fucking idiot again and didn't specify a timetable. She's going to try to hold Zehra for as long as possible to ensure we cooperate. I think she might keep Zehra as a bargaining chip with Vincent, in case her plan with Gloria fails."

I didn't tell him I overheard Ms. West trying to sacrifice her to the god. It was just as well, because Ayaz was already on his feet. "We have to get Zehra out. *Now.*"

I shook my head. "Greg's told us that the weight room is heavily guarded – that's why there are so few teachers. The Deadmistress knows I might try something. I could send the shadows or a couple of you Edimmu to get her out – the teachers couldn't hurt you, but I worry they might hurt Zehra instead."

Ayaz's head fell into his hands. "What do we do?"

"We watch. We pretend that everything is okay, that we're merrily playing along with West's game. We wait for our chance to strike."

His lip twisted. It wasn't quite a smile, but for Ayaz, it was quite something. He looped the *nazar* around his neck. "What's this dangerous mission Quinn was talking about? I'm intrigued."

CHAPTER SIXTEEN

"Are you sure you're okay to do this again?" I asked.

In response, Trey pulled on a tailored blazer that definitely didn't say 'I'm about to hike through a forest.' He did look damn fine, though.

I tossed him Dante's old hoodie. Trey wrinkled his nose like it would give him a disease, but when I pointed out that it would be a better disguise if he *didn't* look like the son of an arrogant billionaire, he pulled it on.

Quinn pouted. "No fair. I want to go for a walk with a pet stone and take Hazy out for ice cream."

"I agree. Ice cream sounds nice," Ayaz piped up.

"That's not what we're doing," Trey snapped, adjusting the hood over his perfectly-styled hair. "We're sneaking into a hotel where at least some of our parents are probably still holed up to visit a woman who may or may not have the answers we need. If we get caught it will ruin the whole plan, so forgive me if I don't want Mr. Everything's-a-joke and Mr. Betrayed-Hazy-and-can't-put-weight-on-my-legs on the case."

"Besides, Ayaz has a binding spell to start on, and someone

has to stay behind and watch out for the other scholarship students," I added.

Quinn waved a hand. "Pssssh. Andre has more than proven he doesn't need help from the likes of me."

Ayaz didn't look happy about it either, but instead of arguing, he swept me into his arms and planted a smoldering kiss on my lips. "Be careful," he whispered.

Quinn's eyes raked over my body. He didn't offer any good-byes, and I pretended I didn't care.

I pulled on my leather jacket and followed Trey through the dorms and down to the atrium. We didn't bother with the secret passage this time. My Docs squeaked on the marble floors. Even though it was past the official curfew, no one stopped us. The teachers barely had a presence at all after dark – they were preoccupied with other things, like guarding the gym while West finished whatever she was doing to Zehra.

Please be strong, Zehra. We're coming for you as soon as we figure out a way. I just hope we're not too late.

Hand in hand, Trey and I strolled out the front door, descended the stone steps, crossed the lawn, and entered the forest.

Even though I'd made my way through this forest several times already, I still couldn't distinguish the different routes. Trey led the way with ease, picking the easiest path around fallen trees and over the craggy rocks jutting from the earth.

"For a pretty rich boy, you seem comfortable here in the wild," I said.

"Twenty years living in hell with this forest as a boundary, you learn the land as well as I once knew our Martha's Vineyard second home." Trey turned to help me over a fallen log. His hands rested on my arms, steadying me. That was Trey – a rock, a solid force. When he was my bully, standing up to him had felt like pushing back against a stone statue – cold and immovable. But now that he was on my side, now that he had my heart and I his, it was like he'd build a wall up around both of us. Nothing could penetrate it.

It was such a strange feeling, this protection.

Trey picked up the rock he'd chiseled from its hiding place and placed it with reverence into his backpack. We continued down the peninsula into the town of Arkham, sticking to the bushes as much as possible. I hoped Trey's hoodie would be enough to keep his identity secret. After all, it wasn't as if people in the town regularly saw the students.

After a time, we reached the base of the peninsula. Here, the gravel road gave way to asphalt. We kept to the trees as we entered the village, ears pricked for sounds. We emerged from the forest opposite the Arkham Grand Hotel, crouching behind the bushes and peering up at the grand facade. As promised, Deborah waited out front, her three dogs fighting their leads and her eyes scanning the horizon. Leopold sat up, his ears pricked. He barked three times.

I nudged Trey. "He's excited to see you."

"He is not. That's just what dogs do." Trey practically bounded across the street. Leopold knocked him back on the grass, licking his face while Trey convulsed with laughter. Deborah helped him up.

"I'd better get you all inside," she said. "We don't know who's watching."

Deborah's room wasn't in the hotel itself, but a cheaper motel room in an annex at the rear of the parking lot. "These were the only rooms where they'd allow me to have the dogs," she explained as she opened the screen door and ushered us inside. "But they're more private and none of the parents would deign to stay in such sub-par accommodations, so I think it worked out for the best."

Trey took a seat on the faded sofa. All three dogs immediately mauled him with sloppy kisses. He laughed as he tried to scratch

Leopold's ears while Roger pawed his chest, demanding attention. Trey's laugh was so rare.

I leaned against the kitchenette counter. I folded my arms, unfolded them, put my hands behind my back, at my sides, tucked them behind my neck. Nerves tickled my abdomen. I had no idea why. *Deborah has done nothing but try to help us so far, and she'd driven all the way to give us this news.*

That was it – why drive here and stay near the school where it was most dangerous, when she could have told me over the phone? I didn't like it – I knew I didn't have the whole picture, and that made me nervous. When I was nervous, I got fiery.

Deborah bustled around the kitchen, banging cups on the counter and opening a bag of cookies. The coffee machine beeped, the sound stabbing at my brain.

"What did you want to tell us?" I demanded. My fingers flew to the scar on my wrist.

"In a moment." Deborah fussed with the coffee machine. "Do you want a hot drink? Trey, there's dog treats and more snacks on the table. I figured you guys would appreciate that."

Trey shrugged. "Not me, but Hazel should probably eat something. She's running on adrenaline and righteous indignation."

"Hazel, do you take your coffee black or—"

"Tell me," I snapped.

Deborah froze, her hand gripping her cup so hard her knuckles had turned white. "Of course. I'd forgotten that you don't have the patience for small talk. Sit down next to Trey."

"I prefer to stand." I didn't like how cornered I felt in this room, as if there was no escape. I moved around the table to stand by the door.

Deborah perched on the arm of the sofa, her eyes flicking from me to Trey. She set down her cup and pulled a stack of papers from her bag. She dropped them on the table in front of me. I glanced at the first page, but all I saw was a lot of scientific jargon and graphs with wavy lines.

"I started to suspect this when you first came to visit me," she said. "When Hazel demonstrated her powers. I didn't want to say anything until I knew for certain because... well, you'll see why. I didn't want to give you something and then take it away again. But the tests confirm it, so I..."

Her voice trailed off. Her fingers traced the edge of the paper.

"What?" *This is tedious. Why can't she just say what she has to say so we can get back to the school—*

"My sister Jessica ran away from home. Our father was... a monster." She squeezed her eyes shut. Her kinky hair bounced on her shoulders. "A pedophile, if you want the technical term for it. He mistreated me for years, until I got old enough to fight him off. I tried to protect Jess as much as I could, but I was only a girl myself, and you can't understand what a master manipulator that man was. We always talked about leaving together, but we were dirt poor and we had no other family to turn to. He kept us quiet through intimidation and pain. I counted down the days until I turned eighteen. I planned to take Jess with me to another state. I'd fight for custody if I had to. But Jess couldn't wait anymore. One day, I came home and she'd left. She'd taken her clothes and some photographs of the two of us and food and money and... she ran." Deborah's shoulders shuddered as she suppressed a sob. "She was sixteen years old."

That sucks, but I don't see what this has to do with anything. I wanted to tell Deborah to get on with it, but Trey held up a hand to silence me. "Please, Deborah. Take your time."

No, don't fucking take any more time.

After a few deep breaths, Deborah continued. "I tried to find Jess for many years, but she'd hidden too well. After a while, I stopped wanting to find her. It was a selfish decision. I needed to focus on getting through college, on securing scholarships and working two jobs so I didn't have to go to my father for anything. I wanted to believe Jess was safe somewhere and she made a better life for herself, because it made me feel good to think so. I imagined picking up the search once I finished my degree. But then came my doctorate and a demanding job and these three dogs and I... I was so secretly happy to be free of my father I wasn't in any hurry to dive into my past, and the years ticked by and now I'm too late."

"What does this have to do with me?" I demanded. "Does this Jessica have the same power or something?"

Deborah flashed a sad smile. "Yes, and also no. Hazel, your mother is my sister. She must have changed her name when she fled. I'm your aunt and you... you are a descendant of Rebecca Nurse."

CHAPTER SEVENTEEN

Her words were too strange to register. Sister. Aunt. Descendant. I'd never had a context for those words before. It had always just been me and Mom. No one else. Until Dante. And then I had no one.

Tears sprung in Deborah's eyes. She watched me, expectant, hoping to see recognition or hear something profound from me. But I had nothing. I felt nothing. It was just too... too much.

"I've mourned Jess a hundred times since. A thousand times. Every time they wheeled in a new cadaver for me to study, a part of me expected to see her face. And now that I know you're alive and that you have no one else, I want to give you the love and protection I was never able to give her." Deborah opened her arms. "I'd like to hug you, Hazel. My niece. Would that be okay?"

I shook my head. I couldn't... I needed to think about this. "I don't need protecting. And you won't want to love me when you find out what I did."

"Hazel—" Trey warned.

"What's happened? Tell me," Deborah insisted. "Nothing you do could change how I feel about you. We're family."

"Hazel believes she's responsible for her mother's death. She

caught her mother having sex with her best friend, a *minor*. She
was angry, and we know what happens when she gets angry." Trey
mimed flames burning.

Deborah's hands flew to her mouth. Her wide eyes studied
me, hoping I'd deny it and put back the shattered pieces of her
vision of me.

Too fucking bad. This is what I am. This is what your genes made me.

"Jessica," she whispered. "What have you done?"

"It's not *her* fault," I growled.

"No, Hazel. We do no good passing blame. What my father
did to her left its scars on her. Trust me – I've had ten years of
therapy to uncover mine. Those scars thread through every
future relationship, every encounter with another human. Jessica
craved attention – she'd do anything for a kind word or a sign of
affection. Even at a young age, she chased after the wrong kinds
of men, wanting someone to treat her like a princess, to rescue
her. This friend of yours, he was a good guy – protective and
kind?"

"He was." Dante's face flashed in front of my eyes. Guilt
tugged at me. I hadn't thought of him as much since I got
involved with the Kings. If I was honest with myself, I pushed
Dante out of my mind because being with them felt like a
betrayal to his memory. He was my first love, even if he fancied
my mother instead. I remembered how he'd drop everything to
walk me home from Mom's club, or how we'd curl up together in
bed and tell each other stories to distract us from the gang fight
on the street outside.

Deborah continued. "That makes sense. She saw a person who
could be her knight in shining armor – who could protect her and
you better than she ever could. And she was terrified that she'd
lose him, so she did the only thing she knew how to do to keep a
man. Perhaps she didn't even see it as a betrayal, because to her
he was just part of the family, and she'd been taught what family
did to each other and what adults you trust make you do.

Violence and horror beget the same, and that heritage is passed on through generations, like your powers."

"My mother never burned anything. I'm the only one with that curse. That's why we moved around so much, why she couldn't go to college and get a real job, because of me." Heat prickled against my skin at the memory. "She was afraid of me, sometimes."

"I never had the power, either. Like many genes carried on the X chromosome, the power will often skip a generation." Deborah took another paper from her bag and rested it on the table. It was a newspaper article about a car that spontaneously caught fire. "My mother – your grandmother – set her car on fire while she was still inside. It could have been a mistake – she was always lighting fires accidentally. I thought it was just normal. In my darkest days, I think she did it on purpose to escape that man."

Beside the car was a photograph of a woman in an old-fashioned hairstyle. My finger traced her face. *She has my mother's eyes.*

My palm grew so hot it stung. The edge of the paper caught fire. Swearing, I dropped it on the floor and stamped out the flame.

Deborah placed a shoebox on the table. I peered inside at a bunch of random junk – some old cosmetics, candy wrappers, hair ties, and some battered books covered in floral paper.

"I wanted to give you this," she said. "It's some of your mother's things, all I was able to save when I left home. The books in there are her diaries. Don't rush to read them. There's a lot of pain inside."

I stared at the stack of books and shook my head. It was all too much. Confronted with my mother's past – a past I'd never known about and couldn't even imagine – brought it all back to me, all the things she'd done to keep me safe and oblivious, all the dumb decisions she made.

The way she clung to terrible men – a repeating pattern of violence and horror. How she relied on Dante almost as much as I did – she would always ask him to fix things around our flat or walk her to clients' homes at night. How she made up stories – she liked to stand in the treehouse in the rusting playground behind our apartment block and pretend she was a damsel captured by pirates or a princess trapped in a tower. Dante and I would have to rescue her.

Or maybe it was just Dante.

My fingers traced the spines. Once I read those diaries, my mother would be forever changed in my mind. Her story would become the one she wrote for herself as a desperate, abused young woman. I wasn't ready for that story, not yet.

I turned away from the box, but that was worse because there was Deborah, tears streaming down her cheeks. She held out her hand again, but I still couldn't take it. "Do you think I want you to read those diaries and understand my own part to play in your mother's torment? I should have done more. I was too afraid. That is exactly why I'm giving them to you – I can't undo the damage I've done, but I can help you however I can to save your classmates."

Take her hand. Take her hand.

Or say something. Anything.

But I couldn't. I just stared at her while my palms grew hotter and hotter.

"Thank you," Trey said. I wasn't sure the words conveyed what I needed to say.

"Please, it's what you do for family."

"I need to talk about something else." I stood up, stepping over Leopold and Loeb to pace the length of the room. I dug my nails into my scar so hard that a ribbon of blood snaked over my wrist, trying to drive down the gnawing urge to raze the building to the ground.

Trey must've seen the look in my eyes. "We've been busy. Hazel had a very productive conversation with the god. If he's to be believed, we can save all the students."

While I struggled to regain control of myself, Trey explained what we'd discovered about the god and his children. Deborah's eyes grew wider and wider until I swore they were going to slip off her face. "As a scientist, I'm struggling to believe all this talk about souls. But this is something the scientific community has considered for a long time – just because life on earth is carbon-based, does not mean there isn't other intelligent life out there that functions on a completely different plane."

"How do you know so much about genetics?" I asked, my interest piqued.

"I need to stay on top of the latest research for my job. Blood also carries genetic material that can help us understand more about human life. And death."

"What about the god using the students to create children?" Trey asked. "Does that sound... logical?"

"It's farfetched, but not impossible, especially if Ms. West intended the student population to remain a closed system. From a population the size of the Miskatonic Prep's student body, it would be possible to create a bottleneck situation where rapid genetic changes would occur in each new generation of children. Those children could breed with each other, and this cycle repeated through the generations. Over time and with isolation a divergent genetic race could develop, especially if helped along by external forces. Perhaps the god has done this elsewhere, on other planets, seeded a new..." she paused. "Listen to me, I sound like I'm in an Arthur C. Clarke novel."

"The important question is – if we give this power to the parents, how do we stop them or their offspring from using it?"

"I'm not sure we can, and that means they're probably the worst candidates for the god's progeny. I'm guessing, of course... things were different when I thought Hermia just rapidly slowed cellular decay somehow. This isn't as simple as getting ahold of her lab notes." Deborah shrugged. "Cosmic god-offspring is outside of my field of expertise."

My eyes flicked to Trey. He sat rigid, his back straight, his eyes forward. "It's okay. We're not doing it unless we can stop our parents from causing more damage to the world. I never expected to get out of this, anyway."

The resignation in his voice chilled me more than anything Deborah had revealed tonight. "I'm not giving up. This whole thing happened because the Eldritch Club wanted power. I wonder if Ms. West had simply told them this in the first place, they would have volunteered to be the children themselves. But then Vincent would have got rid of her and she wouldn't have access to the god."

The god intended his children to colonize this planet. And I know that colonization was always disastrous to the first nations. In this case, the human race.

We'd be annihilated. The screams that made up the god's voice would be inconsequential compared to the horror that would follow. It might take two-hundred years or two-thousand for the descendants of the Eldritch Club to evolve to a state where they require souls to sustain them, but it would happen, and they would gorge themselves on the entire human race.

I couldn't be part of allowing that to happen. Nor could I condone the guys live with that on their conscience. I couldn't let them wallow in the pain of being responsible for more horrors.

Trey's fingers trailed over my cheek, bringing me back from my thoughts. He tucked a strand of my hair behind my ear, where it immediately flopped back – a reminder of one of the tortures the monarchs inflicted on me. Their bullying felt like a million years ago.

"What are you thinking, Hazy?"

I shook my head. These thoughts were for me alone.

"There's something else," Deborah said. "I *might* have followed Vincent Bloomberg and his friends into the woods."

"You... you did what?" I found it hard to imagine Deborah in her tailored suit and ballet flats sneaking around the pitch-black forest. But then, Trey had tried to walk down here in his blazer, so maybe it was just a thing people did – hike around in the forest wearing inappropriate clothing.

"I know you said not to, but I thought it might be the only opportunity we'd have to gather information about their next plans. I left the dogs in the bedroom with enough pig's ears to keep them quiet for hours, pulled on my sneakers, and tailed them through the wood. I know it's getting late, but do you want to know what I saw?"

"Fuck yes."

"The parents walked for maybe twenty minutes or so. By that stage, two of them who were surgeons had gone around and looked at all the burn victims, given them some relief. By this stage Vincent was on a stretcher. The doctors kept telling him that he needed to go to hospital, but it was like he was possessed, he was so angry. Anyway, they walked and I followed – they came to a small cabin. I noticed one of Parris' symbols etched into the stone chimney. A meeting place known to all of them. They crowded inside, lighting lanterns that flickered in the windows and gave me a view of the proceedings. I crept up to the wall and hunched against the side of the cabin, beneath the open window. Vincent's voice carried on the crisp breeze. He made no effort to temper his anger.

"Damon Delacorte had one arm in a sling. He used the other to wave his mobile phone around. He showed them a video the teachers sent him with Gloria Haynes, bound and held prisoner at the school. Mr. Haynes was in the cabin, but he kept yelling about extraterrestrials and a CIA conspiracy until someone punched him. They argued for a time about what to do. Someone suggested they leave Gloria to the teachers' devices and walk away with what they had. The idea had some supporters, but Vincent had someone throw them out the door. 'We're going back for her, and they will regret crossing us.' They agreed that their experiment had failed. That the students and staff at the school would need to be exterminated and new sacrifices found. There was a mention of nuclear weapons, and of assassins hired from Honduras. Vincent ordered each and every one of them to return to their homes and to call in every favor they had. Then he passed out and they called a helicopter to airlift him and the other burn victims to a hospital." Deborah paused. "The Eldritch Club will bring down the full force of their empire on the school."

"You know what?" I forced a smile through my aching mind. "Let them do that. Let them come at us with bombs and assassins and UFOs. We'll be ready. Bring it the fuck on."

CHAPTER EIGHTEEN

Before I could drag a protesting Trey away from the dogs, Deborah laid a hand on my knee. "I've taken an indefinite leave from work, so I'm here as long as you need me. Sneak down and see me any time you wish, and text or call me with information."

"I will." I nodded to the box under my arm. "I'll look after this."

I still wasn't quite able to thank her. That might come in time. I did give her a quick side hug.

Goodbye... aunt.

What strange words.

The sun was coming up as Trey and I trudged back through the forest. My thighs burned and the box of my mother's things weighed a hundred pounds as we scrambled up the steep slopes and pulled ourselves over rocky outcrops. I complained loudly and bitterly, as was my right as a free woman. Trey smiled wryly as he dragged my wretched body up another rock face.

"Thanks." My foot scuffed his satchel, and I winced as pain shot through my toe. "That thing must be killing your shoulders. Want me to carry it for a bit?"

Trey shook his head, his dark hair catching the moonlight –

the edges tinged with crimson, like the piping on his uniform blazer. "No thanks. I don't think I could bear the whining. Besides, I don't like to be separated from it."

"Fine. I hope you and your rock are happy together."

His breath came out in ragged gasps. I thought again how odd it was that he was supposed to be dead and yet he could get out of breath.

But that was just it – Trey wasn't dead, not really. The god gave him immortality, and Ms. West had buried him, but that did not a true Edimmu make. I was beginning to see just how insidious the Deadmistress' lie was – she let the students create their own mythology about themselves to prevent them from discovering the truth.

Nerves pricked at my stomach, but not about Ms. West. I knew Trey wouldn't let me get back to the school without trying to dig inside me. Sure enough, when we reached the outer edge of the school perimeter, he turned to face me, blocking my escape with his broad chest. "Hazel, we've got to talk about—"

I shook my head.

"Tough," Trey growled. "We've dealt with a metric ton of shit over the last couple of days, but the only thing I care about is what my girl's going through. You've stood up to a cosmic god and dealt with death without batting an eye, but Deborah tells you that you're related and you look like you've seen a ghost. When you walk into the dorms tonight, Quinn and Ayaz will see something is wrong, too. You either talk about it with me and I'll get them off your back, or you can deal with all three of us."

I folded my arms. "It's no big deal."

"Bullshit."

This is the problem with people caring about you. They won't leave you the fuck alone.

I rolled my eyes and slumped in the dirt, setting down the box beside me. "Fine. Put down your stupid rock. I'll talk, but you might not like what I say."

Trey grunted as he set down the satchel. He slid his legs over the edge of the rocks, pressing his leg against mine. He wrapped his arm around my shoulders. I knew I should tell him to remove it, but right then I couldn't bear the thought of losing his touch. I rested my head on his shoulder.

We were near the top of a ridge. Through a gap in the trees, the sun rose over the violent surf, painting the sky in streaks of red and pink. A bitter wind blew off the water, slamming into our faces. But with Trey's arm around me, I didn't feel cold.

It struck me how alike this moment was to all the times Dante and I curled up in the treehouse behind my apartment block, smoking weed and watching the sunrise. How alike, and yet how completely different.

"I don't trust Deborah," I said. "I wish I did. I know she's trying to help us, and she's given us every reason so far that she's on our side. I believe what she says about my mother... that they're sisters. That we're family. But..."

"You don't trust easily." Trey pressed his lips to my hair. With my thick dreadlocks gone, I felt his lips through my short, feathery layers. "I had to carve that stupid rock out and come after you for you to trust me, and I'm not even sure you do yet."

"Right." I stared at my hands. "But you get it. You don't trust easily, either. Being joined by blood means shit and you know it."

Trey didn't move, didn't say anything. He didn't need to – his hatred of his father rolled off him, as violent as the waves crashing against the rocks below.

"Maybe family is what you make of it," he said finally. "You. Me. Quinn. Ayaz. The other riffraff you've collected. Look at what you've built in the short time you've been at school – a group of people who never would have been friends all looking out for each other. That's what family is."

"Mmmmf." I didn't want to acknowledge that I'd thought the same thing. That maybe all this time I'd been filling the gap left by my mother and Dante with the intensity of my Miskatonic

Prep relationships. Not just with the guys, but with Greg and Andre and Loretta, too. And now Tillie seemed to be reaching out, tentatively seeking something from me she wasn't getting anywhere else.

"So Deborah could be a part of that family?" Hope crept into Trey's voice. "And the dogs, too."

"Maybe. It'll take time." I nodded to the box beside me. "This is a good first step."

"Do you think you're ready to read those diaries?"

"Nope. But I'm going to do it anyway. Mom never talked about her past. Every time I asked she'd dodge the question or distract me or invent some story about running away from an ogre..." My finger pressed into the scar on my wrist. "Maybe that part wasn't make-believe."

"You know that what your mother did with your friend is statutory rape," Trey said. "Now that you know about your mother... about her past... can you see how maybe she didn't realize that she hurt you?"

"Do we get to keep blaming the past?" I asked. "It's not a get-out-of-jail-free card. Your dad bullied you, so you become a bully. My mother was raped by her father, so she stole the first guy I loved. I was betrayed, so I burn the betrayers. It's like Deborah said – just a cycle of violence and horror."

I shuddered as I thought about the fire ripping through the auditorium, how much I wanted my bullies and their parents to burn. I was part of the cycle, whether I wanted to be or not.

Trey was silent for a long while. When he spoke, his voice was barely audible over the roar of the waves. "When I was eight years old and Wilhem was six, my dad threw this big Christmas party at our home for his investors and executives and Eldritch Club members and important people. They'd set up a big screen in the ballroom to watch the launch of a new deep-space probe the team had spent five years building – it showed a live feed from the launch site and it was really exciting. I couldn't believe my dad built something so *cool*. I told him I wanted to run the company when I grew up. He beamed when I told him that – one of the few genuine smiles I've seen. I think it was the last time he ever smiled at me like that.

"I was expected to circle the room with my father and make small talk with the executives. At first, it was fun – I had this tiny port glass and Damon Delacorte kept refilling it. I told everyone who'd listen how proud I was of my dad and what he'd achieved. I stood with this group of executives who were all pretty plastered. During their conversation, it came out that to create the launch site, the company felled a huge chunk of native forest in Chile and displaced several endangered species. A bunch of environmentalists protested their presence, and so my dad hired a local gang to sneak into their camp and massacre them."

The waves slammed against the cliff below. White foam rolled over rocks that jutted from the surf like rows of teeth. Dark waters swirled in wait, swallowing the horror of Trey's words into the fathomless void.

Trey continued. "My father had those people slaughtered, and he was laughing about it with his friends like it was some funny party trick. I let go of his hand. My knees went weak. I asked him if the protesters were really all dead, and he told me that of course they were, he only hired the best assassins. He said there'd been a family there with two kids and a dog, and they killed the kids so they wouldn't 'grow up to be a nuisance.' They even killed the dog so it couldn't raise the alarm.

"I started to cry right there in the middle of the ballroom. Everyone was looking at me, and my father's face was red and stormy. He commanded me to pull myself together, but you know when you're a kid and someone tells you to stop crying and it just makes you want to cry harder? All I kept thinking about was my dad shooting two kids and a dog. He didn't pull the trigger but to eight-year-old me, it was the same thing."

"It *is* the same thing." I squeezed his hand.

"Wilhem punched me in the arm and told me to stop being a baby, that is was 'just business.' He was six years old, but he was just parroting our dad. I said if assassins killed our parents would it be just business, and he laughed and said that would never happen. And he sounded so much like Dad that I ran from the room. Dad found me huddled under his desk and he dragged me into a cupboard and locked me inside. I was terrified of the dark at that age, and he knew it. He yelled through the door, 'you're to sit in the dark and think about why you're being punished.'"

"I sat in the dark for hours while the party raged all night. I banged on the door but no one came to rescue me. My stomach growled and I got angrier and angrier – at first at my Dad for locking me inside, and then at myself for being stupid enough to cry and make a scene, and then at those innocent people, because if they hadn't been protesting then Dad wouldn't have had to do what he did." A shudder ran through Trey's body. "The darkness closed in on me, and I could no longer tell reality from my nightmares. Over and over I saw my dad lift a gun to his shoulder and shoot a dog. Sometimes, the image was me. I could feel my finger squeeze the trigger as the dog panted hot breath in my face.

"Dad left me in that closet for two days. By the time I came out, I was babbling incoherently, weak from hunger and dehydration. I spent the next two weeks in bed recovering. Dad never once came to see how I was. But when I got well enough to walk around the house again, he found me and said, 'Tell me why I punished you.' Do you know what I said?"

I shook my head. My fingers closed around Trey's and squeezed. I knew I didn't want to hear the next words.

"I said, 'You punished me because I was weak. I'll never be weak again.'"

Yup. That was as bad as I expected.

Trey sucked in a shuddering breath. "But I didn't understand what weakness was. That night at the party I'd stood against a powerful man for the first time, and I'd suffered for it, but I hadn't lost. People at that party saw me break down, they heard me wailing about the family. Dad lost a couple of important investors that night, and they had to close the Chile operation. I'd won a victory against him, only I didn't know it. From then on, every time I chose to do his bidding, I gave in to my weakness. Every time I defied him, he found new and imaginative ways to strip me of my power and freedom – but I couldn't understand that meant I was having an impact – I was more powerful than ever. It wasn't until you strode into Miskatonic Prep with that 'don't fuck with me' look on your face that I learned what true strength was."

Trey stood up. When he withdrew his leg, my body reacted with shock, desperate to hold him close, to tell him he never had to be afraid of the dark again. But of course, I couldn't do that. It was a lie – the dark was coming, closing over us. Soon it would tear us apart forever.

There were so many layers to unpick – and that was only one trauma that Trey Bloomberg lived with every day, only one spoke in his own wheel of violence and horror.

I stood up on shaking legs and followed Trey along the ridge. We trudged the rest of the way in silence, arriving at school just as the sun made its final assault for freedom. The spires pierced the grey clouds – a threat of violence for any stranger who dared approach.

The front doors remained unlocked. We slipped into the atrium, my boots thudding across the marble. All was in darkness – faint grey light from the French doors illuminated the marble floor, but the stairs and hallways were cloaked in shadow.

As we sprinted up the stairs as quietly as we could, a light flared on the landing. I froze, raising my palm and thrusting it toward the other figure that stood in shadow beyond the flickering candle.

"Show yourself or I'll light you up like a Christmas tree." My voice carried more power than I felt.

"Wait, don't burn me."

The figure stepped closer. Candlelight danced over Dr. Morgan's face. I thought about it for a moment. I lowered my hand.

"It's best not to sneak up on me," I said.

"I'm not the only one who's sneaking." Dr. Morgan gave me a half-smile that I might've once imagined was friendly. "Why were the two of you outside?"

"We walked down to the ocean. I wanted to see the sunrise." I held Trey's arm. "It was romantic."

"I see. What have you got in that satchel, Trey?"

"Food and a bottle of Champagne," Trey said. "For the romance."

No way will she believe this tripe.

She didn't. Dr. Morgan lowered the lantern and gave me that 'I'm smarter than you' smile of hers. But she wasn't of a mind to punish us – perhaps Ms. West had said that I had certain privileges. She indicated we follow her into the darkened hallway. "Come to my office. I want to talk to you both."

"We can talk right here." I yawned. "But we're pretty tired. What with the romance and all that."

She glanced over her shoulder. "I can't risk it. You don't know who might be listening."

"That's right. We don't. And that's why we're not going anywhere."

She grabbed my arm, pulling me so close that her breath hissed against my ear. "Fine. But you must listen, because I can't risk repeating this. The teachers know you're having your party on Friday night. They're planning a little shindig of their own, in the faculty lounge, to celebrate the successful capture of Gloria Haynes."

"So?"

"So..." Dr. Morgan pressed something into the palm of my hand. "If you can get your friend on the maintenance staff to slip that into the staff coffee machine before last period, you'll find them indisposed for at least three hours. Hermia replaced the lock with one that's not supposed to melt, and the key hangs from a loop on her belt. Dr. Atwood has another in his pocket. You'll need both of them to unlock the weight room."

My mind whirred. The whole faculty would be out like a light for three hours. Provided Zehra was in any shape to move, we could get her quite far away by then.

Trey squeezed my hand. We exchanged a glance. *Can we trust her? The vial feels real enough, but I don't understand why Dr. Morgan would want to help free Zehra.*

I slipped the vial into my pocket. "Why are you helping me?"

"You're not the only one who thinks Hermia's let the god get into her head." Dr. Morgan ran a finger through her auburn curls. For the first time, I noticed how pretty she was. She had to have been only in her late twenties when she agreed to become one of our jailers. Now she wore her youthful face like a mask. Only her eyes gave away her true age – glinting with the horrors she'd witnessed and been forced to partake in. "At first, I thought it was so exciting, being part of witnessing the birth and evolution of a new race. But after twenty years in this cursed place, I'm done. You students weren't the only ones who left a life behind. I don't have a family, either – most of the faculty members are either orphans or estranged. I fought with my parents over my college major – my dad wanted me to become a surgeon, like him, but I wanted to teach history. He disowned me and we hadn't spoken in five years when Ms. West sought me out. What she offered was so amazing... the chance to be part of something bigger than myself, of complete freedom to create a curriculum that would do so much more than help students pass tests – to teach the possibility of actually *learning* from history, to make sure this new race didn't repeat humanity's mistakes. But it was all a lie. Ms. West didn't want the students to *think* – she wanted to cultivate their cruelty and avarice. I'd traded one overlord for another, only at least my parents came from a place of love. They just wanted what was best for me. I hated my dad so much for trying to control me and now I want nothing more than to fall into his arms. I don't even know if they're still alive..." her words broke into a shuddering gasp.

Heat flared in my palms at the sound of her sob. I'd thought little about the faculty since I'd discovered the truth about Miskatonic Prep. They were the ones who tossed students to the god. They plotted to hurt me and the people I loved most. For the first time, Dr. Morgan gave me a glimpse into what might have brought them here to become pawns in Ms. West's game.

Freedom. Power. Revenge – all desires I can relate to.

Dr. Morgan sucked in a breath and rallied herself. "I've seen Hermia try to extract information from Zehra Demir. She tried to sacrifice Zehra, but the god wouldn't take her. Hermia's now convinced Zehra is here as an agent of Vincent – since her brother is his favorite. Your friend is strong, but she won't last much longer. Use that vial. Get Zehra out of the school, before she becomes the next casualty of Hermia's megalomania."

"And then what happens?"

"You tell me, Hazel Waite." Dr. Morgan's lips curled back into something that resembled a smile. "There are teachers on your side, even if they remain in hiding for now. You're the one who's really in control of Miskatonic Prep, and everyone except Hermia knows it."

CHAPTER NINETEEN

I knocked on Ayaz's door. In the corridor, students skirted around me, pressing their backs against the walls and refusing to lift their eyes from me until they were out of firing range.

Classes had finished for the day, although I hadn't attended any of them. As soon as we got back, Trey and I fell into bed and slept the whole day. I must have needed the rest because not even the god could penetrate my dreams. I woke just as the final bell ring with the overwhelming urge to speak to Ayaz.

It might have had something to do with my mother's box sitting on the shelf in Trey's room, calling me, taunting me.

But it was mostly the fact that I'd made a promise to Ayaz. The Deadmistress had Zehra because of me, and seeing his face pinch every time someone mentioned his sister twisted that knife of guilt deeper into my gut.

Thanks to Dr. Morgan I might have the chance to reunite them.

If I could trust her. I turned the vial over in my hand as I waited for Ayaz to answer. Was this really some kind of sedative? Or did Dr. Morgan have some other plot in mind?

"It's open," a delicious voice called from inside.

I pushed the door open, revealing the Scandinavian furniture and calming colors of Ayaz's dorm room. At first, I didn't see him – he wasn't lying on the bed reading or curled up on the white sofa playing video games. A moment later, Ayaz emerged from the bathroom, a towel wrapped around his narrow hips, his bare chest on full display – all hard planes and perfectly-healed chiseled muscle and beautiful ink. Droplets of water glistened over his shoulders, and the scent of his rosy aftershave curled off him.

Saliva pooled on my tongue. Fuck. I wasn't ready for this. I was supposed to be resisting. I had to keep Ayaz at arm's length to save both our hearts, but if he kept surprising me with nudity I'd be writhing underneath him in minutes...

No, no. I shook my head. *Be strong.*

I tore my eyes from Ayaz to shut the door behind me, letting the CLICK of the lock jolt me back to reality. I stared at a spot on the wall and reached for my pocket to grasp the vial.

"Hazel, what is it?" He stepped closer, but I held up my hand for him to stop. His scent made my head spin. "Did you and Trey—"

"Yes, we saw Deborah, and she had a lot to say and it was... confusing as fuck. But that's not what I came to talk about. I mean, it is, but there's something else and I would've come sooner but I didn't sleep all night and—" *Stop babbling.* I took a deep breath. "We're breaking Zehra out."

Ayaz flew across the room, his hands circling my arms. "What? When?"

"Friday night. Dr. Morgan caught Trey and I coming back inside. She says she wants to help us take control of the school. Apparently, the teachers are planning a party of their own. I know their parties usually take a turn for the occult, and I don't want to give them the opportunity to do something to Zehra. Dr. Morgan's given me a sedative that she said will knock them all out. She's also told me the location of the key. If she's right, we'll have enough time to sneak into the gym and get Zehra."

Ayaz wrapped his arms around himself. His eyelids fluttered shut again, the dark lashes tangling together. Seeing him like that only made me want him more. I dug my nails into the scar on my wrist. *Be strong for him. For all of them.*

His eyes flew open. "Wait, why is she helping us?"

"She thinks Ms. West has gone crazy. Can't say I disagree. Or she's really working for West, and this is some ploy to walk us into a trap. The only way to find out is to try it."

Ayaz slumped back down. "It's risky. What will we do with Zehra?"

"We could keep her here, but I don't want to risk Ms. West finding out and telling Vincent. Ms. West believes Zehra might be Vincent's spy in the school, but we know that's not true. We need to get her off the peninsula – if we send her to Deborah, she'll help Zehra hide somewhere safe. Zehra's resourceful and she's eluded Trey's father for decades – she'll do it again."

Ayaz reached for my hand again, pulling me onto the bed beside him. I tensed, ready to jerk away if he tried to kiss me. Instead, he squeezed my hand, and his serious face broke out into a brilliant smile. "Zehra's always been resourceful – no matter where I hid my toys, she'd find them and break them. She was advanced for her age – more than I ever was – and she had my parents wrapped around her tiny finger. Sometimes I hated her for that. She was only four when my parents sent me to America. She was so angry with them that she blocked all the sinks and flooded their house." He laughed at the memory. "That's Zehra – a slave to her passions, but fierce in the face of what she sees as injustice. I adored her after that. She has that effect on people."

"I believe it." I smiled, remembering the first time I met Zehra. Except for Dante, never in my life had I met someone and so instantly clicked with them. It felt like we'd been sisters in another life.

I wanted the chance to get to know her for real, to be the friend to her that she deserved. Yet another cord binding me to this world that I would have to cut loose if I wanted to save them all.

Ayaz continued. "After I moved in with Trey, we'd talk a few times a month over video chat, and I text her every day. She always made me laugh. Trey was a bit jealous, I think. His younger brother Wilhem was a creep, and his dad barely acknowledged his existence. Even he would talk to Zehra sometimes, and she'd always win him around. She was so clever, she never seemed like a younger sister, and now she's grown older and I haven't, and it almost feels…" He shook his head. "Zehra may not be an Edimmu, but she's missed out on so much. If it weren't for me, she'd be a doctor or a Fortune 500 CEO or the first president of Mars."

"It's not your fault, Ayaz."

"It's *not*." He spat the words, his hands balling into fists. "I have much to feel guilty about, Hazy. So much evil weighs on my conscience that I'll never be rid of the burden, but for ruining Zehra's life I blame Ms. West and the Eldritch Club. And I cannot let them go unpunished."

"And we will punish them, I promise. But right now, we're focused on Zehra. If we can pull this off, she'll get her life back." I reminded him. "Will you survive till Friday?"

"Only if you distract me." Ayaz leaned in, his beard brushing my skin, sending a delicious flicker of heat through my body. He grazed his lips over my cheek, laying a trail down to—

I leaped to my feet and went over to the stack of books beside the table, desperate to put some distance between us. "We've got work to do."

"Hazel—" Ayaz's feet slapped on the marble as he padded over. His eyes burned into me. I didn't dare look up, knowing I'd crumble under the intensity of his gaze.

"We want to know about everything we can about this pillar, and why it's appeared *now*." I pulled over a stack of books and opened one at random. "I need to know if I'm being tricked by the god. He says it's a piece of something, and the rats tell me it's a lock and I'm the key. But a key to what? Is the god trying to get me to free him so he can devour the entire human race? That wouldn't sit with his plan to populate the universe, so then what—"

Ayaz chuckled, sliding into the chair opposite me. "As you Americans say, no pressure."

"Right." I handed him Rebecca Nurse's diary. "I've found a few things. We tried to chisel a piece off the pillar to take to the lab, but the stone broke all our tools. Greg did a couple of tests for his geology project, and as far as he can tell the stone isn't made of anything that exists on earth. That could mean we don't have the right lab equipment to get better data, or it could mean..."

"...that you're avoiding kissing me," Ayaz cut in.

"Don't be ridiculous." Fire raced along my veins. "That's not true."

"Trey and Quinn said the same thing," he whispered.

"Well, it's not true." I slammed the book shut a little harder than I intended. "I just have bigger things on my mind right now. As I was saying, it could also mean that no human could have carved that symbol... or for that matter, built the pillar itself. And the rock didn't come from our planet."

Ayaz stood. "I need to see this pillar."

"Why?"

"Because I'm not going to sit here while you lie and pretend there isn't something you're keeping from me. Because I'll be able to understand more once I've seen it for myself. I was a bit... unconscious from crippling pain by the time it appeared on the scene."

"I'm not keeping anything from you, I swear." The lie stung my throat. I threw everything I had into smiling at him. He needed to believe everything was fine – if he found out what I'd agreed, he might do something stupid and mess it all up. I held out my hand to him, knowing that his touch would burn me inside. I had to endure it if I wanted to save him. "We're going there right now – all four of us. I can dream with the god. Maybe that will give us some answers."

Ayaz stared at my hand for a long time. Behind me, a clock ticked on the wall, marking the seconds as hours while my love turned over whether he trusted me. Agonizing moments where he laid our relationship bare in his silence and chose to believe my lies.

Finally, he stretched out long fingers and entwined them with mine.

"Let's go talk to a god," he said.

CHAPTER TWENTY

Ayaz and I found Trey and Quinn in Trey's dorm. Trey sat at his desk, bent over his books as he studied for exams. Quinn slouched on the sofa, playing some video game with the volume on mute in deference to Trey's need for concentration. This was lovely, except for the fact that Quinn was supplying his own running commentary – which was equal parts annoying and hilarious – and Trey's shoulders grew tenser by the moment.

"...feel the sting of my steel! Your own man has betrayed you. In the land of the witless and gullible, you would be king—Oh, hey Hazy. Ataturk." Quinn paused the game and jumped up.

"Thank fuck you're here." Trey rolled his eyes at the TV screen. "Maybe you can take Quinnanigans for a walk or throw a stick for him or something."

"Trey is proof that even cosmic gods don't have a sense of humor. I'm glad to see you guys." Quinn jumped up and wrapped his arms around me, his controller bouncing off my shoulder.

His touch shot heat straight to my core, and I had to grit my teeth to stop myself from meeting his embrace with a smoldering kiss. After Quinn's fear of my fire, this was such a big step – a grand gesture of trust and faith and love as only Quinn could. I had to endure it, instead of sinking into it and basking in the glow of Quinn's renewed passion.

I tried to return the embrace with as much sincerity as I could without being drawn into Quinn's magnetism. He went to kiss my cheek and I ducked down, pretending to tie my bootlace. Quinn and Ayaz exchanged a glance.

Shit. They suspect something's up.

Of course they do. They're not idiots.

An awkward silence descended. I straightened up and started talking before they could all gang up on me. "Ayaz wants to see the pillar tonight, and I think it's time I talked to the god again. You guys want to come?"

"Hell yes." Quinn tossed down the controller with glee. "There's nothing I love more than sneaking around creepy phallic objects."

Trey glanced at his watch and frowned. "We'd better hurry. The teachers will start their rounds in an hour, and I want them to find us safe in our beds."

We crept down the hall without speaking (a difficult feat for Quinn), not wanting any of the students to waylay us. Sounds from the dorm rooms bled from under the doors. Expensive sound systems booming old-school tunes, students fucking and talking and crying. It was amazing how even as everything had been turned upside down, this part of student life stayed the same.

We made it across the school to the auditorium without anyone seeing us. Quinn cracked the stage door and ushered us all inside. "I'll stand guard here," he whispered, crouching amongst the props stacked behind the door. "If anyone comes in, I'll distract them. I'll make a lot of noise."

I kissed his forehead. As my lips brushed his skin, the fire inside me flared to life, begging for more of him.

Trey and Ayaz flanked me as we picked our way around the ruined stage. If possible, the auditorium looked even worse than before. It certainly smelt worse – damp fabric and charred wood and behind it, the scent of rotting flesh. The scent of the god's chaos.

In the center of the room, the pillar gleamed, pristine and perfect amongst the ruin around it. It had *definitely* grown – the sigil had disappeared through the ceiling and was no longer visible from the floor. I lurched forward, my palms drawn to touch it. The hum shuddered through my body. Trey held me back.

Ayaz circled the pillar, studying it without touching it. He spent a long time looking up, twisting his head this way and that as he tried to conceptualize it. The pillar had this weird way of warping the space around it – when I stared at it I got a sense that I only saw part of it, like the tip of an iceberg poking above the surface.

"Non-Euclidean geometry," Ayaz muttered. "Cyclopean."

"Is that a particular school of architecture?" I called out, struggling to free myself from Trey's grip. "Because I'd just call it 'giant and terrifying.'"

"That's basically what Cyclopean means. It's used to describe large blocks of dry stone fitted together without mortar, like the kind used on Mycenaean palaces. This work is so fine that it's impossible to see the joins in the stone." Ayaz squinted harder. "It's definitely the same stone as the god's cavern is made of."

"That's all the answers you're going to get from it." I wrenched my hand away from Trey's grip. "My turn."

"Don't touch it," Trey warned.

"Don't tell me what to do," I grinned. To spite him, I slammed my hand against the stone.

The strange... *strangeness* of the pillar wrapped around my fingers. The hum echoed through my body as my mind toppled into the stone. The edge of my vision blurred with black shadows – the servants that would step forward at my command.

With my other hand I held up my chalk stick and drew the sigil on the pillar – the one that allowed me to call the god into my dreams. Keeping my fingers against the stone, I slid down onto my ass, resting my body against the pillar. The stone hummed against my back.

I closed my eyes.

Sleep came instantly, unnaturally. Someone flicked a switch inside my brain. One moment I was in the auditorium. The next, I stood inside a vast burning sphere. Smoke stung my eyes, and the heat felt like it stripped the skin from my bones. I looked down, expecting to see my body boiling away — but I floated inside the flames, apart from them but painfully aware of their presence.

My back still pressed against the pillar, the cool stone the only relief from the primordial heat around me. The flames parted, revealing a ruined landscape of burning peaks and valleys crimson with liquid magma. The air burned in my lungs – thick and viscous, tasting of ash and poison.

The smoke swirled, revealing two more pillars standing in front of me, forming a triangle. Their tips were invisible in the miasma. The geometry of them seemed all wrong. Every time I blinked, the angles appeared different, out of touch with the others, as though each face yearned deeper into some other place beyond where my eyes could see.

I edged my foot forward, and my boot slipped across a platform of smooth, faceless stone. Its edges fell away into the burning landscape below. From beneath its surface, I felt the strangling tendrils of some cancerous horror reaching up, circling my ankles, rooting me in place.

I'm just some poor, smartass girl from Philly. I can't deal with this.

And yet, here I was.

"Where am I?" I screamed into the void.

This time, the god's screams came from all around me, from the smoke and the primordial mountains and the poison air. *You stand in the origin of all, in the place where I fell from the stars.*

I understood then that I stood exactly where I was – on the

grounds of Miskatonic Prep, only years in the distant past. Perhaps a millennia. Perhaps even during the formation of the earth itself.

"Why are you showing me this?" I demanded. "Why is this same pillar now in the middle of my school?"

What has risen will sink, and what has sunk may rise. Loathsomeness waits and dreams in the deep, and decay spreads over the tottering cities of man.

"Okay, right. So the pillar signifies the beginning *and* end of something. Where are the other pillars?" I gestured to the two flanking me.

You have not called them forth. I need more of your power. More of your... truthness. And they too will rise.

I gathered that in god-speak that meant he needed me to burn more shit down. In the moments before the pillar appeared, I'd been in a murderous frame of mind – the same way I'd felt right before I unleashed a hail of flames down on my mother and Dante. Only this time, there'd been a voice inside my head stoking the flames. The god and I had been one. He'd needed someone like me to act as a conduit and call up this blasphemous architecture.

He needed me to do that twice more, to raise the final two pillars. But why?

To free himself? To attract more souls? To act like a giant speaker system broadcasting his power across the world? Or something else – something about his children?

"I promised I'd find you new children, but I'm not going to do anything that will hurt the human race. You said you would stop taking sacrifices and giving out your power, so you can't—"

I did speak this. I am my truth. But I cannot control what stirs beneath, what is preparing to ascend. That is your domain, because you are the light, and light is required for ascension.

"*What* is preparing to ascend?" My head was all twisted around from his words. It reminded me of that scene from The Hobbit when Bilbo Baggins bamboozled Gollum at the riddle competition. Only in this case, I was Gollum and I was going to lose the most precious thing of all if I couldn't figure out this riddle.

My children cannot survive here. They must ascend. You are the light to guide them home.

My head pounded. "You're lucky you're amorphous and inside my head, because I want to kick your ass right now. I don't understand. Let's try something else... why do the pillars attract me? They're like magnets sucking me in."

The fire around me shifted, the smoke recoiling from my skin, giving me a view across the platform and out over the edge. Far below, volcanic activity deep below the surface reshaped the earth before my eyes, forming the fissures and peaks that would become the earth's surface and the ocean floor. The sky crackled with fire.

And I understood. All around the god was nothing. Not even an amoeba to talk to. *He'd endured the formation of the earth alone. Completely alone.*

When the god spoke again, his voice shuddered with pain. *It calls to you because I am...*

The god searched his human vocabulary for the right adjective. But he didn't need to. I knew the word well.

"You're lonely." The word choked on my lips. I gazed out into the world as it once was, to the prison where a god who traveled across space had been trapped.

I am lonely.

When the god spoke the word, it was as hollow as its void.

And I saw then that the god was truly not the faceless force of terror we thought him to be. He could not help the malevolence that seeped from his core, any more than I could help the fire that poured from my fingers. He'd left his family (I guessed family was the right word? He spoke of children, so his race must have some concept of family) to journey across the universe to start anew. Sure, he'd fallen victim to the old colonial attitude of 'bringing civilization to the savages,' only the savages were the creatures of earth. I couldn't blame him for that – we'd done it often enough ourselves. He was supposed to land with his godly girlfriend, do the vertical mamba god-style, and give birth to a new race. He should have been surrounded by children – proud parents birthing new gods. Instead, he'd lost the love of his life and he was alone, imprisoned, the only company human jailers who could not possibly understand his mind and hadn't even seen that he suffered from the most human of afflictions.

And maybe he wouldn't have suffered if we hadn't tried to steal his power and mix our energy with his and give him our emotions. Maybe we caused his loneliness. Or maybe we'd simply given him the only way he knew to recognize and name what he felt.

I tried to imagine loneliness stretching over aeons, and what that might do to my mind, how that would twist me into a monster. I was already monster enough.

That was the key. In his slumber, the god sensed me. It recognized me as one who had started to become like himself. A kindred spirit. The god had, for want of a better descriptor, *fallen in love*.

As the realization coalesced in my mind, the god fed my imagination, showing me glimpses of the hell he had lived in, of the hope that Parris had raised within him, only to bury him deeper within his prison. Of how it had not known the existence of hope.

Yessss, he hissed with his choir of tortured voices. *You know my truth*.

Last quarter, when I spoke to the god, I'd asked if he could go home if I took away his feelings. I thought the feelings made the god weak. But maybe those human feelings – this loneliness, this compassion and utter *humanity* – were all that stopped the god from unleashing his malevolence. Maybe the cage wasn't made of stone or magic. Maybe the god's cage was his own conscience.

He felt sorry for his children, because he had imprisoned

them. He had made them lonely and broken, just as he was lonely and broken. That was why he was so willing to help me.

The pillars were not a trick. The god didn't understand tricks or lying. I truly *had* raised something from the deep, something that had been buried with him since the earliest days of the earth.

Raise that which been sunk, and I shall have new children. The god's voice shuddered inside my head. The pillar vibrated against my back, and tendrils of darkness slithered from the smoke, surrounding me, dragging me back.

CHAPTER TWENTY-ONE

My body slammed against cool, humming stone. I groaned, raising my hand to touch the tender skin on my head where my skull had cracked against the rock. Warm hands grabbed me under the arms, lifted me, pulled me back.

I reached out, clawing for the stone. A whimper escaped my throat. I didn't want to be away from it. The god's loneliness hung heavy on my heart, and it drew out the loneliness that snuck up on me as I withdrew from my Kings.

"No, no. *Hazy*."

Hands grabbed me, dragged me back. I kicked and screamed and tore at my captor, caught in the fire-trance that bound me to the god. I needed the god, and he needed me. I could drive out the blackness in his heart, and he would do his best to sate the impossible void of their absence.

Emotions rushed my body – dark lumps of coal that I'd left untouched inside me since the fire, knowing that they would ignite a horror inside me that could never be put out. Now they burned to life, sparking through my veins and pushing out flames that rolled across the floor.

"Fuck!"

Ayaz leaped out of the way as Trey stomped out the fire before it could reach him.

"Hazy." Quinn smashed me against his chest. *He didn't run away.* Instead, Quinn clasped me tight, and bit by bit the warmth of his body and his beautiful big heart seeped into my skin. It cooled the flames inside me, and though the coals still smoldered, they no longer threatened to burst.

I was under control. For now.

Sort of.

My cheeks felt wet. I swiped my hand through the liquid. Tears. I'd been crying.

I *never* cried.

Maybe that was a problem.

"You are *never* doing that again," Trey growled, pressing his body against me, wrapping his arms around Quinn and I. For the first time, I didn't feel the urge to argue, to tell him that he didn't control me.

The scent of honey and rose invaded my senses as Ayaz joined the embrace. I rested my head on his shoulder, succumbing to the protective spell of their presence.

What I'd just seen and experienced was too big, too terrifying, to endure without going mad. I should be a gibbering mess on the floor and yet, I was here, my heart and mind bruised and battered, but intact. And it was nothing to do with me and my strength. It was because of them.

Because in their arms, I knew I was completely safe. And I'd never felt that before. I thought I had that with Dante, but I'd seen it stripped away in a moment by my own hand. But my Kings... they had taken the worst of me and yet they still stood to protect me.

That was love. That was family.

Fuck. More tears poured down my face. Trey offered the corner of his sleeve to wipe my cheeks. And just like that, a piece of the coal lodged in my heart disintegrated, because here was perfect Trey letting his clothes get all snotty. For me.

"Where did you go?" Trey struggled to keep his voice even.

"Back in time." I shoved my freezing fingers into his armpits, trying desperately to warm the chill inside me. "Like, *way* back. I think I saw the world being formed."

"Shit," Quinn swore.

Ayaz's fingers stroked the nape of my neck, raising the tiny hairs on my skin and a lump in my throat. "As soon as you closed your eyes, the room grew cold. So cold even we Edimmu felt it in our bones. Did you get answers?"

I rolled my eyes. "Sort of. As much as the god is capable of giving answers." In between shuddering gasps, I explained to them what I'd learned about the pillars, about the god's loneliness, about what we had to do. By the time I was finished, our little group was swaying gently, and Quinn squeezed me so hard my joints cracked. "When three pillars rise, something that has been buried will be revealed. I don't know what that something is, but I'm guessing it's bad."

"The god will rise," Trey whispered. 'That has to be it."

"I don't know. That seems like the most logical explanation, but the god said something about his children. And last time I talked to him, he said he couldn't go home because his feelings trapped him here. And—"

Ayaz's lips pressed against mine, crushing the words in my mouth with the force of his kiss.

It was a kiss that drove out the loneliness in both of us. Another coal of my heart disintegrated into dust. I would wait for him across time and space on the force of that kiss.

Ayaz yanked away, his eyes flickering. At first, I thought I saw fear there, but it wasn't fear – it was excitement.

"I've got it," he yelled.

"You do, you bastard." Quinn gave him a gentle shove. "You've got our girl, and I think it's my turn—"

Ayaz shook my shoulders. "I figured it out, Hazy. I know what's going on. I know how to stop everything. I can't believe I didn't see it before."

"Explain," Trey demanded.

"I will, but we have to go back to your room. I left my map there." Ayaz tore himself from our embrace and darted off toward the door. Trey and Quinn started after him. I followed in a daze.

Hazy. He called me Hazy.

It was Quinn's nickname for me, but even Trey had started using it. I'd never had a nickname before, and I held it close to my heart. For Ayaz to feel comfortable enough around me to use it...

Ayaz darted through the empty halls. I had to jog to keep up with him. Trey unlocked the door to his room while Ayaz hopped from foot to foot, his mouth pursed in a thin line like he was trying to contain the words.

We tumbled into the room. Ayaz scrambled to the coffee table and rolled out the map of the building and grounds. It was an older map from when the building had been a residence. We'd used it to locate Ms. West's original lab in an abandoned icehouse. Ayaz had scribbled lines and arcs across the map, showing an arrangement of sacred geometry and the placement of sigils and other strange happenings within the school. It looked like a child had scribbled all over it, but it somehow made sense to Ayaz.

"You saw three pillars." Ayaz hunted around under the table for a pen. "The three corners of a sigil. I knew the building's arrangement was significant, but I thought it was part of Parris' cage. I never imagined—"

"Ayaz, slow down. I don't understand what you're saying."

Ayaz's dark eyes glittered with excitement. "The god isn't from earth. So how did he get here? We thought it was through like a crack in space-time or something, but what if he flew here the old-fashioned way?"

"Like, in a ship?"

"*Exactly* like in a ship." Ayaz drew lines across the building, his hand moving so fast it was practically a blur. "We think of a space-ship as a metal tin can with a fuselage, but that doesn't mean that's how the god's race build ships. They'd use the material they had on hand – like a creepy black stone veined with foreign matter, a stone that doesn't exist anywhere else on earth. Maybe the shadow creatures that you control are part of the god, and they're like worker bees... I don't know. The important thing is, the god had to get here somehow. What if instead of rocket fuel, he used the soul-energy or whatever it was that is to power his flight? *And* what if that ship crash-landed into a planet and the god became trapped inside the wreckage?"

The god said his partner was the light that went out. He's made of darkness. Without her, he couldn't see. He couldn't navigate. Of course, he crash-landed. "You're saying that the pillar is part of the god's ship. But what about the sigil on it? How did Parris put it there?"

"I think Paris got the sigils *from* the god, not the other way around. The sigils are part of the god's ship, probably a navigation system – maps of the cosmos, or a path to lead him home. Maybe... maybe this was never meant to be a one-way trip. Maybe the god was going to fly here, poke around, take some samples, have sexy-times with his goddess, lay a bunch of god-eggs to colonize the empty planet, then go home. Only something went wrong and his goddess died and he crash-landed into the earth. If his ship was damaged, he'd have no way to fix it. Maybe he showed the sigils to Parris in the hopes he would be able to help him get home, only instead of helping the god the way he promised, Paris kept it trapped..." Ayaz's voice trailed off as he studied the sacred geometry he'd scrawled across the map.

And maybe Rebecca Nurse was trying to use sigils to jumpstart the god's ship so he could go home? "But he's been here since the earth was young. Surely he would have fixed his ship by now."

"Maybe it's not the kind of thing you can do on your own. Maybe..." Ayaz's dark eyes studied mine with an intensity that made me squirm. "Maybe he's been waiting for the right tool to

come along. Maybe he could sense there were humans out there
with Hazel's power, and he just needed one to get close enough."

"Rebecca Nurse's descendants," Trey breathed.

My heart pounded against my chest. What Ayaz was saying
sounded completely insane, like a bad episode of Startrek SG-1 or
whatever it was (Dante loved sci-fi, not me). But it also... made
perfect sense. It matched up exactly with what Rebecca wrote in
her book (Ayaz had figured out that Rebecca was using her sigils
to create a ritual, but she didn't finish it) and what the god himself
said.

Ayaz nodded. "There probably are more, too. It would explain
why he treated some humans different from others. Remember
the pirates who hid their loot in the caves? The god turned them
insane. He tried to give power to Parris but that backfired. But
Rebecca Nurse had enough power to stop Parris, even though it
killed her. Perhaps it's something in the female genome."

*That explains why only non-Edimmu women can see the fire flaring in
the sigils.*

"When you unleashed your power, Hazy, you acted like a... a
starter ignition. Your power is fire – maybe you're the light he
needs." Ayaz drew loops and swirls radiating out from the location of the first pillar. "Look at this; this is the placement of all
the sigils I know of around the school. If we account for a few we
haven't found yet, and join them together, they form two giant
sigils – one made by Parris, the other by Rebecca. Parris' sigil
incorporates the entire school. *The building itself is a sigil* – one
designed to keep the god trapped within the wreckage below.
Only every renovation made to the building probably makes the
god weaker. Rebecca's sigil is laid over top of it, and it must come
from the god itself because it places three points at its focii."
Ayaz jabbed his finger at the pillar in the auditorium, then
pointed to the center of the gym, then finally to the grotto in the
pleasure garden.

"The three pillars?" I asked. Ayaz nodded.

"And I'm betting if you did the same thing again in these locations, you'd call up the pillars. What has sunk will rise. The god's spaceship will be ready for launch. He could take all his children home."

That's perfect. We could send the Eldritch Club to another planet. They would go far away, back to the god's own universe. Our planet would be safe.

"I've been moving around that boundary sigil," Trey pointed out. "Do you think that's weakened Parris' sigil?"

"I'm almost certain it has." Ayaz tapped his chin. "And there is something else... your friend said there was nothing unique about our DNA? No weirdness that set us apart."

"Nothing."

"If we were truly the start of a new race, we'd see evidence of that on a cellular level." Ayaz the artist looked to Trey for confirmation. Trey nodded.

"That's my understanding. But I'm not a geneticist. We can ask Deborah to confirm."

"Good. Yes, we should do that. Because if our genes haven't changed, the only thing I can conclude is that the god's power is keeping us in this... stasis? That was probably something Ms. West was experimenting with. The god seems to be immortal, and the power he gave to our parents made them age slower. So his power makes us the Edimmu. If we can fix his spaceship and send him back to his home..."

"...we'll turn back into ordinary teenagers," Quinn cried.

"Either that, or drop dead," Trey finished.

The four of us exchanged a glance. For the first time in a very long time, true hope flickered her warmth upon us. We *knew* we'd cracked open the final mystery of Miskatonic Prep. We had a way forward, a plan.

Now we just had to figure out how to repair an ancient spaceship made of stone that existed nowhere else on earth.

No problem, right?

None of the boys seemed daunted by the task ahead of us. Quinn rubbed his hands together with glee. "Sounds like fun. What's the first step to freedom?"

"We've got to activate the two remaining pillars," Ayaz said. "Easier said than done, since we don't know how Hazel activated the first one."

"I do have an idea," I said. "I got angry and I lost control of the fire. The god was able to creep in under my defenses and become part of me. Like the Deadmistress said, I became the conduit for his power, and he used me to call the pillar that he couldn't call himself."

Ayaz's face looked like an expectant puppy. "So you could maybe do it again?"

"Hazy? Get angry. Highly unlikely." Quinn cracked up. I punched him in the arm.

"Yes. I could do it. I'm not even sure it needs to be anger, just whatever emotion stokes my fire."

"And what else stokes your fire?" Quinn waggled an eyebrow. I punched him even harder.

"That's for me to know and you to find out."

"Can we find out now?" Quinn's arm slid around my stomach, pulling me against him.

"Keep it in your pants, Quinnanigans." Trey turned the map toward him, studying the lines with a frown. "We'll get the one in the gym when the parents come for graduation. It won't be hard to make you angry then. That only leaves the one in the grotto."

"How are we going to get that one?" Ayaz asked.

"The one thing Miskatonic Prep students know how to do better than anyone else on earth," I grinned. "We're going to party."

CHAPTER TWENTY-TWO

"I'm calling it the apocalypse party because graduation is the final showdown between us and the senior Eldritch Club." Tillie reached across the table to grab a piece of bacon from my plate. The meat crunched between her teeth.

"Hey, I wanted that." I stuck out my lower lip. "You can't even taste it."

"Ghost bacon is better than no bacon." Tillie took another bite. "Students are going all-out. My body is ready for all the booze, all the drugs, all the wanton debauchery I haven't yet partaken in – it's happening in the pleasure garden on Friday night. If this is gonna be the end of life as we know it, I'm going out with a bang."

"Good. I just need your enthusiasm to rub off on everyone else. Every single student needs to be at this party, and they need to listen to me."

"On it." Tillie bounced off to chat with a group of students on the next table over. They darted glances at me, and this time it didn't look as though they were afraid of me. Ayaz's arm casually draped over my shoulders might've helped with that.

It was weird, going from standing at the sidelines while the students avoided me like the plague to being the one instigating the biggest party of the decade. As Tillie continued her rounds, word of what to expect at the party passed in whispers. No one wanted to be responsible for the teachers finding out.

Of course, the teachers knew. They were planning a party of their own, which was about to be thoroughly crashed.

Friday, last period.

The note landed on my desk, folded into an elaborate origami dragon. When Dr. Atwood turned away to write something on the board, I unfolded it, my heart hammering as I read three words in Andre's neat script.

SADIE DID IT.

Between classes, the teachers all rushed back to the faculty lounge to refill their coffee cups from the barista machine. Sadie was the one responsible for making the coffees and cleaning the machine, so all she had to do was spike the beans and all the teachers would be singing lullabies. I'd worried that she'd get caught or wimp out at the last minute, but my fears were unfounded – Sadie was made of strong stuff. She had to be, to survive Miskatonic Prep.

All we had to do was wait.

We didn't have to wait long. Midway through a discussion of essay topic prep for finals, Dr. Atwood lurched forward. His eyes widened. He grabbed at his desk to steady himself, but his legs collapsed beneath him and he slid off to the side.

"Mmmmmmmf." He tried to make a noise, but his lips had stopped working. His fingers jerked the air. A few more moans and twitches, and then he lay still, the only sound he made faint, labored breathing.

I leaped from my seat to bend over him, slapping both his cheeks in turn. He didn't move or open his eyes or acknowledge me in any way. I turned back to Trey and gave a thumbs up.

"School's out!" Trey yelled. Students whooped and tossed their papers to the floor. They streamed into the hallway, heading for the dorms to prepare for tonight's party. John Hyde-Jones kicked Atwood in the head as he walked out.

Trey ran to the door and peered down the hall.

"Quick." Trey slammed the door shut and leaned against it. "Dr. Halsey just walked past. She's trying to herd the students back to class. I don't think everyone is out yet."

I fished in Atwood's pockets, pulling out a set of keys on an old-fashioned brass ring. One of the keys was shinier than the others – brand new. The key to the new lock on the weight room.

I dropped the entire loop in my pocket and stood up. "Ready."

Trey shoved the door open. I followed him into the hall. The place was chaos – Dr. Halsey had succumbed to the drug and lay across the corridor while students decorated her prone body with rolls of toilet paper. Paul and Nancy drew matching dicks on her cheeks with a Sharpie. Someone had a boom box pumping sweet 90s jams while Courtney and Amber did some kind of sexy hip-hop dance. Barclay had lit a joint under the smoke alarm, so that was buzzing. A few teachers who were still standing tried in vain to contain them. As I watched, Mr. Dexter's legs collapsed from beneath him and he toppled against the lockers.

Another one bites the dust.

At the top of the gymnasium stairs, we met up with Quinn and Ayaz. "I came from Mrs. West's office," Ayaz said. "She's unconscious." He thrust her key ring into my hands.

"What were you doing in her office?" He wasn't supposed to be there – we were going to go straight to her chambers from class.

"She called me from class." Ayaz's dark eyes were unreadable. "Luckily, she passed out just in the nick of time."

I shuddered at the thought of the Deadmistress laying her hands on my Ayaz again. She must have believed that she still controlled him. But I had to push aside the overwhelming desire to head to her office and kick her in the face myself – Ayaz had bought us some extra time, and we couldn't waste it.

"Even Morgan is out cold," Quinn said. "I saw her sleeping on a sofa in the faculty lounge. I guess she wanted to cover her tracks. Smart woman."

"Good." I held up both keys. "Let's go."

"Go where?"

A shrill voice stopped me in my tracks.

I whirled around. Courtney stood opposite us, flanked by Tillie and Amber, her hands on her hips and fire in her eyes. She jabbed a manicured nail in the direction of the pleasure garden. "The party is *that* way. Or is there some other reason you've knocked all the teachers out so we finished class early?"

I don't have time for this. "There is another reason. We're going to tell you all about it tonight. In the meantime, you gotta trust us. Can you do that?"

"Don't worry, Courts. It's not a real party until I show up," Quinn blew her a kiss. I expected Courtney to demand to know what was happening, or to come with us, but she only laughed and flounced away.

The keys jangled in my hand as we turned back to the gym. Down, down, down, we crept into the darkened hallway, past the rusting old lockers and dusty storage closet that led down to the god's cavern. His presence hung thick in the air, and I sensed the edges of his mind tugging at me. He watched us in his dreams. In the darkness, his shadows lurked – commanded by me now, they were ready to leap out at anyone who tried to stop us.

I braced myself for the horrific odor leaking from the gym, but it wasn't as bad as I remembered. The rotting scent still clung to my throat as we walked, but it no longer choked out everything else. As we approached the rolling door to the gym, I heard fans whirring from inside. The teachers must be trying to clear out the stench of their evil before the dance.

I sucked in a deep breath and shoved the door.

It rolled back just enough to allow us entry. I slipped in first, followed by the guys. I clicked on my phone's flashlight function and swung the pale beam around the vast space. The place wasn't nearly as oppressive as last time we visited. Someone had swept the court, so dust no longer swirled in tall columns around us as we walked. Some of the bleachers had been dismantled, and the wood was stacked in neat piles beside the outer door. Extractor fans worked to clear their air of the noxious odor of death.

As we stalked across the court toward the weight room, a scritching noise started at the top of the bleachers and rolled toward us. Even though I'd heard the approach of the rats enough times now to know they were on our side, I couldn't help the tightness in my chest. Those tiny feet and sharp claws scratch-scratch-scratching... it never failed to incite terror.

Rats bounded across the court to circle us. They faced away from us, watching the doors, their little noses twitching with nervous anticipation. *Our guards.* They would alert us if any teachers woke from their stupor and came after us.

A lock that looked like it would be more at home on the safe from a spaceship had been installed on the rolling door. I slid Atwood's key into one of the locks and tried to turn it, but it wouldn't budge.

"Try both at once," Trey suggested.

I shoved Ms. West's key into the other lock and turned both at the same time. The lock clicked open. I hurled up the roller door, revealing a darkened room beyond.

The first thing that hit me was the smell. Now that much of the dead stench had disappeared, I was able to articulate the unique odor of this prison. It reeked of human filth – blood, shit, piss, sweat clinging to an unwashed body, tears left to dry on parched cheeks. I clamped my hand over my mouth as bile rose in my throat.

My flashlight beam swung around the room, leaping over dusty equipment, the laboratory benches along the center of the room, the closed door of the sauna. *Where is she—*

"Took you long enough," a voice croaked.

Zehra.

She clung to a steel weight rack that had been bolted to the floor. Beside her, a filthy mattress and bucket containing I didn't want to know were stacked by the wall. Her eyes bugged from her haggard face as she recognized us.

"Brother?"

Before I could stop him, Ayaz barreled across the room and scooped her into his arms. Her tiny figure was lost in his broad shoulders as he smothered her in his embrace. She collapsed against him, clinging to his neck as if he were the only thing holding her upright. I noticed dried blood on the end of her fingers from where her nails had been pulled off.

Ayaz let out a sob that rent my soul. "What's that witch done to you?" He cupped Zehra's face in his hands, tracing the cuts that crisscrossed her cheeks and the blistering burns on her earlobes.

She shook her head. "The important thing is that you're here now. And you've brought reinforcements. Hi, Hazel."

I knelt down beside her. "Let's get you out of here."

We didn't have keys for the locks that bound Zehra's chains, but they were old and malleable. Ms. West didn't expect anyone to get past her new lock. I held the chains in my hand, calling up the righteous anger inside me until a flame burned in my palms. The metal bubbled between my fingers, and a moment later, the shackles fell away from Zehra's wrists.

She rubbed her wrists, wincing as her fingers traced red welts. Trey stepped forward, sliding his arm under her shoulders. Ayaz went to the other side and hauled her up. She couldn't stand under her own weight, but with the two of them guiding her, she staggered toward the door.

"Wait. Aren't you going to help her?" Zehra gasped.

"Help who?" Quinn whipped his head around the room. His eyes widened as he fixed on a shape in the far corner. I followed his gaze.

A woman slumped in a leg curl machine, her wrists and ankles chained down, her eyes bound and a gag stuffed in her throat. Her head lulled to the side. She moaned and tried to lift her head, but she couldn't seem to do it.

Even with her hair silver from age and streaked with filth, her skin wrinkled, and her clothes torn and bloody, I recognized her.

Courtney's mother, Gloria Haynes.

"I don't have time to explain, but we can't take her." I made to turn away, but the fire inside me flared to life. Inside my head, the god whispered.

I see your mind. I see what you desire.

The rage burned like magma in my veins. In front of me was a parent who had given her child to the god in exchange for power. Gloria Haynes jerked her head up, and a muffled sob came from behind the gag. It sounded like she was crying for help.

I'll help you, Gloria.

I stepped toward her. Trey grabbed my arm. "Forget about her. We don't have time."

I jerked my arm from his grasp and stalked across the room, yanking the gap from her mouth. Gloria snapped her jaw. "Help me," she croaked. "I'm being tortured. There must be a mistake. I don't deserve this..."

I tugged down the blindfold. Gloria's eyes watered as she struggled to focus. When my features came into view, she shrunk away, her body spasming with fear. Watching her jerk her head away, her limbs brittle sticks inside her bonds...

I liked it.

No, I *loved* it.

I loved the terror in her eyes.

I relished the acrid scent of urine soaking through her ruined dress.

I gorged myself on the sight of her silvery-grey hair and crinkling skin.

I *gloried* in the power I held over her.

Yessss, the god hissed in my head.

"No... not you..." she whimpered.

"Why not me?" I leaned in close, letting my gutter whore breath caress her cheek. "Why should I not be the one to take your life, as you took the lives of your children? Tell me, has it all been worth it? Has watching Courtney remain a teenager for two decades, trapped forever between these walls, been worth the heights of your career and the admission to the Eldritch Club?"

Even as tears streamed down her cheeks, Gloria stuck out her jaw in defiance. "You want the truth?" she spat. "It was a *relief* to get rid of that brat. While she was in our house, my husband had no time for me. He was too busy doting on his perfect little girl. He only supported my company because he thought I was building it *for her*. Well, I showed him, didn't I? I sent his perfect girl to Ms. West and she turned into her someone he feared. Courtney will never take what's mine."

"Oh, won't she?" I slapped her cheek. Gloria cried out, and I noticed a fresh burn reddening her skin. I held my palms in front of her face, letting her watch the fire leap between them. "You're right – you turned your daughter into a monster. Well, it takes a monster to defeat one, and you and the rest of the Eldritch Club will reap what you sow."

"Hazel, come *on*." Quinn tugged my arm. He sounded frantic now. "We have to get Zehra away, remember?"

I shoved him away and turned back to Gloria. Her cheeks glowed with wet tears. Her jaw trembled, and her face collapsed in terror. I pressed my hand against her chest, between her breasts, over her heart. I felt it race beneath my fingers, the beat speeding so fast it seemed ready to burst through her chest.

Yessss. What is sunken will again rise. You are the conduit, my star-twin.

The god cried with triumph as the fire flowed through me. Flames leaped from my palm, and I pressed them into her skin. She screamed, her body jerking. A warm joy spread through me at the pain I caused.

This is who I am – the biggest monster of all.

Someone tackled me from behind, dragging me back, tearing my hand from her chest. The flame flared across the room before sinking back into my skin. Gloria's screech pierced my ears as fire tore through the ruined fabric of her dress, wreathing her face in an orange glow. My breath caught as I looked into her eyes and saw my mother. The god yelled in protest, but the connection had broken. The rage within me turned cold.

Quinn held me while Trey rushed over and smothered the flames. I buried my face in his shoulder, gripping his shirt, begging him silently not to let me go.

I can't believe I did that. It was so fucking stupid. I hadn't come here with murder on my mind. We were getting Zehra out. We needed to leave the pillar beneath the gym, and we needed Gloria alive for now, or the parents wouldn't come to graduation.

But when I'd ignited the fire inside me, I *wanted* Gloria to burn. I'd relished the anticipation of her suffering. How much of that was me, and how much was the god's influence calling me, begging me to become his conduit once more?

"Fuck," I whispered. "The god... he got inside my head. He wanted me to burn her. *I* wanted to burn her."

Quinn's arms held me steady. This time, he wasn't going anywhere. "We all want her to burn. It's not your fault, Hazy."

"He was trying to raise the pillar," I mumbled as Quinn dragged me toward the door. A wild thought occurred to me. I dug my phone from my pocket and snapped a picture of Gloria's slumped body, just in case I needed it as evidence or for blackmail.

"Of course he was. His influence is stronger here than anywhere else." I leaned into Quinn as Trey shut and bolted it behind me, muffling Gloria's pain-soaked cries. Ayaz was already halfway back across the gym, carrying his precious load. The rats scurried out of our path as we scrambled for the exit and tore up the stairs.

As soon as I stepped into the first-floor corridor, the god's hold on me broke, leaving my body and mind bereft. Quinn squeezed me and smiled his easy-going smile, and for a flicker of a moment, I believed that everything would be okay.

Quinn's still here. He saw the worst in me, and he's still here.

As quickly as we could, we carried Zehra through the deserted school and across the field into the trees. As we walked, Trey and I filled her in on everything that had happened since we last saw her and our plan for graduation, with Quinn interrupting to 'dramatically re-enact' his favorite parts. His impression of Trey was particularly entertaining, and despite myself, I laughed until my ribs hurt.

I found the tree where we'd hidden supplies earlier. Ayaz set Zehra down, steadying her as she stood shakily on her own legs. I handed Zehra a backpack.

"There's food, water, and cash in here, and some other things you might need. I've put a note with my mobile number in the front pocket. As soon as you buy a phone, text me so we can stay in contact. You're going to the Arkham Grand Hotel – around the back is a motel unit. Deborah has left her back window open. She's in number three. Don't let anyone see you crawl inside. She'll get you cleaned up and move you somewhere safer."

Zehra nodded. Ayaz held her close, locking his arms around her, pressing his cheek to hers.

"She doesn't have to go," he whispered. "We could keep her with us."

I got it. He'd just got her back. He didn't want to send her away into the great unknown again.

I shook my head. "We can't hide her in the school."

Ayaz locked his arms around his sister and stared at me with defiant eyes. "*You* stayed hidden for an entire quarter."

"That was before we had a crazy plan to free you all from this curse."

Zehra wriggled out of her brother's arms. She hoisted the backpack onto her shoulders. "Listen to your girl, big brother. We'll have plenty of time to catch up on two decades of shenanigans once you have your life back."

"And Vincent Bloomberg is out of the picture," I added.

Zehra couldn't keep the grin from spreading across her face. "By Allah, I can't wait for that day."

Ayaz reached for his sister again. "I can't protect her out there. She could be walking straight into Vincent's arms. You know she's not going to sit around and wait for us."

Zehra darted away, sticking her tongue out at him. I wanted to laugh, but the crippled look on Ayaz's face stripped away all mirth. Saying goodbye to Zehra again was tearing him apart. Now that he had her, he couldn't bear to let her go.

This will be me when it comes time to go with the god. I have to be strong, or I could ruin everything.

"I'll be fine," Zehra stared down her brother with those dark, expressive eyes. "But you're right about one thing. I'm not going to hide away like a frightened kitten while you fight. Give me a job to do."

Ayaz shook her head. "You're staying away from this."

"Nope. I've fought too hard and too long to get your freedom to step aside now." She turned to me. "You must need someone on the outside, someone who moves in different circles to this Deborah person."

I thought for a moment. "When the Miskatonic Prep students leave the school, they can't walk back into their old lives.

It'll be too suspicious – people will ask too many questions. They need new identities. Yesterday I made contact with someone I know in Philly who will organize passports, but I'll need other paperwork. I assume you used criminal connections to hide for so many years, so—"

"I know people." Zehra grinned. "I'm even owed a few favors I can call in. I'll get you anything you need."

Ayaz looked aghast. "You shouldn't be mixing with the types of people who sell illegal identities. Either of you."

It spoke to our kindred nature that both Zehra and I ignored him. I longed to hear more about Zehra's exploits over the last decade, but not while her annoyingly, adorably protective older-younger brother was around.

"I can do more," Zehra added. "What if the Eldritch Club decides it's too risky to come back to the school? Maybe they figure they have enough power already. You said they spoke in their cabin about finding another source of funds so they could afford to sacrifice Gloria. What if I made it so they didn't have a choice *but* to come?"

"How?" I was intrigued. This had occurred to me, too. Someone suggested it at the meeting Deborah overheard. Vincent kicked them out for it, but for all we knew he'd lost control over the Eldritch Club. We needed them *here*, and they could always choose not to come. It was the biggest weakness in our plan.

"I've been gathering information about them for years, including their insider trading, shady business deals and political bribes, their fraud and their human rights violations." Zehra tapped the side of her head. "I have enough secrets to write a book stored up here, and evidence to support them tucked away in safe places across the country. All it will take is a few well-written emails to empathetic journalists and I can sink the fortunes of the entire Eldritch Club like they're the Titanic and I'm a fucking iceberg of doom."

"Hell yes. Do it."

Zehra hitched the backpack up and stood on tiptoes to kiss her brother's cheek. Adoration beamed from her dark eyes. For a brief moment she appeared younger, and I was transported to her year at Miskatonic Prep – to innocence shattered, to a wild night rowing a boat on a violent ocean, to outsmarting assassins and uncovering hints of the truth. This school had taken everything from her; except for her resilient spirit. She was itching for her own revenge.

"Smell you later." Zehra flashed a brilliant smile and stalked away into the trees. Ayaz flung himself after her, but Trey pulled him back, placing him in a chokehold until he stopped struggling.

"She's leaving." Ayaz slumped in Trey's arms.

I knelt down beside him and kissed his forehead. "Of course she is. She's spent her whole adult life trying to get you out. Now that we've found a way to make that happen, you're seriously going to keep her out of it because you want to be the caveman protector?" Ayaz frowned. "I didn't think so. We've all got a role. Hers is to ensure the Eldritch Club makes it to the school. Yours is to be a King. And that means honoring your royal subjects with your presence in the biggest party of your decades-long high school career."

"The last thing I want to do is party," he muttered.

I grabbed his hand, yanking him back toward the school. "Tough. I need you. The whole school needs you to do what you do best – give in to your base urges and get absolutely, completely, monstrously freaky tonight."

CHAPTER TWENTY-THREE

By the time we clambered down the steps to the pleasure garden, the party was in full swing. The air swam with the alluring scent of wild drugs and sexual tension. Students passed around pipes and openly tossed pills down their throats, washing them down with bottles of expensive Scotch and champagne from their private stash. What seemed like every student who could play a musical instrument jammed together on a makeshift stage while others stamped their feet and danced in giddy circles. The maintenance staff circled around, dressed not in their grey uniforms but in bright clothing borrowed from the students. Tables groaned under the weight of platters of food and even more booze. Ayaz told me that the Edimmu didn't need to eat – that placing food in their mouths only elicited the ghost of its true flavor. But I knew that some of us took great comfort in our ghosts.

As I stood at the edge of the grotto, surveying the scene, Courtney ran past wearing nothing but a silver thong and a pair of nipple pasties. She'd painted her entire body like a tabby cat, complete with stripes and whiskers across her cheeks. I noted with glee that she'd teased her hair up into cat 'ears,' which looked completely ridiculous, but wouldn't result in her having to cut out clumps of hair after I had glued them to her head previously. She yelped in faux protest as Derek and John took turns slapping her bare ass cheeks.

I glanced at my phone. "It's only 6PM."

"Right on time." Quinn grabbed me and Ayaz and dragged us toward the dance floor. "Let's make Ataturk forget about his sister."

"That's not possible," Ayaz growled, but then we were surrounded by gyrating students and Quinn was twerking against Ayaz and laughter bubbled up inside me as I gave myself over to the music. Ayaz turned to me, and the moonlight glinted off the fathomless depths of his eyes and I knew that, right now, he was one hundred percent in the moment with me.

Trey's hands skimmed my thighs, drawing lines of heat across my skin. Quinn's lips grazed my bare shoulders, sending delicious flickers of fire all down my spine. We'd all left a change of clothes in the tree where we left Zehra, and I now wore the black dress with the white lace collar Greg had found in the costume department. He'd chopped up and re-sewn the neckline and now it was a halter-neck with an open back, which in the hands of my Kings was fucking dangerous.

"You look amazing, Hazy." Ayaz placed two fingers beneath my chin, tipping my head up so he could claim my lips in a searing kiss. As his tongue stroked mine, rising the flame higher inside me, he spoke with his body what he couldn't say with words – that as much as he was here to fight for Zehra, he was also fighting for me. That he trusted me. That he might not remember how we fell for each other the first time, but he was falling again.

I poured my own feelings into that kiss, knitting my fingers through his hair and pulling him closer, longing to fall into him and lose myself. In my mind, I saw those pictures he'd drawn of me – the way he'd conveyed me on a page with strokes of ink, not an exact image of me but of how he saw me in his mind. A warrior with fury and soul behind her eyes, a foil for his introspection and the fuel for his passion. My artist who'd never had the chance to truly express himself. *I will give you a future. And it will be so wonderful that one day you will forget me. And you won't be sad. And that knowledge will carry me across the stars with joy in my heart.*

While Ayaz kissed me, Trey's lips trailed across the top of my shoulders, the nape of my neck. Not to be outdone, Quinn's fingers brushed over my breasts, and I hung between them, suspended, while Trey's erection dug into my thigh and the fire inside me raged into an inferno—

"Fuck!" I shook the corner of my dress, putting out the flame that had sprung up. Dancers shuffled away from me, eyes wide and frightened. Ayaz pulled me out of the fray.

"What happened?" Quinn touched the scorched corner of my dress.

"I got... um, *excited.*"

Quinn's smile could have lit up the sky. "You know, you'd be less of a fire risk if you took your clothes off."

"Somehow I doubt that." An ache followed the trail of fire through my body. My skin still burned from their touch. All I wanted was to have them pressed up against me again.

But it wasn't time for that. Not yet.

Trey swallowed and stepped away. The tension crackled between us, and I knew he used every ounce of willpower not to throw himself at me. "You should give your speech now, before everyone is so off-their-face they don't remember it."

I nodded, not trusting myself to speak. Quinn stuck two fingers in his mouth and let out a piercing whistle. A couple of people turned their heads, but the party went on without incident.

"Time to pull out the big guns." Quinn flexed his muscles. He sucked in a deep breath, opened his mouth, and...

Feeling emboldened, I flipped my palm up and let a pillar of flame cascade toward the heavens.

That got a reaction. Heads whirled around. Students screamed and clutched each other. Amber teetered on her six-inch spiked heels and fell on her ass. A glass bowl shattered as Nancy dropped it on the rocks. Instruments squealed as the band ground to a sudden halt.

Hundreds of eyes bore into me, wide and terrified, as they once again grappled with my command over their greatest fear. I cut off the flame and folded my arms, meeting their gaze with firm confidence. Tonight, I had to make the whole school listen to me, believe me, accept me – the gutter whore. I couldn't let them see weakness or feel the nervous flutter of my heart in my chest.

"Now that we have your attention, gather round, everyone." Quinn waved his arms. "We can return to the drinking and shagging forthwith. But first, our fearless leader wants to say a few things."

"I don't see nipples!" Derek yelled, beating his naked chest. His bloodshot eyes and slurred speech suggested he was already well gone. "I'm not listening to her unless she shows us her tits!"

A shudder ran through my body as I flashed back to that night in my bedroom, where Courtney had Derek and John and some other guys break in, where they were going to...

No. I shook it off. I had to believe that if I gave them back their lives, what these kids had been through was enough to scare them straight. Derek had tried to rape me – he was a monster, born of a monster, groomed to give in to his darkest urges. When he was free of Miskatonic Prep, would he retain his monstrosity? Would he rape someone?

I didn't like to think about that question. Forcing the students to confront what they'd lost at the performance should have been enough to show them that they needed their humanity. But Derek didn't seem to have learned a thing.

I longed to shrink away from him, to step behind Trey and let him take care of Derek. I could tell from Trey's balled fists and tight jaw he intended to do exactly that. But I couldn't show weakness now. "We're going to have a friendly chat about your future, *Derek* — if you're willing to stop being gross and *listen*. I've found a way to free you from the school *and* restore your lives."

"What is it?" John Hyde-Jones demanded, his eyes the same bloodied color as Derek's, although hard and dangerous as flint.

His voice made bile rise in my throat. Of all the guys in the room that night, John was the instigator, the one in command. I'd never forget the words he spat out while his friends held me down. *Spread her legs.* Ayaz squeezed my hand, steadying me. Quinn moved in closer, his arms folded, his usually-jovial face immovable as a cosmic obelisk.

Trey's voice rang hard and clear. "Hazel isn't going to address her would-be rapist, so shut the fuck up. But for the rest of you, Ms. West has informed us that our parents have been invited to attend the graduation dance. The faculty believe they have enough leverage to entice the Eldritch Club to grant any one of us who wishes it the ability to leave the school grounds."

Excited whispers rose from the students. Trey swiped a hand through his dark hair. Already, he looked at home being in charge, with every eye at the party focused on him. "Don't get excited. It's not a real solution. We'd still be immortal, the children of the god. Our parents will never allow us back into their lives — there would be too many questions. You might be able to scratch around in Arkham, go to Walmart or whatever inane activities they deemed appropriate, but as for a future, a life? It's not possible. We'd still be prisoners — they'd just be extending the prison yard. Ms. West and the faculty want this deal because they want to keep their immortality — but I believe we can do better."

"Why would our parents agree to that?" Courtney demanded, suspicion creeping into her voice.

I turned to Courtney. "Because they're holding your mother hostage."

She gasped. "That... that's ridiculous. My mother is at Paris Hilton's birthday party right now."

"Do you know that for a fact? Because I've just come from the gym, where they're keeping her trussed up on an old weight machine. You don't believe me?" I dug my phone from my pocket and showed her the picture I'd taken. "The Haynes fortune is propping up many of the efforts of the Eldritch Club, including political campaigns and failing companies. Right now, even Vincent's aerospace company is losing market share to Elon Musk. As the members lose their influence and their looks, Haynes money is practically all they have left. Evil as she is, Ms. West may be right to assume they can't live without your mother, and I have agents on the outside making sure that is true. So they've put her up for ransom. The price? The Eldritch Club must come to the dance, and they must use their occult prowess to deactivate the boundary sigils."

"What do you think, Hazel?" Tillie asked, her voice pleading. She actually cared about my opinion. The other students leaned forward, waiting for my response.

"I think, fuck them and the occult magician they rode in on. We can do better," I declared. "I also don't want Ms. West running around in the real world after what she's done to all of you. But I don't see any reason to pass up a perfectly good dance."

"Why would we go to *that* dance?" Courtney demanded.

"Your parents are going to be toasting the twentieth anniversary of killing you and trapping you here." I grinned. "We're crashing the party."

It took a long time, and lots of stopping and starting, but I explained to them what the god really was and where he came from, what had been done to them by Ms. West, the lies they'd been told, and how we planned to give them a new future. The only thing I left out was my bargain with the god. "You each have a choice to make. This is your life or un-life at stake, and I'm not forcing any of you to do something you're not into. That's your territory. But I need to know right now, are you willing to give this curse to your parents? Are you willing to make them the children of the god, knowing that you will then be sending them into space, far away where they can do no more harm to anyone on earth?"

I'd barely got the words out when Courtney stepped forward. "I'll do it."

"You realize this means you're sending your mother—"

"I fucking heard you the first time, gutter whore," she snapped. "Personally, I'd rather see you roast them all alive, but blasting them into space should do the trick."

"What will happen to the teachers?" Tillie asked.

"And the maintenance staff?" Greg called from the back. Beside him, Andre's hand fitted into Sadie's. I'd never seen him look frightened before, but now his face was shadowed with fear.

"Both the faculty and the maintenance staff will have their immortality removed, just like you." A few students grumbled. "Trust me, it'll be punishment enough for Ms. West. Because they're not children of the god, they don't have the same energy inside them. The truth is, we don't know exactly what would happen. But they should just become ordinary humans – a boon for Sadie and the other ex-scholarship students, penance for the faculty."

"Vote now." Trey's glare touched every student. "If you're in, raise your hand. If you're out, walk away from this party now. We're not doing this unless everyone agrees."

Trey raised his hand. Quinn pumped his fist in the air like he was at a rock concert. Ayaz leaned over to kiss my cheek as he too raised his hand.

In front of us, hands shot in the air, waving like blades of grass in the breeze. In moments, every single student and member of the maintenance staff had their hands raised.

"Very well, we will continue with the plan. In the coming weeks, I'll need some of you to help us with certain things, but not tonight – tonight is for you, for all of us. If everything goes according to plan, another pillar is going to appear soon. You don't have to be afraid of it – it can't hurt you. I just wouldn't go into the grotto. Next week, we're going to pass around some lists – we need to organize your passports and other paperwork. You need to create a new identity. But don't worry about that now. Tonight, we party."

Trey nodded to the band, and they struck up a Radiohead song. Immediately, students surrounded me, jostling me between them as they boasted in loud voices about what they would do when they were free. They hemmed me in on all sides, blocking my escape. In the moonlight their faces contorted, and I no longer saw jubilant teens celebrating their potential freedom, but the faces of Courtney and the guys as they surrounded me in my room.

The god's voice whispered at the edges of my mind, drawing me back to that dark place that had haunted my dreams.

John Hyde-Jones clapped me on the shoulder and yelled something. My resolve snapped. I was back in that room, to the boys kicking me and holding me down. His words echoed in my mind. *Spread her legs.* I spun around and slammed my fist into his face.

My knuckles smushed his nose with an angry *CRACK.* The pain arcing through my hand brought me back to the present.

"Bitch." John staggered back. "What was that for?"

I shoved my way through the crowd, desperate to breathe. I caught the flash of Trey moving forward, his eyes locked on John as he descended to dish out his own justice. Tillie grabbed my arm and dragged me out of the circle. Two girls stepped toward me, but one look from Tillie sent them back.

"I understand why you did that," she whispered. "He's hurt a lot of girls over the years."

A shudder ran through me as I fought to keep my shaking limbs under control. John had never succeeded in hurting me with more than his fists, but to think he'd done it to others... and I was going to *reward* him with his freedom.

"I'm unleashing that monster on the world," I whispered. Suddenly, everything I'd been working toward seemed stupid and dangerous. I'd been so focused on how the Kings had changed. They saw that they had done horrible things, and they'd already started on the path to redemption. But they were only three of the 245 students. These students had spent twenty years locked inside this hellhole, believing that they could do whatever they wanted to the scholarship students and the staff who served them. And until now, that had been true. They'd had no consequences for their cruelty. So why would they stop?

"Trust me, when John Hyde-Jones gets out into the world, he's going to be watched carefully," Tillie hissed, and the venom in her voice sent a chill down my spine. "And not just by me. But wherever he goes, I'll be there, and if he makes one false move I'll report him to the police. Or cut off his nuts."

The venom in her voice stung the air. I believed her. "What about Derek? What about everyone who tortured scholarship students? I can't watch all 245 students. There's no way to..."

"To make everyone obey the law? To turn us all into upstanding citizens and liberals? You're right – there's no way to do that. And you shouldn't try. There are monsters among us; I'm not denying it. Hell, I was a monster once. But I think I've changed. Or at least, I want to change. And I'm not the only one. The wanting... you made us feel that, and maybe it will be enough, but that's out of your hands. It's not your responsibility to save our souls, Hazel. You've done more than enough by saving our lives, even though we don't deserve it."

I didn't know what to say to that. "Um... you're welcome."

Tillie laughed. She wiped her eye, and I noticed a tear forming in the corner. "When you first came to school, I hated you so much. Trey couldn't stop talking about you. Hazel this, Dead Meat that. He put more effort into torturing you than any of the others. That's how I knew he liked you, and I hated you for it. Isn't that fucked up?"

I nodded in agreement. "That is the *most* fucked up."

"The truth is, Trey and I were never a good match. We dragged each other down into our own misery – because that was the only thing that connected us. But seeing him with you... he's a different guy. A better guy. It's like his eyes have been opened, and he makes me want to open my eyes, too. But not as much as you. I've been a seventeen-year-old girl for twenty years, and I still don't know who I am. Not like you, Hazel. You've always had such a... determination about you. A solidity. That's why he loves you – because you're the stone wall he can throw himself against, and you won't break. The way he looks at you... maybe I'll meet someone who loves me like that one day, but I have to figure out who I am first. And even though I was horrible to you, you're giving me that chance. You're all right, for a charity case." Tillie held out her cup for me.

"And you're okay, for a stone-cold monarch bitch." I grinned back. We clinked cups, splashing alcohol over each other.

Quinn danced over. "Ladies, you need to be on the dance floor, grinding against me. That's an order from your King." He yanked us into a lopsided circle where students bumped and ground against each other to the eerie, tribal beat. A thick fog of sweetly scented smoke clung over the group.

"What's this stuff?" I waved my hands in the swirling mist.

Quinn took a drag from a long-stemmed pipe. He held it out to me. "Paul's dad gave it to us a few years ago. It isn't even on the streets yet. Want me to hook you up?"

I shook my head.

"I've seen enough horrors at this school without a head full of drugs." My brain already felt fuzzy from the confrontations and various substances mixing in the air. I didn't know if it would impact my ability to draw my fire.

Hands clamped over my thighs. I stiffened. The familiar whiff of fresh herbs and springtime caressed my palate. "This party is awesome," Trey yelled over the noise as he danced in close. I relaxed into him, his body raising heat where it grazed mine. "There's only one problem – where's this pillar of ours? I thought you were going to do it when you swung at John – you looked angry enough."

I smiled. Beneath my feet, the god rumbled in anticipation. "Nope. I have another plan for pillar-raising."

I took Trey's hand, stroking my fingers over his knuckles. With my free hand, I picked up Quinn's wrist, draping his hand across Trey's. I looked up. Without me needing to do anything, Ayaz shoved his way through the crowd and stood before me, the corner of his mouth twitching into a smile. He laid his hand on top. Three pairs of eyes met mine – one ice, one warm amber, one dark as night.

I sucked in a breath. I deliberately hadn't told them about this. I didn't want to give them time to think it over, to back out, to come up with excuses. I didn't want them to wonder why I'd been pushing them away, only to draw them to me tonight.

I didn't want to explain that I wanted one last, wonderful memory to carry me across the cosmos before I said goodbye to the Kings forever.

My three bullies. My Kings. The three guys I loved more with every breath, who challenged me and infuriated me and made me giddy with the force of my passion.

"Come with me," I spoke my wish into the air.

"Where are we going?" Quinn raised an eyebrow.

"To the cabins." I met their eyes, letting my desire pool. "I need all three of you. Tonight. With me."

CHAPTER TWENTY-FOUR

Quinn's lips curled back into a smile. "You mean, slacks off, cocks out, Hazy's body at our mercy? I thought you'd never ask."

Trey's eyes narrowed. "You're asking—"

"For the three of you to come with me to that cabin. For us to spend the rest of the night together. I know you've... done it before." I didn't like to think of them with other girls, especially not Courtney or Tillie, but I knew from things they'd said that they'd shared girls before.

"Those meant nothing." Trey's fingers tightened around mine. "Those girls were just a distraction."

"We wanted to see how far we could get," Quinn grinned. "I never thought any of them would go for it. Immortality makes everyone horny as fuck."

Ms. West's probably been lacing their food with aphrodisiacs.

I tugged on their hands. "I don't want to talk about your other conquests. *I'm* horny as fuck. Isn't this a much better way of *raising* the pillar than me torching half the forest?"

Trey and Ayaz exchanged a glance, holding one of those silent conversations between them. Trey shook his head. "This isn't right. You shouldn't do this for the sake of the god."

"You... you're everything to us, Hazy," Quinn blurted out. "We don't want to you to feel like you have to be with us."

This is ridiculous. They're all manwhores. Why are they rejecting this?

"Let me get this straight," I said slowly, trying to hold my rising anger in check. "You're saying you *don't* want to have a foursome with me?"

Quinn winced, his hand flying to his crotch.

"The exact fucking opposite," Ayaz growled.

Trey leaned forward, his lips brushing my ear. "Do you know how many times the three of us have talked about this, about what we'd do to you when we finally had the indomitable Hazel under our spell?"

"I..."

Trey's teeth scraped my earlobe, sending a flare of heat straight to my core. "I'm hard just thinking about it. Of course we want it. We want *you*. But for the right reasons. And raising that pillar is not the right reason. You have to want this."

"I *do* want it." *Mmmmm, yes I do.*

"You want to help us." Ayaz trailed his fingers down my back, raising the hairs on my skin. "That's not the same thing."

"What if we hurt you?" Trey murmured, resting his hands on my hips, letting the heat of his skin draw out my flame. "Did you think about that? What if—"

I burst out laughing. "Hurt me? This from the guys who burned Dante's journal, who tarred my hair and held me over the side of a cliff to make me believe I was about to die? I'd like to see you fucking *try* to hurt me, Trey Bloomberg."

Trey's lips curled back into that cruel smirk that had always sent a shiver down my spine and heat coursing through my veins. Before I could react, he'd wrapped hot fingers around my neck, twisted my head toward him, and covered my mouth in his.

Holy fucking Great Old God.

I'd been pushing the guys away ever since I learned what I had to do. I knew it was the right thing for our shattered hearts. I needed the Kings to forget me so they could move on when I was gone. I wanted them to have all the good things – the true riches that had been denied them: love, peace, hope. They couldn't have that with me, and the sooner I stopped pretending, the happier we'd all be.

But...

Trey's lips seared mine, hot and possessive and savage. Here was the baddest King of the bullies laid bare. Violence bubbled beneath Trey's skin – the predator within him who'd once decided I was his prey and now... and now I was his lioness. And he tasted my growl.

But... I was nothing if not a sucker for heartache. I ran headlong into trouble instead of fleeing the other way.

What was the harm in one last goodbye? One last beautiful memory to carry with me in a spaceship made of black stone and broken memories?

A hand snaked around my shoulders, fingers walking across my naked flesh, raising goosebumps in their wake that had nothing to do with being cold. I could just make out Quinn's cheeky smile behind Trey's ear.

"Let's get to that cabin." Quinn's voice strained with lust.

I turned to lead the way, but Quinn picked me up, tossing me over his shoulder so my ass pointed to the sky. He slapped it playfully. "You're ours tonight, Hazy."

Fuck yes.

Trey and Ayaz took off into the trees, their steps long and urgent. Quinn raced after them, bouncing me over his shoulder. His hand slid along my inner thigh, slipping beneath my short velvet skirt. Nails scraped skin, teasing me as he dragged me away to his cave.

The forest canopy obscured the moon and stars. Quinn didn't seem to need light to see where he was going. I guess they'd been down to the cabins enough times to know the way by heart.

Don't think about it. Not tonight. It doesn't matter how many times

*they've been here before, and with whom. Tonight they're yours and you're
theirs, and that's all that matters.*

The line of pods came into view, their fiberglass shells shimmering under the waning moon. Quinn slid me off his shoulder, setting my feet on the ground and kissing me with desperate urgency. My lips exploded with his touch – Quinn Delacorte knew how to fucking *kiss*. When I was in his arms, I felt like the only woman on earth, like he'd been lost in the desert for years and I was the first sip of water on a parched throat. He kissed like he needed me to breathe.

"You're not afraid of me anymore." I struggled to catch my breath between kisses.

"I don't know what I was thinking." Quinn's eyes glinted with something that might've been regret. "You're the only person who has ever fought for me, who has ever believed I'm worth fighting for. You aren't a monster, Hazy – you're a gift."

I staggered back, stunned by the depth of his words. Quinn looked like he didn't quite know what to do with himself either. He ran a hand through his sandy hair. "I'm not good at being all deep and poetic and shit. That's more Ataturk's territory. But yeah... I'm not sure I was afraid of you so much as I was afraid of how I felt about you. All my life the people I've loved have hurt me, so I try to keep them at arm's length. I make jokes because it gives me distance – it's like pulling a little box over my heart where I can hide. But you came along and fucking kicked in the box with those vicious Docs of yours. I'm out here all exposed, and it's scary. But exciting, too. Especially..." Quinn leaned in to kiss me again, his fingers stroking my cheek with unusual tenderness. "Especially now that we stand a chance of getting out of here. Now that I can imagine a future with you in it."

I knew that wasn't true, and I hated keeping that secret from him, but his lips devoured mine and his fingers laced in my hair and I lost myself in his fruity scent and sweetness and I wanted so badly to fall into his delusion that we'd have a life together.

But I could fall into him – into all of them – instead. In some way, maybe what the four of us had would endure beyond the stars, living on in our memories even when we were ashes and dust.

Ayaz and Trey waited on the porch of the largest cabin, the one the Kings always reserved for themselves. I shoved my hand in my pocket to dig for the key, but Ayaz drew back his arm and thrust his fist through the tiny window. Glass smashed. Ayaz reached inside and unlocked the door.

"I had the key," I told him.

"Fuck the key. I'm not waiting another moment." Ayaz swept me into his arms and crushed my lips with his. His hands trailed over my body, wrapping me in that rich scent of his that takes me out of my body to some faraway place where things are different and fairy tales really do come true. When Ayaz touched me… it was tinged with bittersweet longing and vicious desperation. The intensity of it sloughed off all my edges, leaving me a mess of feelings and nerve endings and hot, urgent need.

We staggered across the room, shoving and tugging in urgency. My shins hit the edge of the bed and I sank back, falling into the sheets. Ayaz crawled on top of me, his hardness grazing my thigh. He claimed my lips again, driving me into the bed with the force of his need.

This was a different side of Ayaz to the sweet guy who I lost my virginity to in my creaking single bed. Ayaz cupped my face in his, and he teased out the darkness that cloaked my heart, igniting the flame inside me that burned for him. He was wild, impassioned, the artist finally free of the shackles of his servitude.

I loved it.

The bed creaked as Trey and Quinn climbed up, one on either side of me. Ayaz tore his lips from mine and sat back, and I stared up at my three Kings. It was hard to believe that only a few short months ago they were the source of all my misery, and now the thought of being without them made my chest tight.

The look in their eyes made my chest burn with heat. But behind the hunger, there was something else. Something deeper than words, more powerful than the rage that had kept us all prisoner. Something that might endure across eons and beyond stars.

"Hands up," Trey commanded. I lifted my arms above my head. Trey gripped my wrists while he and Quinn worked the velvet dress over my body. The fabric caressed my skin as they yanked it over my shoulders. Quinn flung the fabric against the wall.

"Don't come back!" he yelled at the offending clothing.

I wanted to laugh, but hot lips on mine stifled that idea. Trey held my wrists above my head, pressing me into the bed, willing me to submit to them. I sucked in a breath at the sudden loss of my power. His weight against my hips, his hands circling my wrists... if I wanted to escape, I'd never be able to throw him off.

Good thing I didn't want to be anywhere else.

I'd never been one to like to give up control, especially not to an arrogant bastard like Trey Bloomberg. But in that moment, I fucking dug it.

I arched my back, begging them for more.

Bring it the fuck on, bully boys.

I'm about to be with three guys at once. I should have been afraid. Back at my old school, girls whispered horror stories about this exact situation.

Trey was asking me to trust him, to trust *them*.

Heat crawled through my body. I tipped my head back, exposing my neck and parting my lips, offering myself.

For tonight, for one night only, they would be mine, and I theirs. I dragged away the broken glass surrounding my heart. I let them inside me, even though each kiss tore jagged cuts across my soul. Because I knew it would be my last.

The guys exchanged a silent conversation while my skin flushed with anticipation. Trey's words nagged in my mind. *Do you know long we've thought about this?*

What did they want to do to me? What did I *want* them to do to me? Everything. I had to live off this night for eternity. I wanted to savor every exquisite moment and every depraved action.

Ayaz was the first to bend toward me, his lips finding mine. While we kissed with frenzied urgency, Quinn's lips circled my nipple. His teeth scraped the sensitive skin, the slight pain of it only driving the fire higher. Heat circled my palms as I lay them across Quinn's back. He shuddered for a moment, then surrendered to trust.

Trey let go of my wrists to strip off his shirt, folding it neatly and dropping it down beside the bed. He slid off his slacks and crawled up beside me, his lips laying a trail across my cheek and along my jaw. He fought for my wrists again, trapping them over my head. Like fuck I was going to stop him, not with Quinn's lips wrapped around my nipple and Ayaz attacking my mouth with his.

Trey slid himself up beside Ayaz. Their eyes met, and a silent message passed between them. They were brothers in all but blood, and they'd been in close-quarters for more than two decades, so they knew each other's thoughts as if they were their own... or was this all part of the plan they'd devised for me?

It must've been, because Trey nodded and Ayaz crawled down the bed. He slid my panties down my legs, his touch featherlight but tense with need.

He bent between my legs, his tongue tasting me softly, quietly, in just the right spot. His skin against mine brought back memories of our first time together. Of *my* first time. Memories I'd thought tainted by his betrayal but I now clung to as he made the fire inside me dance anew.

Ayaz's beard tickled my thighs as he slid his tongue inside me, tasting, lapping. He swirled around my clit, perfectly matching Quinn's speed as he sucked my nipple into his mouth. I gasped and writhed beneath them.

Trey loomed over me, holding my wrists down while he studied my face. The intensity of his gaze unnerved me, and I closed my eyes.

"Keep your eyes open," he commanded. Despite myself, I responded to that authoritative tone in his voice, and my eyes flew open. A dark smile played across Trey's lips. I tried to bend my head up to kiss him, but he held me tight.

"I love watching you lose control," he whispered.

With my eyes open, I couldn't help but be acutely aware of the three of them, naked and close as they stoked the flames inside me and brought me closer, closer to losing control. My clit throbbed with need, and Ayaz's gentle strokes drove me wild. I bucked my hips toward him, begging him for more, but he only chuckled and held my thighs down with strong fingers.

Quinn turned his head to the other nipple, sucking it into his mouth just as Ayaz did the same with my clit. Bright stars danced in front of my eyes. My body wrenched from Trey's grasp and I nearly threw Ayaz off the bed with the force of the convulsions. The scream that tore from my lips would have floored a lion.

Fire touched every part of my body. For a moment I hung in this exquisite place where pleasure and pain were one, where I'd become a burning ball of a star gone supernova. And then the pleasure crested and the fire retreated, leaving me with a delicious warm flush all over my body.

"We've never done that before." Quinn smiled at the wall above the bed as he lay his head beside me. I turned my head to see a charred semi-circle across the wall. *That's why Trey's holding my hands, so I point my palms away from them.*

That seems fair. I licked my lips as I watched Trey discard his boxers, revealing his long, thick cock. *The last thing I want to do is burn something so perfect.*

I reached for it, wrapping my hand around his shaft. Trey's eyes fluttered closed for a moment, and a tiny sigh escaped his lips. I claimed his mouth as I tightened my grip and moved my hand slowly along his shaft. The tip was already wet, and in a few strokes I had enough lube that my hands slid easily along it.

Trey's eyes flew open. "This is supposed to be about you..."

"Tough. Maybe this gutter whore *likes* sucking cock." And before the King of the school could protest, I bent down and took the tip of him in my mouth.

I wasn't exactly experienced at giving head, but from the tight noise he made in the back of his throat, I guessed I was doing something right. He tasted amazing, like Trey – fresh and herbal – only with that hint of musk and salt and sex that clung to all of them. I swirled my tongue around Trey's head and tried to pull as much of him as possible inside my mouth, pulling out before sliding it back in with a steady rhythm.

"That feels..." Trey tangled his fingers in my hair. "Fuck, Hazy..."

"That's the plan," Quinn quipped. The bed creaked as he tried to move around behind me, his fingers trailing along my spine. But I wasn't done with him yet. I removed my hands from Trey and wrapped one each around Quinn and Ayaz, gripping their shafts hard and moving my hands with the same rhythm I used on Trey.

On my left, Quinn's whole body stiffened. On my right, Ayaz trailed his hands over my back, raising trails of fire over my skin. He made a tiny gasping noise that stoked a fresh fire inside me.

One King in my mouth, two in my hands. All three of them at my mercy.

I'd never felt so powerful in all my life.

I didn't need fire. Right now, my heart ignited from the trust they placed in me, from the tension in their muscles as they fought for control. My fingers tightened as I sucked Trey as deep as I could. The tip of his cock quivered in my mouth. Quinn jerked in my hand.

Quinn tore himself away, panting hard. "Damn, Hazy. We don't want this night to be over too soon."

"Mmmmm." Trey slid out of my mouth, tipping me back against the bed. "You might think you're in charge of this show, but we have plans."

"Oh yeah?" I met his eyes with a challenge of my own. *Go on, Kings. Tame me. Make me yours. For tonight I will take everything you have to give.* "Bring it the fuck on."

"Condoms," Trey barked. I shook my head.

"It doesn't matter."

Trey grinned. I think he thought it meant something else – that I believed Ms. West that they were sterile. I didn't trust that bitch one bit. I just didn't want anything, even a tiny piece of latex, between us. Not tonight. If I carried their child into space, then at least I would have a piece of them with me. Stupid and irresponsible and completely unlike me – I had no desire to have children, *ever,* and *especially* not on a spaceship that didn't appear to have any facilities – but this wasn't your fucking typical teenage hookup.

Trey pulled me to him, rolling me over so that I was on top, straddling him like a cowgirl. His fingers clawed the back of my head, pushing my face against his, mashing our mouths together in a furious kiss. I needed no invitation, grinding my hips against him, letting his hardness rub on my clit and drive a wave of heat through my core.

With commanding ease, Trey placed my hips above his. He drove up into me, bare and wild. Nothing between us, not even our own bullshit. My head bent back as he filled me, as I took all of him in. Quinn's lips kissed around my neck.

Trey pulled out and drove back in, hard and heavy, panting as he gave me everything. I rode him with equal force, our wills crashing against each other like waves against the cliffs, trying to wash each other's pain away. Every thrust, every movement sent fresh waves of fire flaring inside me, dragging along with them something from the deep.

"My turn." Quinn's nails dug into my thighs as he pulled me

back, tearing me off Trey's cock and entering me with a single thrust. I let out a gasp of surprise as I was filled with a different cock. Quinn wasn't quite as long as Trey, but he was wider, and the way he slid into me with such sly confidence, the way he touched different places inside me... oh, it was exquisite.

Seriously. Every girl should try having three guys at once.

My hips slapped against his as I drove myself back against him. Quinn's fingers dug into my thighs, his teeth scraping along my collarbone as he tasted my skin. And the fire... the fire was no longer a single flame but an inferno that burned through every limb and turned my veins into rivers of lava.

Beneath me, Trey rolled to the side and Ayaz slid in beneath. Dark lashes tangled together as he gazed up at me with those dark, soulful eyes. I threw my head back, reveling in his gaze as his friend penetrated me.

Wordlessly, Ayaz placed his hands over Quinn's and guided me off his cock and onto his, the movement so fluid he didn't even skip a beat. I expected Quinn to complain, but instead, he pressed his chest against my back, his slick cock now positioned between my ass cheeks. When Ayaz moved beneath me, Quinn moved too, skin against skin against skin. It felt so, so good, so *right*.

"Hazy..." Quinn purred in my ear. "Would you perhaps be interested in having two guys inside you at once?"

His cock twitched against my asscrack, the tip pulsing with excitement. It took me a moment to figure out what he meant. I leaned back against Ayaz's hips, driving his glorious cock deeper inside me, touching all the darkest places that longed to be touched, and I grinned. "I thought I said you could bring it the fuck on."

"Woohoo!" Quinn kissed my neck as he bent over to grab something from the nightstand. A tube of something... lube? I'd never done this before, obviously, and I should have probably felt nervous, but right now, riding Ayaz's cock with the god's voice screaming in ecstasy from beneath, all I felt was powerful and free.

Quinn squirted something between my ass cheeks. His fingers trailed along my back. Ayaz leaned up to kiss me, his lips holding me, haunting me, while his cock did things to me that made my body purr. Quinn swirled a finger around in the cool lube and pushed inside me.

At first, it felt like nothing at all. But then he pushed a little deeper and I could feel the pressure of his finger against Ayaz's cock, with just a thin layer of me between them, and my mouth opened with surprise. I froze, lost in the new sensation as Ayaz withdrew his cock and slowly, slowly, slid back in. His beard tickled my neck as he chuckled.

"She likes it," he murmured. "I knew our Hazy was a little deviant."

"Then I'd better keep going. Wouldn't want her to think we couldn't handle her." Quinn pushed another finger inside me, and I gasped. It felt amazing, so tight and hot and perfect. The pressure building inside me and the fire pressing against my skin was almost unbearable. But in the best possible way.

"More," I cried, the words strangling against my lips as I gave another inch to Quinn, and to the god.

"As you wish, M'lady." Quinn withdrew his fingers and a moment later, the head of his cock pressed against the opening. Over my shoulder, his eyes locked on Ayaz, and they did that thing where they communicated instructions to each other in the silence.

They really have planned this. I wonder—

I lost the thought as Ayaz pulled out just as Quinn pushed his head inside me. I cried out as he entered me, and the new tight sensation took over my body. Quinn held himself there, his breath hot on my skin. I tried to push myself back against him, to send him deeper, but Ayaz gripped my hips, holding me still.

"Don't move," he said, his voice like silk. "Quinn and I will drive. All you have to do is *feel*."

That I can do. I held my body where Ayaz had placed it, hovering just over his cock, my pussy aching for him to fill me. After a few moments, Quinn pushed himself a little deeper. His lips closed around a spot on my shoulder, his teeth biting into my skin.

"Hazy, you okay?" The moan that escaped my lips indicated the affirmative, so Quinn drove forward another inch. Bit by bit he filled me, waiting for my body to adjust, giving me time to relish this new sensation.

When he was inside me as deep as he would go, Ayaz arched his hips, sliding inside me in one fluid motion. I gasped as his cock filled me, the pressure of Quinn against his too much, so much, just right.

It feels amazing.

I want...

Quinn drew out slowly, and the two of them wrapped strong arms around my body, holding me in place, propping me up. They started to move in a rhythm, one pulling out as the other drove in.

I stopped thinking at all, lost in the wild sensations that assailed my body as my Kings worshipped me between them.

Ayaz drew back, giving Quinn more room to get properly inside me. I moaned as Quinn stretched me wide.

"Oh, fuck, Hazy." Quinn's ragged breath teased my earlobe.

I turned my head to Trey, my lips finding his, desperate to have all three of them on me, in me. But his kiss wasn't enough. I needed more of Trey inside me. I murmured my command against his lips and he complied, kneeling on the bed and lifting his cock to my face.

My lips closed around Trey. He moaned as I took him in. All buttoned up, the King who had to be in control. To see him utterly undone made something shift inside me, and all that fire that had been dormant ignited in one great spark.

Yessss, the god hissed.

Beneath us, the earth shifted. What had been sleeping awoke, and the earth parted and made way for the next piece to reveal itself. Suspended between my three Kings, I no longer felt my body as it once was. I'd become a ball of flame, a pillar of fire, a vessel for the god's triumph.

I am the conduit.

I moaned around Trey's cock, feeling him tense in my mouth.

Pinned between Quinn and Ayaz, I could do nothing but surrender as they moved in and out in a building tempo. From the moment they synced their movements, their cocks like one long member sliding right through me, I lost track of the world. The entire thing was one long orgasm as I burned the world, suspended between them as they drew out the fire that I'd suppressed for so long.

Release. I feel you. I feel your... need.

Release your light.

I closed my eyes, reveling in the exquisite sensation of it all, of being the complete center of their sun. While my Kings poured all the love they'd been afraid to feel into my body, placing these gifts at the altar of their adoration, the god gave me the things that he'd hidden within his screams – the human feelings he'd tried to deny. While they loved and needed and surrendered to me, so did he.

I am the conduit.

Five of us joined together – Trey, Quinn, Ayaz, and the god, all penetrating me at once, our fires melding and burning bright as the stars from which we came.

"Hazy," Ayaz gasped, clenching his lower jaw in a completely adorable expression. His whole body stiffened. His cock hardened inside me as he came, his dark eyes wide with surprise and delight.

Seeing Ayaz lose control like that and feeling his cock hard inside me sent me over the edge again. My final orgasm blinded me completely, burning me up in the inferno of my own making.

Heat flung from my fingers, from my solar plexus, from every part of me. Blue flame tore through the cabin, hot and brighter than the brightest star. It leaped through the open window. I couldn't aim it, but from the way the conflagration tugged at me, desperate to be free, I knew it would find true.

When I surfaced, I tasted Trey's orgasm on my tongue. Quinn shuddered against my back. Flames licked along the windowsill, and a charred circle had singed into the wood around the bed. Heat and power still sizzled in the air around us. I was amazed the building hadn't burned down.

Ayaz collapsed against the sheets, his chest slick with sweat as he slid out of me. I lay across his chest, my breath coming out in ragged gasps, my fingers grasping at his smooth skin, now completely healed of burns.

"I hope that doesn't start a forest fire," Ayaz mused.

"Don't sound so smug," I gasped, listening with my body, trying to feel the god's next move. The ground beneath us rumbled. From the woods, screams reached my ears. *It's happening.*

I rolled off the bed, scrambling for my clothes. I found a towel on a hook on the wall and used that to wipe myself off, then yanked the dress over my head, adjusting it across my tits as I leaped down the steps and crashed into the trees. The ground tossed me, and I slammed into a trunk.

"Easy." Ayaz grabbed my arm. Trey and Quinn surrounded me. Wordlessly, we picked our way through the forest, passing terrified students running for the campus as though their lives depended on making it inside the walls.

I'd told them not to run, not to be afraid. But that was easy for me to say.

We reached the stone steps just as Greg flew up, his mouth wide.

"There you are, honey!" he yelled. "You'd better come quick. Another of those pillars has risen out of the grotto."

CHAPTER TWENTY-FIVE

Two down, one to go.

The four of us stood rigid, staring up at the pillar that jutted from the middle of the dark pool. It was identical to the one in the auditorium – all creepy geometry and angles that didn't resolve correctly to the eye. Heat rumbled through my veins.

This proves that Ayaz and I are right. We can do this. We can raise the god's ship from the deep.

Around us, students charged in all directions, scrambling along the slippery rocks. I noticed a couple fleeing down the path to the cemetery. Their terror must have voided their senses – I knew how much the students all hated it down there.

"Stop!" I yelled. "Listen to me. I told you that you had nothing to fear from the pillars."

But it was useless. Perhaps it was all the drugs in their systems making them see monsters, or maybe they'd just seen too much, felt too much, and the pillar pushed them over the edge. They fled back to the school to hide in their comfortable beds. Greg waved at me as he linked arms with Loretta and followed them back. He'd keep an eye on them, spread the word that everything was okay as soon as they calmed down.

All was silent in the pleasure garden, save for me and my Kings.

"That went about as chaotically as I expected," Trey mused.

"We might as well head back. There's nothing else to do here tonight." I clung to Ayaz as the hum of the pillar called me closer. I needed to put some distance between us before I was unable to resist. I didn't want to be sucked into that primordial vision again – I'd had enough excitement for one night.

My body ached in all kinds of good ways as we trudged back to school. As we stepped through the doors into the darkened atrium, Ms. West flew through the faculty wing and threw herself at me.

"You!" she cried, fingers like talons reaching for my throat. "How dare you drug me and violate our trust!"

Trey and Ayaz slid in front of me. Ms. West slammed against their hard bodies. They didn't hold her back, but she couldn't get to me.

I snorted. "I betray *you?* We're supposed to be working together, but you were still hurting my friend. You said Zehra would be free, and I was making sure you kept your promise. As for drugging you, consider it payback for what you did to Ayaz."

Ms. West's eyes flashed. Ayaz stiffened as she rested a hand on his shoulder. "Such a pliant mind, so ready to believe the lies I placed there."

So it is true. She just admitted it. She altered his mind.

Ayaz grabbed her fingers, twisting her wrist around. She yelped in surprise as he forced her arm into a hold, her back bent awkwardly over his knee, her head pointing to the floor. "Move an inch and I'll snap your arm. It won't heal the way mine does. But don't worry, I'll do far worse unless you give me back what you took."

"Boy, I took nothing from you but your virginity, and you didn't seem to mind that too much."

"You took my sister! You kept her locked away from me, and

you tortured her for your own amusement." Ayaz seemed to grow an extra foot as he tightened his grip on Ms. West. His dark eyes blazed with hatred born of hurt. "You took my life and locked me away in this place and made me hurt people. And then, you took my memories – the one beautiful thing to ever come out of this hellhole, and you stripped it away."

Ms. West gasped as he wrenched her arm tighter, but it was a gasp of triumph. "Those cannot... be restored. The erasure is permanent."

With a howl, Ayaz shoved her hard. She skidded across the room, her heels sliding on the slick marble. She slammed into the wall and crumpled to the floor in a tangle of black fabric. A candle sconce clattered to the floor beside her, the glass bulb smashing to pieces.

The Deadmistress tilted her chin, glaring at Ayaz with defiant eyes.

"Keep them," Ayaz whispered, his voice edged with steel. "You'll need something to heat up your cold, dead heart in the nights to come. I've made new memories with Hazel and with my brothers, and you won't take those or anything from me *ever again.*"

At his words, Ms. West's eyes flooded with cold realization. She no longer had control of us, and she had an inkling that we might not be entirely going along with her plan. "You're playing with fire, Ayaz Demir, and you and the rest of your friends will burn up in her inferno if you're not careful. I've waited too long and worked too hard for things to fall apart now. We have one shot at freedom, and I won't have you messing it up for all of us with some ridiculous scheme."

"No schemes here." My lips formed what I hoped was an innocent smile. "We're *so* looking forward to being able to walk around outside the school and hold hands like normal teenagers, until I grow old and die and these three can build a shrine to me."

Her eyes darted between us, but the Kings weren't giving

anything away. Ayaz's shoulders heaved – it took all his resolve not to throttle her with his bare hands.

"If I find out that you're playing me, I'll be *most* upset." Her voice remained calm, but the threat lurked behind it with cold precision. We all knew what she was capable of. "It won't be you four who pay for messing this up. I'll let the Eldritch Club destroy every student, and you can watch them all die before I force you all to impregnate Hazel to produce the next generation of the god's children. If you truly are the Kings of Miskatonic, you will protect your subjects from the real enemy. Or else all hope is lost."

CHAPTER TWENTY-SIX

"My nails are *ruined*," Courtney whined, throwing down the chisel to suck on the tip of her finger.

"Suck it up." I couldn't help the pleasure that crept into my voice. "You're learning an important lesson about how the rest of the world works for their money."

It was a week after the party, and we were back in the forest with a small group of students we trusted. Courtney Haynes would not have been top of my list, but Trey and Ayaz fought for her inclusion. Of course, she'd then immediately gone and spilled the beans to John and Derek, so they were here too, which I was not happy about. I'd rather fuck a cactus than trust those two.

We were about to embark on the most ambitious part of our plan. Zehra had made contact on her new phone. She'd found her people who could get us the documents we needed, but they expected to be paid.

A *lot* of money.

245 Miskatonic Prep students and 76 members of the mainte-nance staff needed new lives. Even without helping the teachers – we decided they could fend for themselves – we would need some serious cash to get the basics sorted. And that was before we

considered how everyone would live and eat and buy plane tickets while they got as far from the smoldering remains of the school as they could get.

As I turned over the challenge of how to get our hands on mad scrilla, my thoughts had drifted back to Trey's black card and the enormous balance it carried after twenty years of non-use. I wondered how many other Miskatonic students had money sitting in accounts and on cards they might still be able to access if only they could leave the grounds.

All it took was a whisper of a promise to Tillie, and she had a list of the most likely suspects. We'd slipped a note under each's dorm room door. *Come to the cabins after midnight on Friday night if you want a taste of freedom. Be prepared to get dirty. Don't tell anyone else.*

Of course, when Courtney heard the word *dirty*, she imagined something very different, which was probably why she'd told John. She showed up wearing a sparkly halter top, booty shorts, and heavy makeup, and looked completely confused when I handed her a mallet and chisel and told her to remove one of the border sigils carved into an ancient cairn.

Courtney hit the chisel a few more times, then dropped the tools at her feet and stuck out her lip in a petulant pout. "I don't see why I'm doing all the work. I thought you said we were supposed to be a collective – equal work in, equal out."

I rolled my eyes and pointed to another cairn a little way down the ridge. A large hole marred one smooth side. My foot rested on a stone wrapped in cloth at my feet. "Because I've already finished chiseling that one out of the rocks. But if you really can't do it, you can go back to the school and forget about crossing the boundary—"

"*Fine.*" Courtney gave the chisel a few half-hearted taps. A few minutes later she yelped again. "Ow. It hurts!"

Not-quite-undead-children-of-the-cosmic-god sure do know how to complain.

"Out of my way." I grabbed the chisel and shoved her aside. "I liked it better when we were enemies."

I slammed the chisel into the small split Courtney had made and bashed it with the hammer. A chunk of stone flew out and skittered across the ground.

"Wow. You're good at this," Courtney remarked.

"It's easy. I just imagine I'm hammering your perfect nose."

Courtney snorted with laughter. After a few more hits, I felt the chisel slide through to meet the first cut. I bashed out the last of the loose stone and lifted out the sigil, my tired arms struggling with the weight. I dropped it into Courtney's lap. "There you go. Are you ready for a walk?"

"Hell yes." Courtney strained to push the sigil into her backpack. Once she'd drawn the string around it, she threaded her arms through the holes and tried to stand, only to slide back down again.

"I'm never going to be able to carry this."

I smirked. "Not even for the chance to go to a real nail salon?"

Courtney bit her lip and struggled to her feet. She wasn't used to being ordered to do things that made her uncomfortable. There was always some boy ready to help her. But not tonight.

Once Courtney looked steady and like she wasn't going to try to palm off her sigil to me, we hiked along the ridge to meet the others. Trey had gathered the group in a semicircle. There were about forty of us, including me and the Kings. Eleven bulging backpacks were stacked in the center. Courtney's and mine made thirteen sigils in total. We'd left the sigils carved into the cliffs that bordered the raging sea. In front of us were all the stones from across the peninsula – boundary stones that sealed the Edimmu within the school.

I stepped into the circle, meeting the eyes of every person there. When I got to John Hyde-Jones, he turned away and scowled. *Great. Why's he here again?* "We're splitting into groups. One sigil per group. Taking your sigil with you extends the boundary of the school to where you are. You won't be able to move in front of it, but you can carry it as far away as you want. You have to stick together in your group or you risk being hurt as the sigils move. The most important thing is to come back with cash – as much as you can carry, but I'm giving you free rein to do whatever you please while you're outside the boundary, as long as you don't hurt anyone else and you don't get caught. You have until the sun comes up to be back at Miskatonic Prep – drop the money into our dungeon room in the basement, and get back to your dorms before you're caught. And don't think about skipping out or reporting to your parents. I've got spies watching you."

I clapped my hands. Through cracks in the rocks, shadows sprang up, circling the sigils with hissing cries. Amber shrieked and clutched Tillie's shoulder. Other students shuffled away from my servants.

I clapped again, and the servants rose into the clouds, scattering across the sky, waiting and watching. "We chose you because we believed we could trust you. Don't disappoint us. As far as the teachers and your parents are concerned, tonight never happened. Are we clear?"

John grabbed one of the sigils and raced off, Courtney hot on his heels. The others whooped and yelled as they leaped over the invisible line that had divided them from the real world for two decades. In their glee, they made those heavy stones look as light as feathers.

I watched them disappear with a sense of trepidation. Tonight was about more than just a means to get our hands on much-needed funds – it was a test, although they didn't know it. Could I count on them to leave Miskatonic Prep without becoming a scourge on the world? Would I live to regret my part in making them free?

The shadows swooped after them, promising that my dreams would soon be filled with reports of the students' activities.

"Why are they going back that way?" I demanded as I

watched Courtney, John, Derek, and some others doubling back toward school. *Great. I'm already regretting my decision.*

"Probably to get Courtney's car." Trey picked up his satchel and followed them.

"Courtney has a car?"

"Of course. Lots of us do. Our parents left them behind after the fire. What's an abandoned luxury vehicle to them? There's an old stable building near the entrance to the school, but you wouldn't see it unless you knew to look for it. Courtney's Lambo and Quinn's truck and my Porsche are all inside. In the early days of being Edimmu we'd drag race down the driveway, but that got old. It's tough to get excited about driving fast when you can't go anywhere. But Paul's a bit of a hobby mechanic, so he's been keeping them in working order."

I glared at him. "Why the fuck were you trying to shove me into a boat when you could've just given me some keys and let me drive away?"

"Are you kidding?" Quinn laughed. "That car is Trey's baby. He wouldn't trust anyone else behind the wheel."

"True." Trey smiled. "But that wasn't the reason. Like all the mobile phones, Ms. West keeps all the keys locked up some-where. Ayaz tried to find them on at least two occasions, but no luck. We didn't have the resources we do now."

"You mean, like a scrappy thief from Philly?" I dug Ms. West's keychain from my pocket. A couple of keys on there looked suspi-ciously like they belonged to cars.

Trey's lips found mine, and his kiss seared with danger. I could feel the excitement rolling off him at the thought of getting behind the wheel again. "C'mon, our little thief. It's time you discovered how Kings like to play."

Trey was right – I never would have noticed the stable hidden in a thicket of trees. A round arena out front had grown over with thistles that reached nearly to the roofline, completely obscuring the entrance. By the time we arrived, Courtney's group had already flung open the door and flattened a path out toward the drive. Even so, Trey got several thorns in his arms hacking his way inside. Judging by the grin on his face at the thought of seeing his beloved car again, he didn't feel a one.

I cared. My arm stung like fuck from tugging out thorns. And I was concerned about all the evidence of our escape – the flattened weeds, the tire tracks, the sound of engines. "Walking would be much less conspicuous."

"True, but the teachers never come out here." Trey pointed. "We got sick of them breaking up our parties, so we had Ayaz put up some kind of sigil that makes anyone who's not invited feel a crippling sickness if they get near. Come on, you won't believe what we've got in here."

I followed Trey inside. The stable was a long wooden building with a mezzanine floor where a stablehand might once have slept. Every spare inch of space on the ground floor had been crowded with cars. And not just any cars – the place looked like the impound lot of 'Lifestyles of the Rich and Tacky.'

Trey flicked through Ms. West's keys and tossed one to Quinn. "Move your piece-of-shit truck so I can get the Porsche out."

"Why are we taking your car?" Quinn shot back. "Mine's right in the front, and it's bigger so it can fit more. It's also got these kickass off-road tires and a snorkel. Does yours have a snorkel?"

"I don't need a snorkel, because I have self-respect and a beautiful Cayenne—"

"If you two don't stop arguing, I'll be the one driving," Ayaz shot back, grabbing for the keyring in Trey's hand.

"Argh, no! Fine." Quinn stuck out his bottom lip. "We'll take the Porsche. But I get to drive a bit after Trey. *Only* me." He shot Ayaz a worried look.

"Why don't they want you to drive?" I asked Ayaz.

"Ataturk is a speed demon." Quinn slid into the driver's seat and gunned the engine. "He won all the drag races."

"And he lays on the horn," Trey added.

Ayaz shrugged. "In Turkey, there are forty-three things you can say with your horn."

"In America, there are only two things you say with a horn," Quinn shot back. "One. I'm about to fuck up, and two, I'm a twatwaffle who can't drive for shit and blame the rest of the world."

I turned to Trey. "You don't think the teachers will notice all this noise?"

He grinned. "Not since I had Dr. Morgan add some of her wonder drug into their dinner."

"Trey! We shouldn't do that again – not with Ms. West already suspicious. We don't know if we can trust Dr. Morgan—"

He laughed. The randomness of it caught me off-guard. The last time I'd seen Trey this... relaxed, it was when we'd first visited Deborah, when we were sleeping on an air mattress and walking the dogs and eating take-out. "Relax, Hazy. Tonight belongs to us and us alone."

Quinn hopped into an enormous truck painted bright yellow (because of course it was) and pulled around to the side of the stable. Trey slid a sleek red Porsche out into the moonlight. Even though the car had been shut up for years, the engine purred like a kitten. Paul must be a miracle worker. Now I knew where Trey's good mood had come from – it must be amazing to drive a car like that.

Grinning, I slid into the passenger seat. Even though Trey had wiped off the seats when he got in with a chamois, the interior still had a slightly musty smell. Trey flipped through the CDs in the glove compartment (CDs! How quaint) and stuck on one from Ayaz's favorite band, Blood Lust. Sweeping metal guitars and furious drums blasted from the stereo. *Is that a cello?*

Sick. Quinn and Ayaz hopped in back and Trey gunned the engine.

The car roared to life and tore down the gravel road. Trey whooped as he yanked the wheel hard and the back end of the car slid around the first corner. I gasped as the front wheels gripped the road for dear life.

They weren't the only thing gripping for dear life. My knuckles were white against the dashboard as Trey took every corner like a rally driver. If this was what rich kids did for a thrill I'd go back to jacking cars and hard drugs, thanks very much.

Trees whizzed past in a blur as we careened into Arkham. Trey slowed down as we slid along the main street, a wild grin warming his icy features. "What do you think?"

"Ayaz was supposed to be the speed demon!" I yelled. "What the fuck do you call that?"

Trey's smile turned giddy. Seeing him like this, like a normal guy who didn't button himself up or hold himself back, made a new fire ignite inside me. "*That* is what you get when your rich daddy owns a Formula 1 team. I learned to drive on a race track."

"You could have killed us." I fought to control my beating heart. Heat danced across my chest.

"I'd never put you in danger. If Ayaz was driving, it'd be another story."

We shot through Arkham without looking back and hit the freeway. Trey couldn't keep the smile off his face. For being out of practice, he slid into the traffic without a single mistake, merging seamlessly and waving thanks to a driver who let us in. I bet he never used to do that.

In the backseat, Quinn and Ayaz headbanged. Ayaz strummed an air guitar while Quinn screamed unfathomable growly vocals into an upside-down Scotch bottle he was using as a microphone. A hollow ache formed in my stomach – they were so carefree, so normal. It reminded me of hanging out with Dante, which reminded me of things I didn't want to think about right now.

"Bloomberg, I had a boo boo... the bottle wasn't empty." Quinn perched his chin on the back of my seat, his breath warming my neck.

"You'd better not have spilled Scotch over the leather," Trey growled.

"It's fine. No biggie. I'll make Ataturk lick it up."

"Lick up your own whisky." Ayaz let out a howl as the song reached a crescendo.

The longer we drove, the less I thought about Dante. Tonight wasn't about the past. We drove along the shoreline, where waves crashed against the breakwater, sending up pillars of froth and foam. I rolled down the window and breathed in the frigid air. The taste of freedom.

My fears slipped away as I embraced the present moment – each second precious because we lived it fully, the way teenagers were supposed to. Driving at top speed with the wind in my hair, I felt like a real teenager for the first time in... maybe the first time ever.

This is what it's like to be normal.

Right, normal. With three boyfriends who are children of a cosmic god, cruising down the freeway to steal a hundred k. Totally normal.

Fuck.

In the back of the car, we found blankets. They smelled musty, but who cared? Trey pulled up in a parking lot overlooking the ocean. The only other vehicle was an abandoned food truck covered in graffiti. Quinn and Ayaz folded down the seats and all four of us crowded in back with our sigil (and it was a squash – even Trey's four-seater Porsche had precious little room), wrapped in the blankets while Metallica's 'Wherever I May Roam' pounded through the speakers.

I watched Ayaz light up a joint. "Ms. West could be a problem."

Smoke swirled around Ayaz's head as he took a long drag

before he passed it to Trey. "Agreed. She's not going to be happy when she finds out we took away her immortality. How do you know the god won't tell her our plan? You said he didn't know how to lie."

"He doesn't. I told him to go silent. He isn't speaking a word to her at all." I breathed the weed deep into my lungs, letting a wave of calm wash over me. "I think that's what's got her in such a state. She's not used to the silence. It's making her nervous. She can't do anything now, not when it could risk her plan falling through. But if she discovers the missing sigils or decides to jump in at the last second and ruin things, I don't have a plan to deal with it. I guess we just wait and see."

"Can you ask the shadows to deal with her?"

I shook my head. "They're part of the god. They'll be in the spaceship with him."

"What about your little army of plague-carriers?" Quinn piped up.

"The rats? I'm not sure I can command them to do anything. But I can ask."

My phone beeped. It was Zehra. Ayaz read over my shoulder, but Zehra hadn't written anything, only dropped a link to a newspaper article.

"Some family in upstate New York had their assets seized by the IRS," I read aloud. "Apparently, they haven't paid taxes in fifteen years, and now they're going to lose everything."

"The Montagues? That's Nancy's family," Trey looked at Ayaz with an astonished expression on his face. "Your sister did this?"

"She's something else." Ayaz's eyes beamed with pride as he grabbed the phone and read through the article. "I just hope she stays safe out there. The Eldritch Club won't let this stand."

We talked and smoked and kissed until the sun rose over the water – the first sunrise my Kings had seen outside the school in twenty years. The clock on the dashboard counted down the minutes until the nearest bank opened.

Beside me, Trey snored. Grinning, Quinn dug his fingers into Trey's pocket and fished out the keys. Trey woke just as Quinn gunned the engine.

"You fucker." Trey kicked the back of the seat. "Get out of my car."

"No can do." Quinn whooped as he tore off, ramming the car into the nearest speed bump. Trey winced as something on the underbelly of the car scraped over concrete. Quinn bumped and ground his way along the freeway to the next small town. He didn't have nearly as much skill behind the wheel as Trey – I guess that was why he had a truck, so he could flatten any obstacle in his path.

"Stop," Trey ordered as Quinn ground the gears and we turned onto the main street.

I glanced across the road at the tiny provincial bank. "Here?"

"It's as good a place as any."

Quinn narrowly avoided scraping the Porsche along another car as he parallel parked. He and Ayaz waited in the car while Trey and I pulled on the wigs and hats and long coats we'd dug out of the costume department. My eyes flicked to the security cameras over the bank entrance. *Please don't let Vincent be watching.*

Trey stepped into the teller and slid his black card across the counter. "I require a cash advance," he said.

"Certainly sir. For how much money?"

"All of it."

CHAPTER TWENTY-SEVEN

I secretly hoped the teller would give us the money in sacks with dollar signs written on them, like in all the old cartoons Dante and I loved to watch. But she just handed Trey two thick envelopes containing stacks of hundred dollar bills.

Seventy-eight thousand dollars.

They couldn't give us all the money – they didn't have enough stored in the safe. According to the teller, you're supposed to call in advance if you want to take out loads of cash. But it didn't matter. I'd never seen so much money in my life. Hell, I'd never even *contemplated* the idea of that kind of cash falling across my path.

It occurred to me as I slid the money into the satchel with the sigil that I could walk away with it. I could sneak out at night and be halfway across the country before the Kings even thought of following me. Seventy-eight grand would help me and Greg and Andre and Loretta start new lives.

Trey knew that, and he'd given me the money anyway. Either because he trusted me, or because he wanted to give me the chance to make my escape, the same way he'd tried to save me so many times before – by putting me on a boat and floating me out to sea.

Tough luck, Trey Bloomberg. You're stranded with me for a bit longer.

We sped back toward the school. The presence of the cash sobered us – even though Trey had the radio on, no one sang along or made jokes or said much of anything at all. Trey sped through Arkham without slowing and turned the corner onto the gravel road. A figure stepped in front of the car.

"Fuck." Trey slammed on the brakes. I screamed as the car lurched to a stop. My seatbelt bit into my shoulder.

Luckily, the Porsche was such a fucking great car and the tires gripped so well that the front grill had stopped barely an inch from the girl who slammed her fists on the hood, not caring that she'd nearly been flattened. *Who is that and why is she screaming—*

"Courtney?"

I recognized the halter top and booty shorts, but that was where the similarities to the haughty Queen who'd left school last night ended. Her eyes bugged out of her face, and her hair was all matted, with leaves and branches sticking out. Blood trickled from a cut in her temple.

"Fucking John!" she yelled, punching the hood again to emphasize her point. "I'm going to wring his fucking neck!"

"Watch the bodywork." Trey was already out of the car, slamming the door behind him as he dragged Courtney out of the road. She clung to him, yelling a stream of incoherent words.

"Courts, get it together. You're not making sense. What happened? Where's your car?"

"He took off with it, is what happened," Courtney shrieked. "Two groups of us decided to stick together. We had a bit of a party on the beach, then went to a bank in Innsmouth to get John's money. We managed to get fifty g's, but as soon as we threw it in my car, John sped away and that's... that's not even the worst part!"

She broke down into gasping sobs. Trey shook her roughly. "Tell us."

Courtney paled. "Paul was John's partner, and he'd gone across the street to get some drinks while we were in the bank. He must've... he must've been standing in the wrong spot, outside the sigils when John took off, because..."

"What? Spit it out." The vein above Trey's eye was ready to explode from the tension. My fingers gripped the edge of my seat so hard the knuckles glowed white.

"Because he collapsed on the street, and his body turned to dust," Courtney sobbed. "He's dead."

CHAPTER TWENTY-EIGHT

Dead.

No.

Paul can't be dead.

Trey's words mirrored my own thoughts. "That's impossible. How can he be dead? We're immortal."

Courtney swiped at her eyes and pointed toward the gap in the trees where she'd emerged. "See for yourself."

My legs trembled as I stepped out of the car. I noticed rustling in the trees. An animal? A horrible practical joke? For a moment I was transported back to the first quarter, when I was the victim of vicious bullying at Courtney's behest. *I bet Courtney's tears are fake – she lures us into the forest and then John and his buddies jump out and—*

I didn't like to think of anything past the *and*. But Quinn and Ayaz stalked into the woods after Trey. They clearly didn't think Courtney was faking it. I touched my fingers to the burn on my wrist, sucked in a breath, and plunged in after them.

Only a few yards into the trees, we found them. Tillie and Derek held two ends of a makeshift stretcher they'd made of uniform blazers tied between two sticks. Tillie dropped her end on the ground and rushed to embrace Trey, her face stricken.

On the stretcher lay Paul's body.

At least, I *assumed* it was Paul's body. He was impossible to recognize – he wore his school uniform, so only his head was visible, but he no longer looked like the same fun guy who'd welcomed me into the monarchs' circle after the Kings adopted me. Paul's skin had practically disappeared from his bones, save for patches that clung to his cheeks. Instead, the surface of his bones appeared covered in fine dust. Where his hands should have been were only empty cuffs.

As I watched in horror, the body slid down the tilted stretcher. Paul's foot hit a tree root and disintegrated into a pile of dust. The breeze fanned it across the forest floor, leaving the hollow hem of his slacks flapping free and a single ash-filled sock lying in the dead leaves.

I think I'm going to be sick.

As I struggled against the rising bile, Nancy threw herself over her boyfriend's body, clutching his jacket and laying kisses on his forehead. Every time she touched him, more of his body fell away. When she removed her lips, she left a hole in the top of his skull that rapidly filled with dust as the bones crumbled around it.

Rage bubbled inside me. *John did this.*

My ears rang. John's words from that night in my room burned over in my head. *Spread her legs.*

I tried to help him, even after what he wanted to do to me. I ignored the warning in my heart and tried to give him his freedom and convince myself he'd change, or that justice would eventually catch up with him. Now my worst fear had been realized. I'd let a child of the god out into the world and he'd acted *exactly* like a spoiled rich rapist bastard, and now Paul was *dead*.

I'll kill him. He may be running around out there as an immortal, but I swear I'll kill him.

"We thought..." Courtney struggled for words. "Miskatonic

Prep is the closest thing Paul has to a home. We couldn't just leave him on the side of the road."

"You did the right thing." Ayaz laid a hand on her shoulder. Courtney's body stiffened at his touch, and I knew that what had been between them was over for good. She took nothing from his comfort. Courtney needed to be with the person she loved most... herself.

"We'll carry him." Trey moved around the stretcher, his presence calming, authoritative.

"Where are we taking him?" Derek gripped the other end.

"To the Porsche."

"He won't fit in the trunk."

"He will by the time we get there," Trey's voice was grim.

Trey, Ayaz, and Derek lifted the stretcher. With every movement, more of Paul blew away. By the time they maneuvered him into the trunk of the Porsche, all that was left was a pile of clothes and a torso of dust. Derek climbed in the passenger seat next to Trey and us four girls squeezed in back with Quinn and Ayaz. The car was barely meant for four people, let alone eight. I had elbows in places elbows should never be, and I had to hold on tight to stop myself banging around. Courtney sat on Ayaz's knees, tears streaming down her pretty cheeks.

Trey drove carefully to disturb Paul as little as possible, so our climb up the peninsula was slower than our descent. Even so, my head banged on the roof with every corner. After a stop to hide our sigils back at their original locations, Trey backed the Porsche into the stable. We all toppled out and he lifted the trunk. I peered inside, wishing I had the good sense to look away. A ring of dust had settled around Paul's clothing. When the boys lifted the stretcher, more dust cascaded from the sleeves. There was practically nothing left.

"What do we do with him?" Trey asked Courtney. He sensed that she needed something from Paul's return.

For the first time since I'd come to this school, I saw my own pain and horror reflected back at me in Courtney Haynes' eyes. "We bury him."

Paul already had a grave, as they all did – down in the first row, closest to the edge of the cliff, where the trees bent their spindly limbs down toward the churning ocean below. The guys took off toward the forest. Courtney followed, clutching Nancy who still wailed hysterically, while Tillie, Ayaz, and Derek ran up to the school with the bags of cash to gather Paul's closest friends.

Down we went to the pleasure garden, which still bore the signs of last week's party – the trash on the ground, the dirt and sand churned up from dancing, a broken table lying on its side. The black pillar jutted from the grotto – reflecting its surface into the pool of water surrounding it, creating the illusion that I was back in the primordial place. A trail of blue flame shimmered on the surface of the pillar's sigil.

The wind picked up as we neared the shore and I tried not to think of bits of Paul blowing through the air around me. We found Paul's grave just as Tillie and Derek ran up with a handful of other students and, weirdly, some of the maintenance staff. I glanced at Sadie across the crowd, and she shrugged. She didn't know why she was there, either. Tillie carried a shovel, which she handed to Trey.

Of course, Trey would be the one expected to dig the grave for the only classmate to ever truly die at Miskatonic Prep. That was the duty of the King of Kings – and he bore it as he bore all things, noble and remote and determined to be the best. Trey set his jaw against the horror of his task and dug the spade into the soft earth. In no time at all, he'd hollowed out a shallow grave and lowered what remained of Paul inside.

That done, he stepped back into the semicircle we'd formed around the grave. I glanced around the stricken faces. Each one looked at me expectantly, but I'd barely known Paul. It didn't seem right that I be the one to eulogize him. Nancy was still crying, so I nudged Courtney forward.

Now she had an audience, Courtney pulled herself together, wiping over her stricken features with a mask of subdued sadness. She really was an exceptional actress. In a clear voice that rang across the cemetery, piercing through the howling wind, Courtney spoke. "Paul was a loyal friend, a fun guy to hang with, a sweet boyfriend but a mediocre kisser. Most importantly... he was family."

From behind her, Tillie let out a loud sob, but Courtney's features remained hard and focused. Paul's death had shifted something inside her – she stared out at the gathered students with eyes wide open, as though she was seeing the reality of her world for the first time. "Like the rest of us, Paul's family abandoned him years ago, even before he entered Miskatonic Prep. His parents wanted a son because it looked good for the tabloids, but they spent more time jetsetting off to Milan or Paris with their reality TV show buddies than they did looking after him. Paul practically raised his younger brother, who he was hoping to see again soon.

"Despite everything we've been through, Paul always tried to stay positive. He didn't always succeed, but he was better than the rest of us. You all know I dated him for a couple of years before Nancy—" I hadn't known that, but it didn't surprise me. I guessed everyone dated around when you had the same classmates for two decades. "—and they were some of the best years in this hellhole. That was before Paul got sick of my shit and moved on to someone much more deserving." Courtney smiled at Nancy, who leaned into Barclay's shoulder and sobbed.

I'm not sure about that. I remembered seeing Nancy in the grotto making out with Barclay. But I'd just slept with three guys at once, so who was I to judge? For all I knew Paul and Nancy were both dating Barclay. The guy sure looked cut up about Paul's death.

"And yet, after everything we've been through, Paul didn't die because of our parents' evil plotting," Courtney continued. Her eyes met mine, and I saw my own resolve reflected back at me. "He was killed because John Hyde-Jones wanted to escape Miskatonic Prep and screw the rest of us. After everything we've been through together, that fuckface put his own desires over the needs of his classmates, and that's something I know none of us will stand for."

Students and maintenance staff greeted this news with hard, stony faces. John's betrayal had hurt more than what their parents had done.

"We've had our souls cut up and tampered with, but some pieces of our humanity must still survive," Courtney slid a backpack off her shoulders and opened it. I expected it to be empty, since we'd dropped the sigils back out in the forest. Instead, wads of cash toppled out. "This isn't about our stupid pride. It's about so much more than that."

Silence. I leaned forward, my fingers tightening around Ayaz's wrist. *What's she doing?*

"This is some of the money I took from my untouched trust fund last night. I only gave half of it to Hazel, because I was going to keep the rest for myself. I didn't want to share." Courtney held up wads of bills, letting a few notes flutter on the breeze before being torn off the edge of the cliff by the relentless ocean. "I *earned* this money by being Courtney fucking Haynes. It's *mine*. Why should any of you have it?"

Courtney stepped up to Sadie and shoved the cash into her hands.

"I remember you, Sadie Lancaster." Courtney struggled to form words now. Tears streaked her cheeks, sticking strands of her perfect hair against her skin. "You have the most beautiful hair. I didn't like you for stupid reasons that don't matter, and I'm sorry for what we did to you. This money doesn't make up for it, but I hope you'll accept it along with my apology."

Sadie glanced down at the cash. For a moment, I thought she'd throw it back in Courtney's face. Instead, she tucked it into the pocket of her grey shift. She beamed at Courtney, and that smile held equal parts contempt and respect.

Courtney stepped into the crowd, shoving wads of bills into the hands of the other maintenance staff. "This is yours more than it is mine. I want you to have it."

When all the money had been given out, Courtney raised a single hundred-dollar bill between her fingers. "Hazel, would you do the honors?"

I stepped forward, raising my palm toward the note. Courtney nodded. I let my palm form a small flame, the light a beacon against the graveyard gloom. While the students sucked in their breath, I moved the flame slowly to the note until it touched the corner and caught.

The bill burned through in a moment, letting out a faint *psst* as it became ash. Ashes and dust — that was what tonight was about. Burning away the past, once and for all. It just fucking sucked Paul had to die to make it happen.

Courtney turned to me, her eyes blazing. "When we meet John Hyde-Jones in the real world, he will pay for what he did to Paul. And to you. I've done some shitty things to scholarship students over the years, but what we tried to do in your room that night... it was the worst. Sometimes, it's safer to be on the winning side, even when no one but the monsters win in the end."

Something in her voice told me John was her monster to slay, as well.

I cocked an eyebrow. "That how a rich bitch apologizes?"

Courtney shrugged. "If that's what you want to call it, gutter whore. Now, what are you still doing here? You have to go spend my college fund on criminal misdeeds."

CHAPTER TWENTY-NINE

The next day, Monday, the dorms and corridors were so quiet you could hear a pin drop. The story of Paul's death and John's escape passed in whispers between the students.

"Urgent meeting in the senior common room after classes today," I whispered to Tillie and Greg as we walked to homeroom. "Pass it around."

Mr. Dexter didn't notice John's absence as he rarely bothered to take roll now. But during the next period, the two empty seats in the second row couldn't escape the attention of Dr. Morgan.

"Where are John and Paul?" she asked.

No one said a word.

Dr. Morgan met my gaze. I tried to articulate through super-subtle shaking of my head to drop it. It was a good test of her trust – she lowered her eyes to her lesson plan and kept going as if she'd never asked.

Trey, Ayaz, and Quinn flanked me in the hall between classes, but Ms. West didn't show her face. I dared to hope that she wouldn't notice their absence, especially if the teachers didn't spill the beans.

We stopped by my locker to collect my chemistry book, and I realized I needed the bathroom.

"Go ahead without me," I told the boys, and I headed toward the nearest bathroom. I needed to hurry – Dr. Atwood was a stickler for punctuality and unlikely to award me a hall pass.

I shoved open the door of the toilets. Quinn made to follow me in, but I slammed my foot down on his.

"You're not coming in here." I rolled my eyes. "Be serious."

"I'm always serious. We promised we wouldn't leave your side," Quinn pouted. "Besides, it's not like I'm not familiar with the inside of that bathroom. Courtney, Amber and I once—"

Ayaz shot him a warning look, and Quinn snapped his mouth shut. I kicked his foot out of the door. "I don't care what you and Courtney did, but Hazel Waite pees in peace. I'll just be a minute."

With Ayaz restraining Quinn, I managed to get the door shut. A quick glance around revealed a single occupied stall near the door. I walked right to the end of the row and kicked open the stall, enjoying the hyacinth scent that wafted from the pristine bowl. *This is the one thing I will miss about this place when I'm soaring across the stars.* The bathrooms at Miskatonic Prep were palatial, with marble floors and fancy skin products and little rolled-up fluffy hand-towels. Although this stall door didn't lock properly so I had to hold it shut with my boot. *Some things never change—*

My stall door banged open, wrenching my knee painfully. I jumped up in surprise, glad I hadn't peed all over myself. "Quinn, get the fuck out—"

Someone grabbed my arm and twisted it behind me until red spots appeared in my eyes. I yelled as my chest slammed against the wall. A hard body pressed against me, pinning me in place.

John Hyde-Jones. My thoughts spun out of control. I tried to kick out my attacker's legs, but I was in the wrong position to get a good hit. He grunted as I pummeled his shin with my Docs, but it wasn't enough to loosen his hold.

And it wasn't John. Dr. Atwood grunted in my ear. "Make this quick. I can't hold her forever."

I wondered what he meant. A black-clad figure glided into my stall. *Oh, he's talking to her.*

Ms. West's cruel eyes swept across my face. "Hello, Ms. Waite. I'm concerned you're overstepping the bounds of our agreement. The god refuses to speak to me, and now two students are missing from my school. I know you have something to do with it."

Atwood pressed me harder against the wall, bending back my head to press my windpipe into the cold tile. My whole body went into panic mode as I fought to gulp in air.

"Perhaps a little oxygen restriction will do you good." Ms. West wrapped her fingers around my throat, her talons digging into me as she drove the air out of me. "And if I get a little carried away and squeeze too hard, well... that's just your rotten luck. I'm sure the god would eventually forgive me. After all, I am the source of his children. In time, he will come to see me as his *real* consort."

She said some other things, but with her hands clamped around on my windpipe, pressing and crushing and closing, I stopped being able to hear her.

Adrenaline coursed through my body, imbuing me with a rush of superhuman strength. I clawed at her fingers, kicking and bucking and lurching. Atwood nearly lost his grip on me, but West's fingers kept digging, pushing, squeezing. Fire tore from my palms as I tried to drag her hands away. The orange flames flickered against her skin – the pain of it must've been excruciating, but she didn't loosen her grip.

"You took the one thing I loved," she hissed, the words cutting through my panic. "You took the god from me. Turnabout's fair play, Ms. Waite—"

My vision thinned. Stars danced in front of my vision, and weird, ethereal sleepiness slowed my movements, dragged at my arms. *Help me.* I called to the god. *I need...*

From somewhere, I heard a faint *pop*. Through the fog of my mind, Ms. West's face collapsed, and her hands slid off me. She collapsed to the floor.

Air filled my lungs.

Glorious air.

Atwood yelled as someone tore him off me and flung him against the sinks. The mirror smashed, raining slivers of glass down on him as he slumped to the ground beside the unconscious Deadmistress.

I gripped the top of the stall to hold myself upright and gasped and gagged for precious oxygen. My head spun. *What happened?*

I saw shapes moving around me. The god's shadows? But no, they resolved into flesh-and-bone people. Courtney stepped over Ms. West's prone body. Behind her, Greg wiped blood off his knuckles. Tillie rushed to my side, catching me in her arms before I toppled over.

Courtney grabbed Dr. Atwood's collar, jerking his head up so his face was inches from hers. Blood trickled from a wound above his eye.

"John and Paul won't be returning to graduate," she said, and her eyes dared Atwood to cross her. "If you have a problem with that, I suggest you take it up with their parents. Just don't expect them to show up at the dance if they believe something is wrong."

Tillie's arms went under my shoulders, and she took my weight as I leaned against her, still gasping as I pulled up my panties and stockings. My chest burned and tears leaked from my eyes.

"We won't be in class this afternoon," Tillie said in a saccharine sweet voice as she stroked my hair. "A fellow student needs our care. Tell Ms. West we're so very sorry to hear about her *unfortunate accident.*"

Tillie helped me toward the door, held open by Ayaz and Quinn, who stared at my three rescuers with wide eyes. As I stepped over Ms. West, I couldn't resist giving her a kick in the side of the head.

Damn right, bitch.

We stepped outside into a circle of students. They must've heard something, because they hovered with part fear, part curiosity. "Is Hazel okay?" asked Loretta. It was the most concern she'd ever shown for me.

I tried to answer that I was fine, but broke down into a coughing fit that would've landed me on my ass if it weren't for Tillie.

"That bathroom is out of order," Courtney declared, shooting her panther stare around the circle of students. "Nothing to see here."

"We'll take her from here." Quinn's arm went under my shoulders. I sucked in a deep breath of his coconut and sugarcane scent, my head spinning.

"I'm fine," I managed to choke out. "I've been standing on my own feet since I was two."

Quinn bent down and before I could protest, he'd scooped me up into his arms. "No complaining. Let boyfriend Quinn take care of you."

And he did, carrying me back to his room and shoving aside all the porn magazines and empty alcohol bottles to lay me down on the bed. He brought me hot tea and massaged my shoulders and kissed my forehead in a way that made me long for my mother.

"You're good at this," I smiled. "The only thing that could improve your bedside manner is a skimpy nurse's outfit."

"I got sick a lot as a child." Quinn held out another cup of tea. "I had colic as a baby and I dunno, an upside-down immune system or something. Mom took me to a million doctors and specialists, convinced I had the bubonic plague or some rare wasting disease when really I was just a wimp. Dad found it all annoying. Before I was born, Mom went out with him every night to exclusive clubs and events, but now all she wanted to do was stay in with me. He resented it – this weak, sickly child monopolizing his perfect arm-candy wife. Damon Delacorte can't stand weakness."

The words tumbled out of him in a rush. Quinn clutched my empty mug in his hands, looking as surprised as I felt. He never liked to talk about his family or his feelings or the abuse – or anything serious at all. Every time I brought up his dad he'd make a joke and change the subject. Opening up like this was a big deal to him.

I didn't expect Quinn to volunteer any more information, but he seemed to be in a chatty mood. He took a shuddering breath, and continued, "Dad had been hitting my mother ever since I could remember – a bruise or black eye for every perceived slight or imperfection. The first time he hit me, I was six years old. He'd been away on business for a month. I heard his car pull up in the drive. I ran downstairs and threw myself at him, wrapping my arms around his leg because I was too small to reach up and hug him. I was so excited to see him at last, I didn't even think that I was wearing my rumpled pajamas and wiping my snotty nose on his slacks. He'd brought the opposing counsel back to the house to intimidate him with our perfect life, and my snotty nose was ruining his carefully-crafted image. I always remember how he had this smile plastered on his face as he dragged me into a bathroom in the guest wing, where his guest couldn't hear. Behind that smile pulsed a rage that burned so deep so it could never be sated. Dad removed his belt and whipped my back so hard I saw stars."

As Quinn spoke, he hugged his arms across his chest, his fingers reaching to touch his back, tracing the ghosts of that first betrayal.

"Why?" I asked. Tears sprung in my eyes. How could anyone want to hurt a child, especially Quinn? "You were just a little kid."

"Why does anyone do the things they do?" Quinn said bitterly.

"It's all part of the cycle of horror and violence, remember? Dad's father belted him when he stepped out of line, and he'd become the most formidable criminal defense lawyer in America. If you ask him, he'd say it was to make me stronger. 'I'm doing this for your own good,' he loved to say. But I see the truth in his eyes, in that smile. He enjoys it. He likes having power over people. He couldn't turn his anger inwards – that would mean admitting his own weakness. It was always directed at those beneath him – subordinates and assistants at his company, customer service staff, Mom. Me."

Quinn tightened his arms around himself, and I thought again how lucky I'd been that I'd always been safe with my mom. She'd had some abusive boyfriends, but they left quickly when they got wind of the strange things I did with fire. I'd never had to wonder if she was having a good day or a bad day.

"The worst thing was, I was so twisted around that all I wanted was to please him. How I loved him. How I wanted to be just like him. Dad's a charmer. When he's happy he lights up a room, but he had this dark side his peers never saw. I saw how he commanded a courtroom or orchestrated an amazing party and I thought, 'when I become like him, no one will be able to hurt me. I could protect Mom.' But I could never measure up, and eventually I stopped trying, and all I cared about was protecting Mom. I'm completely fucked up, and then I met Trey and Ayaz and piled their shit on top of mine. We fed off each other's fears and insecurities and used the lessons we'd learned from our parents to become the Kings. And then you came along and tore everything apart and showed us what true strength really means." Quinn's amber eyes rested on me with perfect love and trust, not knowing that soon I was going to shatter his heart. "You made me want to be better."

"We should get to the meeting," I croaked, in part because I saw the time on the clock behind his head, but mostly because I saw the hope lurking in his eyes, and I wanted to save him from spiraling into a place he didn't want to go. A place where I couldn't follow.

Quinn shoved my feet into my Docs and knotted the laces, which I usually left undone. I grabbed one of the backpacks we'd stuffed with cash and looped it over my shoulder. He held out his hand, and I took it. As he held open the door for me, I swept past him and planted a kiss on the tip of his nose. "You broke the cycle, Quinn. You're nothing like your father – he could only dream of being half as strong as you are."

Quinn's smile could have lit the world.

Thank the cosmic god for having two notorious gossips on our side. Tillie and Greg made sure that by the end of the day, every student had the word about the meeting. When Quinn shoved open the common room door, it nearly wouldn't open. Every spare inch of floor-space was taken up with students and maintenance staff. I inched my way through the crowd to Trey and Ayaz, who stood on the kitchen island to command the room. Trey pulled me up beside them, and I stared out over the sea of faces who all believed I could save them, and a strange mixture of pride and vomit gurgled in my stomach.

Trey opened his mouth to make a speech, but that wasn't my style. I dropped the bag off my shoulder and dumped the contents out onto the counter. Students gasped and conversations broke off mid-sentence as wads of bills toppled out into a messy pyramid. Amber reached for a stack, but Trey patted her hand away.

"Some of you may have heard that Paul died on Saturday night. He was part of a small group who risked... more than we ever realized to get this cash. Paul didn't die in vain. I've got several more bags where this one came from. This cash is for all of us," I said. "It's going to help you buy your freedom."

Amber wrinkled her nose. "That's hardly enough. How will I be able to afford an apartment in the East Village if I'm sharing that with these plebs?"

Courtney shot Amber a steel glare.

"You're not buying an apartment in the East Village." I shoved the cash into the backpack. "At least, not yet. What you all need to remember is that you've been gone for twenty years. As far as the world is concerned, you died in that fire. If you show up again using your real names and your old identities, people are going to ask questions. Questions you can't answer – at least, not in any way that makes sense. As soon as someone in power gets wind of the fact 245 formally-dead students walked out of Miskatonic Prep without aging a day, along with 76 missing scholarship students who've had their tongues cut out, they're going to lock you all in padded cells and experiment on you for the rest of your lives." My skin crawled as memories from my time at the Dunwich Institute threatened to dislodge my resolve. My time there was a picnic compared with what the government would put the Miskatonic students through.

"We're using this money to get IDs and passports for all of you." Trey handed out a stack of clipboards. "Write down your preferred new names. Please don't be stupid and call yourself Conan or President Bush or something, or I'll rename you myself and you don't want to know what I'll choose. If there's a particular country you want to flee to, let me know and we'll try to secure a visa as well."

"Can we keep our first names?" asked Tillie.

I sighed. "If you must."

"This is not what we signed on for," Amber spat. "I had a promising modeling career. Courtney was supposed to inherit her mother's clothing label. How can she do that if the world can't even tell they're *related*?"

Trey loomed over her. "You haven't grasped the enormity of this. Hazel is offering us a way out of this hell, and all you can think about is money?"

"You're all going to have to work for everything you earn, without the benefits of your family connections or stacks of cash." I folded my arms. "Provided we all make it to the end of this final quarter intact and you pass your exams, your Derleth diploma will at least enable you to apply for college, *if* you want to go. You'll have to get financial aid. Or a scholarship. Or work a second job to support yourself, just like normal kids in America. Now, what's it going to be, Amber Smith or Bimbo McSluttyPants?"

Amber scowled at me, but she grabbed the pen and scribbled something down. The room fell into silence.

"Good." I held out the clipboard. "Who's next?"

CHAPTER THIRTY

What I'd said in the common room seemed to get through. When we collected the clipboards, we ended up with a list of mostly sensible new identities – Quinn had chosen 'Attila the Hun,' but I expected that.

"You have five seconds to pick a sensible name or I'm choosing it for you." I thrust the clipboard at Quinn's chest. "I think you really suit 'Humphrey.'"

"You wouldn't." Quinn looked to Trey for help.

Trey opened a freezer and removed one of his fancy heat-and-eat meals, which he threw in the oven. "I was thinking Aragorn, from *Lord of the Rings*. Did you know that's Quinn's favorite book?"

"Oooh, Aragorn Smith." I picked up my pen to write it in. "That has a nice ring to it—"

"Fine, fine." Quinn threw up his hands. "Put down Quinn Waite."

My heart stopped.

Quinn Waite.

"You can't call yourself that."

"Why not? It's a good name. Short and pithy and not the

name of a fantastical king. It's *your* name, Hazy. You won't choose between the three of us, which means you'll never be able to marry me and take my name. So this is the next best thing. Besides, I can't be the only one who's not part of the family."

Quinn... he's thought about marrying me.

Shit.

I've made a terrible mistake. I never should have kept my pact with the god a secret. I've let him become attached and now...

A lump formed in my throat as I glanced down at the paper. The names at the top read, TREY WAITE, AYAZ WAITE.

My breath caught. Tears welled in my eyes. How I wished that could be my future. How I wanted to be with the three Kings for the rest of our lives. How I wanted us to build a family on the ashes of what we'd lost. But it could never be. In giving them their freedom, I'd lose them forever.

They want to marry me, and I'm leaving them. It's killing me, and it'll hurt them so much...

Quinn flashed me his lopsided smile. "You okay, Hazy? You don't like my name?"

How can I tell them? How can I even begin to explain?

"I love the name. More than you could ever know. But Quinn..."

My phone beeped.

I jumped. My heart thrashed around in my chest.

Okay, it's a distraction. That's good. You need to step back for a bit, decide rationally if it's a good idea to tell the guys.

Newsflash – it's not a good idea.

"It's Zehra. One of her texts must've got through." I swiped my tears away as I read the message aloud. "She says, 'tell Quinnanigans he's welcome,' and there's a link to an article where—"

I scanned the headline and dropped the phone in shock. Quinn scooted over and grabbed it. "C'mon, Hazy. Don't leave me in suspense."

I tried to grab the phone back. "I don't know if you should—"

Too late. Quinn was already scrolling, his eyes widening with every word.

"Well?" Trey demanded, his icy gaze sliding between me and Quinn. "What's the news?"

"My dad's maid is suing him for sexual harassment and physical abuse." Quinn's voice came out breathless. "A whole horde of witnesses are coming forward to testify against him. His secretary. Three law clerks. My old nanny... Holy shitballs, he's going to pay so much money in damages that he'll have to declare bankruptcy..."

A wide smile broke out over Quinn's face. He tossed the phone at Trey and grabbed me, swinging me around the room, planting kisses all over me. "Someone finally stood up to him. And they will win. No matter what happens now, I already feel as though I'm free. He can't come after us now, Hazy. You and me... we'll be able to have our happily-ever-after in peace..." he grinned at me. "With these two bozos as well, of course."

My stomach churned. I couldn't bear it. I couldn't tell Quinn what I'd done to give him his happily-ever-after. I wasn't yet ready to break his heart, even though mine was already shattered into a million pieces.

In the days and weeks that followed, the messages from Zehra kept on coming. Next, she went after John's father. A national newspaper ran an article on the senator's love for extorting third-world governments for campaign funds, based on information leaked from an 'unknown source,' and he was removed from the senate. A string of high-profile fraud cases followed that bombshell, unseating many Eldritch Club members from executive positions and company boards across the country. There were the illicit photos of Barclay's dad taken at the secret Pony Play Ranch which cost him his bishop's appointment, and the Honduran drug cartel that took out Amber's father when they discovered he was ripping them off.

Every night the Kings and I walked down the peninsula until we found decent reception and we'd hold hands under the moonlight and scroll through my phone's newsfeed, taking in the carnage in real-time.

She's hanging them with their own rope, watching and waiting for them to do what they do best and using that as ammunition to destroy them.

For twenty years the students had been collecting this dirt on their parents, storing it away for when it might be advantageous to them. Even though they hadn't known the depth of the Eldritch Club's deception, they'd been taught from a young age how vital it was to wield power over others. After all, the rotten apple didn't fall far from the tree.

Now they came to us in droves, handing over their families' dirty laundry for Zehra to air in the public eye. In the final week of classes, Zehra took down three more parents, sending their fortunes into freefall. We gave them no choice but to obey our summons.

"Your sister is something else," I said to Ayaz after I finished relaying Zehra's latest conquest. He trailed his hands across my shoulders – his fingertips stained with paint and ink. He'd spent every spare moment he wasn't studying creating a beautiful graduation poster, which we'd sent out to all the parents as an invitation.

He beamed that rare and beautiful smile of his. "She is. And so are you."

The first message came. An envelope, delivered by a terrified driver into Ms. West's talons. She read the four words it contained and passed it to me.

What do you want?

Instead of writing a reply, I folded one of Ayaz's graduation flyers and placed it in the envelope for the poor sod to take back to his master.

More messages came, although never in person. Letters delivered by fear-stricken staff. Recordings on old cassette tapes played through the school PA system for everyone to hear. Desperate parents seeking answers. Where had their fortunes disappeared to? What could they do to ensure they wouldn't be next?

The answer was always the same. *Come to graduation.*

Meanwhile, I worked my old contacts, trying to source all the documents the students needed to be free. I must've had the entire Philly criminal underground on my payroll.

On the last Wednesday of classes, while I studied in the library with Ayaz, my phone beeped. My contact had come through with the passports. We just needed to make the exchange.

We waited until class finished on Friday to make the trip. Greg wanted to come too, but I knew he'd stick out too much. At least the Kings looked mean enough I could dress them like white gangsters, but where we were going Greg would have a fist in his face as soon as he stepped out of the car. He agreed to stay behind, as long as he and Loretta could walk with us down to Arkham, where we'd be borrowing Deborah's car (it was much less conspicuous than Trey's Porsche).

"I'd really like to meet your aunt," Greg beamed.

My aunt. I still wasn't used to the idea that I was related to Deborah. My family legacy already weighed heavy on me. It was like Courtney had said, family was forged in fire and blood, and Deborah and I were still in the process of that forging.

We took our normal route down the mountain – Trey walking in front carrying the sigil, Quinn and Ayaz flanking me, eyes darting across the trees, hunting for any danger. Greg and Loretta behind us, their bows slung over their shoulders. Under Greg's tutelage, Loretta had become an unnervingly accurate archer. She said she found it calming, but I think she just liked the powerful feeling of holding a weapon in her hands.

Because we're the murderers.

We circled around the town and emerged at the rear of the motel block. I texted Deborah that we were there, and she ushered us inside, shutting the door behind her.

"I'm sorry for the security," she said. "It might just be my over-active imagination, but I feel as though I'm being watched."

I didn't like the sound of that. "Have you seen anything unusual?"

"It's probably nothing, more a feeling than anything else. Roger has been a bit more alert than usual, but there are lots of exciting new smells so that could be nothing. Please, help yourself to snacks."

Greg and Loretta set down their bows and plowed into the snacks. The dogs jumped on Trey, throwing him to the ground and attacking him with rough tongues. Quinn dived in, rubbing stomachs and scratching behind ears. Ayaz hovered in the doorway, uncertain.

"This is Ayaz." I waved him in.

Deborah rushed over and clasped his hands in hers. "Welcome, Ayaz. Hazel's told me very little about you, but that's her way. I understand you had some amnesia."

He nodded. "The headmistress did something to me that wrote over my thoughts. I remember these things about Hazel that aren't true. I can feel reality lurking behind the lies, but I can't reach it. Ms. West says I never will."

Deborah went over to her purse and pulled out a small container of pills. "These are currently being developed by the people who create drugs for Alzheimer's patients. They're not technically legal right now, but I know people and I figure it can't hurt an Edimmu... take one of these twice a day with food... oh, actually, I suppose you don't need the food. They might help you recover your memories."

"Thank you." Ayaz looked genuinely floored as he stared at the bottle. When he looked up at Deborah, his dark eyes revealed deep gratitude. "For this gift, and for everything you've done for us."

The softness in his voice, the way Deborah had managed to bring all my Kings to her with kindness... for the first time, I saw a glimmer of what the future might be like for my Kings, and it wasn't all broken hearts and betrayal. When I was gone, she'd still be here for them. She'll give them everything they never had from their families, and her connection to me will ensure they'd protect her with their lives.

Even without me, they'll be a family.

Just like that, my mistrust of Deborah Pratt flicked off like a light bulb, replaced by the empty ache that had gnawed at me ever since I'd accepted the god's proposition. They'd be a family, and I'd be somewhere far away.

"Hey, auntie... this is for you." I kicked a bag across the floor toward her.

Deborah's eyes widened at my use of the word I'd avoided until now, the word that still felt foreign on my tongue but that I wanted to get used to saying while I still had the chance. But she knew me better than to acknowledge it aloud. Instead, she peered down at the bag. "What is it?"

"Two-hundred thousand dollars. Zehra needs it – you're probably better off not knowing what for. Can you drive it down the coast to Innsmouth tomorrow so she can pick it up?"

"Of course." Deborah took the bag, staring at it like it was a bomb about to go off. She glanced at the time. "As much as I wish you'd all stay with me longer, shouldn't you get going?"

"Yeah. We've got a long drive."

She tossed Quinn the keys to her Jeep. "Just watch it in third gear – it's a little sticky. And I apologize in advance about the dog smell. It comes with the territory, I'm afraid."

"We don't mind. Quinn, give me those," Trey grabbed for the keys. Quinn dangled them out of his reach.

"Nah-ah. Deborah trusts *me*." Trey lunged, but Quinn was faster. He sprinted out the door and dived into the driver's seat, letting off a stream of maniacal laughter as Trey tried to pull him out the window by his shoulders. Deborah laughed.

"With those boys protecting you, you hardly need me at all."

"I wouldn't say that." I touched her hand, the sensation of her soft skin sending a fire through me. *I'm touching my mother's sister. My mom's name was Jessica.* "Thanks. For everything."

"You're welcome. I just hope it's enough." Her kind eyes flickered over mine – eyes that looked so much like my mom's.

It's enough to free them. And that's what's important.

I just wish I had time left to get to know you, to be a family, to read my mom's journals and cry over them with you. But wishing is pointless.

Deborah pulled my hand to her lips and pecked the knuckles, the gesture reminding me so much of Mom that my chest ached. "Be safe, Hazel."

"I will," I promised. With one final scratch behind the ears, I said goodbye to the dogs and climbed in back with Ayaz, the second bag of money stashed between us.

"We're off." Quinn cranked up the volume on a CD of 90s gangsta rap and gunned the engine. We pulled out of the parking lot and drove out of Arkham in the direction of a place I never wanted to see again. A place where ghosts clung to every building and street corner, where my past had been written in blood and fire.

Back to the badlands of Philadelphia.

CHAPTER THIRTY-ONE

It could have taken us two-minutes or ten hours to reach Philly — the car journey passed in a blur of spinning thoughts and nausea only partly caused by Quinn's driving. I had no sense of time or geography, only a growing terror that crawled across my skin. I was speeding toward a place that every bone in my body urged me to avoid.

We wove through the outer suburbs before I recognized the skyline and realized we'd arrived in Philly. I wasn't used to seeing the city from the outside in — in the Badlands, we all knew that we were never going to escape unless it was under police escort or in a body bag.

Not even I had escaped. Not really. I still carried the Badlands around like a shackle. My fingers tightened around Ayaz's, and he squeezed back.

As we drove deeper into the heart of my old neighbourhood, Quinn's fingers gripped the wheel tightly. For the first time, I saw the burned-out cars, broken houses, kids playing on the street, and graffiti everywhere as the Kings must've seen it. Ayaz had been exposed to poverty in Istanbul — from what he'd told me, Turkey was very different from America — but Trey and Quinn had been sheltered by their privilege and never had to contemplate what it meant to live with a legacy of poverty.

As above, so below. The cycle of horror and violence drones ever on.

I dug my nails into my scar as the memories assailed me. Dante and I skipping school to wander the streets together, laughing at our own private jokes. Me as a ten-year-old having driving lessons from one of Mom's old boyfriends in the empty lot behind the old railway station. I'd barely been tall enough to see over the hood. Mom taking her stripping clothes down to the laundromat and paying extra for fabric softener – the only treat she allowed herself.

The Badlands were part of me, etched into my bones. I might have gotten out, but I never really left this place behind. Even from across the universe, its ghosts would still haunt me.

"This is where you lived?" Trey was trying to sound bored, uninterested. But he couldn't tear his eyes from a grey concrete duplex with windows blacked out.

I nodded.

"What a shithole."

I bit back a defense retort. He wasn't wrong. It was a shithole.

"It's not all bad." I pointed to the corner store. "There's love and community if you know where to look. That store is where we got groceries when Mom got paid. The owner was this jolly Jamaican guy named Tee who was always singing. He used to give free ice cream to the neighborhood kids."

At the end of the main drag, a neon sign with half the bulbs blown advertised naked women. "That's the club where my mom worked. She used to sing in a jazz club in downtown Philly as well, but stripping paid better. It's a total dive, but the girls look out for each other and the bouncer, Manny, is pretty cool. I brought my first ever bag of weed from him – I got so high I ate two whole pizzas by myself."

Trey's eyes darted around the street, and I knew he was trying to see this place through my eyes. I doubted he could do it, but Trey Bloomberg sometimes surprised me.

"There's my school." I pointed to a squat grey building surrounded by a high chain-link fence. It looked more like a prison than an institution for learning. "Before you get inside, you have to step through metal detectors, drug dogs, and security guards on constant watch for weapons."

"Holy Great Old God," Quinn whistled.

"Yup. Pretty different from Miskatonic Prep. But then, they never sacrificed anyone to a cosmic deity, so I guess that makes things even. This is where I hung out with Dante and where I worked my ass off so I could get into a good college. Joke's on me."

"What do you mean by that?" Trey pressed his face to the window, fascinated by this world he'd never known existed.

Oh, just that it'll be hard to go to college when I'm in another universe.

Quinn snorted. "Yeah, have you seen the points table lately? You're right near the top. You're probably going to be valedictorian, which means you'll get into an amazing school."

"All I meant was that I never thought I'd look at my old school and think, 'safe.'"

Ayaz reached across the backseat and squeezed my hand. "One day, when we are free, you will come with me to Turkey, and I will show you around where I used to live. We'll walk the old city walls and relive the ancient tales of prophecies, wars, and vengeful gods, then sip coffee in a cafe beside the Süleymaniye Mosque. In spring, millions of bright tulips bloom across the city, and in summer we can swim in the azure waters."

Fuck, that sounds amazing. I swallowed a hard lump in my throat. "Yup, one day."

"We've got a bit of time to kill before we meet your shady friend." Quinn turned down a side-street. My nails dug into the seat as I recognized the apartment blocks looming over us. "What do you do around here for fun? Apart from stealing cars and buying weed, of course. Maybe we should go back to that ice cream place—"

"Pull over," I demanded.

"Why? There's nothing here apart from a bunch of ugly apartments and that abandoned lot. Or did you—hey!" Quinn yelled as I leaned over his seat and jerked the wheel. He slammed on the brakes and the car shuddered over the curb and came to a stop in front of an enormous pile of garbage dumped in an abandoned lot.

I shoved the door open, kicking mangled beer cans and burnt car parts out of the way. Quinn slid out from behind the wheel, his eyes wide as he took in everything – the garbage, the concrete apartment blocks rising on either side, the ring of soot marring the remains of cinder block walls.

Trey slid out of the passenger seat, his brow wrinkling as he lifted his foot. Something brown smeared across the expensive leather of his brogues.

Quinn kicked a can across the lot. "Hazy, why are we here?"

Ayaz came up behind me. His eyes burned holes in my back. He slipped his fingers in mine and squeezed.

He knew. Of course, he'd be the first to figure it out.

I opened my mouth to explain, but I couldn't find the words. Quinn kicked his can across the lot while Trey used a stick to lift away some of the weeds from the foundation ring. I heard Trey's intake of breath, and I knew he'd figured it out, too. It was obvious from the charred earth and the household debris choked with weeds what this was.

My old home.

The one I burned down in a fit of rage. A funerary pyre for the first two people who ever loved me.

"Fuck, Hazy." Quinn's can skittered away. He dropped his eyes to the debris at his feet. He'd dislodged a wooden box with one corner rotted away. The lid fell open on rusted hinges, spilling out damp, crumpled photographs.

The foundation ring had held up a block of eight apartments, five unoccupied and the other neighbors out for the evening when I burned the place down. Our apartment was on the top floor, which was why the firefighters couldn't get to my mother in time. The objects that survived could have come from any of the rooms, and yet Quinn had laid hands on that box almost immediately.

My mother loved to print out photographs from her phone. She'd often take her dollar tips down to a place in central Philly that had a machine, and she'd come home with a whole stack. We used them to decorate the apartment walls, changing them out as often as we liked. She kept her favorites in a wooden box.

Quinn picked up the stack, his hands trembling as he fanned out the images. Trey and Ayaz crowded around.

They were all of me – me as a toddler, dressed up and posing in some of Mom's clothes, my tiny feet dwarfed inside a pair of red pumps. Me grinning from the swing in the playground, and striking a pose in the doorway of the treehouse. Dante and I when we were eight years old, wearing birthday hats and big smiles, in front of a cheap ice cream cake.

Mom and I – our smiles identical – sprawled out on top of a pile of cushions in a blanket fort we made in our bedroom. The lump in my throat burned as I swallowed.

I will not cry. I will not cry.

"So that's what love looks like." Trey's voice trembled. He held out the picture to me. I took it in shaking fingers.

For the first time since Deborah had told me about Mom's past, I looked into the eyes of the woman in the picture and I saw her, truly *saw* her. She had fled hell itself and carved out a life with me in this place. And maybe to people like Trey and Quinn, our life looked like a nightmare, but it truly wasn't. She made it wonderful.

She did everything for me.

Quinn handed me another picture. *And here's Dante. He's been a part of our lives since I was five years old. In and out of foster homes, used by adults for money, for drugs, he felt safe with us, and there were very few places where Dante was safe.* Mom was broken and Dante was broken, and both of them were desperate for love, for belonging. Mom had so much love to give.

And although I wasn't privy to this secret between them until it was too late, I could see how it had happened – in the moments around me, where I was too focused on being strong, on believing that I didn't need anyone. They were both falling – why should they not crash into each other?

I shoved the pictures into my pocket and picked my way around the perimeter, taking in the details. It was less than a year since I'd watched this building burn, but it felt like forever, like another lifetime. No one had cleaned up the site after the fire. Looters would already have picked through the debris for anything of value – I could see the faint shapes of bootprints impressed in the ash. But other things, useless things, stuck out of the ruins – bits of broken crockery from the mismatched mugs in our kitchen. The aerial from our shitty little TV. Mom's jazz records melted into a puddle of strange shapes.

My fingers slid through the ash, pulling out something that made my breath catch.

A drawing.

Coated in dirt, crumpled and torn at the corner, but intact. How it had survived fire and rain and looters, I didn't know. It had found its way back to me.

I remembered the image like I'd seen it only yesterday. It was the first thing Dante ever drew for me, when he was about ten. He was a great artist even then. I hung this over my bed and it stayed there until the fire.

Three stray cats sat on top of a rusting swing set – one black, one tabby, one slinky and grey. All rendered in colored pencils. The grey one held a mouse by its tail between her teeth, while the other two batted at it with tiny paws, their tails curled over each other, forming a heart.

Mom. Dante. Me.

Family.

Ayaz took the image from my fingers and held it up to the dim light. "He had talent."

I nodded. I knew if I tried to speak, I'd burst into tears.

I lay the picture flat on the backseat of the car, and we picked our way down the slope at the rear of the property, which led to the rusting playground where I swung and slid, and later, Dante and I laid in the treehouse and smoked weed and wished on the stars to be anywhere but here.

Careful what you wish for.

The treehouse was still there. Rough wood jabbed my skin as I flung myself up the ladder and slumped into a dark corner. I held my head in my hands, trying to force back the memories. It was too much, coming at me like a freight train. *How am I supposed to deal with this?*

A face appeared in the doorway. My mind saw Dante – I was so used to his face that I couldn't fix on anyone else.

But it was Ayaz. He didn't say anything. He didn't need to. He climbed up beside me, his back resting against the wall. He stretched out his legs and stared at his shoes.

"I'm sorry we destroyed your journal," he said.

That journal the Kings stole from me and tore up was ancient history, but those words... they opened the waterworks.

Tears fell thick and fast. I cried for all the things I hadn't yet cried for. Because I missed my mother. Because I missed my best friend. Because in a moment of weakness I'd lost them both. And I was about to lose my Kings, too.

Warm lips pressed against my eyelids, kissing the tears away. "Hazy, what can we do?"

My eyes flew open. Without me noticing, Quinn and Trey had climbed up into the treehouse. Quinn knelt in front of me, studying my face with a mixture of awe and concern. Trey bent his body awkwardly around the door, his long legs dangling outside.

They didn't say anything. They didn't have to.

Quinn bent forward, his lips brushing mine. "I know we can't take the pain away," he whispered. "But can we at least give you another happy memory of this place?"

I had promised myself that the night of the party was my last taste of them. I had to make a clean slate so when the time came, I could say goodbye. But as Trey kissed a line of fire along my collarbone and Quinn's hands slid between my thighs, I didn't have the strength to refuse.

Ayaz bent my face to his, and his lips sought mine. This kiss wasn't one of hunger – it was something deeper. Ayaz understood things about me the others never could. He'd been a stranger to their world at first, as I'd been a stranger when I first came to Derleth Academy. He had his own locked box of mixed memories that would take a whole lifetime to sift through.

Three Kings propped me up as I confronted my past. I wanted to be there with them when they faced theirs, as they would again and again in their new lives. I wanted it more than I'd wanted anything ever before.

Bad girls like me never get what we want. We get ashes and dust.

Tears streamed down my cheeks. I pulled back and tried to wipe them away.

"You can cry," Trey whispered, his fingers catching the tears running down my cheeks. "Crying is not weak, Hazel. Your love and your pain make you strong."

Trey's words seared across my soul. I swallowed down a sob that threatened to collapse me as Trey turned my head to his. His kiss spoke of the places in his heart that were also burned out and destroyed by his own hand. *My mirror*.

Trey saw himself in my ashes and dust. I'd ruined everything I touched until I met him. He'd done the same. He longed to rebuild together. His languid kiss dripped with promises and plans for a future he had no idea didn't exist.

My tears flowed freely as Quinn yanked down my panties and pressed his lips between my legs. He raked his fingers along my thigh, cutting me to pieces and fitting me together again. His amber eyes met mine as he circled his tongue around my clit, piling fuel on a fire that had ignited the very first day we met.

Ayaz ran his hot tongue down the curve of my neck. As he bent to kiss my collarbone, his *nazar* pendant touched the bare skin on my throat.

Quinn thrust a finger inside me. His teeth scraped across my clit, arcing molten pleasure through my core.

As the pleasure rose inside me, crashing against the pain, Trey turned my hand over, his fingers knitting in mine. He pressed his tongue to the scar on my wrist.

I came apart under their touch, ashes and star-dust hovering over the treehouse before returning to myself.

In the remnants of my former life, I screamed through an orgasm, not caring who heard me.

We had to scramble into the car to make it to the drop in time. Quinn was the one who took the money inside the abandoned railway station, the doors swinging shut behind him. I bit my nails down to the quick, bracing myself for the gunshot I felt certain was coming. But he came out the same doors a few moments later, whistling a tune as he swung a new duffel bag into the car.

"Got 'em." Quinn tossed the bag into my lap. Trey gunned the engine. I upended the bag. Passports spilled out – hundreds of them, each one containing the photographs we'd taken at school and the fake names each student had chosen. They looked perfect (they'd better, for the money we paid) but it was hard for me to tell – I'd never needed a passport before.

Ayaz held up his passport next to his face. "How do I look?"

"As dapper as always," I said, busying myself with sorting through the pile so I wouldn't have to look at his new name. AYAZ WAITE. My clit still throbbed from the orgasm they'd given me. I felt dangerously close to throwing open the door and hurling myself across the freeway.

I can't lose it now.

I had to take every moment that was given to me, savor my last taste of freedom.

Because I knew something they didn't. In my lap were enough passports for all the Miskatonic students, for the maintenance staff, for Greg and Andre and Loretta. I'd offered one to Zehra, but she already had a stash in some secret location down in Mexico.

There was no passport in this bag for me. No new beginning awaited me on the other side of the god's embrace.

My life ended as soon as we set the god free. Because I was like him – I was a murderer. And I had to face the consequences.

CHAPTER THIRTY-TWO

Our drive back to Arkham was subdued. Nothing like visiting the ashes of your old life to ruin a jovial road trip.

Trey took the wheel most of the way. Apart from a hairy incident involving a squirrel, he seemed to have a decent grasp of the road rules even after twenty years. Of course, he applied his usual intense focus to the task, refusing to turn the stereo on even though Quinn begged.

I spent the entire trip back snuggled into Ayaz's arms, silently turning over my own memories. All I'd wanted to do was find a way to erase them. I'd stamped them down so that I didn't have to face what I did, but they were all I'd carry with me into the great beyond. I needed to hold them close, even the ones that brought me pain.

Ayaz was right – pain made me strong. And I'd need all the strength I had left for what I was about to do.

When we passed the turnoff to the town of Innsmouth, I texted Deborah to let her know we were twenty minutes away. She sent back a smiley face.

We pulled into the parking lot of the motel. Deborah's lights blazed, her door hung open, swaying slightly in the breeze. Odd, considering how nervous she was about someone watching her when we were here yesterday.

Yet, as we slid out of the car with the bag of passports, she didn't step out to greet us or tell us to shut the door. The dogs didn't bark as we approached. Goosebumps crawled along my arms. *Something's wrong.*

Maybe she's just taken them for a walk. But then why leave the door open—

No. Something was definitely wrong. There was a vibe, a trill that sang in the air like a bowstring pulled taut. The Kings felt it, too. Ayaz and Quinn moved close to me, building a wall of broad shoulders and tight muscles around me. Trey flattened himself against the door and peered inside.

"It's been trashed," he whispered. "There's no one there."

Fuck. Fuck. *Fuck.*

This had to have just happened, because Deborah sent me that text.

Unless they've got her mobile phone.

Double fuck.

All the fucks.

The fear rose inside me, overpowering my common sense. I elbowed my way through the guys and burst through the door. "Deborah?"

I took in the carnage – the coffee table overturned, a smashed vase on the floor, a chair in splinters in the corner. The only sign of Deborah or the dogs was a dark smear of blood across the blanket on the dog-bed.

Trey lifted a corner the blood-soaked blanket.

"No." I reached out to stop him.

Too late.

The blanket slipped from Trey's hand, and he staggered back, his face pale, his jaw tight with horror.

Roger lay on his back, one paw cocked in the air, the other disappearing under a spray of blood and gore. Fresh blood still bubbled from the wound in his chest.

"Shit." Quinn grabbed the blanket from Trey's frozen fingers and threw it back over the poor dog. Trey looked like he was going to be sick. Hot rage burned inside me. Roger had done nothing to deserve that. *Nothing*.

There was one person I could think of sick enough to kill an animal without a second thought. And he'd been in this room, perhaps only moments ago.

And he's got Deborah.

Ayaz clamped a hand on my shoulder, his voice taking on the authority of Trey's. When his brother was incapacitated by grief, Ayaz stepped into his place. "Hazel, the bedroom."

His words snapped Trey out of his stupor. I followed Ayaz's gaze across the room. The bedroom door had been shut. It had always been wide open when we visited. Blood smeared the handle.

Bile rose in my throat as I imagined what I'd see on the other side.

A hand squeezed mine. Trey. He stood beside me, his back straight, his eyes clouded with his silent rage. He gripped the iron. He nodded, once. Whatever was inside, we'd face it together.

I grabbed the handle.

Turned.

Blood soaked my fingers.

Whose blood? Whose?

I shoved the door open.

The lights were off. Before my eyes could adjust to the gloom, the barrel of a gun swung from nowhere and pointed directly at my face.

The lights flicked on.

The gunman's face leaped into view. Quinn's father, Damon Delacorte, although much aged, his eyes and mouth drooping. He licked his lips like he was about to devour a juicy steak. A second man I didn't recognize held another gun to Trey's face.

Vincent Bloomberg sat on the edge of the bed, his cruel lips twisted into a smile. "Hello, son."

CHAPTER THIRTY-THREE

Vincent's eyes and his thick, dark hair were the only part of him that resembled the cool businessman who'd first shown up at Miskatonic Prep. Papery skin sagged over his bones, his back hunched and his fingers curled and struggled to grip. Black patches marred the skin on his neck and hands – the remnants of a flame I'd never regret. I read in one of Zehra's updates that he'd been having extensive plastic surgery to rebuild his physique after a mysterious fire at his residence. Apparently, they hadn't got to his face yet because he still had the visage of a hideous old man. His outer appearance was beginning to mirror the monster within.

"That weapon can't kill me." Trey kept his voice placid, even, concealing the rage beneath it.

"No, but it will mess up that pretty face of yours for graduation. And you can't say the same for your little girlfriend."

The guy in front of Trey waved the gun just over his shoulder. "Back up, boys," he said to Quinn and Ayaz. I heard them shuffling behind me, but I didn't dare turn around.

"You had to know I'd discover your secret." Vincent shifted aside, and I saw Deborah – her hands tied to the bed, her mouth gagged with a dog toy, her eyes wide and terrified. Sitting between her legs was the open duffel bag filled with the students' money.

Vincent lifted out a stack of bills and waved them in Trey's face. "You must think I'm an idiot. I've had an alert set on your credit card ever since you entered that school. Last quarter it pinged for the first time in twenty years – at an ice cream store some forty miles from Arkham. I assumed Hazel Waite stole the card during her escape. By the time my team arrived at the shop, they could find no trace of her, or you. Imagine my surprise when it pinged again, only this time to withdraw a large sum of money. I thought to myself, who would be stupid enough to continue to use that card? My son, of course."

Vincent nodded at Damon, who reached across and nudged Trey's backpack off his shoulders. The sigil made a loud clunk as it hit the floor. Damon used his foot to slide it toward the bed.

"When the bank showed me the security footage, I admit you gave me a shock. I could tell it was you even through your pitiful disguise. I figured you'd sent Hazel to take the money, but imagine my surprise to see my son and his friends outside of the school walls. How had you done it? Luckily, Damon and I remembered a strange thing that happened to our friend Senator Hyde-Jones the other week. A drunk teenager rushed him as he was coming out of a meeting, swinging his arms wildly and yelling that he was the Senator's son. Of course, security jumped on him. They removed a backpack containing a large rock with a strange symbol carved into it. As soon as they moved the rock away from the teen, his body disintegrated into dust."

So John's gone. I couldn't say I felt much of anything over his death. But I was anxious that Vincent knew about the sigils.

"Ever since, Damon and I have been staying nearby, watching the school for any more little field trips. Damon has a lot of time for spying on students, now that he's no longer practicing law. We saw you sneak in here yesterday, and this woman left soon after you. We decided to have a chat with her when she returned. Tell me, son, and maybe I'll let your whore live – what are you doing with my money?" Vincent held up a handful of cash. "Who do you have sabotaging our businesses?"

"The money in my account is in *my* name," Trey hissed. "What I do with it is none of your concern. And as for sabotage, I don't know anything about it. It can't possibly be us. We've trapped up at the school at your behest. We don't even have internet, so how are we masterminding any attacks? The Eldritch Club has been doing illegal and unethical things for decades – maybe you just got caught."

"You little punk. How *dare* you? Everything you've been given has come from me." Vincent's smile turned my heart to ice. "For your insolence, Hazel dies slowly and painfully. I'm going to enjoy removing each of her dainty fingers one at a time. Grab them."

While Trey tried to wrestle the other gunman, Damon grabbed my arm and yanked me into the room. He pinned me against the wall, leaning in close to press the barrel to my temple.

An arrow pierced him through the eye.

CHAPTER THIRTY-FOUR

At first, I thought I'd imagined it. One moment Damon loomed over me, whisky breath staining my skin. The next moment, an arrow extended through his skull, pinning his head to the wall. He screamed, but the sound was a whoosh of air as his body jerked beneath me.

"What the fuck?" Vincent whirled to face the window just as a figure ducked below view. "Get them!"

The second gunman turned toward Damon, the gun wobbling in his hand. Trey swung out and punched the guy in the nose. He went down like a sack of potatoes just as a second *whoosh* of air penetrated the room and another arrow embedded itself into the wall where his head had previously been.

Greg. Loretta. Where are they?

I dived for the window over the bedside as the three Kings rushed the room. They pinned Vincent's arms and wrestled them behind his back. Trey grabbed a handful of his dad's thick, dark hair, only to have it come off in his hands. *He's wearing a toupee.* I'd have laughed if there weren't still guns in the room.

Trey dug his nails into the thinning grey hair and fragile skin on Vincent's scalp and jerked his head right back to expose his neck and more burns. Loretta leaned through the window, the string of her bow pulled back toward her shoulder, an eerily placid expression on her face.

"I'm going to enjoy watching you bleed," she whispered.

"Trey, son," Vincent blubbered. "You don't want to do this. The Eldritch Club is planning something for your graduation. I can tell you—"

"Shut up." Trey's ice eyes focused on Loretta. "Lower the bow."

"You joking, Bloomberg?" I demanded.

Loretta didn't move an inch. Her fingers on the bowstring remained frozen in place.

"I'm not going to force you to do this," Trey said, not looking at anyone except Loretta. "If you take his life, we don't get a chance to break the cycle. Plus, we need him alive."

Tension crackled between us, filling the room with electric energy. Loretta's arm jerked. She shot Trey a look that would've burned a lesser man alive, lowered her bow, and turned away in disgust.

"Thank you, son," Vincent blubbered. "I knew you wouldn't be so stupid. You still had it in you to be great, to take over the business. I know that's what you always wanted. I could disinherit Wilhem and—"

Trey shoved his father into the bed. He spoke in that same calm voice, and his words sent chills down my spine. "You're pathetic. And you know nothing about me or what I want. As you walk out of here today, I want you to remember that you have no power over me or anyone else at Miskatonic Prep any longer. We don't care if you know we've found a way to get past the boundary. You're not safe anywhere. The only reason I'm not twisting your head off your body *with my bare hands* is because you will deliver a message to all the parents. We're coming for you, for everything you've built off the backs of your greed and our torture. We're going to tear down every last pillar of the empire you've built. It's already started. The only way to stop it is to come to our gradua-tion. Ayaz, you got a flyer?"

"Sure." Ayaz pulled a folded poster from his back pocket.

Trey slapped it across Vincent's face. "See you there, *Father*. Dress to impress."

CHAPTER THIRTY-FIVE

Trey yanked Vincent off the bed and shoved him toward the door, planting his foot in his father's ass and kicking him so hard Vincent crashed into the wall. Blood gushed from a wound above his eye. His ruined skin couldn't take the abuse.

"Ayaz, help me."

Ayaz reached for him. Vincent held out his hand, thinking Ayaz was helping him, but instead, Ayaz kicked him in the side. Again and again and again. His jaw set in silent rage and his dark eyes blazed with every evil thing Vincent had made him do.

Vincent rolled over and dragged himself through the doorframe. He staggered to his feet and flailed across the room. When he reached the entrance, he clung to the frame and turned, his face twisted into an ugly scowl.

"I raised you out of the gutter, you ungrateful rag-head," he roared at Ayaz.

"May Allah bless your family and wealth," Ayaz replied.

Quinn burst into hysterical laughter. Vincent stumbled out the door. A moment later, the roar of his Porsche speeding away drew me back to reality. We stood in the middle of a crime scene, and if we were caught, it could be a disaster.

The second gunman was only unconscious. But Damon Delacorte was dead as a doornail, his blood and brains splattered across the wall like a grisly Rorschach drawing. Loretta's arrow still stuck out of his eye. Our fingerprints would be all over the room.

This could ruin everything. I can't raise the third pillar from a jail cell.

"Quinn, wait in the car," I barked. Trey and I untied Deborah, and I slid the gag out of her mouth.

"Hazel, I'm so glad you're okay. Is everyone safe? No one's hurt?" Her skin was pale and her hands trembling as I quickly checked her over, but they didn't appear to have done anything worse to her.

Everyone is fine except poor Roger. "We're okay. I'm so sorry they came after you. If I'd known we put you in danger, I never would have—"

"Nonsense." She wiped her eyes. "I went into this with my eyes wide open. You're not the bad guy here."

Don't be so sure about that. "Ayaz, help Deborah into the kitchen. We need to strip the bed."

Ayaz put his arms around Deborah and took her outside. Trey moved to the other side of the bed and helped me strip the sheets. We spread them on the floor and rolled Damon's body on top, then used a spare set in the cupboard to do the same for the unconscious gunman.

I gathered the corners of the sheets around Damon Delacorte's body, knotting them together into handles that would make him easier to carry. Wordlessly, Quinn stepped into the room, his back rigid as he took up two of the corners.

"I told you to wait in the car."

Quinn didn't speak. He also didn't drop the sheet.

"Quinn." I set down my end and glared at him. His eyes were a million miles away. "You know we have to hide the body. If the police find out he's dead, it's going to ruin everything. They'll

march up to the school and haul all the students all away before we can get your lives back. We *have* to do this, but you don't have to be there."

He shook his head.

Trey stepped between us, placing a hand on each of Quinn's shoulders. Their eyes blazed at each other, a dance of will and defiance that had fueled their friendship for so many years. Quinn's shoulders sagged. Trey turned to me.

"He stays. He needs to be a part of this."

I wanted to argue, but we didn't have time. Quinn and I took his dad's sheet, dragging it out into the living area. Trey followed with the unconscious guy and the bag containing the sigil slung over his shoulder. We needed to get him as far away as we could from the crime scene.

Greg sat on the sofa, his head in his hands. Loretta's arms wrapped around his shoulders. He looked up when we entered, and a shudder rocked his body as he saw the bloodied sheet.

"I killed him." Greg curled into the fetal position, as if that would make the horror and guilt go away.

Fuck, I was supposed to protect him from this. I wanted to throttle Greg for following us with that bloody bow, and Loretta for letting him do it, knowing what she knew about carrying murder on her conscience. But he saved my life. So I kept my mouth shut.

"Look after him," I said to Loretta as we wrangled the bodies outside.

With every step I expected someone to run from one of the rooms and accost us. I expected Vincent to have snipers in the trees ready to gun us down. Every footfall on the decking rang as loud as a gunshot. I didn't let out my breath until we penetrated the trees.

Ayaz ran after us, a long-handled shovel in his hands. "I found this in the hotel's storage shed. I figured we'd need it."

Quinn's eyes widened, but he didn't ask what we planned to do with them.

We walked.

Deep into the woods, until the lights of the hotel faded into fireflies and my arms burned from dragging the heavy body. Blood soaked the sheet. Quinn gazed all around – above our heads, into the trees, everywhere that wasn't his father's shroud.

We came to a small clearing. Rain falling through a hole in the trees had left the ground soft. Wildflowers poked their heads through a covering of dead, wet leaves. Trey set down his bundle and picked up the shovel. Without stopping for a breath, he began to dig.

Trey's muscles rippled as he worked. I thought back to the first time I'd seen him do physical work – when he'd chiseled out the bricks in the tunnel so we could sneak back into school. How he'd worked all night under the light of my fire even though it frightened him.

From the way he kept glancing over at Quinn, who roamed around the clearing picking the wildflowers, I knew what frightened him now. Quinn just saw his dad killed in front of his eyes. He hated his abuser, but that didn't mean he wasn't hurting. These things were always complicated. I knew all too well how grief and rage and hurt could be shaken into a potent cocktail of crazy.

Trey hollowed out a foot of earth before passing the shovel to Ayaz. While Ayaz tossed dirt out of the hole, Trey slumped to the earth beside Quinn.

"This burial is too dignified for him," he spat.

Quinn said nothing, staring down at the posy of flowers clutched in his hands.

Ayaz dug until his shoulders shook. The soft earth had disappeared, replaced by thick clay. The hole was barely two-feet deep when he finally leaned against the shovel, panting, his energy spent.

"My turn," Quinn reached for the shovel.

Trey grabbed it from Ayaz and tossed it out of reach. "Sit the fuck down. Let us do it."

"Don't tell me what I shouldn't do," Quinn snapped. "You don't have to protect me like I'm some fucking child. I'm not *sad*. I am more proud that we're ridding the earth of that shitstain than I am of anything else I've ever done, with the possible exception of boning Hazy, cuz she's fucking spectacular."

Despite the horrific situation, I burst out laughing. Quinn would always be... Quinn.

Quinn grabbed the shovel and jumped into the grave. He dug furiously, flinging clay over his shoulder in all directions. It was like he didn't even feel the bite.

When he finally tossed down the shovel, he stood in a hole four-feet deep and about long enough for Loretta to lie down in. Trey helped Quinn clamber out while Ayaz and I rolled Damon's body into the grave.

Quinn reached for the shovel again. I planted my hands on his chest and shoved him back. "Let me do this for you. Please."

Something in my words broke Quinn. He slumped to his knees. A tremor shuddered through his entire body. He was done.

I pushed the clay and earth back into the hole. With each toss, I thought of the whip marks Damon left on Quinn's back, of the little boy who'd been belted for hugging his daddy, of the way Damon openly flirted with other women – shunning the weakness of others while succumbing to his own. None of it made this day any less shit, but it did make me throw the clay down extra hard.

Damon Delacorte would rot in an unmarked grave, and it served him right. He wouldn't join his fellow Eldritch Club members as children of the god, sailing through the stars on their way home to fuck-knows-where. If Vincent didn't make the parents show up at graduation, then as far as I cared, they could all enjoy the same fate.

I knew they'd cook up some scheme to save their asses. We expected it. I just hope like hell we play them before they play us.

CHAPTER THIRTY-SIX

"I'm so sorry." Deborah met us at the edge of the forest as we traipsed out, her arm being wrenched out of its socket by two poodles desperate to get at Trey. He fell to his knees and they licked his face and gazed up at him adoringly like he was a brave soldier returned from war. Which in a way, he was.

We'd left the other guy, still unconscious, a mile or so away from Damon's body. Eventually, he'd come to and stumble out of the forest, hopefully with a serious headache. Or he wouldn't. I didn't give a fuck.

"Vincent is the one who'll be sorry," Trey growled, standing up to look Deborah over. I knew he was thinking of poor Roger. He touched a cut on Deborah's cheek. "Are you sure he didn't hurt you?"

She shook her head. "Not physically."

"Tell us what happened."

"It was awful. I was just getting ready to take the dogs out to relieve themselves. I'd unlocked the door, and I turned around to get the doggie bags off the table, and that's when they ran in and grabbed me. I let go of the leashes. Leopold and Loeb tried to take one of them down, but then he shot Roger and they ran off

into the woods. I should have known they wouldn't be too far."
She nuzzled Leopold's neck, tears swimming in her eyes. "They
came as soon as I called them."

"How come none of the hotel staff reacted to the shot?" I
asked.

"He used a silencer." Deborah shuddered. "That's how I knew
this was serious. That guy was a professional killer. I was so
scared. I kept hoping and hoping that you wouldn't show up.
They kept asking me who I was, how I knew you, Hazel, but I
didn't say a word. They seemed to lose interest in me after a while
– they were here for you."

Coldness settled on my chest as I studied the motel block. I
hadn't planned on covering up a death today. No one had come
out of the other rooms, and there didn't appear to be any cars
parked in the lots outside. "Is there anyone else staying in the
motel?"

Deborah shook her head. "The family next door to me left
yesterday."

"Just in case, could you go and check? Knock on the doors or
peek in the windows – whatever you have to do. Make it quick."

Deborah handed me the leashes and ran off. Trey fussed the
dogs while Ayaz watched him, looking broody. Quinn rested
against me, his head on my shoulder. I ran my fingers through his
thick surfer hair and wished I had a softness to me like his
mother, something that could ease the violence that still hummed
in his veins. Ass-kicking I could do, but comfort wasn't my thing.

Greg and Loretta stood a little away from us, their heads
pressed together as they spoke in low voices. When they saw we
returned, they came running over.

"We took care of Roger," Loretta pointed to the bushes. "And
disposed of the bloody blanket and cleaned the room. It looks as
good as new."

"I'm so sorry." I wrapped my arms around Greg's neck,

wanting to squeeze the bad things out of him. "I wanted to protect you from this."

"You weren't the one who loosed the arrow," Greg shuddered. "It's not like I didn't know what I was aiming for, what it would do when it hit the target."

"I know it doesn't feel like it, but you did a good thing. You saved my life." I squeezed him tighter, hoping to imprint the memory of him in my body to carry to the stars. "I'll never forget that."

Deborah came back. "I've checked out early and paid the bill. There's no one else in the motel. I knocked on all the doors and I even checked the registration book when the clerk's back was turned."

"Good." I handed her the leashes. "You and the dogs need to get out of here."

She shook her head. "I don't want to leave you."

"You have to. You can't come back to school with us, and I don't know who else Vincent told about us and about you. They could come back to try and finish what they started."

"He won't have told anyone," Trey said. "That would be admitting he was wrong, that he let us get the better of him. In the eyes of the Eldritch Club, he'd be responsible for all their woes."

Deborah rubbed the welts on her wrists where Vincent had tied her up. "I don't like the idea of going back to my house."

"Find my sister." Ayaz touched his finger to the *nazar* pendant he wore – the ward against the evil eye that had protected Zehra for so many years. "Hazy can contact her. If anyone can protect you, it's Zehra."

I handed my phone to Deborah. "Ayaz is right. Call her."

After a quick conversation with Zehra, Deborah climbed into her Jeep and Trey tossed her the keys. Leopold and Loeb settled onto their blankets, leaving a wide space for Roger. My heart ached to watch them look around for him. *We've all lost someone.*

Deborah reached through the window and grasped my hand. "Thank you for saving me, Hazel."

Instinct propelled me forward. I leaned through the window and wrapped my arms around her. Our first hug as aunt and niece. I wished it could be the first of many, but it was probably our last. "You saved me first."

As she drove away, I raised my hand, palm facing to the sky, and drew up the dark things inside me, the things that Vincent Bloomberg never failed to draw to the surface. A minute later, smoke curled from beneath the windows of Deborah's unit. Ayaz took my hand, pressing his warmth against the burning in my palm. The scar on my wrist blazed as flames licked up the motel walls. From inside, a smoke alarm blared – too late to save the building.

Hotel staff rushed out with extinguishers. In the distance, a siren rang. We retreated into the woods, our steps silent against the chaos.

Burn it all down.

We trudged up the peninsula, one foot in front of the other. My legs felt leaden, weighed down with the weight of this – of all the deaths burning on my conscience. Greg might've felt responsible, but Damon's death belonged to me. I got everyone into this mess. I made the plan. Another notch to add to the belt, another ghost to haunt my closed eyelids.

Back at school, I left Greg with Loretta, Andre, and Sadie, and the four of us crawled into Trey's cloud of a bed. I slept curled around Quinn, one arm over his shoulders, the other tucked around the bag of passports – our hard-won prize.

Finals week blended together into one long string of anticipation. We studied. We sat exams. We told no one else about seeing Vincent, about Quinn's father's death. Every time there was a noise outside a window or a commotion in the corridors, I expected to see police storming the school with guns at the ready, coming for us... for me.

They never showed up.

Zehra texted me the headlines in the paper – ELECTRICAL FIRE DESTROYS HISTORIC HOTEL. They weren't treating the fire as suspicious, not even with known arsonist and murderer Hazel Waite in the area.

I sat at my desk in the converted dining hall and scribbled essays in the blue booklets, my mind a million miles away across the stars, where my body would soon join it. I didn't remember a word I wrote.

The god came to me only once – a faint shriek in the corner of a dream. His power had waned quickly since he agreed to help us. He needed me now more than ever.

The final piece will be raised. You will be my fire, my light in the darkness, he whispered in the screams of his victims.

I will.

I woke from that dream with tears streaming down my face.

And then, just like that, I handed in my last exam and my senior year was over. Miskatonic Prep was out for good, although no one knew that for a fact yet. Students and teachers wandered the halls in a daze, shuffling from here to there like zombies.

The points tables went blank. No more points could be added or taken away. Students crowded into the atrium before breakfast to see the final class list. Trey squeezed my hand, his shoulders tensed, his ice eyes meeting mine with a hint of nerves no one else but I could discern. The King of Kings was a completely different person from the one who greeted me with a jeer on my first day at Derleth Academy. He'd let go of the need to please his father, and the desire to hurt others on his way to the top.

Although not completely different. He still wanted to be first, to win.

"Make way, move your ass, valedictorian coming through!"

Quinn shoved his way through the crowd, parting the waters like Moses for me, Trey, Ayaz, Greg, Tillie, Andre, and Loretta.

"You don't know who the valedictorian is yet," Courtney grumped.

"Nope," Quinn beamed. "But it's going to be one of this lot."

The blank screen flicked to life. Students crowded forward, jostling each other for the best view. The list streamed past, starting at the bottom. Quinn's name appeared quickly, and he hooted as if he'd won a grand prize. The screens kept flicking over, getting closer and closer to the top of the list. And still, my name didn't appear. I held my breath as the final screen showed up, with the top five students listed in descending order.

5. Greg Lambert

4. Tillie Fairchild

3. Ayaz Demir

2. Trey Bloomberg

At the top – me. Hazel Waite.

Valedictorian of Miskatonic Prep.

No fucking way.

Trey's eyes flicked over to me. Pride leaked through his voice. "You did it, Meat."

I couldn't help the grin that spread across my face. "Not mad at me for beating you?"

Trey shrugged. "I've realized there are more important things in life than being first."

Bodies tumbled against me, Greg and Ayaz and Quinn and Andre and Tillie hugged and yelled at once. I accepted their praise with a stiff smile plastered on my face. In reality, I didn't give a shit. I wasn't going to college, so what did it matter?

I barely ate a mouthful at breakfast. The kitchen had put on a mountain of bacon especially for me, but it tasted like cardboard. All I could think about was graduation and what the parents might be planning. I kept coming back to Deborah's warning about Honduran assassins.

I think we've accounted for everything, but we'd be fools to underestimate Vincent.

When I got sick of listening to 'congratulations, Hazel!' from students who'd done terrible things to me and my friends, I shoved the uneaten rolls and leftover cakes into my satchel. The boys did the same thing. We took them downstairs, where we had one last piece of our own plan to put in place.

I swung open the door to my old room. The twin bed I'd slept in all those lonely nights rested against the wall, giving the room more floor space for our loot. Duffel bags and designer purses filled with cash were stacked in the corner nearly to the ceiling. A few random bills fluttered loose, settling across the floor.

Our freedom stash. All the money the students would need to start their new lives.

There was something else in the room, too – an old black-board I'd had Trey and Quinn steal from one of the abandoned classrooms and bring here, along with a handful of chalk sticks. I hadn't told them what I needed it for – I had a hunch, but I wasn't sure it would work.

I set my bag down in the middle of the floor and dumped out the food. The guys copied me. Bits of bacon and half-chewed bread slices rolled in the dust. I stood back to admire the pile, and behind it, the blackboard and stack of chalk we'd nicked from one of the abandoned classrooms.

Scritch-scritch-scritch. The rats circled overhead, their curiosity piqued by the scent of food.

I peered up at the ceiling. "You can come out. I've brought you a treat."

There was a rumble and a clatter, and the scritch of claws grew louder, more insistent. The rumble became a chorus as more rats poured in from around the school, joining their brothers and sisters in a rapturous dance. One of the pipes crossing the ceiling jolted free, and an avalanche of rats toppled out. They fell upon the stack, tearing the napkins with their teeth to drag out the goodies inside, tiny brown bodies leaping and crawling over each other as they struggled for dominance.

Quinn backed toward the door. I didn't blame him – encountering all those rats in that tiny space *was* a bit disconcerting. But they'd been my friends and guardians ever since I arrived at school. I knew them. I knew their names. They wouldn't hurt me.

One of the rats stopped in front of me, its cheeks stuffed with cake. It clutched a piece of bacon between its claws and rose up on its haunches to present me with its treat.

I laughed and patted its head. "That's okay, I've had some already. I smuggled this out for you."

The rat king bowed graciously and nibbled on the meat.

I held up a stick of chalk. "I got this for you, too. And a blackboard over there on the wall. I thought you might like to write something for me. But first, I'm going to tell you a story, and you can tell me if you think it's any good."

The rat nodded, its little jaw working frantically at its bacon-y treat.

"Okay, so a long long time ago, in a place called Salem, there were many innocent women and some men who were accused of being witches. It started with some young women desperate to avoid the wrath of their sanctimonious parents, and the fires of persecution, hysteria, and fanaticism turned their accusations into a travesty of justice. Nineteen were executed by hanging, all innocent, and their wretched souls were so angry they lingered on earth, terrifying the man who signed their death warrants. When the Reverend Parris succumbed to their torment and died, they moved on to punish his son for the sins of his father. They followed Parris from Salem to his new house on top of a wild peninsula, only instead of sending him quaking in terror, they ended up as sacrifices to his god."

The king rat stopped chewing. The bacon slid from its paws, clattering on the ground. Other rats turned toward me, ears and noses twitching. It was odd to see them reacting to my words, understanding English.

They were never just rats.

I continued. "When a witch named Rebecca cast her spell and killed Parris, the spirits became trapped here, unable to cross over and unable to leave the grounds. The sleeping god had no need of their energy, and so they lingered still, growing fainter and more sorrowful with every passing year. Parris' home became a school, and after many more years, a young headmistress found the spirits lurking in the halls. Hungry for power and scientific discovery, she tried to turn these spirits into the god's children. She sliced their souls into pieces and placed them inside the bodies of rats, thinking the rodents would go forth and multiply in great numbers, quickly overwhelming the earth with the god's seed. But something happened when she tried to give the rats the final piece of the god's soul. It didn't work, because the god needed a certain type of vessel – a creature that related to his malevolence, and the rats knew nothing of this. So she found some other children, and left the spirits of the Salem witches trapped inside a colony of rats. And they've seen everything that's gone on in this school. They've lived in the pipes and walls and watched as countless scholarship students cried themselves to sleep in this very room as the god's children competed over who would break them first.

"One day, a new girl comes along – she's not like the others. She's already broken, but she won't give up. The rats think, 'she's our chance. If we can protect her, she might be able to free us.' How's the story so far?"

The king rat held out his empty paws. I dropped a piece of chalk into them. He wrapped his arms around it and scrambled to the blackboard, where rats had already stacked themselves into a small tower. The king rat clambered over the bodies of his friends to stand in front of the blackboard. The chalk scratched as he dragged it over the surface, creating a message in shaky letters.

YES
WE ARE NOT RIGHT
NOT REAL RATS
BUT CAN'T PASS OVER
SOULS BROKEN

"Holy cosmic god," Quinn whispered. "The souls of the Salem witches have been living in the walls of our school this whole time."

"You're too clever for your own good, Ms. Valedictorian," Ayaz added.

The king rat's nose twitched, begging me to continue.

I knelt down beside the blackboard, so we were practically nose-to-nose. "We're going to send the god back to his home. This will free the students of Miskatonic Prep, and I have an idea that I believe will free you, too. Your souls could cross over. But it's not a guarantee. I'm not an expert at all this soul stuff. That's why I wanted to talk to you. I want your consent. Do you understand?"

The king rat nodded. Behind him, the rest of the rats copied the movement.

Quinn giggled. "It looks like they're all headbanging. Hey, Ayaz, put on your metal—"

"Shhhh." I extended a finger to the king rat. He placed his paw on top, a promise of his loyalty. "The senior Eldritch Club will show up at our graduation ceremony, and they're planning to kill us all. If they succeed... well, let's just say it'll suck real bad. But we've got a plan. They're expecting a fight, but they're not expecting you."

CHAPTER THIRTY-SEVEN

"Pass that comb, would you?" Quinn elbowed Trey in the ribs as he struggled in the mirror.

Trey dumped the comb into Quinn's hands. "Fine. I need to borrow your cologne."

"Why would you want his cologne?" Greg piped up, running gelled fingers through his hair. "Is the toilet water taken?"

The boys laughed and joked as we got ready for graduation in Trey's dorm. I could almost believe we were going to a normal school dance – at least, normal for fancy rich people. Dances at my old school were in the gymnasium with cheap fairy lights and music that was five years out of date.

This dance was in a gym, sure, but Miskatonic Prep had spared no expense. With the god's shadows and the rats gone from the gym, the smell had all but disappeared. Just to be safe, the decoration committee had been running the extractor fans full blast *and* doused the place in some chemical that neutralized the rotting flesh smell. Mostly. Unless you breathed in too deeply or stood in the same place too long.

The decoration committee (headed by Courtney, because of course) were given an unlimited budget. Well, Courtney had commanded it, and Ms. West, now not showing her face in the school after what happened in the bathroom, had no choice but to obey. Students and maintenance staff worked together to tear out the old, rotting bleachers. Ayaz and Greg led a team of artists in dismantling old stage sets and repainting them with new scenes. I hadn't seen the finished product yet, but I was told it looked amazing.

And now, D-Day was upon us and we were going to look the part. Greg styled my short, kinky hair to frame my face and dusted me with dramatic makeup. He made me close my eyes while he poked and prodded with pins and brushes. By the time he was done, I was so tenderized he could have served me with a nice pepper sauce. I had to admit, I looked damn fine.

Trey slipped his arm in mine, his eyes drinking me in. The blush pink gown Greg found in the costume closet swirled around my ankles. Ayaz and Quinn made me a corsage from roses picked from the bushes lining the field, the pink perfectly matching my dress. Laughing, I lifted the hem to show them my knee-high striped socks and comfortable old Docs.

"I'm finding it hard to believe that of all the possible choices, you wanted to wear those *filthy* shoes to the dance." Trey looked as though he was trying hard not to laugh. He also looked fucking hot – his suit fit him to perfection, the sharp tailoring and long lapels accentuating his razor cheekbones and penetrating eyes. His green Miskatonic Prep tie looked stunning against my dress, and his dress shoes had been polished to a high shine. He'd never be caught dead in scuffed Docs.

"These shoes are awesome," I retorted. "If they've been good enough to keep my feet warm and dry for three years, they're good enough to dance in."

"Tell that to my ruined brogues." Quinn lifted his foot to show the scuffs where I'd trod on his feet during our dance practice. Turns out 'ballroom dancing' was another lesson my year of prep school education had skipped over.

"Not my fault if those things are so flimsy. *I'm* prepared for anything, including a small hurricane or a nuclear attack." I whipped up my hem again to show them the knife down the side of my boot.

"I'm prepared for anything, too." Trey grinned as he whipped off his shoe to show me how he'd pre-bandaged his toes. "I figured, why wait until after you crushed them underfoot?"

"You're so fucking dicksome. Let's go." I grabbed my bag. Greg and Trey took one last look in the mirror while Ayaz twirled Tillie around the room and Quinn helped Loretta do up the laces on her dress. She'd chosen a red taffeta gown with a jeweled corset that made her look much older and more sophisticated. She beamed at me from across the room.

I beamed back. Tonight was dangerous and things were likely to go down in a bad way. We had one shot to raise the pillar while all the parents were inside the sigil. Everything rode on my shoulders. But right now, I wasn't thinking about it. I savored these moments with my Kings and my friends – committing each crude insult and silly dance move to memory. They were the last memories we'd ever share, and I intended to indulge every teenage fantasy I never knew I had.

I was going to the dance with not one, but *three* hot dates.

I held out my hands to my Kings. Trey took one arm, Quinn the other. Ayaz placed his warm fingers over my thigh. My Turk's suit clung in all the right places, and with his dark hair and tattoos peeking out from his cuffs and collar, he looked less like a prep-school jerk and more like a brooding rockstar. His eyes bore into mine.

In a white linen suit, with his sandy hair slicked back, Quinn looked like he'd be right at home on the deck of a private yacht in the Mediterranean. Not that I'd ever get to see the Mediterranean. But tonight, Quinn could transport me to places and nights I'd never dreamed of. If only he would smile that cheeky grin of his, my heart would soar.

And Trey – my mirror, my King of Kings, resplendent in his school uniform and his arrogant sneer. Just the sight of him would bring the Eldritch Club to their knees.

But tonight wasn't about the guys and how I felt about them. Tonight was for the students of Miskatonic Prep. I beamed up at my three Kings and at the others who had become part of our circle, and I silently vowed that whatever it took, they would be free tonight.

"You're still bragging that you beat me." Trey placed a kiss on my neck. Inside me, my fire danced and sparked. I was so wired for tonight, all it would take was one little flame to set me off. An electric hum sizzled in the air – the pull of a cosmic god rousing himself from slumber one final time.

Somewhere below my feet, the third pillar called to me. It wanted to be free.

That pillar is ours.

I sucked in a breath, gave Trey's hand a final squeeze, and led the group through the door of his dorm.

Showtime.

In the hallway, we met Andre and Sadie. Greg had found Sadie a sequined gown amongst the theatre costumes that perfectly set off her brown hair and bold eyes. Andre looked like a million bucks in a pinstripe suit found in John Hyde-Jones' closet.

"You ready?" I touched Greg's shoulder.

Darkness passed over his eyes. I'd never seen that kind of black hole in Greg's soul before he shot Damon. But he'd done it because he believed in what we were doing. He believed in me. Not sure anyone except my mom had ever really believed in me before.

Greg nodded.

The nine of us climbed down the staircase and stepped into the main dormitory corridor, where a few students still rushed around putting the final touches on their outfits. Heads nodded at us as we strode past in formation, our arms linked, our bodies tall and proud and strong.

Down the empty corridors, through the drafty atrium, and outside, into the warmth of the approaching summer. The decoration committee opened the two outside doors to the gymnasium and set up a makeshift platform in front of the wall, with a lectern and rows of seats on the grass for the parents. If I squinted just right at the wall behind the stage, I could just make out the shape of the giant red cock Trey had painted there back in the second quarter.

The entire area had been enclosed by flickering torches and braziers. It looked magical, but every detail served a specific purpose.

Maintenance staff circulated with trays piled high with food and flutes of Champagne. A few looked up when we entered and snuck a moment of eye contact before quickly looking away again. A few teachers milled around, and we couldn't risk them ruining our plan. We ducked behind the stage, following strings of fairy lights through a tunnel of vines into the gym.

I gasped as we stood in the doorway and gazed up at the space – the gym had been transformed into a shimmering outer space landscape. Glitter covered the walls, throwing prisms of iridescent light against the backdrop of Cyclopean architecture decorated with flaming sigils. Silver runners crossed the tables, perfectly offsetting the matte-black crockery and centerpieces of green alien tentacles. One corner had become the bridge of a ship, with flickering buttons and computer screens. The decoration committee had truly outdone themselves.

We'd chosen *Back to the Future* as our theme – Quinn's idea. I think he'd imagined 80s movie trash and leg warmers everywhere, but Courtney had given everything her Midas touch and turned the gym into a classy spacey nightclub. She was talking about getting into event planning when she got her new life.

I wondered if the Eldritch Club would appreciate the symbolism.

Probably not.

A faint tinge of the rotting smell followed us as we headed toward our table. I guessed the horrors in this room were etched too deep for a little disinfectant and some flowers to hide. I glanced up at the ceiling again.

Is that a scritching I hear, or did I just imagine it?

Scritch-scritch-scritch.

Excellent. The rats were in place. Everything was ready. All we needed was our final sacrifice.

We'd decided to have a little graduation party early in the day, so the students had this opportunity to celebrate before the adults got here and the *real* party began. Our own private celebration, the ending of one chapter, the opening of another.

The buffet groaned under the weight of delicious-smelling foods. My stomach growled. That poor girl in me that never wanted to overlook an opportunity for a free meal took over, and I descended, snapping up a handful of potato chips and tiny salmon quiches. The best last meal I could hope for.

"Let's dance." Quinn's fingers rested on the small of my back as he led me toward the dance floor. As soon as we got amongst the other couples, his stiffness evaporated – he squeezed my arm and twirled me beneath his, then back the other way until I was dizzy and laughing. He smiled faintly, but couldn't bring himself to laugh.

We dipped and twirled and whizzed between the other dancers. I was supposed to feel apprehensive, to be mourning all I was about to lose. But instead, I'd never felt freer. As we fluttered about like dragonflies, Quinn stretched out a lazy leg just as Courtney spun past on Derek's arm. She tripped over the hem of her dress and fell against him, giving Quinn the middle finger over Derek's shoulder. We all broke into uncontrollable giggles.

"This dance thing is actually quite fun," I said as Quinn and I returned to our table. Trey and Greg sat together, both of them clutching long-stemmed glasses of something pink and sparkling while they talked in low voices about what might happen tonight.

I dropped down between them. "If you two keep looking so glum, you'll give the game away."

"Right." Trey rested his hand on his cheek. His shoulders tightened.

He wasn't the only one waiting, milling. Tension tugged in the air – a breathless, palpable anticipation that tinged each conversation with nervous laughter. Everyone was waiting, tensing.

It was a special day, after all. Graduation day. A day no Miskatonic Prep student ever expected to see.

Across the room, a group hovered in the doorway while the ushers took coats and stoles. My breath caught in my throat as Vincent Bloomberg glided into the room with Tillie's mother on his arm. Behind them were more Eldritch Club members, resplendent in glittering gowns and pristine suits that couldn't mask their aging, frail bodies. They fanned out around the floor, elbowing students out of the way so they could get to the bar.

The parents had shown up.

Of course they did. We knew how to pull their strings like puppets. We knew what they cared about more than anything else, and it wasn't their children.

We'd hit them where it hurt – their money, their looks, their reputations. Which meant that we had power over them. They knew it, or they wouldn't be here.

Trey ground his teeth together. "They're already celebrating," he hissed. "My dad's got something planned, and we've walked right into it. We need to—"

"Ssssh. They won't be celebrating for long." I held out my hand. "You and me, we're dancing. You need to calm down."

I pulled Trey onto the dance floor. Unlike Quinn, he didn't joke around or even seem to notice other students brushing against him. He clung to me like I was the only thing holding him upright, his nails digging into my naked arm.

The back of my neck itched, conscious of eyes watching my every move. When Trey spun me, I searched the faces in the crowd. It didn't take long to spot Vincent standing near the entrance, one foot placed behind him like he was ready to run, a glass in his hand but never once touching his lips.

"I don't like this." Trey's teeth grazed my collarbone as he swung me around the dance floor. "It's too much like last time."

He meant last time he'd been to a dance in the gym, when the parents had burned the whole place down.

"It won't be," I promised. "I saw your dad. He's nervous."

Trey's eyes darted across the room again, resting on his father. "He'll kill everyone in this room."

"Not while Ms. West has Gloria. We've got this. Ignore him," I whispered. "I am. Tonight isn't about him."

That proved difficult. Vincent Bloomberg's eyes followed me as I twirled across the hall in his son's arms. His scowl burned into my back as I dressed up Trey with fairy wings and a wand for the photo booth in the corner.

You tried to get rid of me, you bastard.

Now it's your turn.

Tonight you get exactly what you always wanted.

Trey tugged at his tie, swallowing every few moments. He couldn't breathe in the gym. He felt hemmed in, burning up under his dad's scrutiny. I walked him outside, and the rest of our group followed. We huddled under the glittering fairy lights and watched cars snaking up the long driveway – a river of shiny chrome and sleek fiberglass. The vehicles slid into the empty spaces of the visitors' lot and when those were taken, they fanned out across the field, facing the gym. Probably they were parking close in case they had to escape in a hurry. Bodies floated out, doors slammed.

"Welcome on behalf of the graduating class of Miskatonic

Prep." Trey stepped forward, the Class President in him taking over. He beamed as he led parents to their seats. "We hope you enjoy yourselves."

They played their part, taking the programs and arranging themselves in neat rows, accepting the flutes of Champagne but not drinking them. I noticed more than a few looking at the flaming torches with trepidation.

Good.

The teachers gathered everyone in the gym outside – students standing on the grass, the parents in the seats behind, faculty on stools at the rear of the stage. When everyone was seated, the school band struck up the national anthem. We all rose. I sang the words at the top of my lungs, my fist clenched over my heart.

It was late in my life to develop pride in being a citizen of this country, of this planet. But a lump formed in my throat at the words.

Be strong. You're doing this for them.

The minutes ticked down as the band played on and on. Finally, they set aside their instruments and welcomed Ms. West on stage. She wore a black sequined gown that hugged her body and a look of grim determination on her face. She never once made eye contact with me.

A murmur went through the students as they clapped politely for the Deadmistress. The parents remained still and mute. My grip tightened on Trey's arm. *Soon, soon.*

Ms. West crossed the stage in three long strides, a triumphant smile splattered across her face. She stood, proud and silent, behind the microphone. Her eyes swept the room before settling on mine for the first time that day. Even now, that gaze could still turn my blood to ice.

"Welcome to all our students who have been working hard all year. All *years.* Welcome also to their parents. I'm sure your children are so grateful you came to share this night with them. We have important business to attend to. But first, it's time to announce the valedictorian and salutatorian – our two most distinguished students of this year's class. This is a tradition we've had ever since the school opened, and we do *so* love our traditions here at Derleth." She held a red-trimmed envelope between her long fingers.

Students hooted and screamed as the band played through an upbeat version of Pomp and Circumstance. "We've kept tabs on all the merit points, and we can say that these two students were chosen because of their excellent service to the school, their unwavering loyalty to their friends, and a sizzling romance that has flourished under... trying circumstances." Ms. West thumbed the envelope seal, pulling it away with a tearing sound. She opened the envelope and read the names with care. "Please welcome as salutatorian, Trey Bloomberg. And our valedictorian – the indomitable Hazel Waite."

Vincent's face when he heard my name was worth everything I'd been through. *Everything.* That the empire he built could betray him so openly, that a girl like me could be raised up in the eyes of the other students to stand beside his flesh and blood tore at his reality.

Even though he planned to be rid of us all, it still enraged him that I was up here. *You ain't seen nothing yet, Vinnie boy.*

Trey's hand in mine burned with heat as we took the stage together to accept our sashes. As Ms. West lowered the sash around my neck, the corner of her lip tugged into the faintest smile. "You should enjoy this," she said. "Together, you and I have made history. The world will remember our names."

Not if I can help it.

In another life, before the fires, before I made the biggest mistake of my life, I might have stared out into the audience and seem my mother in the front row, wiping tears of joy from her eyes. Dante might've been beside her, flipping me the bird with a wild grin on his face. Instead, I faced rows of parents who only considered themselves, who bent the world to their will and thought nothing of damning their own flesh and blood for their own gain.

The parents were too afraid to be angry, so they stared in wide-eyed silence as I stepped up to the microphone.

I cleared my throat. Instead of speaking, I raised my hands, palms facing up. I gathered the heat inside me and directed it into two pillars of flame leaping between my palms. Gasps rose from the audience as the fire rose above my head in a perfect arc.

Beneath my feet, the god stirred.

"I have nothing to say to you," I said to the parents. "My words are for the students of Miskatonic Prep only."

Trey's fingers dug into my hip. I looked down at the front row, at Quinn and Ayaz, and although my words were for everyone, I spoke to them alone. "For twenty years, this school has never had a graduation ceremony – even though year after year you completed your studies, you competed in sports, you worked hard to make parents and teachers proud of you, and your sacrifice was never acknowledged. But you'll have one tonight. Graduation shouldn't be about what *has been* – it looks to the future, and you never had a future. Until now.

"All your lives you've been taught that you deserved the best in life – the best education, the best houses, the best jobs, the best seat at any table. What I ask you today is, prove them right. When you step outside this school, prove that you are worthy of all the good things that will come your way. Make the world a better place for your existence in it. If you do that, the horror of what you've witnessed will fade into inconsequence."

There was a commotion at the side of the stage. I couldn't see what happened until someone shoved past Quinn and stormed toward me.

Vincent.

His face was as red as Loretta's dress, his neck muscles bulging through his collar. As he stalked toward me, his toupee slid off his head and skidded across the floor, revealing a liver-spotted egg covered with a few tufts of grey hair.

Behind me, Trey choked. A ripple of laughter ran through the crowd. Laughter bubbled up inside me and I couldn't control it, so I let it roll over me, enjoying the shock on Vincent's face as he staggered toward me on one good leg.

Vincent let out an animalian growl and lunged at me. Trey stepped in front of me, shoving his dad in the chest. Vincent staggered back, crashing into the drum kit.

"The time has come, Vincent." Ms. West snapped her fingers. From stage left, Derek and Barclay wheeled out a chair, upon which was tied a gagged Gloria Haynes. Ms. West stood behind Gloria and drew a silver knife from between her breasts, pressing the blade against Gloria's exposed neck. "You will break the sigils *now* and allow all of us our freedom, or I spill Gloria's blood right here. Her fortune and her influence will be lost to you, right when you need it most."

Vincent just stared at her.

"Come on, time's a ticking." Ms. West pressed the knife so hard a thin line of blood appeared on Gloria's throat. Gloria thrashed and wailed behind her gag, but no one paid her any heed. "Unlike me and your kid, she's not immortal—"

"You're right, she's not immortal." With a wild glint in his eye, Vincent whipped out a gun and shot Gloria Haynes in the face.

CHAPTER THIRTY-EIGHT

Her head snapped back. Blood arced up the fairytale backdrop, splattering leaves and vines with dappled crimson.

"What the fuck did you do!" Courtney shrieked. I'd prepared her for this possibility, but even if you hated your parents, nothing prepared you for seeing them shot in the face. Courtney rushed onto the stage and barreled into Vincent, knocking him to the ground and leaping on top of him. She hammered his face with her fists. Blood spurted from his nose, splattering across her dress before Ayaz grabbed her and dragged her off.

In the audience, parents whimpered. Vincent staggered to his feet, lunging for his gun. Courtney wrestled herself from Ayaz's grasp and hurtled toward him just as his fingers closed around the grip.

BANG.

Courtney screamed. She staggered back, clutching her chest, where a circle of red bloomed on her dress.

"You shot me," she growled, her eyes narrowing as she stepped toward him again. "You shot my mother. That was a mistake."

Vincent aimed again, but Courtney grabbed him first. She

didn't even slow down. She was Edimmu running on righteous anger. She couldn't be stopped.

She twisted the gun from Vincent's hands and whipped it across his face. He dropped to his knees, frantically swiping blood from his eyes. With a wicked grin, Courtney twisted a stiletto into his crotch. He curled into a ball, howling. Not one Eldritch Club member came to his aid.

"Go, Courtney!" I yelled. Trey left my side. I thought he'd try to pull her off. Instead, he slammed his fist into Vincent's face, dragging him up by his collar until father and son were nose-to-nose. Vincent opened his mouth, but only blood gurgled out.

"You want to say something, Father?" Trey growled. "You want to berate me for not being good enough? For being weak? You want to say something about my girlfriend? Go on, I can't hear you."

Vincent spat blood into Trey's face. "We don't need Gloria. Not when we have the god in all his glory. Now!"

As one, the Eldritch Club members rose to their feet. From purses and suit pockets they whipped out small devices that looked like garage door openers. They held them up, staring at their children with triumph.

"We've planted explosives in our cars," Vincent declared, his words gurgling with fresh blood. "A single move from any of you, and we'll send this whole place up in smoke. I don't think even an immortal being will survive being disintegrated into a thousand pieces. A mortal gutter whore certainly won't."

"I don't believe you," I shot back. "You love yourself too much to want to blow yourself up."

"Is that so?" Vincent tapped his breast pocket. "Or is it that I know a sacrifice that large would free the god at last and that he would reward me with eternal life? Even as my body disintegrates, my soul will be complete, and that's what's important in the end. Hermia's experiments proved that out."

Double fuck.

I didn't need to ask the god if that was true, because I knew he had no desire to reward his jailers. But it didn't matter, because Vincent believed it. That arrogant ass actually thought the first thing the god would do when he was free was bring *him* back to life.

They are not truth-tellers, the god rumbled from his prison, his screams growing louder as his outrage grew.

Dude, you don't have to tell me.

If they blew us all up, there would be no exchange. I couldn't raise the pillar if I was scattered in a million pieces on the wind. The god's children would eventually become whole again, but they would never be free. The god would not be able to go home. It would all be *over*.

Trey and Quinn moved closer to me, squeezing me behind them. Ayaz had Courtney in his arms. He'd torn off his shirt and jacket, wrapping them around her to staunch the bleeding.

"Get back, all of you." Vincent snarled, staggering to his feet. "We don't want any trouble. All you have to do is give us Hazel Waite, and we'll let the rest of you live. For now."

The fire inside me raged with triumph. I'd worked so long, so hard, to win this school over. To win over my bullies. When faced with standing beside me and winning their freedom, and going with Vincent and the parents who betrayed them, I knew what their choice would be.

Trey and Quinn exchanged one of their secret glances.

They stepped aside.

As one, the students around me hurried back, leaving a wide circle on the grass. The flames licked the inside of my skin as a cold breeze blew across the field, widening the gap between us.

They left me alone, facing Vincent.

They *left me*.

I glanced up at my Kings, at their faces turned hard and cold. "Trey? What's going on?"

Trey shook his head, and in his ice eyes I read all the malice and arrogance of the bully who'd first greeted me at Derleth. A hint of sadness crept into his voice as he nodded to his father. "The gutter whore is all yours."

What?

Vincent's triumphant leer burned against my skin. "Son, get over here. You have done well. You've obeyed my plans perfectly. You've proven your loyalty and your leadership. I never doubted you."

I never doubted you.

They've been... working together?

"Trey, please, tell me what's going on."

Trey's features remained stoic, unmoved. He stepped forward and shoved me toward Vincent. "Take her," he growled.

My legs turned to jelly as hands grabbed me, pressing a blade to my throat. *What? How?*

This can't be real. It's some trick, some part of the plan that he never told me about because... because...

But there was no reason for Trey to hide this from me. Unless he... unless they...

"Sorry, Hazy." Quinn shrugged. "It's been fun. We've let you plan and scheme for all these months, but we never intended to go through with this. You see, we don't want to lose our power. We want to be the Children of the God."

"Who wouldn't want that?" Ayaz strode over on his long legs, his arm thrown around Courtney's shoulders. "We will be the most powerful beings in this universe."

"I may hate my dad, but we were never going to let you take away our immortality," Trey said. "And thanks to you, we're going to get the freedom we've craved. Our parents know all about what we are now, and they've decided it's time we reveal ourselves to the world. Your life, for a permanent break of the seals. We each get something, don't we, Dad?"

Vincent nodded, his wrinkled face gleaming with pride.

Courtney stepped forward, her feline eyes slitted with triumph. "I get to take over my mother's clothing label."

Amber joined Tillie's side. "I'll be reunited with my sisters, and my modeling contract."

No... it can't be.

"You really thought the three of us – the Kings – would share a gutter whore like you?" Trey spat. "You really thought this would be real?"

His words cut deeper than the knife pressed against my throat.

Inside my head, the god screamed for vengeance – his cries a choir of desperate voices, of souls torn unfairly from bodies. And now, as I sank deeper into the blackness of their betrayal, I realized I was about to join them.

CHAPTER THIRTY-NINE

"Take her into the gym, Vincent," Ayaz said. "It has to be right over the sigil in the center of the court, where the first ceremony was performed. I've written the spell we need to transfer her fire-powers to the god."

"Bind her hands." Vincent tugged off his tie and tossed it to Tillie's mother, who trussed my hands together and shoved me forward. I stumbled, digging the soles of my Docs into the grass. I tripped on the hem of my skirt and toppled forward.

No no no no no.

Vincent dragged me through the tunnel of lights and across the threshold. Flickers like fireflies, like stars, danced over my head as they dragged and spun me. Vincent gave me a shove toward the dance floor. My feet skidded on the polished court, and I stumbled again, this time catching myself before I face-planted.

Hands dragged me across the court, grabbing my neck and forcing my head down. I collapsed to my knees. I was right in the center of the gym, in the circle where I'd first met the god's shadows. Before my eyes, a faint trail of blue fire arced across the paint. One of Rebecca's sigils overlaid on top.

I remembered that I'd seen it the first time I'd tried to shortcut through the gym. If any of the other women saw it now, they didn't say anything. They were too busy betraying me, baying for my blood.

I know you're here inside me, Rebecca. Your power runs in my veins. I don't care about my own life but please, please, I have to stop the god from being unleashed. Please show me what to do.

Vincent loomed over me, his features glowing with triumph. "I'm going to enjoy slitting your throat, gutter whore."

Spittle flew from Vincent's mouth, dotting my shoulders. A knife glinted in his raised hand. "Your death will be the final piece of our greatest sacrifice. Of course, we'd never blow up ourselves or our place of power, but we had to make you believe it. You really would do anything for my son. In the end, your love was your weakness. It was all for nothing."

I gazed up at the face of my enemy, and all the evil and rage in the world coalesced into his icicle eyes.

I smiled.

Snapped my fingers.

I had one more trick up my sleeve. One last, desperate attempt. The guys knew about it, so they might've warned him, but...

The scritching started from the rafters, almost imperceptive, tiny feet scrabbling over wood. As Vincent staggered toward me, holding his hand out to his son, the rat army spilled down the fake vines and trees and dropped onto the surprised parents.

Tillie's mother screamed as rats swarmed up her fishtail skirt, tearing off beads and sending them skittering across the floor. Elena rushed past screaming, trying to tear a rat from her hair. Vincent lashed out, kicking one rat that had grabbed hold of his shoe.

Tearing, gnawing, slashing with claws that had been sharpened for exactly this purpose, the rats worked together, piling one on top of each other to reach the tables where the parents huddled.

They tore the switches from feeble fingers and brought them to the students, just in case they weren't actually fake.

The rats created a barrier between two sides of the gym. Them on one side with the sigil of the five-pointed star. Us on the other side with an exit in easy reach, only I didn't want to be on that side with them any longer.

"Hazy, now!"

Trey leaped across the gym, crashing into me. His fingers slid through my bonds, slipping them free. I pummeled his chest with my fists until I realized he wasn't trying to hold me down, but pull me to my feet.

"It was a trick," he whispered. "I had to make you believe we betrayed you, because I knew you need anger to be powerful. Anger, and love."

And he pressed his lips to mine.

CHAPTER FORTY

Trey's kiss was the spark that started all life in the universe. It reached deep inside me, deep inside the earth, and latched on to a primordial force that was bigger and darker and more mysterious than anything. As he cupped my face and poured himself into me, my fire ignited for a final time, the heat stretching down my legs, deep within the earth, drawing up the cold shadows into the light at last.

The world shook.

Plaster and decorations and debris cascaded from the ceiling. Tables jerked across the gym. Glasses toppled from the bar and smashed against the floor. People might've been screaming, but I couldn't hear them over the roar of the god.

Two more bodies leaped into the circle, even as blue flame danced around them. Quinn and Ayaz. They pressed their bodies against me, stoking my fire with the warmth of their love.

The three of us ignited a flame that had burned inside the earth since its creation, since life first began. We drew it up and fed it on all the goodness we saved from a world of hell, until it rushed toward the surface, ready to gorge itself anew.

Ready to wake from slumber.

Trey tore his mouth from mine and grabbed my hand. "Now. Run!"

The four of us led the way to the doors. Students crowded around us, pumping their arms and waving the switches like they were on a victory parade.

As soon as every student and faculty member was outside, we slammed the door behind us, collapsing on the ground with giddy laughter. Quinn clutched me as I chortled and gasped. Trey and Ayaz slammed a heavy steel pole through the handles, locking the Eldritch Club inside with the rats that weren't rats.

The rats that carried pieces of the souls of Salem witches. The victims that had haunted Parris now worked as one hivemind. And they wanted this cycle of horror and violence to end.

A tremor rocked the earth, knocking my feet from under me. The gym groaned, and more brick and debris rained down. Students ran for the cover of the stage, but I sat, transfixed on the sight before me.

Flames licked through the gaps beneath the doors of the gym. With a final explosion of debris, a black obelisk smashed through the gym roof, shooting a pillar of flame into the sky.

The earth beneath me rumbled. The stage tilted, and students and teachers cried and ran toward the center of the field. Ayaz grabbed me under the arms and hauled me to my feet. "We have to go."

He wasn't wrong. We had to get outside of the triangle formed by the three pillars. Somehow I found the strength to churn my legs, running as fast as I could over the rolling ground, flanked by my Kings who refused to leave my side.

Behind us, the building crashed and the earth rumbled as the other two pillars drew up to their full height – thirty, fifty, a hundred feet above the school. Masonry rained down on the lawn as we dived and rolled out of the way. From the top of each pillar shot a flame of pure light – light of a color I couldn't identify – bending toward each other to create an arch of flame. Tendrils of light shot from the center, beaming across the field to stab at every Miskatonic student and teacher.

The engine of a spaceship.

"Argh!" Trey cried as the light touched his chest. He went to his knees, gasping.

"Shitfuckcunt." Quinn rolled on his back, clutching his hands to his chest. The look of terror on his face froze me in my tracks.

All around me, students fell, alive still, but in searing pain. And that light... it shimmered with an ethereal beauty that held my eyes even as I knew we had to get to safety.

I knew what I was looking at.

The god's voice rang in my ears. *I have kept my promise. I am taking from them what is mine.*

Thank you. Another voice rang in my ears. It wasn't the god, but it had a strange accent. Old-fashioned, almost... Puritan. *You have freed us.*

My rats. Their bodies were being emptied of their broken souls, ready to receive the god's new children.

Thank you, the god screamed inside my head as the ground shook and the lights retreated, focusing their beam on the gym to draw up his new children. *Their souls are black with the stain of their crimes. I will gorge myself upon this feast for all my journey, and in their new bodies they will become the most beautiful children.*

I bent down to help Trey to his feet. He clutched his chest and gasped for air, but he moved, he breathed. I didn't have time to ask him how he felt. I grabbed for Quinn and Ayaz, holding them, feeling the blood still pumping in their veins.

The world stopped.

For a moment, there was silence. The earth stopped shaking. The hum and hiss of the engine stalled. A stillness that spoke volumes hung around us.

Then the ground rumbled.

The god spoke.

CHAPTER FORTY-ONE

His voice rumbled across the earth, made of the screams of devoured souls, but also something else, something deeper and darker – a clap of thunder at the heart of a dying star.

And I knew this time, I wasn't the only one who heard his words.

I have slept beneath your planet since its forming. I have supped of you and taken in your essence, your feelingsss. As I have shaped your race, so too have you ssshaped me. But you are many, and I am one. I have hungered, but not for food. I have hungered for that which you made me understand. For love.

With a roar, the ground tore asunder. A giant crack split the lawn. Tendrils of inky darkness crept across the grass, snatching at limbs, raking claws of ice through warm, human skin, wanting, searching.

For me.

Go home, I screamed into the void. *You are not alone. Out there you will find your family again.*

The ground bucked and swayed. Three men held me upright. My three pillars, mirroring the pillars of light that now beamed high above Miskatonic.

I mussst have my light. Otherwise, I am all in darknessss.

The god's eyes turned over all of us. And he saw me. I was a beacon of light in his eternal void.

For so long he'd been in a power exchange with humans. Just as he'd taken from us, so had we drained him. He'd seen the earth born, known the rise and fall of millions of species before he grew to know humans. He'd been alone before Parris, so terribly alone, and now he had found someone who understood him as no one ever could, as even his children would never understand.

Tears streamed down my cheeks as I faced down the darkness, and the promise I knew I would keep.

He needed someone to be his star-twin, a fire to pilot his ship through the darkness.

He needed me.

CHAPTER FORTY-TWO

The tendrils snaked around me, caressing my skin. They wrapped around my ankles and wrists and pulled me toward the crack.

Hands wrapped around me, holding on tight.

"We're coming with you." Trey's voice echoed through the void. My three Kings pressed tighter against me, melding their bodies to mine, trying to slip into the god's embrace alongside me.

No.

No.

No no no no.

"Get back," I yelled, although whether it was my voice or the god's that screamed in their ears, I could not know.

"Not happening," Ayaz shouted.

"You didn't think we'd leave you to explore space all by your lonesome?" There was a smile in Quinn's voice, even as he trembled against me.

Trey's cheek pressed against mine. "Hazy, you've been pulling away from us all quarter. Don't think we didn't notice. We're not stupid, we figured out what you did. You promised yourself to the god, trading your life for ours. But what you can't seem to get through that stubborn, beautiful skull of yours is that our lives are nothing without you. We're not leaving you, and if that means we go to the stars together, then so be it."

The three of them tugged against me, holding me suspended between them. The two sides of me locked in bitter battle – the human side that loved and lingered, the monster who longed to burn his engines and set off with his star-lover.

"No!" I cried. "You need to live. This isn't for you – it's for me alone. It's what I deserve."

The god's thoughts probed my mind. *You and I are the same,* he whispered, his thoughts not screams this time but spoken in my own voice, one with me. *You have love for them, but they are not of you as I am. They will never feel what you and I feel. They are not the light in the darknessss.*

They are not the murderers.

I had to let them go.

Trey, Quinn, and Ayaz had already lived a thousand punishments for their crimes. I had yet to pay for mine.

They would have the chance to start over afresh. We'd made sure of that, with new identities for each student. But Hazel Waite still had a scar on her name. The police would close in. And Trey and Quinn and Ayaz – they swore they'd never leave me. If I stayed with them, their future would be tainted by my crimes.

I bent my neck to the heavens, to the stars. It wouldn't be so bad... I would be queen of a race of gods. I would uncover the vastness of the universe and its secrets. I would love them from afar, gorging myself of the memories we'd made.

I would never see the Kings again. I'd never feel Trey's lips on mine or breathe in the scent of Ayaz or laugh at Quinn's... Quinnness.

We won't even see the same stars.

I sucked in a breath.

"Trey. Quinn. Ayaz. I love you."

To the god inside my head. *I will join you.*

With a final burst of power, I slammed my arms down, breaking the grip of the Kings. The three of them crashed to the ground, their skin marred with a lattice of blue flame. I threw my arms wide and pitched myself toward the crack.

Quinn cried, "Hazy, you don't have to do this."

I opened my mouth to explain, to order him back, but all that rushed out was a torrent of screams that didn't belong to me. The voices of a thousand victims. My chest ached as the voices tore through my veins – a sound that burned like fire.

"You can't have her!" Trey screamed. "She's ours. Where she goes, we will follow."

My heart tore open. Behind me, Quinn let out a furious sob, and it took everything I had not to turn around again.

I lifted a leg. It was like moving through treacle. I stretched out my hands. My fingers brushed the void, and the god's love reached out to pull me in, to join our souls together for eternity—

Something crashed into me from the side. I staggered against the onslaught. The god flailed to catch me, but I hit the earth first. Someone kicked me in the side. I opened my eyes just as the assailant flung herself off me and raced toward the void.

Ms. West.

She stood before the god's mouth, her fingers trailing through the miasma. Black hair streamed behind her, inky and malevolence.

"This is my reward," she cried. "For decades I have toiled alone, my advances misunderstood by frail human minds, my experiments shunned. I was destined for greater things. I will be his star mistress."

Her mouth opened, and the god's screams poured into her.

"No," I gasped, rushing at her, crashing my body into her and wrestling her hands down. "I have to save them."

"You don't get this honor, Hazel Waite." Her eyes flashed with malevolence. She shoved me back, and the connection between us snapped.

As she fell into the god's mouth, the voice in my head burned with desire.

She issssss beautiful.

He'd never seen her before, not as she wished him to see her. Until now – as his voice filled her and he found in the depth of her blackened soul a light that would guide him. A light made not of fire, but of ice.

The darkness swallowed her. A light of a new color that still didn't exist on our spectrum shot from the three pillars. The beams crossed in the sky, writing a symbol with the light of a star.

Rebecca Nurse's sigil. A map, charting their course across the cosmos.

The ground bucked, throwing up jagged rocks.

"Get out of the triangle!" I yelled at everyone and no one.

Students scrambled over the chairs and headed for the trees, falling over each other in their desperate race for safety. I couldn't feel my legs, but I must've been running, for Trey and Quinn and Ayaz formed a triangle around me.

All I heard was the puff of their breath. All I felt were their hands on me.

Skin to skin – warm, protective.

Mine.

We crashed into the trees and kept on going. "Get to the garden!" Trey yelled. Students passed the shout. Balls of fire burst around us, tossing ancient trees like Pixy Stix.

Down, down, down, we slipped and skidded on the stone steps. Courtney screamed as she fell. Quinn picked her up, threw her over his shoulder, kept running.

Rock and branches rained down on us. A crack appeared down the steps as the earth cracked and splintered. We huddled together under the rotunda, necks craned to the sky. The rocks tumbled from the cliff as the crack grew, spreading like a black web across the ground.

The sigil grew and grew, its fire like a magnet pulling the

pillars toward it. The earth roared as the top of the peninsula broke away. The pillars rose into the sky. Whole trees toppled off the edges. Beneath, a great cone of black stone stretched like the tail of a comet, its tip glowing with an eerie light.

The god's ship.

A lump of solid, cyclopean stone, carrying Miskatonic Prep and all its evil away with it.

As it rose high, high, high, it dragged the heat from inside me. The last vestiges of my power tore from my fingers, pouring into the three pillars to fuel the god's assent. My flame would go with them on their star-journey.

My legs failed me. My head swam. Faces danced in front of my eyes, but I no longer knew if they were real or imagined. A voice called my name, soft and sweet. "Hazel…"

Dante's voice.

Calling me home.

I closed my eyes. I gave myself over to the void of my own making. My power was spent. I had nothing left but love in my heart.

Darkness took me.

CHAPTER FORTY-THREE

From the darkness emerged a light that was more than light – a light that gave off a shimmer that made my heart light and made all my problems a million miles away. In the back of my mind, something itched – a sense that I was supposed to be somewhere else, doing something important. But when I tried to grasp at the thought, it trickled through my fingers.

Two figures emerged from the light, their forms resolving into limbs, into smiles that I thought I'd never see again.

"Mom?" My breath came out in a wheeze. "Dante?"

In reply, my mother stopped in her tracks, opening her arms for me. I threw myself at her, allowing her to envelop me in her embrace. Warmth radiated from her skin – the kind of warmth that soaked into my bones.

"My baby girl," she whispered into my hair.

I pressed my lips against her neck, feeling the warmth of her skin, tasting the richness of her perfume – strawberry and lime, a zesty smell that always made me feel safe and loved.

"We've been watching you," Dante's deep voice reverberated through my bones, grabbing my heart and squeezing it tight. "I saw you got a tattoo. Pretty shitty work – I hope you choose a better artist next time."

Laughing, I fell into Dante's arms. His eyes crinkled at the edges, and my heart skipped. All the things I'd felt for him over the years rushed me at once – all that teen longing had gone, replaced by the love that underpinned it all.

He grinned as he fist-bumped me.

"I'm dead, right?" I looked around at the world made of light. "I mean, you guys aren't ghosts. You're chilling out in heaven. But then why am I here? I should be in the place with the more sulphuric interior decorating scheme."

My mother shrugged. "You could be in heaven, honey. Or this could be the lack of oxygen messing with your brain. But I'm holding you again, so let's not waste a moment questioning it."

She crushed me to her chest, and my heart cracked open. She was right – to hold her again, smell her familiar scent, feel her arms squeezing me... it was all that mattered.

Only...

I pulled back, studying her beautiful face beaming with love. "Why do you still love me? Don't you know what I did? I'm the reason you're here. I'm your—"

I choked on the word *murderer*.

"Hazel Waite, you listen to me." Mom wagged her finger at me in mock annoyance. "You're my *daughter*, and that's what you'll always be to me. This was not your fault. Dante and I... we knew what we did would hurt you, but we did it anyway. Because our lives were so shitty that to grab on to one moment of happiness was worth all the pain."

"We're sorry 'bout that," Dante grinned.

"You can't... you can't *apologize* after I—"

Mom gave me one of her stern looks, and I snapped my mouth shut. "No more. You can't carry around this anger – not for us, and certainly not for yourself. You've been given something beautiful, and I expect you to enjoy it."

I shook my head. "You're wrong. You sit up here in heaven or wherever the fuck, but back on earth there are consequences. I *killed* you. I have to answer for my crimes. That's the only way I'll be free of the guilt."

"Have you not answered for them already?" Dante planted his lips against mine.

His kiss was pure light, so different from my King's, whose lips bore the scars of their inner darkness.

The only thing was... I *needed* that darkness.

Dante's light was not what I wanted any more. If his kiss was meant to draw me closer, then it did the exact opposite – it closed the door forever on what we had. I loved him still, but not in that way.

Not the way I loved Trey, Quinn, and Ayaz.

He pulled back, and his smile told me that was exactly his plan. "Goodbye, Hazel. Or should I say, *Hazy?* You're going to be amazing."

"She already is." My mother's smile faded at the edges as her face melted into the light. A ringing sounded in my ears as she drew away, as the light pulled me back, back, away from them. "I love you, darling."

I stretched out my arms to her, but she was already far away.

"Oh, and Hazy?" Dante called after me, his voice quiet against the roar of the light.

"Yeah?" The light pushed in around me, flooding my veins. I could barely see him anymore. My head throbbed, and a pleasing numbness started in my fingers, spreading down my arms, toward my heart.

"Don't eat *all* the bacon."

I opened my mouth to reply, but the numbness closed around my heart, and my flame became the light.

CHAPTER FORTY-FOUR

"Wakey, wakey, lazy Hazy."

A voice called me back from the white void. A dream? I had a sense that dreams didn't belong in the place where I was, but that voice kept tugging. My mother's face faded back into pricks of light. Stars sprinkled across my vision, even though my eyes were closed.

I opened one eye, then the other. Oh, this was so much better than a dream.

Quinn's face hung above mine, his lips curled into a shit-eating grin.

I opened my mouth to speak, but he covered it in his. Talk about the kiss of life. Quinn's lips on mine shot electricity straight into my veins. I felt invincible, like I could leap a tall building in a single bound or run a marathon or something.

Well, maybe not a marathon. My head was throbbing something awful. But I could at least get out of... wherever we were.

Quinn pulled away, knitting his fingers in mine. He had the same idea. "Come with me if you want to live."

I burst out laughing. It felt good to laugh.

We crawled out from beneath the rubble. As the haze cleared,

I made out the other students, coughing as they pulled each other free of the collapsed rotunda. Two faces stopped my heart – Trey and Ayaz, beaming at me. I collapsed against the guys. Hands roamed my body, squeezing me, probing me, checking I was alive. Every caress lit my veins, but the fire that burned there had no otherworldly power behind it. It was just pure, old-fashioned, totally normal – an utterly *human* love.

I'm alive.

"Hazy, Hazy, Hazy," Quinn murmured my nickname over and over, like a mantra. Like a spell. Ayaz buried his lips into my hair while Trey's arms circled us all, an immovable force against the world.

"Help me stand," I groaned.

Hands lifted me. Not just the Kings, but others. Loretta on my left, a long cut down one side of her face. Greg on the other side, his white-blonde hair streaked with dirt. Behind him, Andre and Sadie, steadying us all. Zehra's beautiful smile peeked in over their shoulders, as well as Deborah's concerned features.

"Hey, Hazel," Zehra grinned. "Deborah and I decided to stop in to witness the lift-off."

I hung between them all, letting their love and relief wash over me. Time had no meaning in this embrace. Slowly, all around me, more students crawled over to join us, crushing me under the weight of their freedom.

"Are we alive?" Courtney asked. A bruise darkened her chest from where the bullet had penetrated. Luckily, she'd already mostly healed before the god took away her immortality.

"I propose a test." Ayaz lifted a sliver of rock and drew it across his wrist, leaving a thin cut in his skin. After a moment, blood trickled from the wound, the red lurid against the dusting that coated all of us.

We stared at that cut, a hundred silent prayers to a departing deity swirling in the air around us.

The wound did not close. Ayaz's body was no longer immortal

– the god had gone and taken his healing power with him. The only thing that would heal Ayaz now was time.

And love.

As the realization rippled through the crowd, students whooped and hollered, and all the hugging began anew.

Trey and Quinn steadied me as we picked our way back up the cliff, first collecting our bags of cash and passports from the mouth of the secret passage where we had them ready. The staircase had been obliterated and the shape of the cliff much changed. Where the grotto had once been was now a pile of rubble, which we used to scramble up. I was surprised at how intact some things still were. There were still trees, although many of the rocky protrusions had been smoothed over. The peninsula, it appeared, had a few extra angles and dimensions, long-hidden beneath a facade of normalcy.

The woods ended on the edge of the school field. We stepped out of the shade of the trees and beheld an incredible, eerie sight.

Ayaz swore. Quinn burst out laughing. Trey's hand squeezed mine so hard my knuckles cracked.

I'd expected a fiery pit, or the entire peninsula to have collapsed into the sea. To be fair, there were a few fires dotted here and there across the lawn, as well as some scattered shards of the black stone pushed up through the field.

But apart from these, the school grounds were exactly as we'd left them – the concrete drive snaking into the trees. The old fountain. The playing fields and hedges of rose bushes. Trees dotted the edges. Everything was exactly as it was.

Except for the Miskatonic Preparatory buildings, which were nowhere to be seen.

Gone were the stone pillars and gargoyles upon gargoyles. Gone was the house of nightmares, the center of a wheel of horror and violence that had turned for centuries.

I kicked off a boot and took a cautious step forward, allowing my toes to sink into soft grass before I pushed my weight down, not certain it wasn't a mirage.

The ground held me. It was all real. It was as if Parris' home had never existed.

"Where..."

I turned to Ayaz. If anyone could fathom what had happened here, it was him.

"Not being an expert..." Ayaz rubbed the stubble that dotted his jawline. "Is it possible that the god's ship didn't entirely exist within our known universe? When it left, it only took what belonged to it, and so the house is gone but not the land that was always part of the earth. Something like that."

I shrugged. It was as good a reason as any. Frankly, I didn't care. Miskatonic Prep was gone forever, and that was good enough for me.

"What happens now?" Courtney said.

I leaned back in the grass, relishing the tickle of each blade against my skin. It was such a luxury to just look at the sky.

"As soon as I can lift my legs of my own accord, we're walking into Arkham and going our separate ways. You all have your new identifications, and we'll share out the money. You know what to do – get the fuck out of here before the FBI descends, and make a new life for yourselves. Whatever you do, don't follow me, because I'm turning myself over to the police."

"You... what?"

I sat up, meeting the eyes of my three guys. Quinn looked completely confused. Ayaz's dark eyes shone with new fear. But Trey... his eyes narrowed with realization. He knew exactly what I was thinking.

"What happened here today doesn't erase the past. I accepted the invitation to Derleth Academy in part because it enabled me to continue to run from my guilt. But I'm not running anymore. I committed a crime. I can't go back and erase that, so I need to accept responsibility for it."

Quinn shook his head. "You can't. I won't let you."

I shook my head. "This is my choice to make. I—"

Sirens screamed along the driveway, cutting me off.

A hollow laugh escaped my throat. They'd beaten me to it. Of course, the universe found a way to take even that choice away from me.

At least twenty police, emergency vehicles, and state troopers pulled onto the field. Men and women clad in black kevlar leaped out of the back of an Army vehicle and fanned out around the perimeter, advancing on the spot where the school had once been, machine guns raised.

Oh well, if you can't beat 'em...

Grinning, I waved at our visitors.

A man in a dark grey suit walked over to us. "I'm Agent Anderson. I'm guessing you're students at the school. What happened here? Where did the buildings go?"

"Uh..." Quinn paused. "Sinkhole?"

I couldn't help it. I broke down laughing. Beside me, Ayaz's stomach rumbled as the laughter caught on, then came Trey's chortle. All four of us rolled on the grass, clutching our stomachs as tears rolled down our cheeks. The laughter caught, and the entire school broke down into uncontrollable giggles.

A fucking sinkhole!

"Is something funny?" Agent Anderson demanded.

"I think they've had a terrible fright." His partner squatted to peer at Courtney as her shoulders shook in uncontrollable mirth. "They might be delirious. Get the paramedics over here. All these kids should be thoroughly checked out."

"I think you need to get that sinkhole checked out." I wiped my eyes. My stomach hurt from all the laughing.

It felt good to laugh. It felt like I hadn't really laughed in a long time.

Paramedics rushed over, dragging stretchers and medical kits. They sank down in the grass, talking to the students. Agent

Anderson fixed me with a laser stare. "They'll take you to the hospital and get you checked out. After that, the FBI wants to have a word with you all. Especially you, Hazel Waite."

Shit. "You're FBI? And you know who I am?"

He nodded. "That's the 'Agent' part of my name. Don't look so worried. Your friend Deborah Pratt contacted me some time ago. We've been monitoring strange activity in this area for several years. At first, her story sounded unbelievable, but as we learned more, it became clear she was at least telling the partial truth. We knew something big was happening when all the parents of past students of Miskatonic Prep started to lose their fortunes. Then, the IRS informed us that large sums of money were withdrawn from their kids' bank accounts, all on the same night. Tonight, we witnessed something incredible, so we thought we'd better get up here."

My chest tightened. "What did you see?"

"A weather phenomenon," Agent Anderson's eyes sparkled. "To the untrained eye, it might have looked like a cosmic deity blasting off from our planet in a ship made of black stone and powered by human souls, but that's obviously completely ridiculous."

"Obviously," I agreed, my throat tightening.

He nodded. "As long as you and your classmates can attest that you saw a weather phenomenon, stay out of the papers, and help us curb any potential hysteria about other things that *definitely didn't happen* here, we can help you. I understand these students need money, new identities, perhaps..." his gaze fell on the tattered robes hanging from my frame. "...college placement?"

"Yes. I mean, for the others, yes. We've already got fake passports and visas, but if you could help them with something more official that would be amazing. But not me. You probably know me already. My name is definitely in your database from a little arson back in Philadelphia."

"Of course." That kind smile never left his face. "Hazel Waite, the brave student who saved her classmates from a freak weather event."

"No, I mean, two people died in that fire. You need to clap me in handcuffs and—"

But Anderson kept gazing at me with that kind expression. "Crimes go unsolved every day in this country, Ms. Waite. Arson is especially difficult to prove, and convictions are rare. I don't see the need to waste the court's time in this case."

Paramedics swarmed around me. A woman lifted my arms, studying my face. "Is anything wrong? Does anything hurt or feel broken?"

Good question. I aimed my palm at the tree and tried to call upon the flame inside me. All I felt was a fizzing spark, like a lighter trying without enough fuel. Nothing ignited.

I lowered my hand and smiled. "Nope. Nothing is wrong at all."

EPILOGUE

Five years later

"Arf!" Fergus barked from the backseat as his face smushed against the window, tongue licking the glass.

"I can't believe they still haven't fixed this road," Quinn muttered as he yanked the wheel around the corner, sliding out the back wheels of the car.

"Don't fucking do that," Trey muttered from the front seat. "We've got precious cargo."

Acting on instinct, Ayaz reached across the seat to hold his hand over my belly, which now protruded so significantly I couldn't see my Docs over top of it. My last midwife said I shouldn't be wearing Docs while I was pregnant, and tried to shove my feet into orthopedic horrors. Big mistake. Luckily, Trey managed to smooth things over with the agency and they agreed not to sue us. My new midwife never mentioned my choice of footwear.

Smart woman.

I knitted my fingers in Ayaz's, pressing his palm against my skin just as the baby kicked. The way my Turk's face lit up as he felt the tiny limb made the pain of it wriggling around on my spinal column worth it.

This little guy or girl was a fighter, just like me.

Even though I was in my twenty-fifth week of swollen ankles and morning sickness, I still couldn't quite believe I was growing a real-life human inside me. Not just any human – a child of my Kings. We'd decided early on not to test for paternity unless it was medically required. I'd put Trey's name down on the birth certificate for the associated benefits, but it could have belonged to any of them. It didn't matter. Our baby belonged to all of us.

We all had a new name now – the same last name. When I'd created my new identity, I'd chosen to take my mother's maiden name, Pratt. The guys had followed suit. It wasn't the same as being able to legally marry, but it made us feel like a family.

Also, 'Pratt' described Quinn perfectly. And now our baby would share it.

Our baby.

I never thought I wanted children. The thought of a tiny parasite growing inside my belly for nine months before being unleashed in a fountain of blood sounded far too close to everything I endured at Miskatonic Prep. But the day that strip turned pink changed my life. Now, I counted down the days until we got to meet a new little human.

Ayaz squeezed my hand. He never recovered his memories – Ms. West had been too thorough – but it was okay. We made new ones. "We don't have to go today if it's too much. They'll understand. It's not too late to turn around."

"Speak for yourself, Ataturk." Quinn's hands yanked the wheel around the next corner. The back wheel spun out again, kicking up a spray of loose gravel. "There ain't exactly anywhere to turn around."

"Arf!" Fergus agreed, throwing his head over the back of the seat to lick my face.

"I'm fine." I forced a smile as I shoved Fergus' head away. "Really. I want to see what they've done to the place."

It was only a half-lie. I did want to see what had become of the place that still haunted my nightmares. All these years since we were carried down from the peninsula in the back of an ambulance into the arms of the FBI, Miskatonic Prep shadowed us. It lurked in the corner of the dorm room I shared with Trey at college. It hunted in the woods where Quinn ran his wildlife safari, it watched and waited as Ayaz graduated *summa cum laude* with his architecture degree and opened a practice. It lay in wait as we went to the animal shelter for Trey to pick our first puppy, who now hopped around the back of the car, panting on Ayaz's head.

Branches scraped across the roof of the car as we rounded the last corner. I caught peeks of grey stone through the trees, and a knot twisted in my stomach. A shining new sign at the gate read. "Welcome to Miskatonic Preparatory Academy. All welcome."

Fuck. They even kept the name.

The car fell silent as we all stared at that sign, as the weight of what it meant to be back sank in. We pulled into a parking lot beside a row of cars. There were the familiar fancy rides, of course – a Lamborghini splattered with dust from the road. A Porsche with a scrape down the door from where it had clung too close to the cliff. But interspersed with them were battered pickup trucks and used cars. Against the backdrop of grandeur, these vehicles seemed silly. But the fact they were there at all was a good sign.

The new school buildings loomed above us – the classroom and faculty wings, the dorms, the gymnasium with its high stone wall. It was uncanny how alike they were to Parris' old home. I searched the windows of the dormitory, finding those that had once housed my friends and my enemies. The tree that had let me out of Trey's room on more than one occasion no longer existed.

The stone steps, where I'd first laid eyes on Trey Bloomberg all those years ago, still stretched up toward twin wooden doors. The very place where he'd warned me away and laughed at my discomfort.

A shudder ran through my body. We thought we'd banished

the ghosts, but would we ever truly be free of the horrors that had chased us?

This is a terrible idea. We should never have come.

The baby squirmed in agreement.

The door flung open. I half expected to see Ms. West's Morticia Addams gown sweeping over the marble tiles, her hard eyes boring into my soul. Instead, two very familiar but very different figures bounded down the stairs toward us.

"Hazy!"

Greg's academic gown fluttered around his shoulders. Behind him, Andre beamed – his broad shoulder blocking my view into the building behind them. Greg kissed my cheeks. "You look amazing. You're positively glowing. Pregnancy agrees with you."

"It doesn't agree with that fucking access road," I muttered, steadying myself against him as a fresh wave of nausea slammed me.

"We'd better get her inside." Trey took my shoulders. Ayaz came up on the other side and held the door open for me. Fergus wiggled out of the seat and bounded out first, barking in excitement as he raced to sniff the flower beds. Quinn rushed in from the car, carrying this stupid tote bag he insisted I have with me at all times, filled with heat pads and herbal supplements and whale noise that helped the baby grow.

Honestly, what happened to my badass bullies? They used to be the Kings of the school. Now my husbands are fussing over me like old maids. When the baby comes, they're going to be even worse.

I say husbands, but we weren't officially married. You couldn't do that... yet. Tillie was running for senator, and she said she was going to change the law, but I doubt she'd get that one past the House. Not even she had the power to work miracles.

Greg's hand on my arm trembled with excitement as he led us slowly up the stairs. "I can't wait for you to see what we've done with the place. It's okay to leave the dog outside."

He flung open the doors and swept us into a high, airy atrium.

My breath sucked in, and for a moment I imagined myself six years ago, stepping into Derleth Academy for the first time. My fingers flew to my pocket, where a brand new iPhone rested against my leg. I remembered clutching my old one for dear life on my first day here before Ms. West slipped it into her robe.

I remembered Trey's smirk, the way his breath brushed my skin as he christened me 'New Meat.'

"—tried to choose materials that closely matched the original structure," Greg was explaining, pointing out details in the moldings. "Of course, we made improvements. The biggest one being laying cable up the peninsula so the entire school has one of the best wifi networks in the state. You can't get lost in the woods around here, and all students have access to university databases and academic resources."

Trey pointed to an empty space above the stairs, where the enormous electronic scoreboards used to sit. "No merit points?"

"Hell no," Andre said, in his deep, rumbling voice. My skin rippled with pleasure from the sound of it. I threw my arms around him. It had been too long.

Over the last few years, after the FBI and some of our class alumni organized enough funds to put him in therapy for his trauma, Andre started to talk. Not a lot, and not often, but every word was a gift. He and Sadie taught us all the basics of sign language so we could use our hands to speak to them as well.

"We decided we didn't want that kind of competitive atmosphere," Greg said. "Don't get me wrong – this isn't a place for lazy kids. But we wanted students to focus on improving themselves. So instead, we track individual progress against a set of self-defined parameters. It's more admin, but it seems to be working. We have one of the best success rates for college acceptance in the country, which is unheard of in such a new school."

Trey smiled. "Well, new-ish."

"Right. If you come this way—" The bell rang, cutting Greg

off. Doors banged and the entire building shook with the rumble
of hundreds of feet. Students erupted into the halls.

I noticed the changes immediately. No longer was the student
body of Miskatonic Prep a sea of petulant sameness. Now, I saw
uniforms resplendent with Native American adornments, faces of
all colors and shapes and sizes laughing together. Accents and
languages from all corners of the earth rose through the space in a
polyglot symphony. An ocean of diversity, wild for its unusualness,
beautiful because of what it meant for the future.

As students raced past on their way to their next classes, they
high-fived Greg and fist-bumped Andre.

As I followed Greg and Andre down the hall, posters adver-
tising a school LGBT club and a multicultural celebration week
jumped out at me. All things that would have been completely
foreign at the school I attended. He showed us the dormitories,
which had been remodeled. Instead of the sumptuous suites for
the richest students, there were collaborative spaces where
students worked together. There was no staff in the dorms – laundry, cleaning, and cooking was all done by the students.

We reached the end of the hall. My hand gripped the
balustrade. A hole in the floor gaped darkness, with a row of
narrow stairs like sharpened teeth ready to swallow me. The basement. The dungeon.

The baby squirmed. A fresh wave of nausea washed over me.

I squared my shoulders and plunged into the void. Down into
the gloom. Only, as soon as my foot hit the third step, a light
flickered on.

"Sensors," Greg grinned. "We don't want anyone fumbling
around in the dark."

The dungeon wasn't exactly as it had been. It was only around
half the size, chopping off the end of the hall where the secret
passage had been. I guessed Greg and Andre had no use for those
old remnants.

Only, they did. Framed pictures on the walls showed some of

the previous alumni and the members of the senior Eldritch Club, along with news headlines about their downfall and strange disappearance – hundreds of the most powerful people in America suddenly missing without a trace, believed to have been a mass hit by a Honduran drug cartel ripped off by the Eldritch Club. There was a whole display about the conspiracy theories abounding on the internet about the 'weather phenomenon' – suggesting it was everything from a UFO landing to a Russian missile test gone wrong.

Without mentioning the god or the dead students, the museum painted a sad picture of the school's history. I peered at the letters laminated under glass, each written by past scholarship students detailing the bullying they suffered. All this next to smiling images of the school's elitist alumni.

"I wanted to make sure we always remembered what division does to us," Greg whispered. "That way the students knew why we do things the way we do here."

I squeezed him back. "It's perfect."

His mobile phone buzzed. For a moment, I was transported back in time, and my stomach clenched, thinking a teacher would come by and punish him for breaking the rules. I grabbed Trey's arm before remembering that Greg was the headmaster now, that he'd set the school up with world-class wifi.

Greg peeked at his phone. "They've all arrived now. Let's go."

He led us back up the stairs and through the dorms, throwing open one of the double sets of French doors leading out onto the quad. I staggered back in surprise, gripping Ayaz to steady myself.

People filled every spare inch of the quad. Familiar faces, many of whom I hadn't seen since the day we clambered up from the grotto.

"It's Hazel!" someone cried. Conversations broke off as faces turned toward me, beaming as if I was some famous celebrity. The guys did a good job of keeping them at bay as we moved toward the dining hall, but there was one face that surged forward whom I really wanted to see.

"Hazel."

Her hair was shorter now and dyed a luxurious brown. But I'd recognize those feline features and that haughty mouth anywhere.

"Courtney Haynes."

"It's Courtney McMillan now," Courtney flipped her hair and smirked at my Docs. "I see you haven't changed a bit."

I took in her designer outfit and feline features. "Likewise."

Courtney smiled then – a genuine smile I didn't think I'd ever seen before. "You might be surprised. I built a sustainable fashion label. All our production comes from ethical factories that pay a living wage to women in Ghana." She glanced across the quad, nodding to Loretta. "My business partner was over there just last month setting up to fund schools and scholarships to local female entrepreneurs."

"Wow. That's... um... that's..." I laughed. "For the first time ever, you've rendered me absolutely speechless."

Greg rang the bell and invited us into the dining hall for dinner. The chefs had laid out an incredible banquet. No fancy food here, just good old fashioned fare. Greg had put in a special order with the chef for me – a side of bacon strips, piled up into a mountain and drenched with maple syrup.

We dug in while Nancy and Barclay delivered a short lecture. They'd taken over Vincent's company following his disappearance and built a probe that was tracking the object now known only by its designation CTHU-LU as it tracked across the sky. "It passed out of our galaxy last month. From now on, gathering data will be much more difficult, but we'll do what we can."

The god was going home. With his star-mistress at his side. I wondered how the Eldritch Club enjoyed being in the bodies of rats.

I still felt as though I got away with murder. I lived with that guilt every day. Imagining my mother and Dante in their void of light helped, but not all the time. Sometimes I still dreamed of flames. Sometimes I imagined I heard the god's voice, but it was usually just the wind whistling through the trees around our mountainside home.

A few months ago, shortly after I finished reading my mother's diaries, my fire returned. That frightened me, especially with a child on the way. Deborah believed it was the pregnancy that ignited the flame inside me. "You have a baby to protect," she said.

What if our baby carried the flame?

Across the room, Courtney met my eyes. She nodded her head. I nodded back, touching my fingers to the tattoo on my wrist. A few years ago, I covered the scar with a *nazar* tattoo – protection from the evil eye. It felt appropriate.

When the plates were cleared away, Greg invited us to a dance. We carried torches and chanted words of magic that the Eldritch Club had made their own – reclaimed now as school songs – down to the old pleasure garden overlooking the ocean.

Students were allowed to join us. We danced around a bonfire, toasting Paul's memory and congratulating each other on the positive changes made in the world. Fergus was the real star, splashing around in the grotto and rolling over to submit his belly for pats. I got into a heated argument about spontaneous combustion with an earnest young scholarship student from New Zealand. It was one of the greatest nights of my life.

After everything that Miskatonic Prep had stolen from these people, here they all were – well, most of them – to hand over the keys of power to a new generation, one that would hopefully not make the same mistakes. The blood spilled for their freedom would not be in vain.

I held my hand to my stomach. Trey kissed my forehead.

"Our child will be King of this school one day," he said.

"What if it's a girl?" I teased.

"Queen, then. Or gender nonbinary ruler."

"Our child will be whatever they want to be," Ayaz asserted.

"As long as they're as hot as I am," Quinn added.

I gathered my Kings in my arms. We faced off against a cosmic deity, parents who tried to sacrifice them, and broken a cycle of horror and violence. Compared to that, parenting would be a snap.

Bring it on, little fire-baby.

Bring it the fuck on.

THE END

Psst. I have a secret.

Are you ready?

I'm Mackenzie Malloy, and everyone thinks they know who I am.

Five years ago, I disappeared.

No one has seen me or my family outside the walls of Malloy Manor since.

But now I'm coming to reclaim my throne:

The Ice Queen of Stonehurst Prep is back.

Standing between me and my everything?

Three things can bring me down:

The sweet guy who wants answers from his former friend.

The rock god who wants to f*ck me.

The king who'll crush me before giving up his crown.

They think they can ruin me, wreck it all, but I won't let them.

I'm not the Mackenzie Eli used to know.

Hot boys and rock gods like Gabriel won't win me over.
And just like Noah, I'll kill to keep my crown.

I'm just a poor little rich girl with the stolen life.
I'm here to tear down three princes,
before they destroy me.

Read now:
http://books2read.com/mystolenlife

Grab a free copy of *Cabinet of Curiosities* – a Steffanie Holmes compendium of short stories and bonus scenes when you sign up for updates with the Steffanie Holmes newsletter.

FROM THE AUTHOR

I first read HP Lovecraft's stories when I was 15 years old. I'd recently discovered heavy metal music in that obnoxious way all teenagers uncover things and feel as though they alone under-stand them on a deep and profound level. When I learned my favourite song was inspired by the short story *The Call of Cthulhu*, I had to know more. What was this word, Cthulhu? What was this mystery I had to unravel?

What I found was a world of cosmic horror that was both beguiling and terrifying. No one can write horror quite like Love-craft. Usually, in a horror story, the fear is of the unknown – as soon as the monster is uncovered and unmasked, it ceases to be scary. It can be defeated. In Lovecraft, the uncovering is the most terrifying part.

(The stories are not without their problems. They can be clunky in places, weighed down by the numerous adjectives Lovecraft adored so much. And the racism... yikes. Because of this, I didn't feel right approaching Miskatonic Prep colourblind, ignoring the fact there isn't a disparity of representation in elite schools that's part of a systemic culture of keeping certain people on the top.)

Numerous writers over the years have contributed to and

expanded Lovecraft's Cthulhu Mythos, and it's been an utter joy to add my own voice to that body of work. To Mr. Lovecraft, I hope my work captures the spirit of yours, even if it might be a bit modern and sentimental for your tastes.

Hazy's story has been a dream of mine for decades, and because of you, dear reader, I got to make it happen. So thank you for coming along for the ride with me.

This series would not have been possible without the awesome people in my life. To the cantankerous drummer husband, for making me rewrite this manuscript until it was perfect and for being my lighthouse.

To Kit, Bri, Elaina, Katya, Emma, and Jamie, for all the writerly encouragement and advice. To Meg, for the epically helpful editing job, and to Amanda for the stunning covers. To Sam and Iris, for the daily Facebook shenanigans that help keep me sane while I spend my days stuck at home covered in cats.

To you, the reader, for going on this journey with me, even though it's led to some dark places. If you're enjoying *Kings of Miskatonic Prep* and want to read more from me, check out my dark reverse harem high school romance series, *Stonehurst Prep* – http://books2read.com/mystolenlife. This series is contemporary romance (no ghosts or vampires), but it's pretty dark and strange and mysterious, with a badass heroine and three guys who will break your heart and melt your panties. You will LOVE it – you'll find a short preview on the next page.

Another series of mine you might enjoy is *Manderley Academy*. Book 1 is *Ghosted* and it's a classic gothic tale of ghosts and betrayal, creepy old houses and three beautifully haunted guys with dark secrets. Plus, a kickass curvy heroine. Check it out: http://books2read.com/manderley1

Every week I send out a newsletter to fans – it features a spooky story about a real-life haunting or strange criminal case that has inspired one of my books, as well as news about upcoming releases and a free book of bonus scenes called *Cabinet of Curiosities*. To get on the mailing list all you gotta do is head to my website: http://www.steffanieholmes.com/newsletter

If you want to hang out and talk about all things *Shunned*, my readers are sharing their theories and discussing the book over in my Facebook group, Books That Bite. Come join the fun.

I'm so happy you enjoyed this story! I'd love it if you wanted to leave a review on Amazon or Goodreads. It will help other readers to find their next read.

Thank you, thank you! I love you heaps! Until next time.

Steff

MORE FROM THE AUTHOR OF SHUNNED

From the author of *Shunned*, the Amazon top-20 bestselling bully romance readers are calling, "The greatest mindf**k of 2019," comes this new dark contemporary high school reverse harem romance.

Psst. I have a secret.

Are you ready?

I'm Mackenzie Malloy, and everyone thinks they know who I am.

Five years ago, I disappeared.

No one has seen me or my family outside the walls of Malloy Manor since.
But now I'm coming to reclaim my throne:
The Ice Queen of Stonehurst Prep is back.

Standing between me and my everything?
Three things can bring me down:
The sweet guy who wants answers from his former friend.
The rock god who wants to f*ck me.
The king who'll crush me before giving up his crown.

They think they can ruin me, wreck it all, but I won't let them.
I'm not the Mackenzie Eli used to know.
Hot boys and rock gods like Gabriel won't win me over.
And just like Noah, I'll kill to keep my crown.

I'm just a poor little rich girl with the stolen life.
I'm here to tear down three princes,
before they destroy me.

Read now:
http://books2read.com/mystolenlife

EXCERPT: MY STOLEN LIFE

Stonehurst Prep

I roll over in bed and slam against a wall.

Huh? Odd.

My bed isn't pushed against a wall. I must've twisted around in my sleep and hit the headboard. I do thrash around a lot, especially when I have bad dreams, and tonights was particularly gruesome. My mind stretches into the silence, searching for the tendrils of my nightmare. *I'm lying in bed and some dark shadow comes and lifts me up, pinning my arms so they hurt. He drags me downstairs to my mother, slumped in her favorite chair. At first, I think she passed out drunk after a night at the club, but then I see the dark pool expanding around her feet, staining the designer rug.*

I see the knife handle sticking out of her neck.

I see her glassy eyes rolled toward the ceiling.

I see the window behind her head, and my own reflection in the glass, my face streaked with blood, my eyes dark voids of pain and hatred.

But it's okay now. It was just a dream. It's—

OW.

I hit the headboard again. I reach down to rub my elbow, and my hand grazes a solid wall of satin. On my other side.

What the hell?

I open my eyes into a darkness that is oppressive and complete, the kind of darkness I'd never see inside my princess bedroom with its flimsy purple curtains letting in the glittering skyline of the city. The kind of darkness that folds in on me, pressing me against the hard, un-bedlike surface I lie on.

Now the panic hits.

I throw out my arms, kick with my legs. I hit walls. Walls all around me, lined with satin, dense with an immense weight pressing from all sides. Walls so close I can't sit up or bend my knees. I scream, and my scream bounces back at me, hollow and weak.

I'm in a coffin. I'm in a motherfucking coffin, and I'm *still alive*.

I scream and scream and scream. The sound fills my head and stabs at my brain. I know all I'm doing is using up my precious oxygen, but I can't make myself stop. In that scream I lose myself, and every memory of who I am dissolves into a puddle of terror.

When I do stop, finally, I gasp and pant, and I taste blood and stale air on my tongue. A cold fear seeps into my bones. Am I dying? My throat crawls with invisible bugs. Is this what it feels like to die?

I hunt around in my pockets, but I'm wearing purple pajamas, and the only thing inside is a bookmark Daddy gave me. I can't see it of course, but I know it has a quote from Julius Caesar on it. *Alea iacta est. The die is cast.*

Like fuck it is.

I think of Daddy, of everything he taught me – memories too dark to be obliterated by fear. Bile rises in my throat. I swallow, choke it back. Daddy always told me our world is forged in blood. I might be only thirteen, but I know who he is, what he's capable of. I've heard the whispers. I've seen the way people hurry to appease him whenever he enters a room. I've had the lessons from Antony in what to do if I find myself alone with one of Daddy's enemies.

Of course, they never taught me what to do if one of those enemies *buries me alive*.

I can't give up.

I claw at the satin on the lid. It tears under my fingers, and I pull out puffs of stuffing to reach the wood beneath. I claw at the surface, digging splinters under my nails. Cramps arc along my arm from the awkward angle. I know it's hopeless; I know I'll never be able to scratch my way through the wood. Even if I can, I *feel* the weight of several feet of dirt above me. I'd be crushed in moments. But I have to try.

I'm my father's daughter, and this is not how I die.

I claw and scratch and tear. I lose track of how much time passes in the tiny space. My ears buzz. My skin weeps with cold sweat.

A noise reaches my ears. A faint shifting. A scuffle. A scrape and thud above my head. Muffled and far away.

Someone piling the dirt in my grave.

Or maybe...

...maybe someone digging it out again.

Fuck, fuck, please.

"Help." My throat is hoarse from screaming. I bang the lid with my fists, not even feeling the splinters piercing my skin. "Help me!"

THUD. Something hits the lid. The coffin groans. My veins burn with fear and hope and terror.

The wood cracks. The lid is flung away. Dirt rains down on me, but I don't care. I suck in lungfuls of fresh, crisp air. A circle of light blinds me. I fling my body up, up into the unknown. Warm arms catch me, hold me close.

"I found you, Claws." Only Antony calls me by that nickname. Of course, it would be my cousin who saves me. Antony drags me over the lip of the grave, *my* grave, and we fall into crackling leaves and damp grass.

I sob into his shoulder. Antony rolls me over, his fingers

pressing all over my body, checking if I'm hurt. He rests my back against cold stone. "I have to take care of this," he says. I watch through tear-filled eyes as he pushes the dirt back into the hole – into what was supposed to be my grave – and brushes dead leaves on top. When he's done, it's impossible to tell the ground's been disturbed at all.

I tremble all over. I can't make myself stop shaking. Antony comes back to me and wraps me in his arms. He staggers to his feet, holding me like I'm weightless. He's only just turned eighteen, but already he's built like a tank.

I let out a terrified sob. Antony glances over his shoulder, and there's panic in his eyes. "You've got to be quiet, Claws," he whispers. "They might be nearby. I'm going to get you out of here."

I can't speak. My voice is gone, left in the coffin with my screams. Antony hoists me up and darts into the shadows. He runs with ease, ducking between rows of crumbling gravestones and beneath bent and gnarled trees. Dimly, I recognize this place – the old Emerald Beach cemetery, on the edge of Beaumont Hills overlooking the bay, where the original families of Emerald Beach buried their dead.

Where someone tried to bury me.

Antony bursts from the trees onto a narrow road. His car is parked in the shadows. He opens the passenger door and settles me inside before diving behind the wheel and gunning the engine.

We tear off down the road. Antony rips around the deadly corners like he's on a racetrack. Steep cliffs and crumbling old mansions pass by in a blur.

"My parents..." I gasp out. "Where are my parents?"

"I'm sorry, Claws. I didn't get to them in time. I only found you."

I wait for this to sink in, for the fact I'm now an orphan to hit me in a rush of grief. But I'm numb. My body won't stop shaking, and I left my brain and my heart buried in the silence of that coffin.

"Who?" I ask, and I fancy I catch a hint of my dad's cold savagery in my voice. "Who did this?"

"I don't know yet, but if I had to guess, it was Brutus. I warned your dad that he was making alliances and building up to a challenge. I think he's just made his move."

I try to digest this information. Brutus – who was once my father's trusted friend, who'd eaten dinner at our house and played Chutes and Ladders with me – killed my parents and buried me alive. But it bounces off the edge of my skull and doesn't stick. The life I had before, my old life, it's gone, and as I twist and grasp for memories, all I grab is stale coffin air.

"What now?" I ask.

Antony tosses his phone into my lap. "Look at the headlines."

I read the news app he's got open, but the words and images blur together. "This... this doesn't make any sense..."

"They think you're dead, Claws," Antony says. "That means you have to *stay* dead until we're strong enough to move against him. Until then, you have to be a ghost. But don't worry, I'll protect you. I've got a plan. We'll hide you where they'll never think to look."

Keep reading:
www.books2read.com/mystolenlife

THESE BAD BOYS MAY PLAY LIKE ANGELS, BUT THEY'RE DETERMINED TO MAKE MY LIFE HELL.

From the author of *Shunned*, the Amazon top-20 best-selling bully romance readers are calling, "The greatest mindf**k of 2019," comes this chilling new dark paranormal reverse harem romance.

Ivan, Titus, Dorien.
These Bad Boys of Baroque may play like angels, but they're determined to make my life hell.

When my mom got sick, my dreams of a career in music imploded. That is, until Madame Usher wafts into my life like a ghost from the past, offering me the chance to study at the exclusive Manderley Academy – a music school for the most gifted and wealthy.

It's an offer I can't refuse—free room and board at the gothic mansion where elite students immerse themselves in mastering their art. But there's a catch, and it's a big one.

I'm her slave.

I clean the rooms. I polish the piano keys. I serve her and the three pretentious a-hole guys who rule this school.

I must endure their bullying in silence. Even when they destroy my things, sabotage my performances, and try their best to drive me from Manderley.

Rich. Arrogant. Cruel.
    They won't have the poor little charity case ruining their fun.
    They've heard me play.
    They know I'm a serious contender for the prestigious Manderley Prize.

These broken muses aren't used to losing, especially to the help.

But they're not the only ones haunting me.

Something twisted and evil shrouds Manderley Academy. Maybe my bullies are the least of my problems. Maybe Dorien, Ivan, and Titus aren't the ones behind the strange noises in the walls, the warnings scrawled on my mirror, and the gruesome murders on the school grounds.

Maybe...maybe Manderley's ghosts are real.

A dark mystery unfolds around musician Faye de Winter in book one of this gripping gothic college reverse harem bully romance by USA Today best-selling author Steffanie Holmes. Warning: Proceed with caution – this tale of three spoiled rich boys with unsettling secrets and the girl who refuses to put up with their shit contains dark themes, a creepy house, a smoldering second-chance romance, college angst, cruel bullies and swoon-worthy sex.

EXCERPT: GHOSTED

Manderley Academy 1

Beep beep. Beep beep.

The machine echoed in my ears like a drumbeat sounding my doom. The sound of everything I'd worked for scattered to ash.

The sound of my mother slipping away from me.

I leaned back in the hard plastic hospital chair, rubbing my burning eyes. I had no idea what day it was or how long I'd been sitting there. A cramp shot up my leg – a dull ache that had nothing on the searing pain in my heart. I stretched out my leg, gasping as the cramp arced down the muscle.

It's like they deliberately make hospital rooms as uncomfortable as possible. Because watching someone you love waste away doesn't suck enough.

My foot brushed the violin case on the floor. Before I knew it, I held my instrument in my hands. The chin rest perfectly fitting my body and the familiar weight of the neck against my fingers gave me comfort. It felt as natural as breathing to run the bow across the strings, to play the familiar trembling notes of Bloch's *Nigun*.

The Swiss composer wrote this piece in the memory of his mother, and it's based on Jewish improvised chants. The idea is that by losing yourself in music, you become closer to God. Right now, I felt like strangling the big bastard in the sky for what he'd done to my mom, but I wasn't playing for him.

Nigun was one of my mother's favorite pieces – I learned it to play for her fortieth birthday. She'd hosted her party in her chic warehouse office in the East Village. All her investors and the executive team watched me in awe while she glowed with pride.

Beep beep. Beep beep.

Now, I played it beside her hospital bed, to an audience of one.

The doctors say she might be able to hear music inside her coma. This might be my only shot at speaking to her, at drawing her back.

Mournful notes rang out as my bow danced over the strings. The grey hospital room came to life in that moment, the sterile edges washed away under a wave of lament. I fancied I saw the shadows of others who had sat in this same chair to cry over their loved ones. I conjured their pain and made it my own.

Music *was* magic.

I needed a little magic right now.

As I played, a cloying scent reached my nostrils. Fake floral – like the bowls of potpourri my grandmother used to leave around her house. Old English roses and hyacinths drenched in sticky toffee and covered in mothballs. The scent tugged at a forgotten memory, a ghost of the past.

My pinkie finger slipped on the string, causing a dull note. I winced, forcing myself to ignore the smell, and kept playing. It happened sometimes when I was lost in the music – the melody conjured images, smells, or feelings from deep in my subconscious. They felt real until I set down the bow, and then I'd realize how stupid that was. *Obviously*, I didn't conjure scented memories with music.

It's just the smell of the hospital disinfectant or something. Don't get distract—

No, it's not. Deja vu tugged at me, bringing with it an ugly fore-boding. *I've smelled that* exact *scent before.*

I reached the end of the piece and lowered the bow. A familiar ache settled along my arm – pain was another thing I never felt until after I stopped playing. I once smashed my foot while climbing on stage. I played Beethoven's entire *Violin Sonata No. 9* standing on a broken toe, and I didn't even notice.

Someone clapped.

What the fuck?

I jumped out of my skin.

My eyes flew to my mother, but she lay in the bed, immobile. The machine beep-beeped behind her. I whirled around.

"*Brava*." A woman stood in the corner of the room. I hadn't noticed her come in. Her Eastern European accent seemed so out-of-place in this ordinary hospital in the shittiest part of NYC. That wasn't the only thing about her that was odd – an old-fash-ioned floor-length gown in black lace and linen clung to her ample figure, and she clutched a large carpet bag with gold clasps. The fake floral smell rolled off her in waves. "You are still talented."

I set down the violin, angry she'd intruded. "This is a private room." The one indulgence I'd made in this entire shitshow, so I could grieve and hope and rage in private. And soon even that would be gone unless I came up with more cash.

"I am aware. I wish to speak to you, Faye de Winter."

How does this strange woman know my name? Her presence tugged at me, the deja vu growing stronger. That smell and her voice were so familiar. Even that black dress sparked some hint of memory, but I couldn't think where I'd have occasion to speak with such a woman. She looked like she'd got lost on the way to a Twilight fan convention.

Beep beep. Beep beep.

Tension sang in the air between us. I didn't want her here, infecting my mom's space with her scent. But I had to know why she knew my name and why'd she'd sought me out. I sighed. "Yeah?"

"Perhaps you do not recognize me. I am Madame Usher."

That name pierced my heart like an arrow.

Of course. The perfume. How could I forget the way it made me choke during music classes, or how it clung to my father when he came home from his private lessons?

I hadn't seen Madame Usher of Manderley Academy since my mother pulled me from her classes when I was nine years old. Alongside her husband on piano, she had been an accomplished violinist in her day but now ran an elite conservatory in the mountains offering expert tutelage for only the most exceptional musicians. She used to come to the city to teach a handful of super-rich students – children and adults, including me and my dad. But ever since Dad's disappearance, her name had been poison in our house, never uttered.

"I see that you remember now. It has been, what, nine years?"

"Ten." I would turn twenty this year.

"You were just a tiny wisp of a thing back then, but you mastered your Bach. The only person I heard play the Chaconne from *Partita No. 2* better was Donovan."

"Don't talk to me about him," I hissed.

"I see you've inherited your mother's bitterness."

"Get the fuck out." I jabbed my finger at the door.

"Excuse me?"

"You don't come into *my* mother's hospital room and accuse her of being bitter. I'd be upset too if I found out the husband who I supported through an expensive music education was fucking his teacher."

"Such foul language." Instead of retreating, Madame Usher stepped into the room and closed the door behind her. "You should know that I loved him with a passion I only ever reserved for music. My husband was a convenience – for the sake of our international career, it made sense to marry Victor. But when

Donovan and I played, it was as though we made love through our instruments."

I balled my hands into fists, resisting the childish urge to jam my hands over my ears. "Read my lips – I. Don't. Want. To. Hear. This."

The smile on Madame Usher's lips boiled my blood. "He planned to leave your mother, and I to leave Victor. We were to run away together. But then he disappeared, and I have never known such pain before or since."

"Get out," I growled, stepping toward the call button. "Or I'll have you removed by security."

Bitch.

Madame Usher continued as though I'd never spoken. "After your mother removed you from my classes, I kept my eye on you, Faye. You might think of me as a guardian angel, hovering in the background, waiting for Donovan's talent to blossom within you. Your father always believed you would one day surpass him, but I admit, I had my doubts. I do not accept just anyone into my tutelage, and you were never serious about your studies, always running about with Dorien."

Dorien Valencourt. I closed my eyes, remembering the little boy who'd been my only friend growing up. Dorien took piano lessons from Victor Usher, but we always paired up for ensembles and recitals. Dorien was rich in a way my family could never hope to be – we practically lived in poverty to fund Dad's career and my tuition – but I was too young to understand the gulf between us or why the other rich kids shunned me so openly. I just knew Dorien's slate-grey eyes gleamed with joy whenever I showed up in class. We'd been the twin terrors of Madame Usher's junior city school. The day Dorien placed his pet iguana in the baby grand and it jumped out just as Victor Usher sat down—

No. I couldn't think about Dorien now, not on top of everything else. That pain still cut too deep.

"Dorien was never serious either, and he's done well for himself," I shot back.

"Ah. So you have followed his career?"

Even if I'd never wanted to hear his name again (which I definitely didn't), I couldn't help but see Dorien everywhere. Every week there was a new article gushing over Broken Muse, the ensemble Dorien formed with two of his friends. The music press delighted in following the trio —who they'd dubbed the Bad Boys of Baroque – as they tore up the European scene with their antics. They were my age, but their flamboyant playing style, modernized Baroque costumes and strings of exotic lovers were giving the stuffy Classical world a playboy makeover. Early last year they stopped touring and dropped off the face of the earth – no one knew where they were, which only added to their mystique. But I wasn't going to give Madame Usher the satisfaction of revealing I knew any of that. So I ignored her question. "Tell me what you want, and leave."

"I've come into the city to speak with music teachers and private schools. For months I've despaired at finding a student to fill our last open place. Your school's music teacher put your name forward, and although I initially dismissed it because of the usual dross she tries to send me, the memory of your father's talent encouraged me to seek you out. I've had a devil of a time tracking you down, but eventually, the trail led me here. I'm delighted it did. There is no need for you to audition – I've heard enough to offer you a place at Manderley if you want it."

If I wanted it? The fuck was she kidding? It didn't matter that I hated her guts. Of course I wanted it. Saliva pooled on my tongue, as if the very thought of stepping inside that hallowed mansion made me hungry.

Beep beep.

The machines pulled me back to reality. Mom's mysterious sickness. The mountains of medical bills. The two jobs I'd been working in an attempt to pay them off. I shook my head. "I can't."

"Faye, an offer like this is not extended lightly, and it will not be offered again."

Don't use my first name. We're not, nor will we ever be, close. I gestured to the prone figure on the bed. "She needs me."

"You do not understand." Madame Usher moved to the end of the bed, standing over my mother and looking down at her with pursed lips. "I am not merely offering you a place at Manderley, but a chance at a future. I expect every musician who graduates to go on to a stunning international career. You cannot do that tethered to a hospital bed. We have the means to help you."

"Help me how?"

"Your tuition will be paid by my late husband's endowment fund. I shall provide your room and board, and an allowance for clothing and necessities. Most importantly, I will pay your mother's medical debts and move her to a more advanced facility closer to the school, so you can visit her on weekends. In exchange, you will extend your services to the school."

"My... services?"

"You will cook meals, keep the house and rooms clean, make sure the instruments are stored correctly, that sort of thing."

"What did your last maid die of?" I muttered.

Madame Usher's mouth tugged at the corner. "A broken neck."

I sucked in a breath. *Is she serious?*

Madame Usher nodded to my phone on the nightstand. "I will not dredge up that unfortunate incident by speaking of it aloud. Look it up if you still have your penchant for morbidity."

She referred to the fact I'd been a strange kid. I was obsessed with horror books and ghost stories. Still was. My favorite thing to do on a Friday night was curling up in bed with Mom and a stack of junk food to watch a spooky film. I knew all the tropes by heart, but I never got tired of hiding under the covers from ghosts and monsters.

I picked up the phone and tapped a line into the search bar. A few moments later, the headline popped up: "MAID DEAD AT

ELITE MUSIC ACADEMY." The maid had been found crumpled at the bottom of the stairs – a nasty fall. A terrible accident. The journalist took a kind of morbid delight in describing the trauma to her skull, suggesting the angle of her body meant that she'd been pushed. Police investigated, but they eventually ruled her death an accident, although the journalist enjoyed speculating otherwise.

Knowing Madame Usher, she probably folded the towels wrong.

Madame Usher frowned at my phone. "As you may be able to guess, it becomes difficult to find new help when the press has made every attempt to suggest your maid died of foul play. Hence, I was inspired to seek you out. We can help each other."

A charity case.

I sank into the chair. The plastic creaked as it sagged under my weight. I was never supposed to be a charity case. After Dad disappeared, taking all our hopes of living off his music career with him, Mom swore that we de Winter women would make our own way in the world. She was sick of working sixty-hour shifts as a taxi driver to support a man's dream. She went back to school for business, and built a successful PR firm from the ground-up. After years living on the skin of our asses, we had money. We moved into a gorgeous East Village townhouse. Mom paid for the best violin tutor money could buy who wasn't Madame Usher. I went to a fancy prep school where I was ignored because I wasn't 'old money,' but the students were all little shits, so I didn't give a fuck. We took vacations in exotic places like Vietnam and Istanbul. We weren't mega-rich, but we were comfortable. We didn't need anyone or anything but ourselves.

Except, as it turned out, we also needed health insurance.

Mom's illness crept up on us without warning. One moment she was taking her team on a spa vacation in Hawaii to celebrate her best year ever, complaining the resort food gave her stomach cramps, the next she was lying unresponsive in the back of an ambulance. I called our insurance company to pay the bills and discovered Mom had forgotten to pay her premium, so they had canceled our coverage.

What started as bouts of nausea and cramping turned into a host of strange gastrointestinal problems, and then her kidneys started failing. She'd been deteriorating over the last two years, in and out of the hospital, while they did tests and tried medications and dialysis, but nothing worked. Every new treatment, every flight to a different state to try some new diagnostic machine, stretched our dwindling savings. I sold the townhouse. I graduated high school (barely), moved her to this cheap-ass chop-shop hospital, and took two jobs to try and keep up. Then, a week ago, she slipped into a coma, and the doctors still had no idea what was wrong with her.

What medical dramas on TV don't tell you is how fucking expensive it is to keep someone on life-support. If I didn't come up with some way to pay the bills soon, I'd have no choice but to shut her off.

My mom was my whole life. I wasn't saying goodbye. Not yet.

I'll do whatever it takes to keep her alive.

If that means bowing and scrubbing for this witch, just call me Cinder-fucking-rella.

I leaned over the bed, pressing my lips to Mom's forehead. How odd it was to see her this still. Mom was always bouncing off the walls, a ball of boundless energy. "I won't slow down – you slow down, you die," she admonished me once after she'd nearly walked out of the house with her underwear on her head because she was so excited about a client's TV appearance. "The only time I'll lie still is if you put me in a coma." Fate is a fucking cruel mistress.

Beep beep, the machines admonished me for my betrayal.

I straightened up and picked up my violin case, hugging it to my chest. All through Mom's illness, even as I sold off our possessions, she forbade me to sell my violin. She had it custom-made by an artisan luthier as my thirteenth birthday present, and it was the most precious thing I owned.

So I'd kept it, even though I'd all but given up hope of a career in music. The money Mom set aside for college had been eaten by her medical bills in the first three months. This was a second chance for both of us – for her and for me.

My father walked out and left us with *nothing*. If I took Madame Usher's deal, then at least something good came of his *trahison des clercs*.

The smile that crossed Madame Usher's face was chillier than the winter I'd just survived in my shitty, non-heated apartment. "Your father would be so proud. Faye de Winter, welcome to Manderley Academy."

START READING NOW

OTHER BOOKS BY STEFFANIE HOLMES

This list is in recommended reading order, although each couple's story can be enjoyed as a standalone.

Nevermore Bookshop Mysteries

A Dead and Stormy Night

Of Mice and Murder

Pride and Premeditation

How Heathcliff Stole Christmas

Memoirs of a Garroter

Prose and Cons

A Novel Way to Die

Much Ado About Murder

Kings of Miskatonic Prep

Shunned

Initiated

Possessed

Ignited

Stonehurst Prep

My Stolen Life

My Secret Heart

My Broken Crown

My Savage Kingdom

Manderley Academy

Ghosted

Haunted

Spirited

Briarwood Witches

Earth and Embers

Fire and Fable

Water and Woe

Wind and Whispers

Spirit and Sorrow

Crookshollow Gothic Romance

Art of Cunning (Alex & Ryan)

Art of the Hunt (Alex & Ryan)

Art of Temptation (Alex & Ryan)

The Man in Black (Elinor & Eric)

Watcher (Belinda & Cole)

Reaper (Belinda & Cole)

Wolves of Crookshollow

Digging the Wolf (Anna & Luke)

Writing the Wolf (Rosa & Caleb)

Inking the Wolf (Bianca & Robbie)

Wedding the Wolf (Willow & Irvine)

Want to be informed when the next Steffanie Holmes paranormal romance story goes live? Sign up for the newsletter at www.steffanieholmes.com/newsletter to get the scoop, and score a free collection of bonus scenes and stories to enjoy!

ABOUT THE AUTHOR

Steffanie Holmes is the *USA Today* bestselling author of the paranormal, gothic, dark, and fantastical. Her books feature clever, witty heroines, secret societies, creepy old mansions and alpha males who *always* get what they want.

Legally-blind since birth, Steffanie received the 2017 Attitude Award for Artistic Achievement. She was also a finalist for a 2018 Women of Influence award.

Steff is the creator of *Rage Against the Manuscript* – a resource of free content, books, and courses to help writers tell their story, find their readers, and build a badass writing career.

Steffanie lives in New Zealand with her husband, a horde of cantankerous cats, and their medieval sword collection.

STEFFANIE HOLMES NEWSLETTER

Grab a free copy *Cabinet of Curiosities* – a Steffanie Holmes compendium of short stories and bonus scenes – when you sign up for updates with the Steffanie Holmes newsletter.

http://www.steffanieholmes.com/newsletter

Come hang with Steffanie
www.steffanieholmes.com
hello@steffanieholmes.com

Made in the USA
Las Vegas, NV
18 February 2022

44170622R00225